D1110302

The One Great Year Series

Book II

Printed in the USA

First printing, 2019

ISBN 13: 978-1-939116-41-3 print edition
ISBN 13: 978-1-939116-43-7 ebook edition

Waterside Productions
2055 Oxford Avenue
Cardiff-by-the-Sea, CA 92007
www.waterside.com

The One Great Year Series

Book II

the Emerald Tablet

⊱ *a Novel by* ⊰

Tamara Veitch & Rene DeFazio

Waterside Productions
Cardiff-by-the-Sea, California

---

*"Those who are able to see beyond the shadows
and lies of their culture will never be understood,
let alone believed by the masses."*

— Plato

Dedicated to Janice and Randy Staub,
Gregory Locklear, and all our wonderful friends
and family who have supported us
along this journey.

We both want to express our gratitude
for our writing partnership.
Without the dedication and skill of
our spouse-muse-partner,
The One Great Year Series would not exist.
With love . . . enjoy!

THE EMERALD TABLET

A translation by Sir Isaac Newton can be found among his alchemical papers, currently housed in King's College Library, Cambridge University.

Tis true without lying, certain & most true.
That wch is below is like that wch is above & that wch
is above is like that wch is below to do ye
miracles of one only thing.
And as all things have been & arose from one by ye
mediation of one: so all things have their birth
from this one thing by adaptation.
The Sun is its father, the moon its mother, the wind
hath carried it in its belly, the earth is its nurse. The
father of all perfection in ye whole world is here. Its
force or power is entire if it be converted into earth.
Separate thou ye earth from ye fire, ye subtle from
the gross sweetly wth great industry. It ascends from ye
earth to ye heaven & again it descends to ye earth
& receives ye force of things superior & inferior.
By this means you shall have ye glory of ye whole
world & thereby all obscurity shall fly from you.
Its force is above all force, for it vanquishes every
subtle thing & penetrates every solid thing.
So was ye world created . . .

Prologue

Present day, Seattle, Washington

When soulmates find each other, regardless of the circumstances, it is a magical experience. When Eden entered Quinn's apartment, the Emissary gawked, suddenly frozen in place. As the tiny brunette stepped out from behind Nate, she was almost completely obscured by the shine surrounding her. Quinn watched the streaming indigo ribbons of energy.

Delirium . . . joy . . . and profound connection overtook Quinn, and all the oxygen in his lungs exhaled. Though Eden was a lovely-looking woman, Quinn could see only the soul that resided within her body. It was his soulmate—Theron!

She's found! Thank God! She's here! Quinn thought. He would have to tell Nate . . . but tell him what? Could he tell him everything? Thirteen thousand years of lifetimes, and all of it culminating in this tiny apartment? Living, dying, searching all the time for this soul, his best friend, Nate's newly declared love, Eden Anderson?

Unlike Nate and Eden, Quinn had past-life memory. In his farthest recollections, he had been called Marcus. Marcus had secretly dared to go against the natural order of things and had consumed a memory elixir; he hadn't wanted to forget the horror of what his adversary Helghul had done, and he hadn't wanted to forget Theron. Since then, navigating countless incarnations, he had been reborn and died, and he remembered every joyful high and excruciating low.

Nate had helped the Emissary on his journey in many lifetimes. More than once he had sacrificed for him. Hundreds of years earlier, as Sartaña's guard, Nate's soul had reunited Marcus and Theron, and for doing so he had been torn from his body by Katari's vicious spear. Quinn owed him so much. Could he betray his ally? Could he make Nate understand?

Nate and Eden have only just met, Quinn rationalized, but his conscience flooded him, reminding him that Nate had already changed his life for Eden. He had left his longtime girlfriend Sarah because of her and was prepared to go on the road filming with Eden for the next four months or more.

Eden noticed that Quinn hadn't moved since she'd entered the room. He seemed odd. Surprisingly handsome, but odd. She hadn't expected that. Having followed his blog faithfully for years, she had often written comments and interacted with him online.

"So glad to meet you," Eden said, stepping past Nate. She reached for Quinn's hand, and he noticed the large Flower of Life tattoo on her forearm.

As the soulmates' fingers touched, electricity pulsed through their bodies, and the shine in the room redoubled. Only Quinn could see it, but Eden tingled from head to toe. She felt the tremor, the magnetism, and the familiarity of all their history running between them.

Finally, jolted to his senses, Quinn stood fully upright, placing his hand over hers. His poise was restored, and every cell of his body wanted to connect with her. He looked down into her green eyes and saw her confusion. Eden was overcome by the powerful force they shared. It was exciting, as if a doorway to some magical world had opened.

"I'm in love, bro," Nate had told Quinn only moments earlier, so he watched Quinn and Eden with alarm. They were both transfixed. He felt compelled to step between them and intervene. They were still holding hands, and he knew he had to break the spell being cast.

Surely, Nate will forgive me, Quinn thought, hoping that would be the case. As he and Eden touched, he felt Theron's energy surging through him, revitalizing and reaffirming the love they shared. In that moment, only *she* mattered.

The soulmates had been reunited, but there was a higher cause beyond Nate's infatuation and Marcus's deep connection to Theron. The Emissaries' lives had always been brought together for a greater purpose. What was the purpose this time?

For Nate, Quinn, and Eden, this reunion was a turning point, and it would change everything.

Chapter 1

The Exodus

13,000 years ago, Atitala

The entity that had bound itself to Helghul's soul prickled him from the inside like coarse wool. It was an uncomfortable fit. This alliance would take getting used to.

"Let me go!" Theron screamed into the deafening wind and pelting rain as she violently struggled against Helghul, intent on returning ashore to Marcus. Helghul was holding her around the waist from behind and did not relent, though she kicked her legs and had bloodied his nose by swinging her head.

The Exodus from Atitala had started suddenly, with a severe tropical storm and earthquake. Marcus and Theron had escaped the fire and falling debris of the quaking city together, determined to board the boats designated for the Emissaries, when Grey Elder had called out for assistance. Marcus had urged Theron forward and had gone back to help, but before he could rejoin her, the gangplank was pulled in. The reed boat was pulling away from shore, tossed by the towering waves, separating the soulmates. When the distance to land was an adequate deterrent, Helghul released the frantic woman.

"What have you done?" she shouted, stumbling as they were tossed onto the deck of the ship. Her green eyes were wild as Marcus grew smaller in the distance. Lightning slashed the sky, and she could see him on the shore, his arms outstretched, beckoning her back from the churning sea.

"We have to get inside! We will be swept away!" Helghul shouted, pulling at Theron's arm.

Her protestations were futile. She knew he was right. The storm was worsening, and Marcus was out of sight and out of reach. Most of the others were already below, except for a brave few securing hatches and urging them to hurry. No one could captain in such perilous conditions. The boat was at the mercy of the storm.

The soaked passengers were strapped in to tautly slung hammocks running in rows down the interior hull of the ship. They tied them closed with knots so they could swing, safely cocooned as the ship was tossed aggressively. They hung below deck, hoping the reed craft would not be torn apart by the enormous waves or shattered by rock debris that had been thrown into the atmosphere from the meteor strike and was now raining down intermittently. The boat was pounded hour after hour, and the passengers were physically battered and green with nausea as the deafening winds whipped the ocean, threatening to tear the ship apart.

There were three violent days in complete darkness. A massive meteor had crashed to earth in the Northern Hemisphere, devastating the planet with its impact. It had caused a dust cloud so great that the Sun, Moon, and stars had been completely obscured. The human population was nearly wiped out by the initial catastrophic events and the famines that followed.

The stench of vomit and waste permeated the hull of the ship. It was a harrowing journey, but there was no time for humiliation or self-pity. The Atitalans on board were the fortunate ones. Their homeland, friends, and families who had been left behind had suffered a worse fate. Anyone who had not been consumed by the fires as the ground split apart and quaked had drowned in the tsunami floods.

The Emissaries had to wait for the winds to subside and the seas to grow calmer before basic communication could commence. Helghul hung in the hammock next to Theron.

"Why did you stop me?" she demanded in the dark, her eyes brimming with tears, and her throat raw from days of grief.

"It was too far! Did you expect me to watch while you threw yourself to the sea?" Helghul replied.

"It wasn't too far! If you hadn't stopped me, I'd be with Marcus now!"

"I saved you . . . and we're Emissaries. We have a higher purpose than your love affair!" he lied.

"You've hated him for years!" Theron said bitterly, and Helghul silently agreed.

As children, Marcus and Helghul had been inseparable friends. In their early teens, in anticipation of the prophesied destruction of Atitala, the boys and Theron had traveled to Inner Earth, hoping to forge an escape plan for their people. However, Inner Earth's climate and inhabitants had been inhospitable, and the mission had been a failure. Helghul had never been the same.

What Theron and Marcus never knew was that while in Inner Earth, Helghul had made a fateful choice. By willingly relinquishing his ability to feel empathy, and murdering Black Elder, he had assumed the infamous Elder's role as King of the Adversaries.

"I will not forgive you for this, Helghul," Theron said bitterly, thinking of Marcus, wondering where he was, and knowing he would be out of his mind with worry.

"I do not need your forgiveness," Helghul answered. Theron's feelings were irrelevant to him. She was where he wanted her. The

Beast inside him twisted and turned uncomfortably, confronted by the love Helghul could not smother.

This one is a problem. You should have thrown her to the sea. She will be nothing but trouble, the Beast growled inside his head.

Helghul unsuccessfully tried to conceal the affection he felt for Theron, but there was nothing he could hide from the Beast.

Helghul had once believed that he and Theron would couple as soulmates—everyone had—but when Helghul murdered Black Elder, beginning the wicked rite to replace him as King of the Adversaries, he willingly traded his ability to feel empathy, for power. His love turned possessive and self-centered, and Theron pulled away from him. As the three dear friends matured, Marcus earned Theron's admiration and affection, while Helghul grew more distant and brooding. Helghul could not see his fault in the breakdown of the relationship, and therefore took no responsibility for it. Feeling wronged, and unable to empathize, Helghul bitterly swore never to forgive Marcus's and Theron's betrayal.

As the storm weakened, the boat continued to be tossed, and Helghul carried on with his plotting. The faces around him were familiar, but there were not only Emissaries on the boat, there were Adversaries. Red Elder watched Helghul suspiciously from the other end of the tubelike hull.

He must be the first to go, Helghul thought, catching his eye. The previous Black Elder had never been welcomed in Atitala. By nature, he had been unable to function in a democratic Senate as part of the greater unitary in a Golden Age, and Helghul was no different. He would not share control with Red Elder—he could not—for their agendas were diametrically opposed.

The Beast disagreed. He saw a threat greater than Red Elder. Though the demon had been bound to Helghul only a short time, it realized that Helghul's love for Theron threatened his ability to be entirely ruthless. His affection for her was a weakness, and her virtue was repugnant.

She must be the first! the Beast countered, and bile rose in Helghul's throat, painfully corroding the soft tissue of his esophagus. His unholy coupling with the entity was affecting him physically, but more, as the voice in his head continually commanded its evil agenda, it would certainly alter him mentally.

><< ><< ><<

The giant swells had subsided to a rough chop, and the weary passengers cautiously climbed out of their silken pods to clean and prepare for when they found land. The sky was grey from the unsettled dust in the atmosphere, and the Atitalans wore cloths over their noses and mouths to filter the air. Helghul was fishing with a small group of Adversaries while others were busy washing their clothes and hammocks. The shine of the Adversaries had turned from the pale indigo that had surrounded them in Atitala to a murky grey, but their fellow students dismissed the change, attributing it to the chaos and fear they were experiencing as they tried desperately to survive. Red Elder, however, knew better. He was aware that the transformation of their shines was significant, and it allowed him to easily differentiate the Emissaries from the Adversaries. Helghul watched warily as the Elder began meditating on the bow of the reed boat.

"How will we get rid of Red Elder without the Emissaries intervening?" Solenna whispered. The raven-haired young woman was beautiful on the outside, but her soul had aligned with ugliness.

"We could suffocate him in his sleep," a towering, muscular Adversary called Abaddon said. The birthmark across his left cheek and ear darkened as his face flushed with excitement.

"Slit his throat?" Solenna suggested, her almond-shaped eyes gleaming. Another Adversary named Thaddeus stood beside her nodding with encouragement and smiling broadly as his shaggy blond hair blew in the wind.

"We cannot underestimate him. I have a plan, Abaddon. You will create a distraction below deck," said Helghul.

"Like what?" Abaddon asked, hopeful the violent tendencies stirring inside him would be called upon. The Adversaries had engaged in a ritualistic sacrifice during the dark rite that bound Helghul's soul and body to the Beast, and Abaddon was excited by the prospect of further bloodshed. The Adversaries' souls had been contaminated by dark passions, and contemplating murder no longer fazed them.

"You will do what you are best at, Abaddon, and start a fight down below. You must draw in as many as you can. The rest of you will call for assistance. The Emissaries will all rush to help—it is their nature. Then, block them in. If they subdue you too quickly, more of you will join the fight," Helghul said.

"They will not subdue me!" Abaddon said, gripping his fist and flexing his bulbous biceps.

"Quiet, fool! Do you want everyone to hear?" Solenna snapped in a harsh whisper, though the crashing waves easily muffled their conversation.

"Where will you be?" she asked Helghul, ignoring Abaddon's petulant scowl. Her face was lit with enthusiasm.

"I will keep Red Elder on deck. While I engage him, Thaddeus will come from behind and hit him on the head. Then we will throw him overboard and return below before anyone notices us missing," Helghul replied, his eyes gleaming, the whites veined red. The Beast was in fervent agreement, and Helghul noticed that when they were in harmony, the entity's presence felt powerful rather than prickly.

Less than an hour later, Helghul stood with Red Elder on deck, having lured him there on the premise of speaking to him privately. The Elder was wearing the long, flowing robes he had been wearing the night of the Exodus, and they flapped in the wind as they sailed.

"I have something important to tell you," Helghul said.

"I have been expecting this, Helghul," Red Elder replied.

"Have you?" Helghul asked, surprised. "What is it you are expecting?"

"I expect that you are going to tell me you have become Black Elder," Red Elder said.

At that moment, below deck, while Theron and several Emissaries were preparing a meal, Abaddon leaned in between them roughly, determined to start a fight.

"I do not want fish! I am not eating this!" he shouted as he swiped his bulky fist across the table, scattering food across the people and floor.

"Stop! What are you doing?" demanded one of the Emissaries, who was covered in food. The Adversaries were calling for help, as they had been instructed. Abaddon continued ranting and throwing fistfuls of fish at the stunned onlookers as passengers came running to see what was causing the uproar.

Abaddon picked up the largest of the fish and, tearing it in half, pushed its dead, staring eyes into the face of the man in front of him. The Emissaries around Abaddon grabbed him by the arms and shoulders, pulling him off, but Abaddon would not be subdued. He swung his body violently, and the Emissaries trying to restrain him were flung like tassels or sent reeling. The other Adversaries shoved and jostled the crowd that had gathered, furthering the mayhem, just as Abaddon, using his brute strength, grabbed Theron and two more Emissaries, lifting them off their feet and mercilessly knocking their skulls together with a spray of blood.

The shouting had the intended effect, and those who were topside hurried below to assist. Helghul and Red Elder, however, stood unmoving, their eyes locked.

"How long have you known?" Helghul asked.

"Since you were a boy, returning from Inner Earth," Red Elder said over the din.

"Yet none of you intervened?"

"Each soul must choose its own lessons. Nothing we could say would teach you what you have chosen to learn."

"Why did you let me on board?" Helghul asked, wiping the stinging ocean spray from his eyes.

"The only thing separating the Emissaries and the Adversaries is choice," Red Elder said.

"I have become who I was meant to be!" Helghul said defiantly.

"You have a new choice in every moment. Each of those moments creates your future," Red Elder replied.

As the Elder turned to go below and rectify the discord Helghul had certainly commandeered, there was a bright flash, pain, and then darkness as he was struck on the head by Thaddeus's wooden mallet.

"Be quick!" Helghul commanded, taking the Elder's legs while Thaddeus hoisted his shoulders. *Up, up, over!* The Elder's limp body was released facedown, his robes flailing, until he landed with a splash.

Helghul surveyed the deck. Solenna watched from nearby, but otherwise it was empty.

"You should be below helping Abaddon," Helghul said, but as he neared her, they embraced and kissed passionately, excited by the energy of what they had done.

When Helghul marched into the fray below, with Solenna at his elbow, he saw Theron standing in front of Abaddon, her face filled with rage. Her slightly crooked nose was bloody, and her hands were pressed against the brute's chest. His arms were extended wide as he held off two strapping Emissaries with either hand.

"Enough!" Helghul shouted urgently. The tenderness he felt for Theron seared the Beast inside him, and the contentment they had found together in murder was reversed. The Beast burned and prickled inside Helghul, more uncomfortable than ever at being immersed in the feelings Theron's vulnerable state had provoked.

The Beast was not the only creature irritated by Helghul's fondness for Theron. Solenna understood that her master must take control of the moment and establish himself as the next rightful leader, but she watched resentfully as Helghul rushed to the woman's side. Helghul's affection for White Elder's daughter had been well known when they were growing up. It was Solenna's love for Helghul and unspoken competition with Theron that had enticed her to become an Adversary. She was hopeful that someday she and Helghul would couple in the Grid and become soulmates, even if it took the entire twenty-six-thousand-year Great Year Cycle to occur. In the meantime, she was determined to establish her loyalty and make herself indispensable.

As ordered by his leader, Abaddon dropped his fists. Helghul commanded everyone up and onto the deck, feigning anger and berating the man as he moved. The King of the Adversaries took charge, and Abaddon allowed himself to be steered topside. Everyone followed them outside.

"Where is Red Elder?" people began to ask. Theron's chestnut hair blew across her bloodied face as she searched the crowd. She had not seen him since the fight began.

"Helghul! Have you seen Red Elder?" Theron asked from his side, looking around the group, still searching. She noticed that many of her cohorts' energy fields had lost their purple hue.

Is it merely a result of the declining consciousness? Does all shine turn grey and dismal as the Ages descend? she wondered.

The Emissary she had sent to search for Red Elder returned.

"He is not on board, Theron," the man said, deeply concerned.

Abaddon continued to sneer and snarl at Theron, and though she was not comfortable having Helghul in charge, she was grateful he was able to control the angry powerhouse.

"What kind of behavior is this for an Emissary?" Theron admonished, glaring at him. "Helghul—" she began, but Helghul interrupted her.

"Call me Black Elder," he said, and his face twisted as the ghostly visage of one of the Beast's ten heads seemed to emerge through his skin. It was as if he had become momentarily transparent, and the group gasped and recoiled. "Throw the Emissaries to the sea!" Helghul commanded.

Abaddon took hold of Theron by the back of the neck and by her hips. He lifted her easily over his head, and though she struggled and kicked, it was hopeless. Helghul looked away, pretending not to care, though his heart and the Beast knew he did, and Abaddon launched her overboard. He then picked up another and another, flinging the frantic, screaming Emissaries into the white-capped water. The Emissaries could not match the rage of the Adversaries, who swarmed their fellow Atitalans, pushing and punching and forcing them overboard into the violent, frigid ocean.

Paddling for their lives and trying to float, the desperate Emissaries called out for mercy, gulping bitter salt water.

The vicious struggle continued on the deck of the ship. Thaddeus preferred to stay out of harm's way and stood back with Helghul while his cohorts wrestled with the Emissaries. He was the first to notice a glimmer of light beneath the frantic swimmers. There was a flickering green glow rushing past them at shark-speed, and Thaddeus pointed it out to his leader. Neither man could make out what it was. A whale, a great white, or some other predator? The Adversaries watched with anticipation.

Theron was scanning around her for any floating debris she might cling on to. Her panic was further elevated when she suddenly realized there was something large gliding below her, creating a significant undulation. She submerged her face in the water to get a better look, but everything was blurry. The water rippled, and fear coursed through her as she pulled her face back above the surface, gasping for air. She prepared for the worst. Death now seemed certain. Theron slowed her movements and breathed as much as possible, hoping the creature would ignore her. She knew it was only a matter of time before she and the other innocents treading water lost their battle, one by one, either to some creature or to the sea.

The luminescent green light disappeared under the boat before breaching the surface, spraying white water high into the air. A powerful gust of wind blew across the deck, and the combat halted. Helghul's hair flew forward; in confusion, he turned to where the others were gawking. Hovering above the reed boat, on some sort of flying disk, was a soaking-wet Red Elder, his drenched robes whipping out behind him. The Emissaries on board and in the water cheered and shouted to one another with relief, as, with a wave of his hand, the Elder targeted individual blasts of sound vibration at the Adversaries. Abaddon was lifted as though he were a leaf on the wind, and he crashed against the distant railing with a powerful thump. The reverberations easily flung the Adversaries across the deck, separating them from the Emissaries who had not yet been thrown to the sea.

"How?" Helghul gasped angrily.

"The Emerald Tablet!" Solenna exclaimed, pointing. Her left eye was swollen and bruised. She had been amid the brawl with Abaddon and the others, ruthlessly pushing and pulling the Emissaries to their doom, when Red Elder's blast had thrown her at least twenty feet.

The Treasure! What power it could give me! Helghul realized. He had not known it was on board. He had not thought of it since leaving Atitala. He had had no idea that Red Elder was the protector of the sacred slab, but now that he knew, he had to have it.

"In our haste, we must have thrown it overboard with him! Imagine if the Tablet had been lost to the sea forever?" Thaddeus said, and Helghul raised his hand irritably to silence him. He would not have his blunders broadcast.

Red Elder's arms were spread wide as he circled the boat, dipping effortlessly into the ocean and pulling victims to safety. At his feet, the Emerald Tablet glowed spectacularly against the grey sky. Theron and the other Emissaries waited as the Elder promptly plucked each of them out of the water and placed them on the ship's bow. The Adversaries were no match for the Emerald Tablet *and* Red Elder, and they knew it.

Helghul watched his murderous plan be undone, hastily plotting his next move. Nearby, Thaddeus hid himself behind his shipmates, hopeful that Red Elder did not know it was *his* hammer that had dealt him a blow.

Once the Emissaries were all huddled, wet and shivering on the ship, Red Elder floated protectively in front of them, just five feet above the deck.

"The Golden Age has ended, but we are far from the Age of Darkness overpowering the Light!" he shouted. The usually subdued Elder's face was menacing as he stared down from the antigravitational tablet at the Adversaries on the stern. His body was strong and burly, his short red beard and chin-length hair blew in the wind.

"There are those among you who have chosen to work with the darkness. Emissaries, be on your guard! Trust your instincts. Regard your fellow students! What do you see?" the Elder asked.

"Their shines have lost their light," a soaked woman said, shivering from where she sat on the deck. The Emissaries were doing their best to warm and comfort each other.

"Never ignore the subtle signs. Soon the ability to see shine and your memory of this Age will die with your body, but you will *feel* shine, and your instincts will alert you to danger. These Atitalans were once your allies and friends, but they are now your rivals. They will be reborn into every lifetime, seeking to destroy the Light you create. They are guilty of attempting to kill another. What should their consequence be?" Red Elder asked.

After some silent contemplation, Theron was the first to respond.

"Forgive them," she said. Helghul and the others were stunned.

How could she come up with such a pathetic answer after what we did to her? Helghul thought.

Do not mistake her compassion for weakness! the Beast snarled in his head.

"They will only try again," another Emissary argued. "Should we wait to die in our sleep?"

"Bind them, and when we arrive at our destination, let the laws of Khem decide their fate," another Emissary suggested.

Helghul's mind raced through the possible penalties the laws of Khem could impose: *stoning, mutilation, slavery, or death in some brutal manner?*

I have memory, a huge advantage that the Emissaries do not have, Helghul mistakenly thought, unaware that his nemesis Marcus also had memory.

Better we take control! the Beast said, and Helghul agreed.

Helghul whispered urgently to his subjects, commanding them to make another dark choice.

"We will be the masters of our own fate. We will end this incarnation now, by our own choice," Helghul declared, and the crowd gasped in surprise. He was determined that his new life as Black Elder would not start in confinement. Helghul did not fear death, by any means. He had memory, and he knew he was eternal. He had nothing to lose by dying, and he would discover for himself what judgment, if any, there was for intentionally causing his own death.

"Such a choice brings its own consequences," Red Elder warned.

"Lifetimes are like days—a new one will come . . . and as you said, each soul must choose its own lessons. Nothing you could say would teach what I choose to learn," Helghul said, stepping toward the edge of the boat.

"Helghul, no!" Theron cried, dropping the blanket that had been draped over her and jumping to her feet.

"I told you to call me Black Elder. See you in the next life!" Helghul yelled, and the Emissaries watched in stunned horror as he dove into the water. Solenna jumped next, followed by Abaddon. The rest of the Adversaries, like lemmings, pitched themselves overboard. Diving deeper, they deliberately gulped salty water into their lungs. Thaddeus was the last to jump.

"Sleep and death are brothers!" he shouted, before completing a skillful swan dive.

The notion of suicide was alien to the Emissaries. It was a phenomenon that had never occurred in the Golden Age. Even the term for what was happening was foreign. It was a word lost along with the ancient languages of previous cycles. Over the Ages, views about self-harming changed. Some believed committing suicide brought disharmony in the afterlife, and one's energy could be trapped in the world between or the Down Below—the chasm from whence the Beast had emerged. Others believed there was no judgment, regardless of the manner one died; there was only judgment as far as how one had lived. One's actions and choices in life determined the path of a soul's next incarnation.

"Stop!" the Emissaries cried out in protest, running to the edge as the Adversaries jumped. It was traumatizing to witness people they had known and loved doing something so unthinkable.

"We have to save them! We cannot let them drown!" Theron shouted, staring into the water.

"They will not be saved, and you will die trying. Their lessons await them on the other side," Red Elder said in a calming voice, still hovering on the Tablet.

"I must try," she said stubbornly, jumping into the churning water, determined to save someone. She could not stand by and do nothing.

Theron swam down, following the bubbles deeper, searching. The water grew colder as she neared the motionless specks hanging in the murky ocean. She spun Solenna's drifting body, but her swollen eyes were dead and staring. She swam to another, then another, searching for any signs of life, but there were none. The Adversaries had not held their breaths for survival; they had inhaled the water, willingly betraying their reluctant lungs. They had paddled as deeply as they could before their bodies shut down.

Theron's chest was burning and filled with grief. She was ready to give up when she saw Helghul, floating motionless. She swam to him, expecting that he, like the others, was beyond rescue. Clinging to one last hope, she turned his face to hers, and at her touch, his eyes popped open. Unlike the others, Helghul's lips were tightly pursed. He was still alive! Theron grabbed hold of him, and kicking her legs, tried to propel them both upward. The Adversary resisted. He did not wish to be saved, but he would gladly take her down with him. He clasped tightly onto Theron's arm, and she immediately realized her peril. She fought against him, but his grip was unyielding. As he stared into her frantic eyes, his face twisted with cruelty.

We will die together, he said telepathically. Theron exhaled valuable air from her lungs as she struggled, sending frantic bubbles to the surface.

You will die alone! Theron transmitted back to him, and with a hard knee to his gut, his final air bubble burst from his lips, and she freed herself. Helghul tried to pursue her, but he had no more air. Still grabbing at her fleeing legs, he gulped his last salty breaths and then slumped motionless as his body slowly sank deeper. Gasping for air, Theron broke through the surface, and Red Elder swooped down to retrieve her.

The dead were left to the sea, and the elementals reclaimed their material bodies. Theron and the other Emissaries were wrapped in blankets as Red Elder stepped off the Emerald Tablet onto the deck. The crowd lowered their heads in grief, and Red Elder led a blessing for their unfortunate shipmates and the others killed at home and around the planet. Together, they cried for the loss and for the corruption of their friends.

"Let us Merge. There will soon come a time when the Unity Grid sleeps along with your memories, but that is not now. Let us connect our loving energy while we still have the ability to do so," Red Elder said.

The Emissaries touched one another with their arms, feet, and hands; and as they did, their shines linked, expanding in beautiful geometric forms. A web of colorful light lifted into the sky above them, and breathtaking prisms were cast as the Unity Grid reflected off the dust particles.

The world they had known was rapidly changing. Red Elder knew that a cosmic event was underway, and the Emissaries and Adversaries were key to the balance of good and evil.

Red Elder had never intended to take Helghul and his followers as far as Khem, for having them along would have posed a constant threat to the Emissaries and the security of the Emerald Tablet. He had planned to leave the Adversaries at the first habitable island, but he had underestimated Helghul's ferocity. It was barely the Silver Age. If Helghul had already embraced his ruthless ambition to this degree, he would certainly be a formidable Black Elder.

⋈ ⋈ ⋈

The Emissaries' journey continued. It was a month later when primitive survivors on the shores of Khem, later called Egypt, greeted them as if they were gods. The people were sick and starving. Their crops and animals had died from the dust and lack of sunlight, and they had none of the technological advancements and higher knowledge that Atitala had enjoyed.

"Why are they so undeveloped in this advanced Age?" Theron asked.

"Many levels of experience and understanding are happening simultaneously," Red Elder replied.

In the coming years, the simple villagers were taught by the great master, Red Elder, and his students. With the help of the Emerald Tablet and the knowledge of the Atitalans, their civilization flourished beyond anything they had previously imagined. The Emissaries and citizens of Khem encoded the secrets of the Golden Age and Oneness in their art and writing. As the generations died out, the Emissaries' firsthand memories of the information were forgotten. Eventually the Adversaries infiltrated the developing civilization, and as was the case in many places across the globe, wars broke out.

The declining Ages took hold, but Egypt remained a beacon of civilization for centuries. The Emissaries were tasked with guiding humankind back into the Golden Age, though first consciousness would fall, and there would be darkness and suffering as a pall of individualism and separation embraced the globe. The Emissaries knew that they must maintain the Light, no matter how dim the flame.

Theron lived out her life in Khem. She died an old woman, her body worn down by years of service to the people. She was surrounded by loving friends but no family. She had never married or had children. She had watched for Marcus, hoping her soulmate would find her, and despite his relentless searching, their paths never crossed.

With her final breath, she whispered, "Marcus, how many incarnations will it be before we are reunited?"

Chapter 2

The Burden of Memory

Present day, Seattle, Washington

It had been thirteen thousand years since the Golden Age lifetime in Atitala, when Marcus and Theron had chosen to become soulmates and Emissaries. Quinn instantly recognized Eden when she entered his apartment with Nate, and he was overcome by the impact of her shine.

When the soulmates touched hands, there was a surge of energy. Eden felt an intense jolt to her solar plexus, and every hair on her body stood on end. Their physical connection ignited her chakras and snaked up and down her spine in an infinite loop. To her, the apartment suddenly seemed brighter, warmer, and less neglected. The lined maps and piles of paper now appeared to be laid by design and orderly. Eden's perspective had shifted, along with her body chemistry. She felt like Alice finding Wonderland, or Lucy entering Narnia through the Wardrobe—as if she'd been transported to another world. Though she couldn't see Marcus's shine surrounding Quinn, her Theron-consciousness remembered him, and the spark between them was inflamed.

What is this? My God, he's so, so . . . What is he? she thought. The attraction and familiarity running between them made no sense. She was flustered, and she imagined him pulling her into his arms and kissing her, without a word. *He's gorgeous!* she thought, admiring his messy dark hair, cleft chin, and gentle eyes. The power of her attraction to the stranger mystified her. *Is he feeling what I'm feeling?* Eden wondered.

"Hey . . . are you crying, dude?" Nate asked incredulously. Until that moment, Quinn hadn't realized that he was.

"It's just my eyes tearing up from working," he explained, finding his voice. He reluctantly released Eden's fingers and wiped away the tears.

"Sorry to barge in, but I'm a huge fan of your blog. When Nate told me who he was staying with, I forced him to bring me. I doubt you remember me, but I comment on your posts sometimes. I'm Anderson88," Eden said, beaming at Quinn. Anderson88 was the tag she used when commenting online. Though her words were calm and composed, the emotions coursing through her were not.

"Anderson88? Impressive. Your posts stand out," Quinn said, his voice full of desire, wishing that she knew him but encouraged by her response. "I always thought Anderson88 was a dude," he added.

"Nope, not a dude," Eden said, smiling, her eyelids lowered seductively, her enthusiasm obvious.

"Lucky for me," Quinn said flirtatiously.

Lucky for you? Nate thought to himself, stunned. This was all wrong! What was happening? Quinn didn't seem the least bit cynical and depressed now, and the energy between Eden and him was undeniable.

Eden and Nate had come to see Quinn for two reasons: First, Quinn's Emissary blog had been instrumental in inspiring her to proceed with the documentary she was creating, *The Arrival—Birth of the Crystal Children,* and she hoped to propose a collaboration. Second, Nate had been concerned for his friend's bleak mental state. Quinn had seemed especially despondent when Nate had left him earlier, and Eden's previous work filming soldiers with PTSD made him think she could help. Nate knew depression was a vicious cycle that caused people to isolate themselves, making their separation and loneliness worse, and though he had only gleaned a tiny piece of Quinn's suffering, it was enough. He wanted to help.

"Maybe we should go?" Nate suggested, and Quinn's brown eyes flashed from him, back to Eden.

"No, please, I'd like you to stay. I've been cooped up here all night. Let's have a drink. I'd love to hear about your documentary," Quinn said, maintaining eye contact with Eden.

Quinn's Marcus-consciousness was frantic. Theron must not leave. The bachelor had traveled the world looking for her. He had settled in Seattle three years earlier, knowing that Theron could be anyone, anywhere—male or female—and she might not even be born yet. He had missed her terribly. He craved her spirit the way an addict craves a fix, and his blood and soul were ignited by her.

"We just got here, Nate. We haven't even asked Quinn about helping on the project yet," Eden insisted. She didn't want to leave. She wanted to linger in the messy little apartment with this beautiful man; and his books, diagrams, and sketches that were pinned up and spread about. Her rational side tried to quash the emotions rushing through her, but she knew for certain that she wanted to stay and venture farther down the rabbit hole.

"Nate tells me your documentary's about Crystal Children?" Quinn said.

"That's what I'm hoping to talk to *you* about," Eden said.

Nate grumbled in protest, but Quinn led Eden to the sofa, where he cleared a spot among his array of climate charts, books, and dog-eared magazines. He chatted about her blog comments, and Nate reluctantly took a seat in the chair beside her. He tried to catch Quinn's eye, but the Emissary intentionally avoided looking at him.

"I only have beer," Quinn said. The apartment was small, and the narrow kitchen was only a few steps away.

"Beer's great," Eden said, and within seconds, Quinn handed one to each of them.

Quinn and Eden sat side by side on the sofa, his knees almost touching hers, and they quickly fell into a deep discussion about the consciousness revolution.

Nate stared at his bottle, muttering sullenly. *What a fool I was, worrying about him, and now Eden has been . . . mesmerized,* he thought, struggling to identify what the hell was happening. Nate was annoyed as he recognized the obvious attraction between them, and the threat Quinn posed to his romantic aspirations.

Eden had never intended to have a romantic relationship with her cinematographer. He was younger, a pleasant dalliance at most, but she never mixed professional and personal business. Eden had known Nate was interested, but she was accustomed to dealing with crushes, and though she hated to admit it, sometimes it helped her to have a slight edge. Eden was certain she could keep the relationship with Nate strictly professional; Quinn, however, was another story. She had the rare feeling she'd known him her entire life. Eden didn't remember ever feeling this way before, not even with her husband. Theirs had been a warm, easy, joyful relationship, but Quinn's magnetism was something new.

Nate was completely unnerved by their connection, and he resented his pal's intrusion into his plans, no matter how unintentionally it had begun. Quinn ignored the bitterness emanating from Nate; he had no choice. He didn't want to injure his friend, but he wouldn't let anything come between him and Theron.

"I want to hear all about the documentary," Quinn chirped, his voice happier than Nate had ever heard him. "I've been writing about Crystal Children for a while. They're remarkable when they're authentic. What made you interested enough to make a film about them?" Quinn asked.

Eden was once again aware of how attractive he was—the muscles in his jaw, the intensity in his eyes—and she struggled to focus. "Your blog helped me recognize that my son, Elijah, was a Crystal Child," Eden said, her voice catching in her throat. "It was a huge relief."

Oh, shit. Seriously? Nate thought. That was big. That was a Quinn-the-super-hero kind of revelation, and he could see the gratitude sparkling in Eden's eyes.

"Wow. I'm so glad if I helped," Quinn said.

"You did. More than I can tell you. Once I realized there were other kids like him, I was able to truly accept him. It's why I want to help other people really understand their special kids."

"Tell me about him. What's he like?"

"He's always been so unusual. It started as soon as he could talk, and that was really early—full sentences at about nine months. He told me about all these dreams and bizarre stories of places and people and inventions. He started drawing detailed pictures, some quite disturbing. He tends to get frustrated easily, which teachers find difficult."

"I can relate." Quinn smiled. "I feel frustrated a lot of the time too."

"My first instinct was to take him to a child psychologist . . . three, actually, but they wanted to 'fix' him and drug him when I thought he was gifted, so I looked elsewhere."

"Like where?" Nate asked, wanting to be part of the conversation. Quinn wondered why he hadn't already heard this story. How could it not have been his first question?

"Everywhere! The internet, other moms, then the shaman of a local native band who's a friend of mine. Eventually, as he got a little bit older, I just asked Elijah if he remembered where he'd been before he was born and came to live with me," she said, feeling sheepish.

"Smart! What did he say?" Quinn asked, smiling. He wanted to touch her. It was painful to sit so close and not feel her skin and complete their connection.

"He said he's a traveler, an advanced soul with a special mission," she said, smiling. "I know it sounds crazy," she added, taking a sip of her beer and sensing the skepticism Nate was trying to conceal.

"But you believe him?" Quinn asked.

"I do, especially after reading your blogs about the Crystal Children. Now, I've seen them for myself. I met a three-year-old who's painting like Monet, and another girl who's playing piano concertos without a single lesson. I've lined up meetings with kids speaking foreign languages and telling stories of ancient times that they couldn't possibly know about. Yes, I believe him."

Nate watched the bonding pair in distress, anxious to jump in, to be a part of the exchange, but he had nothing to add.

"How old was Elijah when he told you that?" Quinn asked, basking in her glow.

"About three and a half. He still couldn't say his *L*'s and *R*'s. He would say 'messenjow' instead of 'messenger,' but the stuff he came up with blew my mind."

"How old is he now?" Quinn asked. He had wondered if the many Crystal Children he had read about were Emissaries. The way they spoke and communicated on the internet implied some past-life memory. They had an advanced connection to their higher consciousness that he hadn't seen in thousands of years. Humankind was ascending into a Bronze Age, so Quinn knew that changes were bound to happen. Children were being born with more evolved cellular memories.

Would all the Emissaries have memory soon? Would Theron? he wondered. There was no way to know.

"Eleven. He just had his birthday," she said.

"I'd love to meet him," Quinn said.

Nate was dumbfounded, aware he was outside of what was happening between them, and he was growing more irate by the minute. Nate regretted his decision to introduce them. He had wanted to pop in, check on his pal, recruit the blogger, play the hero, and leave. Moreover, he was puzzled by Quinn's behavior. A buddy should know better! Guys understood each other, and Quinn was playing dumb, doing it all wrong, and there was no sign of the sad sack he had been just hours earlier.

Nate knew he was a bystander, an obstacle between his date and his best friend. He could not see the shine dancing around the room, but he could feel it moving through them. He was anxious to leave and break the spell that had been conjured up.

"I know you're busy with your blog, but we could really use your help on this project. Not many people are experts on consciousness and alternative history. Plus, your audience is our target market, so your endorsement would be huge for us. And, of course, it's a paying gig," Eden chuckled.

"Definitely! I'm in," Quinn said. She didn't have to convince him. If she hadn't asked, he would have insisted.

"Hey, uh . . . Eden, you said something about getting back for your sitter?" Nate reminded her, desperate to get her out of there.

"Oh, it's getting late . . . um, yeah, I should go," she stammered, looking at the dusty clock in the corner and setting down her still-full beer. Nate was relieved, and he jumped up.

"Call me tomorrow. We can figure out how I'll contribute," Quinn said.

Eden searched her purse for her phone to enter his contact information and realized with dismay that she'd left it in the car. Quinn took her number and promised to text. Once again, their eyes locked, and her stomach lurched. Quinn squeezed her arm and let his hand rest on her elbow. Nate's face was flush with anger as he pushed his way through the middle of them and ushered her out.

Amazing! The whole thing had been extraordinary. Quinn sympathized with how confused Eden and Nate must be feeling. He was overwhelmed with emotion, and *he* understood why.

When Eden got in the car, all the positive feelings surging through her were immediately replaced.

"Oh, God! I missed five calls!" she exclaimed, dialing home. *Shit!* She hadn't checked her phone in more than an hour. *Five missed calls! No time to read the texts! Shit!* She was filled with worry and mother-guilt.

Her stomach was in her throat when the line picked up on the first ring. "Hello? Yes, I'm sorry I missed it . . . in the car . . . but you're okay? What . . . oh, honey . . . okay. Yes! Thank God. No, no, I'm sorry. Yes I'm on my way. No, on my way, twenty minutes. I know . . . I love you too. Twenty minutes, buddy. Okay, bye," she said as Nate sped toward her car.

"What happened? Is Elijah okay?" Nate asked. He knew the boy was all right; he could tell by the way her tone had changed by the end of the call. He was glad she'd shaken herself free of Quinn's trance.

"Yeah, some kids were giving him a rough time. He's okay. I just need to get home," she said, filled with self-reproach. She was fiercely protective of her son. He seemed to have so many challenges relating to other people, and losing his dad had made it worse.

Nate chattered about their upcoming travel schedule as he drove, trying to push any thoughts of Quinn from her mind, but after the initial panic over her son subsided, Nate's words faded into the background, and thoughts of Quinn filled her head. She could still feel his hand on her arm—not figuratively—literally. Her skin was still tingling where they had touched.

"Quinn's something else," she said after a minute.

"Yep. Just what I was thinking," Nate said, pulling into the lot where she had left her car.

"You okay?"

"Sure, no problem," Nate said, not wanting to come off as jealous. She might change her mind about working and traveling with him if he wasn't careful. He'd had plenty of girlfriends, but he had never felt jealous before. His attraction to Eden had been immediate and powerful, and watching her with Quinn had stirred up ugly, competitive feelings in him.

"I'll call you tomorrow," Eden said, anxious to get home to her son.

As Eden parked in front of her small bungalow, the front door flew open. "Mom! Where *were* you!" Elijah cried out as he ran down the crooked walkway into her arms. "You didn't answer your phone! You *always* answer your phone! I thought you were dead! Or kidnapped . . . or—"

"I'm fine. I accidentally left it in the car," she explained, hugging his head against her chest where he'd buried it. *Thank God!* Elijah was okay. The angst in her gut lessened as she ushered him back inside.

"Let me look at you. Tell me exactly what happened," Eden said, lifting his chin with her finger and peering into his face. Under the foyer light, she could see that his eye was bruised and puffed up, and his lip was swollen, with a bloody line where it had been cut.

"I was at the park. There were four kids from school. They pushed me and called me a freak, and a . . . a retard," he said, gulping and crying fresh tears upon remembering. He knew his mom hated that word, and it was humiliating to say it out loud. Elijah inwardly berated himself for being weaker than those kids, and for being hurt by their ignorant words. His anger rose, and Eden hugged him to soothe it away.

"Did you fight back?"

"Yeah. After the big kid punched me in the face, the other guys jumped in, so I started yelling like a howler monkey and swinging like crazy, and they took off." He demonstrated by swinging his skinny arms wildly, and Eden couldn't help but smile.

"You didn't hit first, though?" she asked. It would not have been the first time Elijah's temper had caused him to lash out.

"Mommmm! There were *four* of them! How dumb do you think I am?" the boy replied, rolling his eyes.

"Good," she said, hugging him again. "Where's Lisa?"

"I'm here. Sorry. I tried to call you," the babysitter said from the kitchen doorway, sounding bored. "I thought he'd be fine. The park's only a block away. They were just other little kids," she said.

Lisa left out the fact that she'd been relieved to get rid of the boy for a while and that her face had been glued to her phone the entire time. Elijah was cute, with his short sticking-up hair and thick ruby lips, but he was intense. He followed Lisa from room to room, asking questions about her college courses and occasionally correcting her answers. He was weird, and a know-it-all, and she couldn't really blame the other kids for saying so, or for wanting to sock him.

Eden knew what the babysitter was thinking; she read the disdain in her expression, and she was glad the girl was old enough to drive herself back to her dorm. She closed the door behind Lisa for the last time and swept Elijah up into her arms. He was almost too big. She was small, and he was tall, but she was determined to hug away the hour she had been unreachable.

Children could be so cruel. Eden wished she could take it on for him—being different, feeling like a freak and an oddity among his peers. Elijah was too smart for his own good, and his acute awareness of his strangeness isolated him. She would have borne it for him if it were possible. This mother's love was boundless.

⚬⚬⚬ ⚬⚬⚬ ⚬⚬⚬

The following morning, Eden got a frantic phone call from a mother of a Crystal Child she had scheduled for an interview in the coming weeks.

"He's gone! Missing out of his room since last night! Who have you told about my son?" the woman demanded accusingly.

"Mrs. Rodriguez? No one. Everything we've discussed has been completely confidential," Eden assured her, filling with concern.

"It's something to do with *you*! It has to be. We were fine before you contacted us, and now Miguel is missing," Manuela Rodriguez said, breaking down.

"Have you contacted the police?"

"Of course! They do nothing! They say he's a runaway, but I *knew* I shouldn't have told you anything!" the woman accused shrilly. "I've protected him all these years, and now this!"

Eden had been referred to the Rodríguezes through another Crystal Child, and though Miguel's mother had been extremely hesitant to let him talk to her, she had finally agreed after months of gentle convincing. If Miguel was truly capable of what they said he was, he would be a marvel . . . a literal telekinetic superhero.

Eden hung up the phone and stared at it in her hands, feeling useless and anxious. The Rodríguezes were in South Miami. There was nothing she could do to help find him from Seattle, but Manuela's assertions that Eden was responsible were troubling.

Could there be a connection? Only a handful of people involved in the project knew anything about her scheduled interviewees. *Would publicizing the abilities of the children make them targets? Were they in danger?* Eden thought. She couldn't imagine losing her son, and her heart ached for Miguel's mom. She dabbed the corners of her eyes before finding Elijah and clamping a big hug on him. Elijah pushed free, video game bound, and Eden's thoughts turned to Quinn. A moment later, her phone vibrated in her hand.

Great meeting you. Looking forward to connecting on the Crystal Project, Quinn texted. She left Elijah to his Fortnite and called Quinn right away.

"Greece . . . in two days?" Quinn asked, dumbfounded, as she told him her plans. His happiness upon receiving her phone call plummeted. Theron was leaving, going half a world away after he had only just found her. He felt the misery he knew so well creeping at the edge of his thoughts, threatening to rush in.

"Yes, we fly out at nine Monday night. Didn't Nate tell you?" she asked, surprised that the roommates hadn't spoken. "He just booked the same flight."

It was about two weeks sooner than originally planned, but after Elijah's black eye, and now learning about Miguel, she was happy to leave for the anonymity of the road.

"I need to see you," Quinn said, trying to mask the desperation he was feeling. "I'm going to help with the Crystal Project, and we need to figure out what that looks like. Can you fit me in? Give me an hour?" Quinn asked.

"Yes, of course, thank you," she said. "I won't have long. Tomorrow for lunch? There's so . . . so much to do," Eden stammered.

Nervous—he made her nervous—and excited! She wasn't sure why someone she barely knew suddenly occupied so much of her mental energy, and she was hesitant to begin something she couldn't finish.

"Lunch is great," Quinn responded.

"How about Café Zazou on Capitol Hill at noon? It's close to my place," she suggested. Her stomach flipped with anticipation, yet she was irritated by the schoolgirl nerves he elicited.

Fitting, he thought. Paris and World War II were not so long behind her. Theron had no way of knowing, but still, even without memory, she had been drawn to the Zazou. Over the Ages, Quinn had observed that the-soul-that-forgets was still driven forward with instincts, karma, and purpose—drawn to the people and places that had provided warmth and comfort in lifetimes past.

"See you tomorrow, then," Quinn replied, allowing himself a moment of happiness and relief.

The Emissary hummed while he showered. However briefly, Marcus and Theron were reunited. After so much darkness, Quinn finally felt hopeful, but he knew it was temporary, and even in that moment, his memories tormented him.

Something always goes wrong, he thought. *And where's Helghul?* Quinn wondered for just about the millionth time. Helghul always showed up—somewhere, sometime—and too often Marcus was sadly unprepared. *You're still fucking unprepared!* he thought bitterly, getting shampoo in his eyes and rinsing roughly.

Memories of Theron and Helghul were so entangled with who Quinn was and who he'd been that they couldn't be unraveled. The three were entwined like the strands of a whip. He had not encountered Helghul in this lifetime, and he wondered what fresh hell the Adversary was creating. Quinn's Marcus-consciousness never understood what had made his former friend embrace the darkness, but he knew it was his job to counter it.

The Iron Age had transitioned into the ascending Bronze Age, and the spiraling Great Year Cycle was too slowly emerging from its darkest depths while humanity's consciousness was awakening in tiny jolts and jerks. There had been so much death, so much senseless destruction, over the last twelve hundred years of the Iron Age. Those harrowing centuries had robbed him of his connection to his soul's purpose, but the spiritual winter was thawing, and Quinn knew if people didn't destroy the planet, the Bronze Age would surge upward, transitioning into the Silver Age and back into the enlightened Golden Age.

It was a cycle that had been repeated countless times, and it could be plotted in the cosmic alignments. As the Earth took her twenty-six-thousand-year wobble through the zodiac, civilization cycled, and consciousness rose and fell. It was a slow process from a human perspective. The density and cruelty of humankind was far from finished, and the transition from one Age to the next would be messy. The old paradigms would not go out without a fight.

It was twenty-four hours before Quinn would see Eden again, but that was nothing compared to millennia of longing and searching. However, the Emissary felt every minute slowly tick by, burdened by a profound sense of impending doom and a gnawing worry that she might cancel.

Greece? Of all places? What have I missed? So many lives, so many lessons. Have a puff and relax, he thought. *No! That is exactly the opposite of what I need to do! Greece . . . why Greece?* Greece had been a triumph and a miserable failure for the Emissary, and it was the second time he had been reminded of the country that week. The Seattle Art Museum was having a huge exhibit featuring ancient Greece all month, and he had seen the posters plastered all over town.

Nate hadn't come home last night. *Had anything happened between him and Eden?* Quinn wondered. Eden hadn't let on when they'd spoken on the phone, but sitting around his apartment waiting for Nate to show up to confront Quinn for moving in on his date wasn't something Quinn wanted to do. The Emissary decided to go out and listen to the synchronicity of the Universe speaking to him. He pulled his coat lapels together as he walked Seattle's grey, glistening streets toward the museum. His dark hair dripped down his collar, and he lamented having left his umbrella at home.

Quinn shook off before entering the museum and stared at the ceiling, passing under sweeping banner images of Plato, Aristotle, and Alexander the Great, which were hanging overhead.

Plato had recorded a myth that was especially meaningful to Quinn. According to Greek mythology, humans had originally been created with four arms, four legs, and a head with two faces. Zeus, fearing their power, split them in two parts, condemning them to spend their lives in search of their other half. Quinn could relate. He'd always felt torn apart and had spent eons searching.

Think, Emissary. Remember! Everything that happened in that lifetime matters! Learn, dammit, or you're going to live the same lessons again and again until you do!

Quinn believed he was suffering because he was failing to learn. He believed that when he figured things out, the lessons would change, and though he would undoubtedly have new things to learn, perhaps he and Theron wouldn't be torn apart at every turn. *What am I missing?* he thought in frustration.

As he strolled among posters of philosophical quotes, there were images of the Acropolis, the Parthenon, and hundreds of bits of historic architecture and pottery. The familiar likenesses and artwork triggered Quinn's past-life memories of Greece, and he let them flow over him in waves.

He turned as if someone had called to him. There on a pedestal stood a bust of Socrates immortalized in marble, his blank eyes staring into space—dead but not dead. It was a fair likeness, and his distinct hairline and forehead were familiar—an old friend. Quinn reached out tenderly to touch his face.

Such an inspiration . . . such a waste. One of the wisest men to ever walk the earth, he thought bitterly. *What are you trying to tell me? What do I need to know?* he wondered. Quinn allowed himself to be transported to another time. Surrounded by trinkets and images of an Age long gone, he forced himself to remember. He had visited the museum hoping to recall or understand something he might have missed, something that would help him in this lifetime. He remembered himself on the shores of the Aegean Sea, the scent of olives in the air, his face lifted to the warm sun and the sound of seabirds calling in his ears.

Chapter 3

The Honorable Mentor

Greece, 341 BCE

Aristocles was a child of wealth and privilege who spent his sun-filled afternoons in lessons or at leisure. At eleven, he was an oddity among his peers, preferring the company of adults.

The curious boy was wandering along the docks of Athens, smelling the sour sea air. Commerce and hustle flowed all about him while haggard fishermen lugged their heavy, rank loads by cart or over their stooped shoulders. It was a hard, dirty place smelling of rotted fish and cat urine; he found it exhilarating. His well-made leather sandals were little protection from the foulness of the place, and his fine clothes and coiffed silky hair stood out. Everywhere around him, servants haggled for their masters' dinners, and sellers scowled as they were being coerced to lower their prices.

The boy noticed a quiet alcove cooled by the shade of a nearby warship, with its three banks of oars. Tired and hot from walking, he ignored the filth and sat down to rest. He gazed at the blue of the sea, and it lulled him. Opening his satchel, he withdrew a scroll: the story of *Pyramus and Thisbe*. In this tale, a beautiful girl and her true love are kept apart by their families. When the lad mistakenly believes his love is eaten by a lion on the eve of their elopement, he kills himself. His intended bride, upon discovering him dead, kills herself.

Aristocles had carefully written his favorite tale onto a parchment and had read it many times. He had only just begun rereading it when the scroll was torn from his unsuspecting grasp. Startled, he looked up into the glare of the sun and made out the outline of three boys, slightly older but significantly larger than he, staring down at him with contempt.

"What here, *Plato*?" the tallest, loudest boy snarled. The epithet *Plato*, meaning "fat," was meant to insult him but did not have the desired effect. The bully waved the curling page in Aristocles's stunned face. He tried to get up but was pushed back to the ground, where he landed with a painful thump.

"Give it back!" Aristocles demanded futilely, still planted by a forceful palm to the hard earth beneath him.

"The pudgy *emperor* thinks we are his slaves," the leader crowed. "You do not rule here, *Plato*. This is *our* territory," he said, tossing Aristocles's document into the foul pool of seawater below. Aristocles was helpless to stop them and was now more concerned for his own safety than for his belongings. The boys squared off, legs bent, ready to wrestle. Aristocles prepared for the challenge. The bullies attacked all at once. He was no match for them and could only cover his head with his arms, blocking their blows.

"Ay there!" a stern voice called out, intervening. Aristocles opened his eyes and looked past the three miscreants to see a wide, thick man swaggering toward them. "Bullies and bastards!" the man boomed, shaking a fist in the air as he approached. "To intimidate a boy and steal his belongings is play?" he barked, coming nose to nose with the nervous leader. In one swift motion, the rumpled man lifted the bully by the throat, dangling him like a freshly caught fish over the water and shocking all of them with his easy strength.

"You laugh when your purpose is cruelty? Your ignorance would be improved by reading," he said, dropping the struggling boy with a splash into the filth below. Turning to the troublemaker's two accomplices, he added, "I suggest you two thick-skulled wonders emulate someone with ethics!" The boys ran off, and Aristocles watched gleefully as his would-be assailant splashed frantically toward the edge.

"Retrieve the scroll!" the older man demanded, blocking the boy from climbing out. When the soggy document was ashore, the boy again tried to climb out. "Swim around to the pier and get out of my sight, or I will let that putrid water bloat you like a discarded carp."

The breathless youngster began making his way to shore. Aristocles stood beside the unusual man, studying him, as they watched the swimmer struggle. Aristocles had the sense that the surly stranger would have jumped in for rescue at the first sign of the boy being in distress, but his theory went untested. The bully successfully pulled himself out of the water a few minutes later.

Aristocles guessed that the man was somewhere around the age of forty-five, but he had obviously lived a difficult life. His ugly face was a mass of scars and lines framed by sagebrush whiskers at his brow and chin. His eyelids had white polyps and bumps on them, and his nose was a twisted lump stranded just left of center. His hairline receded well behind his ears, and the strands he did have were stringy and long. When the protector opened his mouth to speak, his teeth and tongue were purple from wine. Despite his ugliness, the boy had never known a man who seemed so comfortable in his own skin.

"Ha! A lesson taught is worth its time!" the man said, clapping Aristocles on the back, unintentionally sending the young boy stumbling toward the water's edge. "Take care! My best effort to spare you will be wasted if you cannot hold your footing and you end up in that rancid soup."

"I owe you my great thanks. They would have left me in a heap," Aristocles said, holding his sopping parchment and grateful that his only injury was a dull ache where he had been thumped solidly on the back.

"What is it you are reading?" the older man asked. He looked carefully at the rotund boy, who was not an adolescent one would typically see at the docks alone. Obviously a son of privilege, he looked unusual. *He must be inquisitive, curious, and fearless to come here alone, or possibly he is an imbecile,* the older man thought.

"*Pyramus and Thisbe,*" Aristocles answered condescendingly. He doubted this unsightly commoner could read at all.

"They meet a tragic end. What have you learned from such a sorry tale?" the man asked, still sizing up the boy. Aristocles rudely rolled his eyes without realizing it. No longer in danger, his confidence and self-importance were restored.

"I have learned, nothing is as it seems, and love is boundless. Are you a . . . teacher?" the boy asked doubtfully, certain that the rumpled man before him was of a lowly standing.

"Aaaach! A teacher seeks to impart only his limited knowledge. I would rather challenge each thought and its process. I wish to encourage others to think," the man replied.

"What is your fee?" Aristocles asked, reaching inside his cloak for his purse. He assumed the stranger had helped him, expecting some gain or reward.

"The conversation is free, for the love of knowledge, *Plato*, but leave your condescension with your wet nurse," the man answered with a crooked grin. He turned as Aristocles frowned, and without another word, the helper disappeared into the maze of the pier.

Aristocles walked home contemplating the man. He could not imagine his uncles dangling a fishing line, let alone a boy, over the filthy dockside. He had never met such a fascinating character.

Aristocles had been a playful, carefree child, but by the age of eight, he had begun to feel ill at ease and was inexplicably in a constant state of "should be elsewhere." Aristocles felt he was different, and that he was destined to do something great, but to others he seemed strange, an old man in children's clothing. As he aged, he discovered gradually that he had an internal voice that eventually became known to him as Marcus. Afraid of ridicule, the boy told no one about his Marcus-voice but grew to trust its counsel implicitly. It was a part of him, a clever and ancient voice within, with many stories and much wisdom to share.

>―< >―< >―<

"Mother, what is this performance that so many have come to?" Aristocles asked, watching the people file along the high stone walls into the amphitheater. He and his mother had bypassed the clamoring lines, using an entrance reserved for high-ranking families and officials. The stone benches earmarked for them had been made comfortable with fine silk and linen cushions, and they sat waiting, with a clear view of the circular stage.

"It is a play called *The Clouds*," Perictione, the boy's mother, replied while greeting her fellow theater-goers as they settled in nearby.

From where they sat, Aristocles could see the recently completed Parthenon, lit by torches and dominating the hilltop in the distance. He marveled at its perfection. The voice in his head recognized its golden ratio and the secrets hidden in the divine proportions.

Anytus, a powerful military general and member of the political assembly, sat nearby. Though they had never met, Aristocles had seen him many times surrounded by the most affluent of Athenian society. He watched now while the pompous peacocks nodded deferentially to the general, and Aristocles wondered about the man's charisma. Though the general's influence and power were far-reaching, Anytus had the shine of an ordinary man.

Sensing he was being observed, General Anytus's spine prickled, and intuitively his eyes snapped toward the staring boy. Their eyes locked briefly before Aristocles looked away, but the boy felt the general's gaze linger on him.

The audience quieted as two actors took the stage: one standing on the ground and one sitting in a basket suspended in the air in front of a backdrop painted to look like the sky.

"What is the narrative?" Aristocles whispered to his mother.

"It portrays the philosopher Socrates. Hush now, it begins," Perictione replied.

Throughout the dialogue, the audience stomped their feet, cheered, and laughed where expected. However, one audience member seemed amused in the most unexpected places, laughing loudly with great vigor and distracting not only his fellow audience members but the performers as well. The actors continued in their dialogue.

"Socrates, what are you doing?" the first actor asked.

"I am walking in the air and speculating about the Sun," the second actor replied. At this, the disruptive audience member laughed noisily.

"And so you look down upon the gods from your basket, and not from Earth?" the first actor continued. At this, the man in the audience shouted.

"That would be treason!" the troublemaker said, causing those around him to snicker. The theater had never been so interactive and interesting to Aristocles. He joined in the laughter and craned his neck to identify the patron responsible. Aristocles was astounded to see the misshapen face of the man from the quay, sparkling with mischief.

"Who is that man?" Aristocles asked his mother as the play continued.

"That is the *real* Socrates." Perictione smiled. "He's quite something, is he not?"

"Indeed!"

Once the play was over, Perictione and her son made their way to the exit. Aristocles peered through the many bodies and tried to catch a glimpse of the eminent philosopher. Socrates saw the boy and called out to him.

"Young Plato!" he said, approaching them. He had a playful glint in his eye as he politely acknowledged Perictione. "What did you think of that mockery?"

"Do you resent the comparison?" Aristocles asked him.

"Why should I resent when an ass kicks me? Come, meet the writer!" Socrates said, leading them toward the stage. Aristocles was amazed. This ugly, scruffy man was the renowned philosopher and mentor. How could it be so? *Nothing truly is as it seems!* the boy thought.

Throughout the introduction, Socrates observed Aristocles carefully. This boy was exactly the reason he had opened his school. He asked thoughtful questions and considered the answers wisely. He was a spark, and Socrates could see that Aristocles's potential and depth had yet to be discovered.

"Let us continue our dialogue another day. I am called to consume large goblets of ale with this playwright and speak to his blasphemy! When you are ready to forget what you think you know, young Plato, I can be found at the Painted Stoa," Socrates said.

"Thank you, Socrates!" Perictione exclaimed, placing her hands proudly on her son's shoulders. She and her brothers had been trying to enroll Aristocles in his school for some time, with no luck.

"Wonder is the beginning of wisdom. It is a door rarely opened. Are you interested in learning its secrets?" Socrates asked.

"I would be grateful for it," Aristocles said, his plump face flushing red.

"Anytus! I see you lurking there! Come, meet young Plato. He may indeed replace you someday," Socrates called out.

The boy was surprised to see General Anytus standing nearby. He had not noticed him while under Socrates's glowing attention. Anytus scowled and turned his back, ignoring Socrates's overture. He walked toward the exit with his wife and an entourage of doting politicians.

"The General and I have a . . . *difficult* friendship," Socrates said loudly, winking at Aristocles. "Thank you for the stirring conversation . . . perhaps another time, Anytus?"

Perictione cringed upon seeing that her son was being used to bait the influential general, but she was proud that Socrates had praised her boy publicly.

⋊⋉ ⋊⋉ ⋊⋉

The next day, a strong desire to learn delivered Aristocles to the door of his new mentor.

"Are you prepared to pursue the truth, Plato?" Socrates asked.

"I am," Aristocles said.

Aristocles was not in school long before it was clear that the nickname Plato would stick. The moniker was thoroughly embraced, and for the remainder of his long life, few people would know his proper name at all.

Plato's Marcus-voice grew clearer and stronger as he matured, and as the years passed under Socrates's tutelage, his inner dialogue fused with every thought. Socrates also claimed to have an internal voice, and Plato had been relieved to share his secret. Plato was comforted to find that he was not alone.

"We all have two voices," Socrates had said. "Know thyself, and take care of which voice you heed."

Plato was a driven and focused student, but despite the close relationship forming with his schoolmaster, he was often forlorn and lonely. Late at night, when his studying was set aside, his Marcus-memories would roll downhill like a boulder, and Plato would become nostalgic for people and places he had never seen.

In his late teens, he was increasingly tortured by remembrances of a girl named Theron, and he craved her spirit. He searched for her shine in every new place and person. Plato felt perpetually incomplete and saw her in flashes: in the colors of a beautiful sunrise, in the petals of a flower, in a tender moment between loved ones. He believed that if she were near, it would quench his unbearable feelings of emptiness.

His Marcus-voice advised him to be aloof and to insulate himself from the emotional peaks and valleys of his lifetimes, but Socrates gave him hope for the world. Though the Age was waning, his corner of Greece was filled with philosophy, reason, and the potential for what humankind could once again become.

Plato's admiration and respect for Socrates grew, and despite warnings from his inner voice to avoid loving too deeply, a powerful connection formed. Marcus had lived and grieved many times, and the weight of his losses made him wary, but his friendship with Socrates came to be one of the greatest he would ever know.

Socrates educated by asking questions, not preaching answers, and he taught his students to question everything, including *him*. Plato demonstrated great aptitude, often challenging Socrates. As a result, he quickly became a favored student.

Plato matured, and his pudgy frame grew solid and wide as he developed into a plain-looking man. He was a head taller than his gargoyle mentor but never matched him for swagger, charisma, and confidence. Plato was unusually astute, and Socrates admired his ability to memorize and recall entire conversations and dialogues verbatim, even weeks later.

"It is a gift and a curse to have a parrot with such an indelible memory always at my shoulder! I rebuff him like a gadfly, but still he natters on," Socrates would jibe affectionately. Plato did not mind the good-natured ribbing; he looked upon his instructor with awe.

Chapter 4

Murder at the Parthenon

It was a difficult time in Athens. With the help of his Marcus-memories, Plato's best calculation was that the Bronze Age of the Great Year Cycle was coming to an end, and they were descending into the Iron Age. The Athenians had just won a battle at sea versus Sparta, but a freak storm had pounded the victors and had separated the fleet. Despite the best efforts of the generals in charge, the ships were lost, and the dead could not be recovered.

There was a public outcry, and the decline in consciousness allowed for extreme reactions and a bloodthirsty call for revenge. The families of the dead and missing demanded retribution and called for the death of the six returning generals. A mob formed and rallied. The politicians in power, afraid for themselves and their popularity, called the Assembly to order for an immediate trial. They would try all six generals together, in one day, without notice. It was an impulsive edict countering Athenian law and order, but it pleased the angry throng.

Thousands gathered to watch at the outdoor court known as the Pnyx. The structure was a series of flat platforms and steps raised above a large open field, allowing many to congregate. It was located below the southwest cliffs of the Acropolis, which was a high, rocky outcropping above the city. Like a sentry over Athens, at the summit of the Acropolis, stood the newly completed Parthenon. Socrates stood on a stone platform. The hostile crowd was divided into tribal groups, and they watched one another's reactions as intently as they watched the orator.

"Our laws state that six cannot be put on trial as one! This trial is a mockery!" Socrates shouted. His voice carried across the assembly of thousands, thanks to the well-designed acoustics.

Plato's thick gait propelled him quickly toward the steps of the speaker's platform, closer to his mentor. The six generals were chained together, stunned by the departure from legal protocol and their betrayal by their countrymen.

Socrates looked out from the platform. The sun rested in the deep lines of his weary face as he focused his attention on those who called out to challenge his reason. He knew he must calm the passion of the surging mob to prevent them from scapegoating the accused.

The families of the dead, dressed in mourning garments, watched from the edge of the crowd; only men were permitted on the floor. The mothers and grandmothers thrust terrified, crying children forward as evidence. They implored their fellow citizens to punish those responsible for the unjust deaths of their loved ones and demanded reckoning for the dishonor the dead had suffered by not being properly buried. To go without burial was an insult to human dignity.

Socrates was sweaty and short of breath from the adrenaline coursing through his body.

"Friends! These loyal warriors are accused of a crime they have not committed. Let us not be swayed by the families who are rightfully grieving but who are too ready to embrace emotion and occlude reason," he said. "We must adopt logic before it is too late. The generals are wrongly tried, and you must remember that they, too, have families!"

"You disregard the dead! Our sons have been wronged by these men!" the opposition answered.

General Anytus stood silently near the speaker's platform, watching. He avoided the spotlight and was surrounded by the accusers and other members of the political Assembly. The poet Meletus and the handsome prosecutor Lycon were nearest to him. It was clear to Plato that they did Anytus's bidding.

Though Anytus did not have the shine of an Adversary, Plato's Marcus-consciousness recognized Meletus, and Lycon surely did. In Atitala, Lycon had been a proud, confident boy whom Marcus vaguely remembered as having been called Thaddeus; and the shadowy, dark shine surrounding Meletus belonged to Marcus's former friend Solenna. He had last seen her in the cavern on the night of the exodus from Atitala. She had been participating in an evil ritual, during which Helghul had allowed a terrible Beast to take possession of him, becoming some sort of sacrificial king. These thousands of years later, the gruesome memory was still abhorrent to the Emissary, and he shuddered involuntarily and turned back to his mentor.

"Do not abandon our laws," Socrates implored the crowd.

"Would you encourage all generals to leave the wounded and dead behind? Would *you* have done so, Socrates?" Lycon asked. He had the ability to easily manipulate others with his extreme good looks and feigned empathy.

"I am not on trial here," Socrates answered. "But if there is something traitorous in surviving while others die in war, I should be, for I have done it and am guilty. Just as many men here have, including your General Anytus!"

"They are cowards!" the mob shouted at the generals. Plato's Marcus-mind could see the dark shine of the Adversaries swirling throughout the assembly, and they incited the crowd by chanting, "Our loved ones must not be forgotten!"

"Have you no honor?" Socrates called over the shouting. "The law is being undone! Each of these men is entitled to a proper trial and defense, just as *you* would be. Would *you* have an angry mob decide *your* fate or the fate of *your* sons?

"Our sons are dead!" a member of the crowd shouted.

"These men are no guiltier than those left at sea! They simply find themselves on *this* side of the storm," Socrates shouted, desperate to turn the crowd to compassion.

"They will join them soon enough," General Anytus said under his breath, aware that Socrates was beginning to sway the crowd. "Finish it!" he ordered in a deep, grumbling tone. Anytus would significantly increase his power upon the death of his cohorts.

The accuser, Meletus, called for an immediate vote. During the vote, Lycon, who had a flair for theatrics, reminded the crowd that the dead soldiers must not be abandoned yet again. His beautiful blue eyes were brimming with false tears.

A show of hands by the Assembly displayed a majority decision.

"The jury has found the six defendants guilty," Meletus, the accuser, announced.

Anytus whispered to Lycon, who rushed to the platform, and with his mouth only inches from Meletus's ear, relayed the general's directions.

"The sentence is to be carried out immediately! Death upon the rocks!" Meletus shouted to the cheering crowd. With the support of the mob, the law had been circumvented.

The doomed generals reacted with violent resistance, trying to throw off the guards who would lead them to their deaths. As the chained men were pummeled by their captors, Plato, Socrates, and three of their students courageously threw themselves into the fray, punching and pulling at the guards to release the condemned. Their efforts were futile.

Despite their bravery, Plato, Socrates, and the six were far outnumbered and were subdued by the armed guards surrounding them. Soldier against soldier, the generals struggled against their captors. More than one guard was sent tumbling by the resisting prisoners. Noses, ankles, and arms were battered in the violent procession.

The beautiful Parthenon, with its war-inspired panels, loomed above them like the gates to Heaven. The carved marble panels above the pillars depicted a cosmogonic battle symbolizing the conflict between chaos and order. The generals were dragged past the steps of the building to the highest wall on the southeast corner. The angry mob had now gathered in the amphitheater at the base of the rocky cliff for a better view.

Plato and Socrates could only watch as the condemned were pushed and dragged by muscle and spear from the Pnyx, up the stairway of the Acropolis to the height of the Parthenon.

The six bleeding generals had been stripped of their titles and dignity and desperately searched for the faces of their loved ones. Their families, drowned out by the thousands of Athenians calling for their death, were now gathered in the amphitheater below the Parthenon.

The condemned men protested the verdict until the last moment. They were in shock. A trial such as this was unthinkable. This judgment, unbelievable. There was no chance for them to say goodbye to their wives, lovers, or children. How had the people of their beloved Athens become so blind?

Socrates and Plato were impeded by the guards and were unable to prevent what was unfolding. They could only follow the procession up the hill, continuing their call for the release of the doomed generals.

Socrates's nose had been broken in the scuffle, though not for the first time, and his white mustache and beard were streaked red. He used the back of his hand to wipe away blood and snot from his crumpled face, unaware of how gruesome he looked. Plato, too, was battered and bruised but was oblivious to his own pain.

"Death!" the mob chanted, having become its own screeching, bloodthirsty organism. The new creation had no compassion or control, and not one man or woman felt any personal responsibility.

The aggrieved convicts were forced to the upper ledge, battered and bloody. One by one, they were pushed to the jagged depths below, where they burst like ripe fruit across the rocks. The mob cheered while the distraught families of the generals fled the frenzied crowd, aware that Athens was no longer safe.

Until the throng dispersed, Socrates, with Plato by his side, continued to decry the foul deed. The Great Year was declining, and with it, consciousness. The Adversaries had created another traumatic event to be cataloged and recorded in Plato's Marcus-memories.

"With the decline of this Age, the deterioration of rational self-consciousness is to be expected," Socrates said sadly.

"The theoretical knowledge does not make bearing the brutality easier," Plato replied. The Adversaries were gaining power, and Plato knew that their cruelty was boundless.

Socrates and Plato had discussed the Great Year Cycle many times. The mentor had learned of it years earlier, when his inner voice was first awakened by the Oracle of Delphi; and shortly after that, Socrates had met an Indian sage who had exposed him to ancient Sanskrit teachings in which the Great Year was called the Yugas.

How much worse can things get, and how am I meant to counter it? Plato wondered.

Following the execution of the six generals, Socrates continued to challenge the politicians. He questioned his young students relentlessly, and they, in turn, questioned their parents, provoking and berating the older generation. His influence continued to grow; and Anytus, Lycon, and Meletus were determined to silence him.

"He causes the youth to rebel," Meletus complained, and Solenna's shine gathered around him gloomily. The admired poet had a melodic voice with a comforting rasp and a beak-like nose. He resented Socrates and found that the philosopher's outspoken disdain was interfering with his popularity.

"They mock and laugh at us!" Lycon said, his handsome face pouting. The Adversary was proud and conceited, just as he had been in his lifetime as Thaddeus in Atitala.

"It is time to silence Socrates," General Anytus declared.

"Shall we have him assassinated?" Meletus asked excitedly, stroking his sparse beard.

"No, that would ensure he would become a martyr. We will use the will of the people against him," General Anytus said.

"How? He is a hero among them," Meletus pointed out.

"We must inflame the people of Athens, as we have done before. We will incite their fear by spreading lies and propaganda. When they can no longer tell lies from truth, they will defer to us. We will use the law to our advantage," General Anytus explained.

Within days of Anytus's directive, a series of statues standing at the city boundary were desecrated, and Socrates's students were mistakenly blamed for a coup against the state. Socrates and his teachings were held accountable, and there were whispers of conspiracy and treason creeping, like fog, through Athens.

✂✂✂

"Master Plato, you must come!" a young student shouted across the courtyard. Plato quickly followed and found Socrates deep in conversation with Meletus and his witness, Lycon. Plato was filled with protective contempt as he saw the dark shines of the Adversaries Thaddeus and Solenna engulfing his mentor.

"Socrates, you have been charged with the capital crime of irreverence and failure to show piety towards the gods of Athens.

You are required to present yourself to the court in four days," Meletus announced.

"Ah, yes, that is our law! I will be present to enter my plea and address the charges," Socrates replied, unperturbed. "But I shall change nothing in what I do, for it is my right actions that show that laws are naught but words and agreements, and like men, laws can be corrupted."

"These charges are serious, Socrates," Meletus warned, irritated by Socrates's dismissive attitude. He had hoped to see the smug man squirm.

"Throw yourself to the crows," Socrates said casually. It was a phrase basically meaning *piss off.*

"To the crows!" repeated the students approaching with Plato. They were intimidated by Lycon and especially Meletus, but they were emboldened under the protection of Plato and Socrates.

Meletus ignored the students and kept his eyes on Socrates. Plato saw Lycon's and Meletus's shines recognize his own, even though they could not see it. The ethereal field around the Adversaries was inching toward Plato like a bloodhound tracking a mark. As indigo ribbons brushed against the dark, flowing threads, they recoiled, seemingly repulsed. Lycon rubbed his hands anxiously, and Meletus intuitively took a step back as their energy was repelled by Marcus's.

"I do not shrink from exposing the flaws and corruption of this democracy," Socrates continued. He turned to the crowd of students who had gathered to listen, and said, "Fear not, for I detest seeing emotion wasted on my behalf."

After Meletus and Lycon departed, their message weighed heavily on everyone except Socrates. He was pleased that he was ruffling the feathers of the politicians and exposing flawed laws. He reveled in the opportunity to expose the defective system.

"You seem carefree, Socrates, but I have no confidence in the law. Laws are often fashioned and perverted by those in power for their own selfish gain. Forget not the generals who were destroyed in one impulsive afternoon beneath the Parthenon. We have witnessed the darkness in men. There is no guarantee that justice will prevail," Plato said. He knew the Adversaries were more than men and that Socrates could not fully understand the darkness he was up against.

"The death of the generals is exactly why I speak out, why I orate and question and challenge the court to bring light upon the failings laid before us. It is the very reason I will not act contrite in the face of these self-serving reprobates," Socrates explained.

In the days leading up to the trial, Socrates remained irreverent and grew more critical of the so-called democracy.

"The enlightened Aristoi of society need to stand out! Stand up and lead! This democracy will be the ruin of humankind. Wisdom and reason should govern our cities! You!" he said, pointing at his students. "You! Men of thought and intellect need to be the decision makers and take care—not guided by the masses who easily accept the lies they are told. In this Age, the unphilosophical man is at the mercy of his senses and emotions, believing them real and mistakenly trusting them. The way a prisoner in a cave, his back to the entrance, might believe the shadows cast before him represent truth, so do the ignorant and the easily led believe their eyes and ears. They are easily corrupted because they put no thought to further understanding themselves. Thus, they remain ignorant of the truth!" Socrates said.

⋙⋘ ⋙⋘ ⋙⋘

The formalities were over, and the magistrate had heard the charges and set the time for the trial. Socrates and Plato approached the Agora, where the trial would take place, and turning the corner, they came face-to-face with General Anytus. Though he was Socrates's severest critic, General Anytus, unlike Meletus, had condemned him in whispers, behind closed doors, though that was about to change.

Plato had last seen Anytus up close many years before at the theater, and he was once again confused by the karmic code of the general. Anytus did not have the telltale shine of an Adversary, though he was a powerful figure and seemed entirely complicit with their agenda.

"General Anytus! Those of us who were there remember the Peloponnesian War," Socrates said in a condescending tone, referring to a controversial incident that had occurred when he and the general had been soldiers together. Anytus had been charged with treason, and he had successfully bribed his way out of it.

"You are too ready to speak evil of men. I recommend you be cautious," General Anytus warned. His dark-brown eyes were piercing, and there was no softness or warmth in them.

"Threats are admissible in court," Plato interjected protectively. Anytus eyed Plato curiously but did not reply. The general was aware of Socrates's favorite and had been keeping tabs on him for some time. Plato was uncomfortable under his gaze but held his ground.

"When did something last change the way you think?" Socrates baited.

Anytus scowled and abruptly turned, moving toward the opposite corner without another word.

"It is unwise to taunt him," Plato said, but Socrates was amused by the interchange.

Plato was worried and once more urged his mentor to take the charges seriously. It was no use. Just as Socrates had laughed when criticized and mocked in the play called *The Clouds*, he laughed now, amused by the absurdity and irrationality of his critics.

Facing Socrates's jury, Plato's Marcus-consciousness recognized the shines of numerous Adversaries among the 501 men.

"Meletus and Lycon are not to be taken lightly. They are devious beyond what they show," Plato cautioned, chafed by their energy.

"Meletus and Lycon are puppets. Athens herself is the puppet master. I will show this jury the audacity of these allegations and expose the weakness crippling Athenian law," Socrates replied.

A herald called the trial to order, and a magistrate rose to preside over the proceedings. Each of Socrates's accusers—Meletus, Lycon, and General Anytus—were given three hours, measured by a water clock, to make their cases. The large jury of five hundred plus was made up of the male citizens of all the different social classes within Athens and sat behind a railing on wooden benches.

Socrates was given the opportunity to defend himself against the charges and spoke for three hours. To the annoyance of many, he surmised that he must be the most knowledgeable of all the men in Athens "for I alone know that I know nothing."

Socrates's condescending manner was unpopular with many of the jurors, and Plato noted their displeasure.

"It is clear to all who observe that your irreverence and lack of concern serve only to enrage the accusers. They are determined to silence you and to punish your apathy and disregard for them," Plato whispered urgently.

"I am but a seed to their soil. By my unwillingness to be silenced, others will be encouraged and will take root," he replied. Socrates appreciated Plato's concern but altered nothing in his behavior.

The gifted philosopher delivered a brilliant oratory to the court, easily debunking the weak charges against him.

"Men of Athens, I honor and love you, but I shall obey God rather than you, and while I have life and strength, I shall never cease from the practice of teaching philosophy. If this is the doctrine that corrupts the youth, my influence is ruinous, indeed," Socrates said.

After the speeches, and without further discussion, each juror cast his vote using a bronze disc dropped into a specified urn; then together, the jurors counted the votes. The jury, many being simple farmers and fishermen, had been alienated by Socrates's condescension and confusing speeches. Anytus, Lycon, and Meletus had been much easier to understand. It was with sincere shock and disbelief that Socrates heard the verdict.

"Socrates has been found *guilty*," proclaimed the magistrate.

The prosecution and the defendant were then each asked to propose a fair punishment. The expected penalty was a fine, and in anticipation, Socrates's students had raised three thousand drachmas to appease the court since he, his wife, and his three sons lived in relative poverty.

"I call for death," Meletus said, his dark shine hanging over the jury box like a hazy gargoyle. His thin lips curled in pleasure, and he looked more birdlike than ever. There were gasps from the Assembly, and Plato was filled with a horrible sinking feeling. He had flashes of his lifetime as Sartaña. He had been a High Priestess, a mother, and wife, and everyone he had loved had been torn from him. The sorrow had been overwhelming, and he did not wish to feel it again. Love was plagued by suffering.

"I call for free meals delivered to me in the center of town," Socrates said, suggesting a sentence equal to the reward given Olympic champions. The audience gasped and snickered, and General Anytus demanded that the magistrate call the court to order. Many jurors were appalled by Socrates's continued cockiness. The bronze ballots were recast and counted for the sentencing, and Socrates's fate was set.

"Death by hemlock," the magistrate announced.

It was a powerful and unexpected blow. Plato found it hard to breathe—hard to think. A rumble coursed through the court and the gallery of observers. Disbelief, outrage, and triumph crashed against one another in violent, emotional waves.

"*Kakos!* Injustice!" Plato exclaimed in disbelief. "You would kill a man for his manner of speaking rather than judging the evidence against him. The charges against Socrates were unjust, and your verdict is excessive. Did you learn nothing from the murder of the generals?"

Socrates reached out to calm his dear friend.

"They have failed my test of their character, Plato. They understand less of ethics than I had hoped, but I am not surprised," Socrates said quietly before calling out above the clamoring:

"This once again shows the ludicrous nature of our system and the impoverished morals of our laws and politicians. Democracy is failing because men are easily swayed by those who stoke their fears, pass them gold, and feed their egos," Socrates said.

"Death will be carried out in one month," the magistrate declared, and Plato saw the vane adversary Lycon's ashen shine billow and expand like the plumage of a peacock.

><× ><× ><×

It was the eve of his execution. Socrates was home, sipping wine and enjoying a fine platter of bread, meat, and olives. Plato bowed to his mentor's wife, and then, upon Socrates's request, she excused herself and went to the next room.

Plato huddled at Socrates's elbow and gave him hopeful news. "Arrangements have been made to get you out of here tonight. I've been told they will not pursue you. They only want you out of Athens. You can live out your days peacefully in the country," Plato said. Socrates hushed him so his wife would not overhear. She had barely stopped crying the entire month since the sentence had been set down.

"I told you, I shall not flee. Please give the ransom to my wife. She will need it when I am gone." Socrates answered calmly.

"They have less desire to kill you than to silence you," Plato assured him.

"I am old; I will not scurry like a rat in a deluge. I have never run from a debate, confrontation, or challenge. I will not become less than the man I have always been. I have earned my self-respect at the end of my life. I will leave this world happily, willingly, into the extraordinary life awaiting me on the other side, finally privy to all the answers I so desperately seek. Only upon my death will I leave Athens. She is my blood, my bones. I am nothing without her walls, her people. I will go out a flame, my friend, a light that glares upon the wrongs I have tried to expose."

"Athens does not deserve you. We are all as insignificant as the skin shed by a snake," Plato replied miserably.

"I do not seek to be remembered. I desire only that the philosophy and knowledge are not lost. Continue to teach the students to question everything; they will pass on the wisdom. Record what we have learned for future generations."

The realization that Plato was about to lose his beloved companion and mentor in such an unjust and preposterous circumstance devoured his patience and regard for humankind. Time after time they extinguished the bright lights, and he was unable to stop it. Plato's Marcus-brain was flush with overwhelming anger and sadness and then . . . nothing. Numbness spread through him like a poison—like the hemlock Socrates would be forced to drink in one day's time.

"Plato, when I am dead, you must leave Athens for a period. I believe that General Anytus will come after *you* next. When it is safe to return, I want you to build a permanent school. Promise me," Socrates said.

"You would not leave, but you ask me to go?"

"You will also return and take up the work; that is the fundamental difference," Socrates said.

Plato knew he should leave. Meletus and Lycon, with the help of General Anytus, were dangerous. Theron had not yet been found, and his purpose in Athens had been stunted.

"You have my word. I will miss you, my friend," Plato promised.

"Give little thought to Socrates and more thought to truth," Socrates said with a grin.

"I will not watch your murder," Plato said.

"I will be surrounded by many tomorrow. It is better we spend our final moments together alone. For tonight, let us forget about death and parting and have the best of all philosophical discussions. I can offer you the most delectable meats and wine, for it seems that when you are nearly dead, people are exceedingly generous!"

Plato and Socrates ate, drank, and challenged each other for the last time. Faced with his mentor's death, Plato felt more strongly than ever that he needed to fulfill his purpose as an Emissary. He chastised himself for indulging in his grief as he walked home into the sunrise, and he was tortured by his thoughts:

There is no true death. My grief is futile. Stop this suffering—it is your own invention! Socrates will transition, just as we all transition. My friend, my dear mentor! He is the best of men. A waste! And Theron, where is she? This grief does nothing to help Socrates! What should an Emissary be doing? Not this!

⤞⤝ ⤞⤝ ⤞⤝

On the day of his execution, Socrates spoke with eagerness about his journey to the next realm, anticipating great clarity and knowledge after death. He was, however, sympathetic to the burden of grief he was leaving behind for his loved ones. He said goodbye to his wife and children and sent them home. He wanted to spare them his suffering and spare himself witnessing their sorrow.

He bathed, so the women of his household would be spared the task of washing his corpse, and he surrounded himself with friends.

"That was a good hemlock, but not a *great* hemlock," Socrates joked after drinking the poison. Chuckling, he walked around the room, waiting for the numbness to set in to his limbs. He finally laid down, knowing that the poison would turn his belly cold and work its way to his heart. He had expected the retching and vomiting, but it was alarming to witness. He sought to console those in attendance but finally grew impatient with their emotional outbursts, grief, and tears.

"What a way to behave! I sent the women away for this reason!" Socrates chastised. "Be quiet and collect yourselves so I may meet my end in calm silence."

His friends collected themselves the best they could, stifling their sadness. As Socrates's breathing became labored and his body twitched and jerked, Plato departed Athens on the same ship he had arranged for Socrates's escape. He was heartbroken and angry, and he wondered what sort of grand lesson he was supposed to be learning.

How does this cycle of continual life, death, joy, and grief evolve? How am I supposed to make a difference in a world where men exe-cute the bright lights and raise up the idiotic, cruel, and self-serving? he wondered.

Plato had firsthand knowledge of the afterlife and the waiting place he later called "The Meadow" when he wrote about it in the *Republic*, but none of his awareness soothed his disappointment at the waste and brutality of humankind.

He found himself roving the dockside, remembering the day when he had so fortuitously met Socrates. He almost smiled at the notion that it was chance that had brought him there, for he knew it had most certainly been destiny.

What now? What now that the foul, foul deed was done? The mur-der of a genius, a beacon to all humankind, had occurred without ceremony, like closing a door, snuffing a candle, and without even a trumpet blast!

Marcus's armor, honed from many lifetimes of loss, registered a hearty dent. The lifetimes of fighting, teaching, and searching for Theron had exhausted him. In that moment, and not for the first time, Marcus regretted taking the potion that had given him past-life memory. One lifetime of winning, losing, birth, death, beauty, and horror is enough to remember.

Chapter 5

The Oracle:
Plato in Egypt

It had been twelve years since Plato had left behind the corruption of Athens. He had spent several years in Syracuse grooming the future leader, young Dionysius, to become the ideal philosopher-king, only to learn that the boy's character was fatally flawed. Dionysius had framed Plato for murder and imprisoned him, but with help, he, the Emissary, had escaped. Through it all, he had searched a large portion of the known world but had not yet found Theron.

Plato's travels brought him to the bustling seaside village of Rhakotis—the ancient land of Khem. He had lived many lives in that part of the world. Egypt felt like a comfortable second skin. Everywhere he looked, every scent he breathed, even the singsong language in his ears, brought memories flooding back as real and as vivid as his current daily life.

Throughout his journey, Plato's studying and writing continued. The oral tradition was over, and guidance was needed as consciousness declined. Moral codes and laws had to be written down to remind people how to live ethical lives. The Emissaries had been doing this work for countless generations, but many of their scrolls and carvings had been destroyed or lost over the Ages. Plato was determined that his writings would survive as an example and inspiration for future generations.

The Mystery School, hidden somewhere in Egypt, was Plato's current destination. While Plato was growing up, his uncle had told him many stories about the schools. They were a haven for evolved consciousness and had been established by the Emissaries to unite the lightworkers and help them further their knowledge and skills. In the darkening days, openly seeking esoteric wisdom could be lethal. Famed Greek mathematician Pythagoras was rumored to have spent many years there, and Plato wondered if he might have been an Emissary.

Unlike the civilizations of the Golden Age, when these schools had operated openly for everyone, the current state of humanity made secrecy a necessity. The hidden schools were difficult to find. Plato searched for Theron's shine as well as that of other Emissaries. He knew they might lead him to the hidden location. He was determined to avoid the pain of attachment and loss that had affected him so deeply with Socrates, so he remained aloof.

He wandered, lost in his thoughts. Around him, the village bustled and squawked, humid and pungent in the noonday sun. Plato smelled the mingled scents of spices, humans, and animals. Despite having adopted the robes of the locals, he was recognizable as a foreigner, and a young boy called out to him.

"Mister, you need?" he asked, in several broken languages, trying each in turn. Plato was struck by the boy's tenacity and language skills, and he turned.

Instant recognition! Plato's cells filled with excitement. There was a familiarity. He did not see the shine of an Emissary, but he recognized the karmic code of this boy as it flooded through him. They had met before. Marcus knew it was the same soul who had been his prison guard in Stone-at-Center and had shown him mercy in his lifetime as Sartaña. It was the same soul who would someday incarnate as Quinn's friend Nate. Gratitude overwhelmed Plato, as it always did when he thought of that friend. It was remarkable to find him once again.

"Yes, I need," Plato answered. "I need . . . School of Mysteries?" he said in a broken Demotic dialect. The boy's eyes opened wide, and he ducked past the shoulder of a fig seller and fled. Plato called after him, but the boy was gone.

Disappointed, Plato continued through the noisy bazaar and purchased his daily meal, still looking for the boy who'd run away and for any sign of other Emissaries. Sweat ran in itchy streams down his back as he munched the hard, dry loaf and popped olives into his mouth, spitting the pits in the street as he made his way to the nearby temple.

The temple was a plain stone structure, fitting the simplicity of its setting.

"I wish to see the High Priest," Plato said to a young boy standing at the entrance and wearing a monk's garb. The youth hurried away and returned moments later with the priest. The rotund man wore extravagant robes with thick gold bands on his ankles and wrists. The dark shine of an Adversary radiated around him.

Plato's Marcus-mind cautioned him.

"What offering do you bring?" the High Priest asked, demanding a donation from the foreigner.

"I have no offering," Plato replied warily. He would not find the Mystery School in the presence of this dark soul.

"You dare not pay tribute to Ra?"

"I assure you, Ra does not require my gold," Plato said quietly, walking away amid the High Priest's protests. He would only find trouble here. Plato was appalled to hear the priest strike and berate the youngster as he departed.

Outside, around a nearby corner, a silhouette emerged. It was the boy with the familiar shine. The comforting glow of the young man's aura delighted Plato.

"The High Priest is bad man. I don't know how to find Mystery School, but I know who does," the boy said in choppy Greek, stepping back into the shadows and beckoning for Plato to follow.

"Did you follow me?" Plato asked.

"Everyone who seeks Mystery School go here, so . . . High Priest rich and fat, but don't know where school is. Him not worthy."

"How do you know I am worthy?" Plato asked.

"You not pay," the boy answered, smiling openly. Plato admired his logic.

The young boy's name was Amnut, and he was older than he had first appeared—about thirteen years. Plato soon learned that he and his uncle worked as couriers and guides across Northern Africa.

"Where are you taking me?" Plato asked, rushing to follow his guide as he scurried through the maze of alleys and carts. The smell of camel urine assaulted Plato's nostrils. Laundry hung overhead in shabby but colorful strips, and bells and metal clanged and chimed around them chaotically.

"It not here. I will take you to Siwa. The Oracle knows where is Mystery School. She decide if you worthy or not."

Plato knew the Oracle of Delphi had been instrumental in helping Socrates unlock his inner voice, though she had died long ago. It was rumored that Delphi had been reincarnated to become the Oracle of Siwa, but Siwa was many days' travel across a brutal desert, and Plato was unlikely to rely on rumors. Though Plato trusted Amnut, he wondered if the boy might be seeking to maximize his profits by suggesting the guided journey.

"I see and hear everything living at street level, with ears below where they looking. Siwa Oracle have all answers for all questions," Amnut assured Plato.

Siwa was nine days away across difficult desert terrain, and Plato needed experienced guides. The risk of encountering a deadly sandstorm was high. Amnut, with the help of his gruff uncle, was efficient and well prepared with camels and provisions, for a price.

Amnut's uncle's colors were dull and gloomy compared to the luster of his nephew's, and his surly disposition was obvious. Plato had had no luck locating his fellow Emissaries in Rhakotis, and the synchronicity encouraged him to follow Amnut.

The journey to Siwa was long and uncomfortable. Plato ached from the relentless jostling, but he loved the efficiency of the camel's physiology. He watched in wonder as the animal's toes spread and gripped with each burning, sandy step.

Amnut was a joker, and Plato found himself laughing out loud as he had not done since leaving Athens. He would have felt truly light and happy in his adventure if he could only have lived in the moment, if he could only have been a man with a single lifetime without the longing for Theron tugging at the corner of his contentment.

They rode across the vast, scorching desert. The sameness of the landscape and the slowness of the mounts gave the illusion they were standing still. It was a different world, and it was hard to imagine that this place existed on the same planet as Athens. On cold nights, they slept under the expansive starry sky, and the Moon and constellations were bright and close. Plato was happy to converse with the curious Amnut. The boy had never questioned the Egyptian view that the soul or personality, called "Ba," lived after the body died. At least they had that in common.

"So you say, everything has . . . soul and moves in patterns? The planets, Sun, and Moon?" Amnut clarified in his choppy Greek.

"Yes, they all have forms. They are alive, just like you. What we experience in this world is only a reflection of the true forms in the realm where body-less souls exist."

"I do not understand," Amnut said. Plato held up his hand in the firelight and cast a shadow.

"Imagine those who can only see the shadow. They cannot see me *casting* the shadow. They think the shadow is real, though the real object is me, and I am not known until their perception changes to include me."

"How do you know this? Why should I believe you?"

"You should not. You should seek knowledge for yourself, not let your head be filled by others. Your questions are well thought out and indicate a strong mind. Have you been to school?"

"My father say . . . school is for weak and wealthy . . . and I am none."

"Your mind is just like clay. If you shape it and mold it constantly, adding new wetness or knowledge, it will stay malleable and changeable. If you let others form it, never seeking knowledge of your own, it will harden and grow brittle and weak," Plato replied.

Amnut's uncle snorted his disapproval from across the fire.

"You disagree? Please share your thoughts. I am a man who believes opinion can always be improved upon," said Plato.

"You would have him believe the lessons of his father are worthless," the uncle said clearly.

Plato was surprised by his mastery of the Greek language. He had not heard more than a few perfunctory words from the older man thus far. "No disrespect was intended. It is only that I see in this boy a great mind, and I hope he will continue to question the world around him and learn to improve himself."

"Who are you to say he needs improving?" the old uncle groused, stoking the fire with a stiff, narrow staff he carried with him. He slumped his body away from the flames, not wanting to offend a customer who had yet to pay.

"Oh, Uncle, only this morning you shout loud for everyone to hear, the many ways I could be improved!" Amnut laughed, and his offended uncle smiled despite himself. The older man watched the shadows around the fire dance. He stuck his stick into the sand in front of the flames, and it cast a shadow behind it. He thought of what Plato had said about the shadows, and he resentfully pulled the rod out, laid it on the ground, and turned away from the fire. He resisted the new way of thinking Plato had triggered.

The temple of Amun in Siwa was a lush oasis, rewarding the weary travelers. The sanctuary and its community rested on the bank of a large lake surrounded by thick vegetation and groves of shady palm trees.

The locals regarded Plato's party curiously. They were welcoming, but cautiously aware of visitors. The village was bustling, and there were many dressed in the robes of priests or monks. Plato was pleased to recognize the shines of Emissaries among them. He tried to converse with them, but their language was unknown to him. They smiled and nodded at one another but got nowhere. Plato left them, determined that he would try again if the Oracle was unable to help him. Amnut accompanied Plato to the base of the main temple.

"We wait outside?" Amnut asked.

"Set up camp, and find some food and wine. I do not know when I will be finished here," Plato said, climbing down from his camel after Amnut directed it to kneel. Plato paid the balance of coins owed for his transit, and extra for new provisions.

The holy temple of Amun was built on a hill of rock overlooking the village. Steep stairs led to the main gate, through which there was an open courtyard. In the center of the compound, near the entrance, a circular stone altar housed a sacred flame. The fire had been blessed by the Oracle and had been faithfully kept burning by the devoted sect of priests who maintained the building and its unusual treasure. People from all around came daily to pray and to light their torches. Many sought an audience with the famed soothsayer and were turned away. The Oracle granted an audience to very few, and only on very specific days. Plato was hopeful he would be granted a reading and had no intention of leaving Siwa until he was.

Plato passed the crowded firepit toward the entrance through a narrow marble archway ornately carved with symbols of gods, animals, and Oracle-inspired motifs. The walls were also painted in the same style, though with bright, vibrant colors. Priests, and others not distinguishable by their clothing, stood talking in hushed tones. As Plato grew closer, the group clustered in front of the door, blocking his progression.

"I have come to see the Oracle," Plato said to those who were impeding his path.

"Many come. Move on, traveler; seek your answers elsewhere," a robed priest answered protectively. Plato's Marcus-consciousness wondered how he could demonstrate himself worthy. He *must* see the Oracle. Surely she could help him find the Mystery School and possibly lead him to Theron.

"I am an Emissary from Atitala. I come with the knowledge of many past lives," Plato said boldly, knowing no dark souls were near.

There was a gasp, and the small group stirred, eyeing him curiously. The ancient legend of Atitala and its downfall was known to them. A revered Emissary was said to have rebuilt the sacred temple on that spot more than eight thousand years earlier after the Great Deluge. The human barrier parted, clearing a path to the door, and an old priest with a humped back stepped forward to lead him.

Plato walked in silence behind the stooped man. The high ceilings were reinforced by enormous doorways and stone pillars framing mud-and-salt brick walls. Torches and candles burned throughout, and Plato breathed in the sweet, fragrant incense as he walked. He felt the positive energy of his surroundings. He sensed the history and the universal connectivity. He knew that this place, like the Great Pyramid of Giza and the earth of Stone-at-Center, was sacred and holy.

The priest guided Plato through an intricately carved wooden door. The walls were hung with colorful tapestries, and the image of the Seed of Life and other sacred symbols welcomed him. In the center of the round room, there was a massive copper scale the size of a large elephant. On the right stood another ancient-looking priest in orange robes. Plato felt an overwhelming enigmatic force in the chamber and bowed his head respectfully, waiting to be approved.

Will she answer all my questions? Was Theron here before me? Was Helghul? he thought.

"Why have you come?" asked the priest in orange. Plato raised his head to meet the dark eyes sparkling in the old man's wrinkled, weathered face.

"I seek the grace and wisdom of the Oracle," Plato replied. The priest looked deeply into his eyes, as though he were searching Plato's most hidden thoughts, and when he was satisfied, he nodded.

"Come," he said, ushering Plato into another much smaller chamber. The room was barely large enough for Plato and the tiny child before him. She was sitting on a small wooden platform. Her legs were crossed, and her narrow shoulders were draped in a finely woven blanket. The Oracle wore the skull and horns of a ram on her head, though she looked hardly strong enough to lift the expansive headdress. Her dark ebony skin was effervescent and shone with fragrant oils. She was rocking forward and back in a slow rhythm, and she spoke as Plato took a seat on the well-worn silk pillow directly in front of her.

"Good Emissary, welcome. You have come seeking answers," the Oracle said in a deep voice that did not match her appearance. Her eyes were rolled up in their sockets with almost none of the pupil and iris visible. He could see only whites that had turned pale yellow and were lined with veins of deep red, and he wondered how she could see him. Her eyelids fluttered but did not blink. Plato was unnerved by the demonstration.

"Yes, I have many questions," Plato replied.

"Understanding the question is half the answer," the Oracle said in typical Socratic fashion. Plato was impressed by her use of the method. "In my life as the Oracle in Delphi, I spent many hours deliberating with Socrates," the Oracle explained.

"I am sorry to tell you that he is dead," Plato said regretfully.

"Something I highly recommend," she replied. "I wonder why you have come so far when you are aware that all the answers you seek are within yourself?" the low voice rasped.

"I have lost hope. In each lifetime, I watch people fall deeper into the great sleep, growing ever darker. How do I help them?" Plato asked.

"You have lost the energy for your purpose," the Oracle said.

"I drown in my own uselessness, despite my best attempts to live better. I do not have the strength to carry this burden alone. If I can be reunited with my soulmate, Theron, I can shed this constant state of vigil and become whole once more."

"Your suffering is born of your perception and desires. You carry *no* burden. You are *never* alone. You are one of three in this destiny. Your fates are woven together like the strands of a whip. In this lifetime, your wisdom will be summoned and will be instrumental in the initiation of a great boy king," the Oracle said.

"A great boy king? When?" Plato asked.

"Time is nothing but a human construct. The choices of others will affect your outcome. Have patience," the Oracle said.

"Can you tell me how to find the Mystery School?"

"You will find it in Heliopolis. The eye of Horus is carved at the entrance. There, a great treasure awaits you. The time will come when you must return to Athens and fulfill your promise to our dear friend Socrates."

"What is the use of building a school in Athens? Soon the people will burn the knowledge and embrace the Dark Age."

"You must honor a promise neglected for twelve years. All will unfold as it should, but do not expect perfection of yourself or others. Do not berate yourself so. The light is within you. It is your memories and experiences allowing you to play your special role. Do not look darkly upon them."

"Tell me, I beg you, will I find Theron in this lifetime?"

"Your search continues," the Oracle answered. Abruptly, she stopped her rocking, and her eyes stood still. "I am sorry, It is all I have," she whispered in the high-pitched squeak of a small girl, then collapsed into the pillows around her.

Plato was upset with himself, disappointed he had squandered his opportunity to find out about Theron.

Amnut and his uncle willingly guided Plato to Heliopolis. Plato had agreed to a very generous payment without bartering.

"What a fool!" the uncle had said behind his back, pleased with himself.

"He is a good and generous man," Amnut had countered.

On the long journey, Plato repeatedly contemplated the message from the Oracle.

⊰•⊱ ⊰•⊱ ⊰•⊱

"We leave you now," the uncle said as they reached Heliopolis. He and Amnut would replenish their supplies with the generous payment they had received from Plato and would return to Rhakotis.

"Use this money for education," Plato whispered, covertly placing a gold piece against Amnut's small palm and sadly bidding him farewell.

"It is too much!" Amnut replied quietly so that his uncle would not hear and seize the gift on his behalf.

"Please," Plato insisted, squeezing it into his fist. "You are a good and generous boy. I have no doubt we will meet again, if not in this life, in another," Plato said loudly, embracing the young man warmly and kissing him on each cheek. The uncle snorted from a distance—a skeptic.

Plato could not easily swallow past the knot choking him. He was filled with melancholy. The soul within Amnut had reunited Sartaña with Inti—Marcus with Theron—and Marcus would be forever grateful. He had been a life-giving spark in a very dark cell. Even in this lifetime, Amnut had been a reprieve from Plato's loneliness and separation.

⊰•⊱ ⊰•⊱ ⊰•⊱

Heliopolis was loud and busy, and Plato had found the eye of Horus carved in many places; however, none of them was the doorway he was looking for. It took days of searching to find the Mystery School, but synchronicity finally lent a hand. There was no grand portico, no signs. There was a steep stairway leading into a cellar beneath a two-story mud-brick building that had been built and rebuilt in the same spot many times. A cart almost blocked the access completely. Plato would have passed by a tenth time if not for a mother hollering from above.

"Hori, time for eating!" she had shouted to her son, Synchronicity. The boy's name was a dedication to the Egyptian god Horus.

Plato's instincts were alerted, and he surveyed his surroundings critically, just as a second woman began pulling in her laundry. To his left, a blanket was removed from a clothesline, and there it was. The sign he was looking for was carved onto the wall above the steps. Symbols were the language of the Universe, and he was listening. Just as he saw it, a young Nubian girl with the indigo shine of an Emissary came around the corner and skipped down the stone steps. She rapped on the wooden door and was quickly whisked inside.

As Plato descended the stairwell, children ran by, and a baby cried for food or sleep. The narrow stairway led down to a thick wooden door, below the carving.

Plato's Marcus-memory revved with anticipation as he knocked on the thick, locked door. Nothing. After a few moments, he knocked again. This time the door opened a crack, and a middle-aged man in a plain brown robe peered out. Marcus recognized his Emissary shine immediately and was filled with joy. There, with the door barely ajar, shone the familiar energy of Marcus's Atitalan friend Bapoo.

"*Unus Mundus,*" Plato whispered. The password had been cataloged with every other significant and insignificant detail in his memory. It meant "unity" or "one world."

As he said it, the man stepped aside, repeating the phrase. Plato slipped inside, and the door was swiftly bolted.

"Have you traveled a great distance?" the cleric asked.

"I have, indeed, my old friend. I wish to speak to the High Priest," Plato said with a wide smile.

"Do we know each other?" the cleric asked in confusion.

"Not in this lifetime," Plato said, and the cleric contemplated him, smiling back.

"Perhaps you will explain?" he said.

"Yes, in time," Plato said, patting the man's elbow affectionately, and though the cleric told Plato his current name, Marcus would always think of him as Bapoo.

The last time Plato's Marcus-memory had recognized Bapoo's shine, Marcus had been incarnated as Sartaña, and she had been imprisoned by Helghul. Helghul had been the brutal invader Katari, and by his hand, Bapoo had been beaten and murdered before Marcus's eyes. It was a horrible memory—one of many.

Plato was grateful to now see Bapoo's shine around this content, peaceful man. It was a blissful sight, but he was eager to move deeper into the Mystery School. His soul tingled with the anticipation of who else might be inside.

Bapoo led Plato into an adjoining room glowing with the indigo hue of multiple Emissaries. Plato searched among the men, women, girls, and boys for Theron's familiar shine while the students watched him curiously. The shines of Kushim and Holt answered back to him in a familiar way. They had known Marcus well when they had been students together in Atitala, and they smiled warmly, but neither of them remembered him now, and neither of them was Theron. Plato's face fell, and he was filled with disappointment despite the abundant comradery of the place.

The small room was lit and sweetened by pairs of beeswax candles placed on each of six rough-hewn tables. The seats were simple wooden benches, grooved and polished from centuries of use. The floor was dry, hard dirt that was often swept and neatly kept.

There were twenty people huddled in cozy study groups. The stone walls were unadorned, and like everything in Egypt, they had a layer of sand clinging to them. Small sporadic holes near the ceiling allowed for airflow but let no light in.

The cleric Bapoo introduced Plato, and those present listened intently as the newcomer accounted for his arrival by way of Siwa. Plato was then led farther into the school to meet the High Priest.

"Welcome," the head of the Mystery School said. He was dressed in simple robes that did not set him apart from the others.

Plato was surprised. He did not have the special shine of the Emissaries; his karmic code seemed like that of a normal man.

"Good High Priest, I am known as Plato. I come to you a humble student, guided by the Oracle of Siwa," Plato said, lowering his head. His Marcus-consciousness was at full attention, and he watched cautiously while Bapoo whispered to the High Priest and quickly left the room.

"My cautious cleric tells me you have indicated past-life memory," the High Priest said. "Welcome, Marcus."

Who is this soul I do not recognize, yet he knows me as Marcus? Plato wondered. His mind was spinning. It had not worked out well for him when Katari had recognized him as Sartaña, and he had vowed then to be more prudent in the future, yet he had already foolishly betrayed himself to Bapoo, assuming safety lay within the Mystery School walls.

"I cannot help but wonder how *you* know *me*," Plato replied, searching the face of the man whose eyes twinkled bright blue in amusement.

"I cannot help but wonder why you . . . unlike your fellow Emissaries . . . have past-life memory?" the High Priest asked.

"Who are you to speak of Emissaries?" Plato asked.

"I am the Keeper of Records. It is essential that I have unlimited memory. As I am sure you have learned, it can be a blessing and a burden in *equal* measure."

"Red Elder?"

"Yes, Marcus, you have known me by that name," Red Elder replied.

"Why am I unable to see your shine? You look like any other man, not an Elder at all!"

"Elders can hide their shine, should we choose to do so. It is important, at times. I needed to know who I was meeting before I revealed myself."

Plato's mind was racing. *Red Elder must have taken the elixir. Could he have been the cloaked director in the caverns with Helghul on the night of the exodus from Atitala? Was it possible?*

"I feel your mistrust, but worry not. I am with the Light," he assured Plato.

It made sense that the Elders would have memory. What good was it to have *no* memory?

"Why did the Elders not give us *all* past-life memory? I see the Emissaries faltering, their auras bright and bountiful, but their heads are foggy and unaware," Plato said.

"You are mistaken. The knowledge of the Universe is woven through their souls. It does not leave them. Once learned, the wisdom stays with them and grows stronger as they learn, deep and eternal. It is a foundation on which great things can be built. What is troubling you so?"

"Theron. Have you seen Theron? I search for her still."

"I have known her many times, and she has made a difference. I am interested in how it is you have past-life memory?"

Plato did not answer but pressed the priest further. "Tell me, is she here now?"

"No, she is not here."

"Do you know where I can find her?" Plato asked.

"You must know that to search is futile. The soul of Theron is well at work somewhere. Only when it is destined . . . will your paths cross."

"I understand," Plato said miserably.

"How is it you remember? How is it so? Leave nothing out; I am not your judge," Red Elder stated again.

"The day Atitala fell, I followed Helghul." Marcus paused.

"Go on."

"It is still not totally clear to me, though I know the images of that day have plagued my dreams and sent me nightmares in many lifetimes . . . I hid from view and watched. I can still feel my fear, my overwhelming horror . . . they murdered the children . . . the missing children . . . but I did nothing to prevent it."

"They killed the innocent to strengthen the dark energy . . . the darkness feeds on murder and sacrifice," Red Elder explained.

"Yes, it did! I could feel it growing. Helghul was there with others, chanting . . . and there was a person in charge . . . someone leading them, though I couldn't tell who it was. Perhaps Black Elder had returned? Helghul was sacrificed. He was cut, and something *took* him. A dark beast entered him. I looked away . . . I cannot explain what it is I saw. It is too inconceivable. Even now my mind runs from it," Plato said.

"What happened next?"

"Helghul drank from a vial. It was said that the liquid would enable him to remember in future lifetimes. I hid until all the others were gone and . . . before I left . . . as I was leaving, I saw it, and I retrieved the discarded bottle."

"You risked dark magic? Were you not afraid?"

"I was afraid to forget," Plato said.

"Is it possible you endure this choice for the love of Theron?" the Elder asked.

"Yes, for the love of one," Plato replied.

"No . . . for the love of Theron. The love of One is something altogether different," Red Elder corrected.

"You remind me of Socrates, with your challenging and reorganizing of my words," Plato said.

"He must have been a wise man," Red Elder replied, and both men chuckled. They spoke for a while longer, over tea.

The students in the Mystery School were broken up into small groups to maximize their skill sets. This process gave Plato a profound appreciation for the real and varied abilities of each individual.

The students were called *initiates* and were identified as either Warriors or Guardians. They would specialize in methods of alignment and transmuting negative energy or leadership and negotiating peace, respectively. Many years later, when writing the *Republic*, Plato would include a third category of service: Producer, which referred to the farmers, artisans, and craftsmen of society who had not been represented at the Mystery School.

Plato remained at the school for many months. He studied the ancient wisdom of the Emerald Tablet that had been expanded into texts centuries before by Red Elder when he was Hermes Trismegistus.

Plato asked Red Elder what had come of the Emerald Tablet.

"It is well hidden," Red Elder answered.

"Could we not use it to help the Emissaries cast greater light into the collective consciousness?"

"The Emerald Tablet has allegiance to neither light nor dark. It is a tool just as easily used to destroy all light and hope from the world," Red Elder explained.

"How?" Plato asked, intrigued.

"It is time I show you the immense power of the Emerald Tablet," Red Elder said.

"Perhaps it is better that I do not know," Plato said. "In another lifetime, Helghul questioned me about it, torturing and eventually killing me. He offered me my son . . . my boy was Theron . . . in exchange. I might have given in. I remember wishing I had the Tablet to trade."

"You underestimate yourself, Marcus," Red Elder said. "Follow me closely, and do not draw any attention."

The High Priest wore the plain brown frock of a shepherd as he led Plato through the streets of Heliopolis toward the Emerald Tablet's hiding place. Red Elder looked behind them often to make sure they were not being followed. The shine of the Adversaries was easily recognizable.

"It is concealed in a secret chamber below the Obelisk of Re-Atum. The granite aids in concealing the Tablet's energy," Red Elder explained. The obelisk was a sixty-nine-foot red-granite monument built upon the Re-Atum Temple.

"Is not the Obelisk in the other direction?" Plato asked in confusion.

"We must enter here," Red Elder said, standing before a small mound behind a row of stone homes. "It is an unlikely place for a treasure."

It was an old tomb that had been broken open and robbed generations earlier. Together, the two men walked down narrow, broken steps into the dry, earthen mound. There was nothing inside apart from a few pieces of worthless, cracked pottery. There was no tunnel. Red Elder climbed up a few rocks and, with remarkable ease, pushed a large slab on a lever, exposing a stairwell that descended into the cool, dark earth.

As they entered, Red Elder tapped the slab closed behind them, shutting out all the natural light and plunging them into complete darkness. Plato gulped.

"Close your eyes and take my arm. The discomfort of the darkness will lessen as you trust. I know the path well without sight."

They walked for a few minutes without Red Elder so much as stumbling on the uneven ground.

"Are we under the Obelisk?"

"To be precise, we are under the temple, *under* the Obelisk. We used the only entrance to this location. It cannot be accessed through the temple or monument," Red Elder said, deftly finding the treasure he sought in the dark and removing the lid. Plato immediately registered the light on his eyelids, and with relief, he opened his eyes. They stood in a roomy cave, and a golden box sat in the middle of the floor with the Emerald Tablet nestled inside, glowing.

"Good God!" Plato exclaimed, overwhelmed by its energy. "There are no guards?"

"In this Age, there are no guards to be trusted. Only you and I know the Tablet is here."

"Not even Emissaries?"

"Without the benefit of full memory, even an Emissary with the best of intentions might be deceived. The Emerald tablet is too valuable to risk."

Plato understood; his Marcus-memory once again set him apart. It was a huge responsibility.

He traced his fingers along bas-relief lettering he knew so well. His body vibrated, rattling his teeth and flooding him with vivid memories. Upon touching the Tablet, his mind was clearer, and his memories were more vivid than he was used to. It took his breath away.

Red Elder lifted the golden box, and Plato's fingers dropped to his side. As the Elder held it, his shine was revealed, and it wrapped him in swirling ribbons of radiant white light.

"I can see your shine," Plato said. It was beautiful, and he was amazed that at one time that same aura had been unremarkable to him.

"The Emerald Tablet reveals many secrets," Red Elder said. "Bring the lid. We will use the glow to light our way out, but we will need to conceal the Tablet again before we exit."

"Exit? Why? Where are we going?"

"Into the desert. To a pyramid, far from prying eyes and malicious energies," Red Elder said, once more masking his shine.

They made their way back through the tunnel and empty tomb, onto the streets of Heliopolis with the Emerald Tablet.

"Is this safe?" Plato whispered as he followed Red Elder to the stables to gather two camels for the journey. It was not! And he knew it.

"We can see the shine of the people around us and can take the necessary steps to avoid those we must," Red Elder said, and they plotted their route.

With the gold-encased Emerald Tablet tucked into a satchel under Red Elder's robe, the two men mounted their camels and rode for a few hours through the evening heat toward one of the many forgotten pyramids in the nearby desert. Once they arrived, the sun's golden light receded into dusk, and stars were appearing in the night sky above the small pyramid. Red Elder growled from the back of his throat, signaling the camels to drop to their knees so the men could dismount.

The pyramid in front of them, like the Great Pyramid in Giza, was specifically aligned with the stars and the ley lines of the planet. Long ago, in the Golden Age, the Emerald Tablet had been used to activate the White Pyramid, connecting pyramids around the globe and suspending the powerful Unity Grid encircling the planet. The harnessing of the Unity Grid allowed them to supply free, inexhaustible, clean energy to everyone.

That information was nothing new to Marcus. There was more that Red Elder wished to show him.

Though this pyramid was smaller, and therefore less powerful, it was isolated, and Red Elder could work with Plato with little fear of discovery. Once inside, Plato could see that the carved walls had been decorated in traditional Egyptian hieroglyphs. Five pointed stars lined the ceiling and still maintained their remarkable color. The pyramid was open and easily accessible. Many people had come and gone over the years, most of them never dreaming of the pyramid's amazing purpose.

"When directed to do so, the Emerald Tablet can be used to . . . open doors." Red Elder said.

"What kind of doors?" Plato asked.

"If one knows the secret command, when inside the pyramids, the Emerald Tablet can tap in to Indra's Web and open portals into time."

Red Elder held the Tablet out in the center of the room and slowly let go, moving his hands away. The Emerald Tablet floated into the air, its antigravitational abilities activated by his thoughts. Red Elder stepped back slowly until he was side by side with Plato.

"Indra, share your secrets," Red Elder said, and the Emerald Tablet began to sparkle as ribbons of green light burst into a vortex and opened into the churning torus of light spilling into the space around it. Instantly, stretching out infinitely in all directions, was Indra's Web, looking like a remarkable, jewel-encrusted quilt. There was no longer a ceiling, nor were there walls. Everything was an expansive four-dimensional web. At every intersecting vector on the net, there was an Emerald Tablet, and they stretched out in every direction. The Tablets were suspended like glittering green stars within the vast web. Plato was amazed, and he saw that the polished surface of each jewel was a reflection of all the other jewels in the web, infinitely in all directions.

"Focus your gaze on one of the jewels, and look closely inside," Red Elder said. "Each of these is a portal to any moment in time. Go ahead, choose one."

At first, Plato saw only his reflection blinking back at him.

"Do not use your intellect, Emissary; use your instincts. Think with your heart," Red Elder said, tapping Plato on the center of his chest.

Immediately, reflected in the Tablet, Plato saw a moving image of Theron laughing in Marcus's arms, above the waterfall near the Great Hall in Atitala. It was their last ride on the glider, the day he had taken her swimming at the quarry. Plato was thrilled by the sight. He eagerly shifted his focus from one to another of the sparkling nodes and saw all his lifetimes: past, present, and future. The jewels were alive with his lives: laughing, crying, working—everything was captured by the magic of Indra's Web.

"What are these memories? Are they real?" Plato asked, once again watching Theron smile from Marcus's arms—*his* arms.

"They are not memories. They are real. It is the past, the present, and every potential probability of the future. They are all happening at this precise moment, but your soul's focus is here and now," Red Elder said. Plato stepped closer to the vision held within the jewel, and as he did, the portal expanded.

"Can I go there? To that time in Atitala?"

"It is not advisable," Red Elder replied.

"Yes, but is it possible?" Plato asked stubbornly.

"It is possible. You need only place your hand on the Emerald Tablet and step into that lifetime, and you will be transported, but your karma will pay a price. Your purpose resides here in this time, and your soul must learn the lessons it has come to learn before it can move on," Red Elder cautioned.

"Can I visit, briefly, and then return here to fulfill my purpose?" Plato asked.

"These portals are not readily available in every moment. In this Dark Age, we cannot harness the energy as we once did. I highly advise you not to make that choice. It is *not* why we are here."

"Let me watch her, just for a while," Plato said.

"Look deeper . . . into *this* lifetime," Red Elder urged. Reluctantly, Plato found the jewel representing his present life. He saw himself orating to a group of students. A shiver ran down the length of his spine and vibrated on the crown of his head. Though he could not see Theron's face, he could see her shine with him, standing before the Parthenon.

"She is coming in this lifetime? To Athens?"

"It appears so. Better to focus on meeting her in this life than living in the past," Red Elder said, lifting the Emerald Tablet away from its current position and breaking the cosmic connection. Indra's Web fell away and disappeared. Plato stood in the empty pyramid where they had begun, but he was suddenly too far from home, and his desire to return to Athens immediately filled him.

"Now you understand why the Adversaries must not gain possession of the Emerald Tablet. Do not be enslaved by memories, Marcus. The learning is in the *living*. For every soul, there is a theme, a path that must be followed and lessons that must be learned. It is so for the Emissaries, as it is for all others. Those who live in the past find misery. Those who live in the future create fear and uncertainty. Live in the present. I know you are weary, but you are early in this journey."

"Why did you show me this?" Plato asked.

"We have to assume that Helghul has learned this information; therefore, it is important that you also have this knowledge. You may need it one day to protect the Emerald Tablet."

It had been early morning when they had begun the journey back to Heliopolis. They were still more than two hours away when they saw black smoke billowing over the blue skies in the direction of the city.

"The Persians?" Plato guessed in alarm.

"We cannot know, but judging by the negativity assaulting me, our school is in grave danger," Red Elder replied. The men urged their camels forward. Plato's heart was racing. He thought of Bapoo and the other students at the Mystery School, and he said a prayer for them.

Before the final miles, Red Elder stopped. The sun in the sky was red through the smoke and ash hovering over the city.

"I will return to Heliopolis alone. Follow this direction; the path will lead you and the Emerald Tablet to safety," Red Elder said. He grunted in the back of his throat and dismounted quickly as his camel bowed. He removed the hidden satchel from under his robes and passed it up to Plato.

"We could hide the Tablet and return to Heliopolis together," Plato said.

"Whatever damage is done cannot be undone. Take the Emerald Tablet to the island of Socotra. By month's end, it will be unreachable due to the monsoons. Hide it deep within the caves at the highest peak before returning to Athens."

"I am not sure I am worthy . . ."

"You are," Red Elder assured him.

But Plato disagreed with the Elder, for he knew that since he had seen himself in Indra's Web, reunited with Theron in Athens, he could think of nothing else.

"You must tell no one. You and I alone will protect this treasure from Black Elder. We will use our memory to locate it in future incarnations," Red Elder continued.

"Black Elder! He lives? You think he has done this?"

"Though you underestimate yourself, do not make the mistake of underestimating your enemies. Long ago, during your misadventure to Inner Earth, Helghul was changed."

"Helghul is Black Elder?" Plato said slowly as the realization hit him.

"Yes. Beware of the soul who would trade his empathy for a shallow title. I must hurry."

Red Elder was determined to return to the Mystery School as soon as possible. Plato reluctantly split off from the Elder and continued alone along the road leading to the Erythraean Sea and beyond to Socotra. Red Elder continued south toward the burning Heliopolis.

As the Elder neared the city, distressed cries carried across the desert. The air was thick with smoke, and evidence of an invasion was everywhere. Homes had been ransacked, and roofs had been burned, with nothing but stone walls, scorched earth, and ash remaining. The marketplace had been completely overturned, and the streets were strewn with spoiled goods and bodies cut down by sword and spear. Families hid together along Red Elder's route, weeping for their loved ones. The path of destruction led directly to the Mystery School.

All the wood tables, chairs, ladders, and thatched roofs in the neighborhood had been set ablaze and were still smoldering. The Mystery School had been destroyed. The weary mother who had often been heard calling out to her child, Hori, had scooped up her son and had run for her life as the laundry lines over her head burned like ghoulish flags.

Alerted by the screams of the townspeople, the Warrior Emissaries had emerged from the Mystery School, ready to fight the marauders. They hoped to ensure the escape of the others, and the small troop greeted the invaders sword to sword. They had waged a valiant resistance but had been far outnumbered. The bodies of Emissaries and many of their attackers now lay attracting flies in the street.

The Guardian Emissaries who had tried to escape with the sacred scrolls had also been cut down. Red Elder saw the texts scattered in the mud—ignored and trampled. The invaders had clearly been searching for something else. Red Elder thought of Plato—alone and unarmed—riding toward the coast with the Emerald Tablet.

How had they been targeted? Who had recognized their shine? the Elder wondered.

Three marauders, two with the shine of an Adversary, remained at the scene on watch, waiting. The sentries noticed the unremarkable old sage too late. Red Elder had approached slowly on foot, his head bowed, and then swiftly, with the agility of a much younger man, he picked up a sword in either hand. With three skillful swipes, he killed the Adversaries, and their dark shine dissipated into the ether.

"It seems that you are more than you appear, old man," General Anytus said from the adjacent rooftop. The out-of-place Greek stood with a line of archers on either side of him, their arrows drawn and aimed at Red Elder. "Where is the Emerald Tablet?"

"I do not fear your arrows," Red Elder said bravely.

"Take his swords!" General Anytus ordered.

Just as the men moved to obey, Red Elder swung both arms with all his might and launched a sword at General Anytus. The archers released their arrows, and in unison, General Anytus and Red Elder fell. Each man had been pierced through the heart and dropped dead on the spot.

Chapter 6

Squaring the Circle

After parting from Red Elder, Plato continued the long journey to Socotra with an anxious heart, and his mind filled with the uncertainty of what he had left behind.

Once the Emerald Tablet was secured and the monsoon season ended, Plato returned to Athens. Upon arriving, he was disappointed to learn that though he had seen Theron's shine in Indra's Web, she was still nowhere to be found. Moreover, he was stunned to hear that General Anytus had been killed on a military campaign . . . in Heliopolis. The dates lined up. It was the same attack he had avoided.

Socrates had warned him that Anytus would target him, but that had been nearly two decades earlier. Had Anytus been looking for him? Had the general been responsible for the fire and carnage at the Mystery School? It now seemed probable.

Plato never mentioned his trip to Socotra, and he had used a false name while on the island to ensure anonymity. There was no evidence he had ever gone there. The Emerald Tablet was well hidden, and Plato was relieved that the responsibility was no longer solely his.

As directed by the Oracle, Plato turned his focus to ensuring Socrates's legacy. In 385 BCE he opened a school in the countryside of Athens and took his place as headmaster of the Academy. There, he waited for signs of Theron. He wondered if she would be the boy king about whom the Oracle had prophesied. "Three strands of a whip," she had said. But as time passed, Theron did not appear, and his wondering turned to doubt.

Did I see her shine at all? Was it this time? Has my potential future somehow been altered?

Plato continued to orate and write, painstakingly recording the philosophical observations of his day. He further developed theories on geometry and contemplated its great secrets. He enjoyed leading his students around the grounds in deep discussion, just as Socrates had done. The acclaimed Academy flourished and grew, but he continued to feel that his purpose was unfulfilled.

Many years passed, and Theron's karmic colors did not appear. Plato progressed through his forties and into his fifties, never marrying. He wondered if he would do better if he were guided solely by intuition, like the other Emissaries. Did they falter so uncertainly in this declining Age, feeling doubt and confusion about what they should be doing? Or was it the agonizing result of having taken the memory potion? Did his intentions, choices, and consciousness create his world, or was the future set no matter what he did? Plato pondered these questions, and pessimistic Iron Age thinking slithered its way into his thoughts.

Plato's sixtieth birthday came and went. Decades earlier, Red Elder had assured him that he could not force destiny, and the greater plan of the Universe was not his to manipulate. Marcus could not find peace or acceptance. Having seen into the eyes of

Indra's jeweled web, he contemplated many times returning to Socotra, taking the Tablet back to the pyramids and using it to finally find Theron.

Plato was now tortured by the past *and* the future.

Chapter 7

Plato and Aristotle: Platonic Love

Plato had been ill for several weeks, and he was glad to finally be returning to his students. It was early in the day, and the morning sun cast beautiful gentle hues over the portico and gardens. The impressive grove stood out on the landscape, and his spirits rose, buoyed by the view of it. The stately stone stairway leading up the hill to the entrance of the Academy was purposefully designed as an assembly point. He smiled as he looked upon the sea of white togas gathered there, as an enthralled group of students engaged in conversation, debating their ideas. Above them in the white marble fascia of the building was inscribed: *Let no one ignorant of geometry enter.*

Plato slowly climbed the stone steps. Age had eroded his joints, and he cursed his younger self for designing such a steep incline. Only the view had interested him back then.

The sun illuminated the assembly in front of him. The light was too white, and he raised his arm against it, squinting, realizing with a happy surge that there was an indigo karmic glow from within the group. He stopped abruptly, midstep, his heart pounding and his ears and scalp tingling—it was Theron's shine!

"A true friend is one soul in two bodies," a soft, fluid voice intoned. Plato craned his neck to find the owner of the words. The sun's beams were blinding, and only when he grew nearer did the glaring mass of faces become discernible. Plato's eyes skipped over the folds of the fabrics, the arch of each forehead, and the bridge of each nose. He stood at the edge of the group, now anxiously stretching and shifting to get a better view of the person beneath Theron's indigo shine.

"Friendship is essentially a partnership," Aristotle said from the center, answering his professor while turning to face Plato head-on.

Plato's energy expanded in every direction. Violet and indigo light rippled through him, and his Marcus-consciousness soared. The karmic colors were intertwining, mingling, and touching his soul in every way. Intense beauty, love, and joy recognized and encircled him. He caught his breath. The familiarity and lightness of Theron's being radiated from Aristotle.

Plato saw with his soul—Marcus was calling to Theron, and immediately her energy had rushed to his. Tears, overwhelming relief, and pure happiness surged through him. Aristotle looked kindly at the much older man, who appeared overwhelmed and ill, and interrupted the dialogue to call out to him.

"Are you well? Do you need assistance?" he asked. Plato's body was again electrified by the voice, the underlying timbre and rhythm so familiar, so loved. Plato collected himself, every hair and whisker still at full attention. An electric current ran through him as his soul rose to meet the creature before him.

"Who are you that offers me assistance?" he asked. The professor, Eudoxus, approached him enthusiastically, but Plato irritably waved him away, beckoning to the young man who had affected him so strongly.

"I am Aristotle. It is a great honor to meet you," Aristotle said, moving past the other students and standing before Plato. He looked up at the face so full of hope and optimism, already inches above him, and wept inwardly with joy. At long last, after so many lifetimes and so much disappointment, he had found her.

Marcus was grateful for the potion allowing soul recognition, and he cursed the will of the Universe that kept Theron sleeping and unaware of him.

At last, eighteen years after returning from Socotra, the day had finally arrived. Plato was trembling. The spectators wrongly assumed that the older man was fatigued from walking up the stairs in the warm morning sun. Aristotle steadied him, assisting him up the final steps and inside the building. Plato let himself be led. Aristotle's hands on him were like hot stones in his bed on a cool night. Once seated, Plato was handed a silver goblet of water, which he drank in one gulp.

How long has Aristotle been here? How many weeks have I lost due to the illness in my lungs? Plato wondered, grieving for every lost second.

Plato looked up from his cup to the radiant, smooth face of Aristotle. The younger man, not yet twenty, looked at him with clear admiration in his pale-blue eyes.

Eudoxus broke their gaze by exclaiming, "If you would lead the oratory today, it would be a pleasure!"

"You flatter me, though you know I abhor it, Eudoxus. Today I have more to learn than to share. A wise man knows when to speak and when to listen," Plato answered, smiling. "Return to your dialogue; I would like to absorb it for a while," he said, standing, once again strong and steady. Together, Plato and Aristotle—Marcus and Theron—returned to the group on the steps in the sunlight.

For the next two hours, Plato listened in rapture to the dialogue and discussion, every molecule and cell of his body vibrating in ecstasy. Aristotle felt something magical and energized. He assumed it was Plato's charisma and his own nervous excitement at meeting the legend. He did not understand how every ounce of him remembered this soul and magnetically reached out to him and was embraced.

Plato was barely able to restrain his happiness. Aristotle looked upon him with awe. The young student was promising and impressive, and Plato took him under his wing. He taught him to question and to challenge every thought and assertion, no matter how small, just as Socrates had encouraged him to do.

Plato continued his life at the Academy with unprecedented vigor and optimism. The founder and his favorite student spent endless hours in study and discussion.

Walking in the garden one day, Aristotle questioned Plato about his many years away from Athens.

"Was it for *Eros*? Was it for love you went searching?" Aristotle asked.

"Perhaps, but my love has only ever been here," Plato said, though Aristotle did not realize Plato was referring to him.

"I left Athens after Socrates's murder, and eventually I traveled to Siwa, where I received a prophecy from the Oracle," Plato said. He told Aristotle about his travels, but left out searching for Theron and the Emerald Tablet.

"The Oracle said I was one of three in a destiny, and my wisdom would be summoned in the initiation of a great boy king," Plato mused.

"Do you still believe you will find a boy king and that the Oracle can predict future events?" Aristotle asked skeptically. Both men knew that the student believed no more in oracles than in centaurs.

"Yes," Plato replied.

"I do not believe in mysticism. Nor do I embrace the notion of fate. I have observed that each man is his own visionary. There is no foregone conclusion, no predetermined future. Yet the prediction by one who is trusted may very well affect the behavior of the hearer, who then, by his actions, causes the foretold to occur."

"Perhaps we are born with our knowledge, and it is revealed to us as required . . . or as we are ready to bear it. It is possible that there are many choices and paths leading to the same result. Could our free will be an illusion? Perhaps we merely choose *how* we will arrive at the ultimate predetermined outcome," Plato said.

"The soul does not exist without the body, without material cause of life. No one can know if I will spontaneously reach for a mango as the asp slithers past or lean too far from my window and fall to my death. Our choices and paths are just that. There is no goal or result," Aristotle replied.

"You cannot prove; therefore, you cannot be certain, that death is the end. Nor can you be sure that oracles cannot predict. You certainly have no evidence that the soul does not go on outside the body," Plato said.

"The evidence is the absence of life. There is no evidence that anything goes on. The soul is the final cause of the body; the body dies when the soul dies," Aristotle debated.

The men continued to consider, to counter, and to connect. Aristotle was inspired by Plato and sought his counsel and company. Their friendship quickly grew.

Marcus felt Theron in every moment and rejoiced in their time together, but at times he was lonely even with her spirit nearby. Their closeness was not close enough. He wished so fervently that she would wake to him, that her kindred soul would be conscious again and know him as he knew her. As he sat or walked at Aristotle's side, he would concentrate and send streams of color, light, and energy into him. His student would respond warmly, sometimes in a way implying a glimmer of recognition, but then, just as quickly, it was gone. Plato was left desperately alone in his awareness.

One afternoon Plato wrote tirelessly while Aristotle worked nearby.

"Why do you write your dialogues without your voice and name to the philosophies on the page?" Aristotle interrupted.

"My name is irrelevant. My philosophies and personal beliefs are likely to change and grow with my understanding and experience, and I do not wish to be forever fixed to one way of thinking. I do not seek to record one true answer, only the myriad of necessary questions. A conversation is so much more entertaining than a lecture," Plato told him.

"But you have an opinion. You are bursting with opinions. Will you not claim them?" Aristotle asked.

"I would rather show an argument and let the reader deduce reasonably how he would think," Plato said, and Aristotle shook his head skeptically.

"There is obvious leading in your words. You claim to present an argument, but you are not unbiased; you seek to sway the reader."

"I cannot create balance. I cannot create an equality of ideas where they are unequal," Plato laughed.

"Your neutrality is false, Plato. You seek to sway others but will not admit it."

"There is no falseness. I seek only to shed light on contemplation and ideas and the importance of reflection. What is irritating you so?"

"By writing in dialogue, by speaking through characters, you distance yourself from your statements. I think you should claim your beliefs and give them the power of your status."

"My status is fleeting and false. It is a pretense and a flaw of our society born from the desire in the belly of men who seek notoriety. Humility is a virtue, Aristotle. The ideas are what matter, and they were here before I came and will be here after I am gone."

"What if we are here only once? Here and gone, nothing before or after. Your words will guide those who come after you. Do you not wish to claim them?"

"It is not a question for me whether I have lived before and will die and be born again. I know it to be so. I would shed this corporeal body today and rejoin the incorporeal world if I knew you would be there with me, surrounded by the proof of the ideal forms," Plato answered.

"You beg others to question all, yet in unguarded moments you speak definitively about the world after death. Where does this certainty come from?" Aristotle challenged.

"I cannot pretend not to know what I know."

"I believe in proof . . . in the value of my senses to understand reality," Aristotle explained.

"Show two men the same image, and they will each report differently," Plato argued.

"If they discuss and study its form . . . they must find agreement," Aristotle reasoned.

"Yet experience has taught me that they do not. Truth is subjective, and senses are faulty."

"Truth can be found through solid deductive reasoning where proof is evident," Aristotle argued.

"And again, we disagree," Plato said, smiling.

"I am glad that we can still be such good friends, though our philosophies so often clash," Aristotle said.

Marcus was overjoyed to be near Theron, and their relationship flourished despite the fundamental differences in their philosophies. He felt complete, and he wrote prolifically.

Occasionally, Plato would get the sense that Aristotle was growing more in tune with Atitala. Plato had a plan to try to spark Aristotle's past-life memory. For the first time in all his lifetimes, Plato openly revealed the story of Atitala, in the *Critias* and *Timaeus* dialogues. He wrote of his homeland's beauty, perfection, and downfall. And though the name Atitala would be lost and mistranslated to Atlantis in years to come, many of the details would be immortalized. He described the layout of the city, its politics, its aesthetic beauty. He explained the higher thinking, emotion, harmony, energy, and Oneness with God and each other that the citizens had gloried in.

Plato was not only interested in inspiring Aristotle's memory, he also hoped to present Atitala as an example of what humankind should aspire to. The Emissary remained true to his memories of the fair land and warned of the darkness and deceit that had emerged, threatening all societies. He was passionate and, at times, melancholic while he wrote of Atitala. His soul longed for his home as he remembered the beauty and closeness of Theron in their final days.

>◦< >◦< >◦<

As the years passed, Aristotle graduated from student to mentor at the Academy. While his reputation grew, Plato withdrew, concentrating instead on his writing. The Emissary was truly happy and fulfilled for the first time in centuries.

As Plato aged, his eyesight and hearing grew poor. He would often miss bits and pieces of conversations, and he became increasingly moody and cantankerous. The students at the school began to avoid him, and only Aristotle, now in his late thirties, sought him out daily. Plato, nearing his eighty-second year, was frustrated and betrayed by the breakdown of his human shell. His mind was still sharp, spry, and young, and his days had become increasingly focused on his time with Aristotle. They chatted often and argued and debated less.

Plato's life was nearing its end, and he hadn't thought about the Oracle's prophecy in many years. Once he had found Theron, he had lost interest in the prediction. The Oracle's prophecy had amounted to nothing. The boy king destined to change the world had not materialized. The Oracle had foretold that Plato was one of three: fates woven together like the strands of a whip. She said that Plato's knowledge would be summoned in the young regent's initiation, but it had not come to pass, not yet.

>◦< >◦< >◦<

Aristotle stood on the luminous, white Academy steps surrounded by students. The sun was bright, and the gardens around the school were at their most lovely. A young servant ran into the fold of scholars and beckoned timidly to the professor. He had a message from Plato.

Aristotle rushed to the bedside of his ailing friend. The headmaster's humble chamber was cool and dark as he entered. The old man lay in his bed, small and frail. What remained of Plato's hair was white and coarse; his eyes were heavily lined from years in the sun and years of broad grins, and his lids sagged loosely, ready to close forever. He smiled as he felt the familiar aura snug against his own like a snail in its shell, and he reached his feeble hand to him. Aristotle moved to his side, taking the arthritic fingers in his own.

"You have given me the most valued friendship of my life," Plato croaked dryly.

"My dear friend . . . drink," Aristotle said, reaching for the water beside him and placing it to Plato's lips. The patient refused with a subtle shake of his head.

"Death, which people fear to be the greatest of evils, may indeed be the greatest good. But for me to be parted from you is a tragedy," Plato whispered. Aristotle's eyes filled with tears, and his dying friend attempted to soothe him.

"My dear Aristotle . . . must not all things at the last be swallowed up in death? No evil can happen to a good man, either in life or after death."

Though Plato sought to ease Aristotle's grief, his Marcus-consciousness was in turmoil, bitterly resisting the inevitable outcome. He would die and once again be separated from Theron. He lay there, steeped in the vigor of her shine. She was everywhere. Light, sound, and energy resonated between them at the most basic molecular level. The love of Aristotle had been earned and enjoyed, and his friend stood grieving before him. Marcus was suffocated by the reality that he was losing her once again.

"*Philo se*, I love you," Plato said. Marcus wondered how many years, how many lonely, difficult lifetimes, he would have to endure before he found her again. He breathed in her violet shine and basked in her light. As he began to slip away, he wondered if he had done enough as an Emissary in his lifetime as Plato.

"Socotra," Plato said with sudden urgency. "Socotra holds the key to unlock the secrets of the end of the world," he mumbled, suddenly thinking that Theron should know. Aristotle could be trusted.

Aristotle cataloged the declaration as the nonsensical ramblings of a dying man. His only thoughts were to comfort Plato.

It happened quickly. Plato's soul passed unseen through the room, through Aristotle, mingling with Theron's soul like dust particles in a sunbeam. The Emissary was reclaimed by the Source. Marcus was once again flowing through the Grid, destined for the place in between—The Meadow, Plato had called it in the *Republic*. He was at complete peace, in harmony with the divine Source and all creation, and he suffered no conscious, separate thought. Marcus was met by Socrates on his journey into the afterlife.

"Nothing is as it seems," Socrates reminded him with a wink, free of the density of human form and able to communicate from the pure point of view he had so anticipated before his death.

Marcus existed in complete bliss, lightness, and color until he was reborn. Each lifetime had its own highs and lows, lessons to learn. His childhoods would be unfettered by past recall. But eventually in each life, his memories would come to him in shouts or whispers. They would always come, piled upon one another like a wardrobe from countless centuries, layer by layer, weighing him down.

Chapter 8

Eden Found

Quinn was trancelike as he walked home in the rain. When a neighbor noticed him and called out in greeting, he was inordinately startled. His exaggerated response made the woman jump too, and she hustled away, nervous and embarrassed. Quinn's brow was drenched in sweat, and he was sorry he'd frightened her.

His PTSD sometimes made him jittery. Post-traumatic stress disorder. *At least they have a name for it in this century,* Quinn thought. But labeling it hadn't helped deal with the symptoms, nor did it make him feel less unhinged. Quinn knew memories weren't passive. They were snakelike, and they sank their fangs in over and over, releasing the venom in unexpected bursts. Hideous moments came to him in flashbacks and nightmares. An innocuous trigger: a smell, a word, a whistle, or a loud noise might transport him to another time and prompt a memory of when the slamming door had been a prison cell, a whip, or a gunshot.

Quinn was still contemplating his lifetime in Greece as Plato. Eden would soon be headed to Greece with Nate.

What was I meant to learn? Is it about the Emerald Tablet or Indra's Web? Quinn found it hard to concentrate. His inner voice irritated him. It was always bombarding him with higher-purpose rhetoric. Always so demanding and perfect, trying to help him feel better.

Am I mentally ill? Maybe I'm not an Emissary. Maybe none of it is real—the voices, the past lives. What if I'm exactly like the guy on the corner who thinks he's Jesus. Maybe he is Jesus? For fuck's sake, I need a puff! he thought as he entered his apartment.

It was Marcus's hope versus Quinn's depression, and they battled within him. He was sick of conflict. Twelve hundred years of war had broken him down.

He just wanted to get high, tune out, and do nothing, but his inner voice resisted.

Fuck this righteous life. Fuck people. Fuck this bullshit. People were a constant disappointment.

They are you! What happens to one happens to all, he reminded himself.

"People aren't learning!" Quinn shouted to no one.

Later that afternoon, the Emissary had distracted himself, charting earthquakes, wars, and weather anomalies. He pondered increased climate control and the effect of the thawing oceans releasing CO_2. He wondered if the Adversaries were intentionally destroying the planet, or if it was purely human ignorance. He scrolled through the world news but quickly became enraged by the waste and brutality the media reported. He tossed the papers on his desk. He was *not* having a good day

Just then, an email alert popped up on his computer screen. *Eden.* The absolute bright spot in his life . . . *lives.* She had sent him a trailer for the documentary. Quinn clicked on the link.

Eden's intriguing clip was just finishing when Quinn heard a latch click. As he turned, his apartment door opened slightly.

Quinn assumed it was Nate; he'd been dreading the conversation that would have to occur about Eden, and he took a deep breath.

Nate didn't enter; no one did. The door now sat open about an inch.

"Hello," Quinn called out, but no one answered. Quinn moved cautiously toward the door. The threats against him on his blog had grown in number and detail. But so far he'd been successful in protecting his identity. He pushed the door open, but the hallway was empty except for Mr. Olufsen and his little dog.

I probably didn't close it all the way.

"I'm losing my mind!" Quinn muttered to himself before locking the door. He returned to his computer and checked his blog comments.

"You're going to hell!"

"Get a real job."

"I hope you die a horrible death."

The trolls were diligent, but their venom was the last thing he needed today. He closed his laptop in disgust.

Quinn cracked open a beer and lit a joint, melting into the back of his sofa and trying to decompress. *Come on, Emissary, get it together,* his Marcus-mind urged. Now that he had met Eden and found his soulmate, the last thing he wanted to do was mess it up. He was excited by their scheduled lunch date the next day, but Socrates's words played over and over in his head like a song he couldn't stop singing. *Nothing is as it seems,* he thought again and again.

Quinn returned to his books, trying to bring order to his thoughts.

He studied history intently and was thankful for the gaps in his lives that historians were able to fill in. He wanted to know what had occurred in the lifetimes woven in and out of his own.

Quinn braced himself when he finally heard Nate's key in the door. He was at his computer, blocking a troll who had described a painful and gruesome death for the Emissary.

"I was hoping you'd be out," Nate said without looking at his friend. He walked across the room and began picking up his belongings from among the disorder.

"Listen, Nate, I know I have some explaining to do," Quinn began, and Nate rounded on him, his eyes flashing furiously.

"Seriously? Dude, *seriously*? You tried to back-door me! I *told* you how much I like her, and you just . . . you tried to sweep her up into your charisma or whatever! You blow off *everyone*! All the women I've seen hit on you, and you move in on *her*? Why?"

"What's happening here is bigger than you know. I think you were meant to bring us together, Nate," Quinn said simply, still seated.

Nate fumbled with some shoes and a pair of pants. "Fuck you, you condescending prick!" he said, his face dark with anger.

"Nate, listen to me, please," Quinn said, getting up and walking toward him. "There's something I have to tell you . . . I . . . you've always said you felt like we've known each other before. Well, we have. Many times, but she and I have too. This is how it's supposed to be."

"Nice for you! And who are you to say how it's *meant* to be? And suddenly this talk of *knowing* each other before—that's convenient! Bullshit!" Nate snapped, sounding like a wounded animal.

"The truth is in you . . . you've just forgotten."

"Save it. Save your shit, man. I told you I loved her," Nate countered.

"You just met her."

"Not according to *you*! I'm outta here, man."

"Did you spend the night with her?" Quinn couldn't help but ask.

"Yeah, I fucked her brains out," Nate said venomously. He stuffed a few more items into a bag, and he grabbed the cord of his phone charger with an angry tug, breaking it as it ripped from the wall, sending pieces flying in different directions. He threw the shrapnel down at his feet and quickly left, slamming the apartment door.

Eden had chosen Café Zazou, a French restaurant named after the ultrastylish Parisian youth who had resisted the Nazi regime and the Vichy government in Paris during World War II. Though she had no idea how profound her choice was.

The Capitol Hill community was a mixed bag of characters, but Quinn could see shine, and he knew true threats versus freaky filibuster.

"God will strike you down—repent!" a scrawny, tattooed skinhead shouted from across the street. Quinn kept walking. He had seen the man many times before. He was often on that corner, and Quinn had avoided the Adversary identified by his murky aura. His name in Atitala had been Abaddon, and he had been hulking and muscular even as a teen. In his current incarnation, he was a far cry from his former physical perfection, and once again he displayed a large red birthmark on his left cheek and ear. His scabs and twitches indicated a meth addiction; and his racist, paranoid rants cleared the sidewalk around him. He held a tattered sign with dates and Bible verses, and Quinn noticed that the other homeless people who lived on the streets avoided him as well.

"Sinner! Blasphemer!" he yelled, but Quinn didn't look back, even though he knew the man was focusing on him. He was sure it was his indigo shine that was blindly offending the stranger. The street preacher marched into traffic, ignoring the screeching brakes and honks. He followed Quinn, but the Emissary pretended not to notice and walked faster. He knew better than to feed darkness's need for confrontation and drama. When the distance between them increased, the zealot gave up and wandered back to his post, still yelling and mumbling.

Angry, tension-filled situations aggravated Quinn's PTSD quickly, so he took deep breaths to keep his adrenaline in check. As he turned onto the next block, he could see Eden in the window of Café Zazou. She was sitting in an old-fashioned burgundy velvet booth, and the sight of her sent a wave of excitement through him. When she saw him out on the sidewalk, she felt the same baffling euphoria he did.

"No Elijah?" Quinn asked, sitting down across from her, grateful they were alone.

"He's at home with his granddad. I can't be long. Elijah's shaken up from the other night, and I'm still packing."

"What happened the other night?" Quinn asked with concern.

"Just an incompetent babysitter and some bullies pushing my son around at the park. Little bastards," she said with a half smile.

"Maybe I can teach him a few moves," Quinn said with a grin. Eden took it as a joke, but Quinn had been sincere. He had become an accomplished combatant, and though he only fought if he had to, he could protect himself. It was a skill honed over many lifetimes, and he was happy to share his expertise.

"I don't want him fighting, but if I change my mind, I'll let you know," Eden said thoughtfully. *Maybe it would be a good idea to teach Elijah some self-defense,* she thought.

"I'm glad you've agreed to help us with the Crystal Project. None of it would be happening if I hadn't started reading your blog and looking into all the information on consciousness and ancient wisdom you've shared." Her chestnut bangs fell over her forehead as she took a sip of green tea. "I'm just wondering, do you have any concerns . . . about the safety of the children?" Eden asked, fishing, and thinking about the missing Rodriguez boy.

"I think your documentary is really important. Are you having concerns?" Quinn asked. He knew what people were capable of. He had seen it over and over, and he had kept his identity secret on his blog for that very reason.

"I'm starting to worry. What if revealing the Crystal Children and confirming their highly evolved abilities leads to invasive genetic testing, isolation, or worse?"

"You mean like dystopian, Chrysalids-Divergent type shit?" Quinn said.

"Yeah, exactly! I didn't worry about it at first, but it's suddenly become a real concern!" she said, recounting her call with Mrs. Rodriguez. "And Miguel still hasn't been found," she finished, her concern pinching her face.

"How old is the kid?" Quinn asked. His mind flashed to the brutal rite in the cavern so long ago. He remembered clearly the night when Helghul had been entered by the dark entity. He'd often had vivid dreams of the screaming toddlers as they were murdered in the cave. For nearly thirteen thousand years, the memory had haunted and tortured Marcus. He stayed silent.

"Seventeen."

"Oh, thank God. There are other reasons a seventeen-year-old might not show up home for a day or two. It likely has nothing to do with you," Quinn offered with a sigh of relief. "What are his parents like?"

"*Parent.* She's a big personality. Actually, she can be a little overbearing," Eden said kindly.

"Maybe he just needs some space, or he has a girlfriend . . . something nonlethal."

"You're probably right," Eden said, smiling. She felt better about the situation, seeing it from another perspective.

"This documentary has the potential to change the way the world looks at evolution. But we do have to protect those kids. They're our hope for the future, and we need to let the world see what's possible," Quinn said.

"They are. I know . . . it's true," Eden agreed.

"I'm looking forward to working with you. I'll do whatever I can to help," he said, though he was looking forward to more than working.

"I need you for the way you think, for what you know. Don't forget, I'm an Emissary blog devotee! You can help take this thing big—viral, I hope!"

"You overestimate me," Quinn said, remembering that she always had.

"I don't think so. I'm a very good judge of people. I need help with the website, social media, tweets—all the stuff I won't have time for. It's a lot to ask. I know you barely know me, and I'm asking you to share your audience . . . I understand if you don't want to do it. And we can pay. Oswald Zahn has agreed to bankroll everything." She smiled, feeling quite proud that the renowned philanthropist was assisting her. "It's his passion project."

"Zahn? He's big-time! Mr. Moneybags! That's great, but money's not *my* motivator, and I actually do feel like I know you. How would you feel about me joining you on the road? I can pay my own way and make an adventure of it. I can write my blog from anywhere, and I'd like to be there for the filming, if that's okay," he said, reaching across the table and taking her hand in his. He had wanted to do it from the moment he'd seen her.

Kapow! Their connection sent shivers up both of their arms, once again visibly raising the hairs.

She gave his hand a squeeze but pulled away. Quinn withdrew his empty hand.

"I feel like I know you too, Quinn. To be honest, it's a little unsettling. I'm happy you'll join us for the shooting; we could always use another mule," she joked. "But . . . everything's just too complicated—"

Quinn felt as though he'd been kicked. He had pushed too hard. Why hadn't he asked her about Elijah's father? He hadn't wanted to know. He hadn't asked because he hadn't wanted to entertain the possibility of anything keeping them apart.

"I'm sorry. I should have read you better," he interrupted.

"You read me exactly right, but we can't . . . If we're going to do this project together, and I think we are *meant* to do this project together . . . what with meeting Nate, then you and your blog . . . it's too much synchronicity. There must be a higher purpose, right? I just don't want to screw it up. I feel it, right down to the roots of my hair—it is so important that we do this. We can affect a lot of lives."

"Okay, I get it . . . no matter what, I'm on board. Will you tell me about Elijah's dad?" Quinn said, and Eden took a deep breath.

"He was killed in Syria just over a year ago. I'm still in shock most of the time. I'm so used to him being away, sometimes I just forget he's . . . *gone*-gone. I just expect him to show up, you know?" She absentmindedly played with the ring dangling around her neck while she spoke. She hadn't said "dead"; she had said "gone."

He was still alive for her, and Quinn understood how hard it must be. If there was one thing he had learned in his many years, it was empathy for loss and grief.

"I'm so sorry. Was he a soldier?"

"No. When we met, Jamie was the chief of a relief agency working all over Northern Africa and the Middle East, and I was filming a documentary about soldiers suffering from PTSD. After I had Elijah, I set up a home base here near his parents. Jamie was an engineer and stayed with the relief agency, traveling back and forth."

"Sounds like a good guy."

"He is . . . *was*. It's been especially hard on Elijah. We were supposed to meet Jamie in Egypt this June. It was going to be the summer we got on the aid trail . . . this time as a family. I plan to homeschool Elijah. I guess I was just waiting until I thought he was old enough before we became full-fledged vagabonds again."

She had planned to return with Elijah in tow, to Egypt—the land of the Giza Pyramids, and of Alexander the Great. *Interesting,* Quinn thought.

"And now? What will you do when you finish this project?" Quinn asked.

"I've thought about opening a school, especially for Crystal Children."

"Like the ancient Mystery Schools," Quinn said, nodding. It fit Theron. She was perfect for it, and if the kids were in danger, they would need a haven. Who better to run it?

"Your blog was the first place I read about those," she said, smiling. "It's a long way off, though. I've learned not to plan too far ahead. Life always throws curves, and plans fall away. Now, I try to live in the moment, and I know life will unfold as it is meant to, as long as I stay open and watchful."

I was watching for you, Quinn thought, but instead he said, "Absolutely right," and they sat in silence for a moment.

"Friends . . . professional? We need to keep focused," she said. "You okay with that?"

"Do I have a choice?" he asked, forcing a smile. He was flirtatious and casual on the outside, but inside he was churning with alarm that his longing for her would go unanswered.

"Oh, Quinn, there's always a choice," she said. "Nate was upset the other night. I hope I didn't lead him on," she said kindly. Theron was shining through, and Marcus basked in her glow.

"Well, when he finds out you shut me down, he'll be fine," Quinn laughed, though it hurt him deeply to say it.

"Oh God, you do say what you think, don't you?"

"Always. And Eden, after the bulk of the work is finished, I want you to promise you'll see me then . . . if you want to."

"I can't promise. Postproduction is very time-consuming. You could very well meet someone in the meantime or change your mind. We never know where we'll be," she insisted.

"I can guarantee *that* will not happen," Quinn said, smiling, and resisting the urge to kiss her. *Oh God! The next few months are going to be hell,* he thought. And he was right.

The hour had flown by, and Eden had to rush off. As she got up to leave, she wondered if she could travel and work with Quinn daily and still ignore her attraction to him.

Quinn didn't notice the desire in her eyes. He was looking past her, out the window, at a car waiting outside. Inside a 1958 red Plymouth Fury sat three men; two of them were Adversaries. The skinhead, Abaddon, who had been shouting at him earlier, was standing by the passenger window, holding his sign under his arm and pointing at Quinn through the glass. The Emissary filled with dread. He never knew how he would die, and this moment was full of life-ending potential.

"Is there a back door?" Quinn called to the server, gently urging Eden away from the window. There wasn't. Old building, old bricks. There was a rule they had to have two exits, but they were on either end of the dining room, and both led to the same stretch of sidewalk. There were only two other couples in the restaurant, and they were tucked in the back corners, oblivious to the drama mounting outside.

"Who are they?" Eden asked. She reached in her purse and pulled out a can of pepper spray.

"Stay in here until I get rid of them. If they get past me, use it right away. Don't wait, understand?"

There were four of them, all with shaved heads and camouflage or black clothing. They were now leaning and pacing around the bloodred car, staring at Quinn through the window.

"Let's call the police," Eden said, peeking out around the window frame.

"And tell them what? There are four scary-looking guys hanging around on Capitol Hill?" he said. She knew he was right. Intimidation and looking mean was hardly a crime. "I can handle it. Call the cops if I look like I'm in trouble, then you'll have something to report. Just promise me, if they get past me and walk through that door, you spray them." He kissed her on the head and strode toward the door.

"Don't go out there," she called as he opened it, but he didn't hear her over the man who had once again begun shouting.

"Blasphemer! The redeemer will strike you down! We are his cavalry!"

Abaddon, the Adversary, with his sign and booming voice, was the least of Quinn's worries. The other three men had come armed. He could see a knife, a baseball bat, and a tire iron, and he hoped they hadn't brought guns. Quinn approached the men with his hands raised, trying to negotiate a harmless passage. There was no doubt the troublemakers were there to see him, since three of the four were Adversaries. Quinn cringed to see their swastika tattoos, openly displayed. It reminded him of some of the most base years in the history of the world, a hateful time he had painfully endured. Quinn filled with anger and resistance in the face of the bastardized symbol. The veins on his neck were standing out, and his jaw was clenched tightly as rage engulfed him. He was determined that they must not get past him to Eden. Her pepper spray wouldn't be enough to protect her.

Eden screamed as the first man lunged, swiping with a blade about four inches in length. She and the restaurant owner were both dialing 911 as Quinn knocked the attacker to the ground with a roundhouse kick to the head. The second and third attackers pounced, bat and tire iron swinging, while Abaddon jumped up and down screaming and swearing, calling on some evil version of his God to smite Quinn.

Quinn was fast and skilled, and his heart raced, burning with hatred for the foul souls whose daily task was to tear the world to pieces, creating fear and discord and terrorizing humanity. He was happy to lash out. Elbow to the nose, knee to the groin. He grabbed a fallen bat and used it to smash his charging opponent's grimy fingers, breaking them and forcing the man to drop his weapon with a metal clang to the sidewalk. A black belt for nearly three thousand years, Quinn was quite accomplished. The power and bravado that had buoyed the Adversaries, prompting them to attack the Emissary, had now transformed into ratlike self-preservation. Only the street preacher, still high on meth, felt invincible against Quinn's disciplined blocks, kicks, and punches. As the other three crawled and staggered to their car and sped away to the sound of approaching sirens, Abaddon pulled a small handgun from the inside pocket of his floppy military-style coat. Another kick, and Quinn's foot connected with the man's jaw, near his birthmark, lifting him off his feet. The man landed unconscious with a heavy thump, and his head bounced off the pavement.

The ambulance had departed, and Eden and Quinn had finished giving their statements when they cuffed the Emissary and put him in the back of the patrol car. His cheek was bruised, and his ribs had taken a beating, but Quinn was better off than the four attackers. There was one additional cop car, and other people on the street were being interviewed as witnesses.

"It was self-defense!" Eden said angrily.

"It's a possible homicide, lady. Your boyfriend won't be just walking away this afternoon. We're going to the station to book 'im. When he's been printed and processed, he'll be arraigned before the judge, and then you can pay the bond and pick him up, probably tomorrow."

"You don't understand! I'm flying to Greece tonight," Eden insisted.

"Then someone else'll have to bail him out," he replied. But there *was* no one else. There was just her and Nate, and even though she and Quinn had just met, it made her desperately sad to realize that.

⤬⤬⤬ ⤬⤬⤬ ⤬⤬⤬

The holding cell was large and filthy, and Quinn tucked himself into a corner, away from the other prisoners. It was a sleepless night full of disgusting sights, sounds, and smells, but he didn't care. He had to think!

They knew me. How did they know me? It makes no sense, Quinn thought. *Is it Helghul? Did he find me and send his goons to get me out of the way?* he wondered. *Why is his life purpose so intent on sweeping her away from me? It must have something to do with Helghul! There must be something I don't understand! Something between them . . . and between the three of us!*

"Three connected like the strands of a whip," the Oracle of Delphi had said.

Yes, we have always been tied together, the three of us. Where's Eden now? Is she safe?

By morning, Quinn had black circles under his eyes, and a few more bruises had appeared as evidence of his fight the day before.

"Max Quinn!" an officer shouted. The prisoner had been bailed out, and he was grateful that Eden had postponed her trip, even for one day, to help him.

"You must be present for a hearing in three to four weeks. You or your lawyer will be contacted with a date and time. You must appear on that day or bail will be forfeited, and a warrant for your arrest will be issued. You must not leave the country. Do you understand?" the officer asked without looking up.

He did. He would not be joining Eden and Nate abroad as quickly as he had intended. He found himself hoping that the injured Adversary, Abaddon, would make a full and speedy recovery. His death would complicate things, and Quinn was no killer.

As Quinn was released, he searched the room for Eden.

"You Quinn?" an older man with greying hair and deep wrinkles in his face asked.

"Who are you?" Quinn said.

"Eden sent me."

Disappointment. Crushing, depressing disappointment filled him.

"She said to tell you she'll call you as soon as she gets to Athens. She asked me to drive you to your car."

Theron was gone. Once again, she had appeared and then slipped through his fingers, consumed by her own life purpose, ignorant of their connection and promise.

The old man was wearing a fashionable blazer with a Native American–art eagle design on the back and slim, dark jeans with a wide, shiny buckle. His hair was just above his shoulders and was smooth and stylish. Quinn recognized the man's aura from a lifetime long ago and was surprised by how similar his face was. They had once been in the same clan, the same tribe. Was it a coincidence? Quinn didn't believe in coincidence.

What is the Universe trying to show me? Why has the old shaman turned up now? Quinn asked himself as he stepped out onto the street, shielding his eyes from the glare.

"I'm parked right over here," the small man said, motioning to a Ford Mustang parked on the street.

Quinn was studying the eagle art on the old shaman's jacket as he walked behind him down the courthouse steps. The Emissary jumped, overreacting to the shriek of the automatic door lock.

Quinn walked around the back of the car and saw the Mustang emblem of a horse in full stride on the trunk. In Mongolia, where they had known each other before, life was lived on horseback. It was another synchronicity reminding him of their tribe long ago. Quinn climbed into the front seat of the convertible.

"Nice car," he said.

"Thanks. I call her my wind horse. You mind if I drop the lid?" the old guy asked.

"Please do."

"Buckle up, it's the law," he said before pulling away.

After a minute, Quinn learned that the man who'd bailed him out was the shaman of a local Native band. He had been the person Eden had called upon years earlier when trying to diagnose Elijah's "problem." They had stayed close friends.

A small Native drum and mini beater hung from the shaman's rearview mirror. Attached to the front of that were two small convex mirrors.

There's a lot of reflecting happening there, Quinn thought.

Quinn wondered how the old man could be so much the same after all these centuries. He had been a powerful and important mentor, full of wisdom and sage advice.

What was it he always used to say? Quinn couldn't recall. He *should* remember; he'd heard it a thousand times from the man. Was it his PTSD or just memory overload? There was so much to catalog that it was sometimes hard to keep his thoughts straight.

The old shaman looked at him sideways, recognizing his suffering. They continued driving in silence. Quinn focused on the wee beater—the leatherwork was so fine and intricate. The tiny drum was perfect—a work of art. It swayed back and forth, lulling him into a half-conscious state. The old shaman was a reminder that Marcus had forgotten something important. He had lost his ceremony, his reverence, his practice. Quinn's eyes swayed with the drum, unable to see the city outside the windows as he was transported to another time.

Chapter 9

Chilger and Borte

Mongolia, AD 1171

A band of riders raced across the Mongolian steppe. The diminutive animals looked more like ponies than full-fledged horses, but the riders rode with skill unmatched anywhere in the world. Nearby there was a large gathering of the tribes. They came together to buy, sell, and trade their goods once a month, though the location changed as the nomads moved. This month there was a big turnout.

Borte ran unchecked through the marketplace; sheep, wheels, grain, and large wrestling men were all obstacles to be avoided. The tips of her plaited hair, dark and glistening, blew free of her fur cap. Her black eyes sparkled with the chase, her cheeks permanently ruddy and burnt by the constant winds cutting across the plains of her homeland.

The crowd was loud and moved deliberately, ignoring the children as they darted and played joyfully. A small circle of shamans stood in deep conversation nearby wearing traditional clothing, with mirrors and shiny things attached from shoulder to toe. They, too, had once played on the steppe, but now they were a motley crew of men worn down by life and baked by the sun. Deep creases carved their faces, and one had a blind eye.

Chilger and Borte, laughing and running, stopped breathless behind a shelter, unnoticed by the adults nearby. Chilger opened his hand and produced a date, easily snatched in passing. He held it out to Borte, and she took it happily, biting it in half and returning the other portion to him. He popped it in his mouth, flashing a broad white smile, and suddenly, without a word, they were off again. She looked back, her heart racing. How close was he? Bam! She slammed to an abrupt stop. The tribal leader, her father, solid as a stone wall, loomed unyielding over her. She bounced off like a pebble, and he easily caught her before she hit the ground.

"Ay, ay!" he grumbled. Her smile already wiped clean, she was contrite and lowered her head respectfully as her father steadied her and used the moment to subtly scold her under his breath. He hurried her along, and his swiftness unnerved her. It was unlike him to move quickly or say much, so she thought he must be quite upset with her to act in this way. He was a quiet, contemplative man, typically cautious to smile but unlikely to anger—very good qualities in a chief.

Chilger watched from a distance, sorry he had caused his friend to suffer her father's disapproval. Borte's father eyed the boy cautiously and waved his arm in the air toward him once, as if swatting a fly. Chilger sadly watched Borte go; they were from different clans, and he looked forward to their chance meetings at the market or the seasonal festivals, as they always had great fun together. Chilger observed as Borte and her family disappeared into the distance. There was something unusual about her.

The daughter had been loaded onto the family cart, and they were making the long journey home in customary silence. They crossed the endless grassy landscape, empty to the untrained eye, aware of every rabbit, fox, and magpie for miles. Even under the bright sun, the temperature cut hard and cruel as they rode; the wind from all directions stirred the dust and grass in alternate sweeps.

It was the early months of autumn. The days of snow would come soon to make life difficult, but the people of northern Asia would endure heartily. In tune with the elements, the heavens, and the Earth, they survived the bitter cold by hard work and planning—the furs must be plenty, and the food stocks full. The angry cold and blizzards could hold them captive for weeks at a time, isolated and dependent on their herds, which needed grazing land to survive.

The nomads positioned themselves as best they could to accommodate their need to be self-sufficient, often going months without the option of trade in a shared marketplace. Common sense and preparation were second only to pleasing the gods in their beliefs. There was no chance; events unfolded as they were meant to at the pleasure or displeasure of the countless deities who abounded in the living, breathing land around them. Borte smelled the snow that had not fallen yet; the sweet, flowery scent of summer had gone and been replaced by the frigid crispness, warning them to make haste.

Borte and her father arrived at their nomadic tent, which was one of a group of fifteen *gers*, or yurts, spread out along that section of the remote steppe. Their fellow tribespeople were busy with their work and did not stir as they arrived with the dust billowing around them. Their horses and sheep herd, back from the pastures for the night, milled around them, and Borte's father forgot her, busy with his work. She climbed out to help unload the goods before milking the mare for dinner, and the distant horizon drew her eye. She saw something there, a cloud, an unusually large smudge of movement approaching their camp. She pointed.

Her father turned, his square silhouette momentarily obscuring her view of the evening sunset.

"Go, daughter, there is much to do. They come quickly," he instructed, nudging her toward the shelter. Her brothers had already joined their father in attending to the cart, and he directed them with few words to position the sheep for the night.

Borte was unsettled at being sent inside. Her father was acting strangely—her ten-year-old mind reflected on the marketplace and Chilger, and she assumed she was to blame. She knew that she was getting too old to behave in such a carefree, childish way, and she felt shame that she had disappointed him.

In fact, she was responsible for his preoccupation, but not for the reasons she supposed. Though she remained unaware, it was a monumental day in her life. Borte was being introduced to her prospective husband that night, and if the meeting went well, an alliance would be made and a contract agreed upon. The fathers were both tribal leaders, and they had met months before to discuss the possible alliance of their like-aged children. It was a time of discord and uncertainty between tribes, and wars were not uncommon; an ally would be welcome.

"Daughter, you may meet your husband tonight. You see, they approach. Come quickly and be washed and dressed," her mother said as she entered. Instantly she noticed that the ger smelled deliciously of roasting lamb tail and fragrant tea, and she was grateful for the warmth of the healthy fire in the center of the room. She saw that the traditional circular dwelling had been neatly arranged to receive guests at the north side near the altar, respecting Father Sky, Mother Earth, and the ancestors. It was laid invitingly with their best furs, skins, and carpets. Borte walked clockwise the short distance east to the women's side of the quarters. She stood compliantly while her hair was tightly rewoven, and her over-clothes were replaced with fresh ones she had only ever seen folded carefully in her mother's personal belongings. Her mother and grandmother rubbed and dressed and cleaned her, the entire time clucking around her like hens.

"This is a special day, Borte," they explained briefly in their spare but happy singsong way. "You will always remember the first time you see your husband."

Borte's mother stepped away from her, attending to the food preparation and arranging tea and spirits, while her grandmother continued to fuss over the wide-eyed girl. Borte noticed that both women had also taken special care with their dress and had scrubbed themselves and retied their hair. They were beautiful; their wide, round faces were perfectly symmetrical and kind. Even the elder woman, in her late forties, had an unusual sparkle in her almond eyes.

"Will they take me away?" Borte asked bravely. Her respected grandmother's face creased into cheerful lines, and, smiling widely, she displayed the gap where she had lost a side tooth. She held the girl tightly by the shoulders.

"Good girl to be so strong," she said, nodding. "You won't go now, not until your thirteenth year, at least. This is the time to make sure the choice will stick and your temperaments are in balance. If it is Heaven's will, he will join us here to serve your father until the year of the marriage ritual," she said, while at the same time rubbing her thumb superstitiously across the girl's forehead in a protective sign.

"But who is he?" Borte begged to know, her excitement and curiosity building.

The dust cloud grew closer—ox and cart and more men on thick, wide, heavy horses. Father rushed around the outside of the ger, still preparing, then pounded the dust from his layers of clothing. The sun was barely a sliver on the scarlet horizon, and the cold of evening was settling upon them. Each breath and word hung like smoke in the air. A blazing outdoor fire had been built to welcome and comfort the visitors; and the sheep, their long winter coats growing in, had been gathered nearby to rest for the night, where they could be heard bleating occasionally.

Tribal members from the other gers just beyond the chief's began to gather a few hundred paces away, anxious for a firsthand view of the visitors.

Nine-year-old Temujin approached, accompanied by his father, Yesugei Khan, his uncle, and numerous attendants. The group had traveled on horseback for three long days, but they were a traveling people and were unfazed by the journey.

The men arrived, looking stern and intimidating. They were an impressive sight, and it was obvious their clan was large and prosperous. They brought gifts of spice, grains, and textiles for their hosts. Borte's father led the honored guests through the southern tent flap into the traditionally appointed ger, warm with fire and food. Her brothers stayed outside with the remaining entourage and gathered at the fire, where they enjoyed a simple meal and exchanged stories and shared good humor.

"I hope you find your sheep's tails fat and your sons strong," Yesugei Khan began, demonstrating his friendly intentions to his hosts as they entered. His uncommon ginger hair and beard were bright against his fur cap, and his weathered face was nearly the same shade.

"You are generous and wise. I hope your horses have the muscle of many," Borte's father answered graciously.

As was mandated by custom, the men walked clockwise around the ger to the northern side and took their comfortable, warm places among the furs. Borte thought compassionately of her brothers left outside. Though they were well accustomed to adapting to the rapidly changing environment, the night had become harshly cold compared to the heat of the day.

A gust of wind shook the felt panels of the ger, and a strange chill ran through Borte.

The spirits are active tonight, she thought with a shiver, and though she was nestled warmly inside, her instincts raised her flesh into chicken skin.

"We bring well wishes and good luck from our tribe to yours. You are hearty, powerful people. It is with satisfaction and humble pride that I introduce my son, the future chief of the Borijin, Temujin."

The young man had been silent up until then, but he bowed his head respectfully and expressed his gratitude at being honored in their home. Borte listened intently, studying the underlying temperament revealed as he spoke. He was not silly or arrogant, as she had feared he might be; he used very few words, but they were well chosen, and she decided to like him.

The prospective bride had not yet been introduced, and she sat excited and silent at her grandmother's side. Her head was lowered, and she peeked curiously through wisps of hair that had once again broken free of their leather ties.

Temujin stole sidelong glances whenever he thought he would not be seen, but nothing went unnoticed as the adults watched the pair with amusement. He was anxious to see the girl's face; he cared not whether she was beautiful, but rather, hoped that she was not proud. He did not want the headache of a proud wife; his father's experience had taught him as much.

The meal was offered first to the gods, and then it was shared and properly appreciated and acknowledged. Finally, the youngsters were brought together so they could interact. Borte was small and thin for her age, unlike the thick, hearty-looking body type more common to her people. She stood especially erect, pushing out her chest to puff up and compensate for her scrawny frame. She kept her eyes on her warmly wrapped feet, her naturally rosy, round cheeks flushing deep crimson.

"T-t-t," her grandmother scolded, nudging her chin upward with a lumpy root of a finger. Borte's innocent brown eyes met those of her future husband. Even though he was a full year younger and only nine, he already looked like an adult to her.

Temujin felt a jolt at his core, and electricity shot through him. The light and dark within him sparred and danced up and down his spine, and something awoke inside him. His Helghul-memories stirred, dropped like a bead of ink into a clear well, spreading and polluting his purity. Innocent ignorance was replaced with something ancient and tainted—suddenly awakened. The extent of Helghul's knowledge was yet to be realized in this lifetime.

Temujin struggled to breathe evenly. He was confused and overwhelmed as every hair on his body stood at attention. He became aware that beautiful waves of indigo encircled Borte and filled the ger with light.

Can anyone else see it? Can anyone else feel it? he wondered, searching the faces around him. The others were unchanged and oblivious as they continued stupidly nodding, greeting, and attending to social formalities. Suddenly, he saw that he, too, had a field of energy around him. He didn't yet remember that it was called shine, but he could see the grey and black waves encircling him. He began to perceive the karmic code of each person present, though none of them was as spectacular as Borte's. None of them affected him as hers had.

Theron, he heard in his head. *How did I not see it before?* Temujin thought, struggling to make sense of shine.

The door to his Helghul-memories had been unlocked, and slowly it would open, until eventually, flung wide, he would have total recall. It was not only the Helghul-memories waiting to be remembered; the Beast within him was biding its time.

Temujin instinctively understood that Borte's power and energy would grow as she aged, and for the first time he had a glimpse of his own potential and power. He decided he would certainly have her.

Borte watched the boy, unsure what to think. He was behaving very strangely; his eyebrows arched and twitched, and she wished he would ask her a question or at least pay her a perfunctory compliment. Finally, he spoke, and then he behaved admirably, hiding his inner turmoil. In keeping with custom, he wished her the blessings from the gods, and then remarked on her home and her dress garments, and again praised the food.

Temujin struggled valiantly to appear at ease and comfortable, convinced he must win Borte over and have her as his wife. The humble gathering continued, and no one noticed the difference in him. Outwardly he was unchanged, but as he spoke calmly of livestock and family members, his mind journeyed through cloudy past lifetimes filled with blurry pictures, impossible places and faces, and memory after memory played like a dream sequence in his head.

Borte decided she liked Temujin, more by way of rational thinking than by feeling. It was nothing he had done or said. He had been odd and wooden, unlike her brothers and the other boys she had grown up with, but she decided it was most likely just his nerves, and he would eventually relax and become a worthy mate.

The next morning, Yesugei Khan said goodbye to his son and started out across the expansive plains toward the distant mountains to return home before the season's first snow. Temujin was left behind in the care of Borte's father. He would remain with them for three years until he was twelve, at which time they would marry and return to his tribe together.

Borte admired Temujin's stoicism; if he was sad to be left behind, he hid his feelings well. She could not know that the farewell was the least of his concerns. No one suspected how he was reeling as he contemplated the all-knowing voice and confusing images filling his head.

Are the stories and memories real? Temujin wondered, questioning the health of his thinking. But feeling more powerful and manly than ever, he surmised that the great Mongol gods Tengri and Gazar Eej, also known as Father Sky and Mother Earth, were communicating to him. He embraced his new awareness as evidence of his divine function in the world. He was a tool of the gods, sent to the plains with a divine mission yet to be understood. He soon became unwavering in his practice and devotion.

Borte was clearly important; she had been a catalyst for him. It had been her gaze that had catapulted him into a whole new level of understanding. Her light and virtue, so foreign to him, were familiar at the same time. The process of recall, at least this time, had just begun—there was a great deal of painstaking work yet to be completed before Temujin would have any true understanding of the Great Year and who he had been. He would have to be patient and do the work. In the meantime, he would develop his relationship with Borte and follow the path that had opened before him.

Temujin had intended to spend the next few days sorting out the shadowy images bombarding him, but before nightfall, his plans changed. Horsemen rode across the steppe toward their humble settlement, and Temujin could see men from his tribe.

He was informed that his father had been assassinated. His uncle and a few fellow tribesmen had come to return Temujin and tell Borte's father that a passing tribe of Tatars had customarily offered the chief an exchange of food and then had poisoned him. The murderers were long gone before anyone realized what they had done. The boy remained stoic.

"I must go," he said, mounting his broad steed, prepared to return to his tribe and claim his place as chief. Borte was impressed by his bravery.

"Are you not afraid they will kill you as well?" she asked.

"I am not afraid. I will return, Borte. Will you wait for me?"

"I will wait," she promised. Their eyes locked, and there was a connection and an awareness that solidified their commitment to one another.

Temujin left to rejoin his clan, vowing someday to exact vengeance on the Tatars. Borte watched as her betrothed galloped into the horizon.

Temujin's party returned to their kin three days later, their fur caps obscuring their faces, making them recognizable to one another only by wardrobe, mannerism, and voice. The season's first snow covered them, sticking to their hats and beards.

The body of the dead khan had arrived earlier that day with the other half of the original party. The shaman had begun a sacred fire ceremony to ward off evil spirits and was beating his drum and chanting while the polished metals of his clothing flashed in the firelight.

Though it was unlucky to speak of the dead, Temujin was unafraid and wasted no time. Immediately upon returning, the nine-year-old—with his uncle's support—addressed the elders and the men of the village. He proposed that he should inherit the title and position left unfilled by his father's murder. The men refused outright and mocked the boy.

"In his ninth year and hardly able to hold his own cock!" "His only hair is on his head!" they jeered. Temujin was irate but powerless, and he was sent away from the gathering, humiliated and denied. His purpose would not easily be fulfilled.

Temujin's mother, Hoelun, now a widow, was left to care for five young sons and a daughter. The wife did not cry; she did not mourn. There was work to be done. In the days to follow, she canvased the village for a sponsor. Any man—old, young, married, single—she cared not. She knew she needed a protector to exist in the tribe, but atypically, no one came forth. No one accepted her. Temujin, with his newly remembered ability to see shine, would soon realize that his mother glowed with the soupy-grey shine of Solenna, the Adversary. Beautiful, but notoriously proud and outspoken, Hoelun was more than any man was prepared to live with, and she was left to fend for herself and her children.

True to her acerbic nature, Hoelun projected her anger outward and accused the tribesmen openly of being too weak and insignificant to be worthy of her. She called the women stupid, ugly, and jealous, and the few who had held any pity for her turned away in disgust. Hoelun, with her pride and arrogance, had doomed her family, and they were soon abandoned by their nomadic tribe.

It was a brutal, deadly winter, but accustomed to the hardship of life on the plains, Hoelun and her children beat the odds and survived. They were a part of no tribe and had to fend for themselves. They had no herd to sustain them; their possessions had been ransacked and appropriated by the new chief when they had been abandoned. Their remaining shelter was a barely adequate ger of wood and poor-quality skins, but somehow they had the fortitude as a family to get through the next nine months of frigid battery.

They ate wild currants and blueberries that Hoelun and her daughter had collected and dried for winter; and they hunted small game, mostly mice. They had fire and prayed many times a day to the fire god, grateful for the life it gave. The days were short and the nights were long, and Hoelun regaled her children with stories of better days: tales of ancestors, strength, and triumph.

Hoelun anticipated their return to clan life someday and prepared her brood for that eventuality. She taught them the ritualistic offerings and assured them they were favored, and as little as they had to eat and drink, they always shared first with the gods. They learned to be wary and cynical, and as a former khan's wife, she explained the ins and outs of the region's politics and her thoughts on how to gain advantage over others. Temujin's Helghul-voice continued to fuel the hatred burning inside him.

Hoelun and her small family remained independent and alone for many years. Temujin continued to grow and thrive and was at least a head taller than his brothers, including the eldest. He looked remarkably like his father—his red hair thick and wiry, his dark eyes hard and cold.

Temujin had changed drastically since his meeting with Borte and the death of the khan. The Beast had awakened him to his own perceived greatness, and his ego thrived. His focus was on survival and on devising a plan to return his family to a place of sustenance, power, and honor. His twelfth birthday had come and gone unobserved; the marriage agreement, impossible to fulfill, was unavoidably ignored but not forgotten. He had become sullen and suspicious, and he manipulated his family, constantly challenging his older brother's authority in their small camp.

It was a beautiful, warm spring day. Thirteen-year-old Temujin and his brothers were stalking the plains, a sea of multicolored, fragrant flowers laid out for miles around them. The gorgeous weather was a welcome reward for bearing a brutal seven months of harsh cold, but it had been an unlucky week. As the boys hunted, they were acutely aware of their hunger and the oncoming short-tempered desperation the too-familiar pangs brought with them.

In a flash of movement, the band leapt at a noise. Temujin had speared a marmot, and it lay squealing and struggling in the field ahead of them. Temujin ran to the animal and bent down to it. Taking his spear, he breathed in the marmot's last breath, and the Beast inside him luxuriated in the sacrifice. His brothers crowded around and knelt, honoring the spirit of the animal. It wasn't until the methodic, ritualistic butchering and division of the spoils had occurred that the merriment was quelled by an argument that erupted between Temujin and his older brother.

"The heart is mine," said the older boy as Temujin deftly removed the coveted organ, according to tradition.

Temujin was in no mood to step aside. "The marmot is mine. You eat only by my skill," Temujin retorted, covered in blood and still cutting deep into the animal to expose its prized bits.

His brother came closer, his hunting knife drawn, to retrieve the animal's heart. Temujin went against custom and denied his older brother, refusing to unhand the carcass.

"You will have to take it . . . you know I am the stronger hand," Temujin warned as his brother got within striking distance.

The older boy sprang, and the fight was on. The two square-brick young men, heavy with their layers of clothing, wrestled on the grass, tangling themselves up in the blood and guts of the beast.

"Off the meat!"

"Watch out!" the other brothers shouted, excited by the battle but conscious of the disrespect being shown. Surely the spirit of the marmot would be angered by such disregard. They were used to wrestling and scuffles among them—it was a way of life. Temujin grunted hard and managed to flip his attacker onto his back, and now he sat wild-eyed on his chest, staring down at him.

It should have ended there, as it had many times before, but Temujin, panting, realized how close he had come to losing this time.

One of these days he will overpower and submit you! Get rid of him now while you can! the Beast inside his head said.

With that thought in mind, Temujin deliberately and unexpectedly raised his hunting knife, still gory with the blood of their dinner, and sank it deep into the throat of his brother. The victim's hand had come up in self-defense and was pinned to his flooding neck.

Gasps and yelps rang out as the younger brothers howled in disbelief. Blood poured unchecked from the fatal wound. No one dared come near. The siblings ran back to their camp, forgetting their food, forgetting their hunger, and terrified by what they had seen.

Temujin felt no shock or sorrow. He climbed off his older brother and cleaned his knife on the corpse, power surging through him. He felt invincible as the Beast within him stirred with satisfaction.

Take control of your destiny, boy! it said.

The marmot heart was his, and he was now the undisputed head of the family. Blood-soaked and victorious, he threw his dinner over his shoulder and headed home.

Chapter 10

The Trials of the Shaman

Chilger had not seen Borte since years before in the market, though he had casually searched for her at every opportunity. They had first met when they were very young. She was the only girl he had ever noticed, and her energy had resonated with him. For as long as he could remember, she had looked like an angel to him. Just as a child can fail to notice a difference in hair or skin color, Chilger had been oblivious to the warm violet glow surrounding her like a thick second skin. It had been visible only to him, but he had not noticed it was different. As they matured, his Marcus-memories had begun to stir—not a thunderbolt this time, but in whispers and confusing, comforting flashes. He was older now, and their childish play should be long forgotten, yet the memory of her continued to haunt him.

Chilger had become a promising horseman and hunter, and by twelve years of age he had proven himself an asset to the Merkit clan. Always profoundly spiritual and in tune with the natural world, he had a way of communing with animals and birds that was extraordinary, even among his people, who were fundamentally holistic and in harmony with their natural surroundings. The clan's shaman was impressed by the youngster's insight, depth of contemplation, and understanding. He had identified Chilger's gifts and was following the boy's progress and growth with interest.

Midway through his twelfth year, Chilger's destiny was laid out. It was early autumn, and the sun was living lower in the expansive blue sky. Eagles soared and swooped above, floating effortlessly on the cool breeze. The plains were filled with the poetry of birds, in harmony, making plans for the changing season.

Chilger had felt the strange energy of the day even before anything unusual had happened. He had felt a tingling in his hands, his feet, and the Tengri-god center at the top of his head since he had awakened that morning. This vibration was usually accompanied by strange visions, yet that day, none had come.

The pictures he saw in his mind were a secret. He told no one about the confusing stories and images filling his head. Only the shaman had ever spoken of visions and premonitions; and Chilger's father, a hunter and herder, was far from understanding such mysterious concepts. He lived a simple life, fulfilling his duties, praying and giving offerings as he was taught, without question. Chilger searched for deeper meaning but learned early that too much conversation and too many questions were met with stern glances or a firm hand. He kept his metaphysical contemplations to himself. He lived like the other boys his age—hunting, wrestling, and riding, always preparing for the coming grueling winter months—but he was different.

Chilger was alone when he entered the woods, out of view of his clan's camp. He saw the beams of sunlight breaking through the golden canopy of the larch forest, lighting the woodland floor. Mother Earth and Father Sky touched one another and danced before him, filling him up. The forest was alive with spirits, and Chilger was at one with the Earth. The faces of nature were alive within the branches, and the leaves nodded and turned with the wind, observing the young rider as he passed.

The boy's horse began to favor one leg, so Chilger dismounted to see to the injury and let him rest. They had entered a sunny clearing perched up on the hillside, and he tied the horse to a small group of birch trees glowing in the evening sun. Chilger noticed a particularly abundant berry bush a short climb down a rocky cliff. Hunting had been unsuccessful that day, but the ripe berries would help soothe the defeat. He removed his bow from his back and laid it on the grass near his horse so it would not interfere with his climbing down. His stout pony, its reins secured, rested happily in the shade eating while Chilger filled his pouch and munched sweet fruit.

In his reverie, singing under his breath, Chilger hadn't realized how late it had gotten. The sun was slipping below the horizon, and the light had grown dusky when he heard a twig snap. Immediately after, there was a distressed whinny and the sound of startled hooves shuffling and pounding the earth. A ferocious growl, then another; the boy's horse continued to nicker and bray in distress. Chilger urgently climbed up the rock face to investigate.

Wolves! A small, aggressive pack, five in all—were crouched around his horse, poised to pounce. The Mongolian wolf was large and savage and could easily pull down a mare. The wolves' silver shackles were raised, and their lips curled and twitched, revealing sharp teeth as their deep rumbles resonated through the forest. The pony swung his head frantically, trying to free himself of his reins.

He can't escape because I've tied him! I've killed him! Chilger realized with horror. Reflexively, Chilger reached for his bow. It was as much a part of any Merkit man as his own arms and legs were, but it wasn't beside him where it should be. It lay on the ground, unreachable, in the middle of the wolf pack.

The lead grey wolf howled, and Chilger worried that the call would summon others and increase their numbers. Birds and small prey scattered farther, and a marbled polecat sprayed in defense, leaving behind the pungent evidence of fear as it fled.

It was easy to identify the alpha male, for he was the largest, and the others awaited its lead. Its broad shoulders glowed silver-blue. It was a beautiful coat, and the wolf would have been an impressive kill. The meat was stringy and unappetizing, but the fur would surely have been coveted by the clan. Humans were the wolf's only predatory enemy, but today it was the boy who was at a disadvantage.

"No! *Hah! Hah!*" Chilger began shouting, unsheathing the knife at his waist. It would be a lame, slow defense against the ruthless canine daggers, but it was his only defense. Chilger didn't feel the spiny bushes scraping his legs as he sprinted forward. He bounded past the wolf and expertly launched himself onto the pony's back. He reached to untie the reins, and the wolves snapped and lunged at him.

The wolves, unwilling to abandon pursuit of their prey, lurched forward, signaling their offspring to attack. There was another loud whinny as the male wolf sank its teeth into the pony's hind quarter. Chilger thrust his knife, turning his face away. The wolf's jaws tore into the animal's right thigh, and the pony reared, flipping backward and landing with a thud on Chilger. The boy's leg was crushed, and a rock smashed against the back of his skull, knocking him out as he landed.

The pony kicked and bucked frantically, trying to scramble back to its feet and pounding against Chilger on the ground underneath him. The bucking and stomping only momentarily stalled the attackers. The snarling, hungry pack was relentless, and the horse whinnied in pain as the alpha female clamped down her powerful jaws on its neck.

Chilger lay unconscious as the wild-eyed pony was dragged down. The alpha male and female asserted their dominance, and the smallest, weakest omega wolf, having been rebuffed, turned its attention to the vulnerable boy on the ground. Wolves did not hunt humans, but they had been known to maul them. The canine sniffed Chilger's motionless body.

The old Merkit shaman had been collecting medicinal roots and bark, but signaled by the setting sun, he was returning to camp when the howling and commotion interrupted his tranquility. Everything about the shaman looked weathered and old, but his mind and senses were strong.

A wolf pack so close by was a threat to the livestock and never to be ignored, but what else did he hear?

A horse? A man? Great Tengri! Someone is in trouble! Without a thought for his own safety, he mounted his horse and rushed toward the uproar. The metal panels on his apron and kaftan rattled and clanged as he galloped.

Through the trees, the shaman saw the lifeless boy being sniffed and nudged by the smaller wolf while the other four fed on the fallen pony. The ancient one charged his horse through the trees. His withered face was fierce as he approached at a full gallop. His bow was ready, and with a prayer of mercy, he ripped an arrow through the neck of the smaller wolf, killing it.

"Not today, my friend. The horse is enough. There will be no more," the old man said while he released a second arrow. Startled, the other wolves ran off, dragging the pony's bloody carcass down into the trees, just far enough so that the man was out of sight.

The shaman couldn't rouse Chilger, and he could see by the unnatural angle of his gored leg that it was badly broken. The boy's head had been bleeding down his neck, had begun to clot, and was now matted to the grass. Ever alert and rushing, lest the wolves return, the old man mustered the strength to lift Chilger onto his short pony. Then, with a grunt, he placed the dead wolf behind the boy on the animal's rump. Pulling the reins, he made his way for home.

"Boy, you have one foot on the Earth and one foot in the sky. You must choose one or the other," the old shaman said as he walked.

They were an alarming sight as they returned to camp. Chilger was unresponsive and near death, his clothing soaked with blood. The initial attack had left ugly wounds across his right shoulder and forearm. These injuries, coupled with the broken leg and gash to the head, made his survival unlikely.

Chilger remained unconscious for days. Within hours, a fever set in. In his delirium, he saw strange and terrifying visions. He called out, sharing the disturbing images in languages unknown to his family. Soaked with sweat, the boy yelled and writhed. The stooped shaman attended him hour after hour, his gravelly voice croaking, chanting, and praying while he applied healing salves to the boy's body and water to his lips. He beat the goatskin spirit drum and used a spear decorated with white horsehair called a *sulde*, to draw in the spirit of the wind and sun to revive the wind horse, or soul, of Chilger. His scepter acted as a drumstick and pounded, sending messages and vibrations through the entire clan into the soil and Heavens. The steady thump of the drums called to the Great Spirit.

The old shaman listened intently to Chilger's rants and joined him, trembling and wailing. The shaman's eyes rolled back white in his head, and the ger was filled with the old man's calls. He begged his god Tengri to spare the boy's life. Mirrors were laid all around the boy and placed on his chest to frighten away the evil spirits that might choose to possess him, in his weakened state.

Chilger had cried out about Atitala, the deluge, and the Emerald Tablet. He had called to Theron; he'd seen giants, flying machines, oceans, pyramids; he watched his son die before him, murdered by a spear. He walked up white steps in white robes, visited the land above and the land below, and understood he was a dot, connected to billions of smaller dots. The trees, the birds, the people, the mountains, and his thoughts were all the same. Everything came from the first dot.

And he saw Borte. Over and over, the little girl from the market returned to him in his fevered state, always when he was closest to Tengri. Always when he thought he might move into the brilliant, welcoming glow ahead of him, he would see her face, and she would smile and call to him.

"Come back," she said.

"You have one foot on the Earth and one foot in the sky. You must choose one or the other," the old shaman repeated throughout the boy's delirium.

Chilger *did* come back. His fever broke on the fifth day, and the exhausted shaman who believed the boy was a gift directly from Tengri made arrangements with his relieved parents for him to train as an apprentice.

"His wind horse is ancient and powerful. Though your family has no history of the gift, he is meant to be a shaman," the old healer told them. Chilger's fevered ravings had left them frightened and unnerved, and they were happy to know he would soon be under the full-time care and guidance of the wise one.

"Chilger told many tales. He has traveled among the spirits and has lived many lives," the shaman said.

Chilger heard the shaman's words, and in his sleepy haze he heard his simple father grunt his assent; it would not have occurred to the parent to do otherwise.

The clan chief, an Adversary, was unhappy with the old shaman's choice. He had always found Chilger irritating, and he did not wish to elevate the boy's status. The shaman, however, was convincing, and he played upon the chief's fears and superstitious beliefs to ensure Chilger's path.

Chilger healed, though he had many scars. He trained with the old master through his teen years and proved to be a profoundly gifted spiritualist. His Marcus-consciousness generated wisdom and an understanding of life. That history, combined within this lifetime, belonging to a people united with the soil and sky, helped him tap into a profound and powerful psychic energy. He shared that connection with his village. His wise mentor realized that the abilities of his prodigy would soar beyond him.

Chilger's visions and dreams continued after the wolf incident, and one vivid and gory dream began recurring. He saw and felt thousands of dead—people slaughtered, dismembered, and left to die on the steppe, plains, and hills of northern Asia. Chilger shared his visions with the old shaman, and together they sought clarity, for when the spirits sent images, there must be a reason. It would be many years before they would understand the visions.

In his fifteenth year, Chilger rescued a large golden eagle with a wingspan beyond eight feet. Its left wing had been damaged defending a kill from a challenger. Chilger had approached the injured bird cautiously, humming, droning. He had lowered himself down a sharp cliff to reach it. His own shaman-eagle feathers not yet earned, he had looked more like a wolf in his fur coat and cap than the bird he would later embody as a full shaman. The vulnerable eagle struggled and thrashed, its claws and beak, like razors, viciously defending itself.

Chilger called for wisdom, for comfort. He had killed a rabbit earlier, and he gave it to the bird while he sang his intentions, offering help and healing in a language known only to the pair. The eagle calmed down and hooked the rabbit in its beak, allowing Chilger to help it. Its wing was broken, and against all reason and nature, the eagle allowed him to place a blindfold over its eyes.

Chilger tenderly folded its muscular wings into its body, and it screeched, dropping its meal and pecking his arm, a reminder to be gentle. The eagle had torn through his thick fur jacket and opened a bloody gash. Though it was in pain, the bird understood that Chilger was a friend. It allowed him to continue, no longer afraid. Chilger stroked the back of its neck and continued to hum, undaunted and ecstatic. He wrapped a long silk strip, pulled from his waistband, around both folded wings, preventing attempts at flight and further damage. He then scaled the precarious rocks again and carried the massive bird back to camp.

Chilger was a miraculous sight with the giant eagle resting on his thick arm, proud and erect. Alarmed clan members gasped, and animals fussed and retreated as they passed. Those at camp emerged from their gers and left their duties to witness man and beast in complete harmony. The eagle slowly rotated its regal head, and though its eyes remained covered, it was unafraid, at one with its host.

The wounded eagle survived its injury. Once healed, Chilger released its silk bonds, and it soared joyfully free into the vast, open sky.

Be free, he thought in awe, hoping he would see the eagle again and certain he would recognize its call.

He watched in wonder as the eagle returned to him, seeking his company. He sent it off again, riding away, dropping his arm so it would fly free, but it refused to leave him.

When it became clear the eagle would not be put off, Chilger decided to train it. The bird was intelligent, and they communicated easily. Chilger had been earmarked by the spirits before birth, and his connection to the natural world continued to grow. The eagle remained a constant companion to him, a thick leather saddle blanket strapped to his left forearm for their mutual comfort. They learned to hunt together, and the eagle brought him trophies and gifts. He treated the bird with sustained respect and reverence and spoke to it in hoots and hollers but never presumed to give it a name.

Generations of Merkits would have spoken of this amazing scene in fire dances and tales. They would have sung of this young shaman-to-be, this gifted boy who had walked into camp with a golden eagle for a friend, if they'd had the chance . . . had the tale not died with them.

After many years of training, Chilger was in his ger preparing to receive the accessories and kaftan inherited when he completed his journey to become a shaman. Beside him, the old shaman, who had insisted on the boy's advancement, was in ceremonial attire. On the table nearby sat the headdress of the golden eagle, intended for Chilger. The mask was an artistic masterpiece with a large beak made of golden material wrapped around molded leather, with cascading feathers down the sides resembling wings. Its hollow eyes stared while they methodically proceeded through the traditional steps. Soon Chilger would be the only person to observe the world through those sacred sockets.

They burned juniper and blessed the process while the mentor helped Chilger dress in traditional clothing and trims that had been painstakingly prepared for him. The first layer was symbolic and infused with ancestral energy. The old shaman explained the significance and importance of each piece of the wardrobe. For the first time, Chilger donned the leather belt hung with mirrors he would wear daily as a shaman. The mirrors would reflect his inner and outer selves and ward off evil spirits. Once complete, heavy leather strips fell in bands dangling from his arms and hems like feathers, swinging and swaying dramatically as he moved.

"Today you will fully unite with your totem, the golden eagle, and join me in being an intermediary between the spirit world and the human world. Our people will look to you as an example and for guidance," the old man said.

"And I will look to you. The chief still resists my placement. I hope I will live up to your expectations," the Emissary said humbly.

Though he was seventeen, and by all accounts a man, Chilger was nervous to hold so much responsibility within his tribe. His Marcus-memories were still unclear to him in this lifetime. They remained an inner restlessness that he avoided confronting.

"My advice will be as unnecessary as a second arrow into a dead kill. You surpassed my ability to know Tengri when the eagle chose you two summers ago. No man could be prouder of a son."

"No son could value a father and teacher more. My scars are proof of your bravery and sacrifice," Chilger said with a lump in his throat. Chilger and the shaman had formed a profound friendship within the clan. Chilger's birth parents, simple herders, had struggled to understand him and had been distant.

"I have always told you, you have one foot on the Earth and one foot in the sky. It used to be because I wanted you to focus your attention, but through your trials and practice, you have become like a tree, with deep roots in the Earth and strong branches reaching to the Heavens."

The young man was deeply moved. He knew this kind of love; Socrates had taught Plato like this. He had taken him under his wing and had mentored him in a way that had helped him grow, but Marcus had suffered for the attachment. Though he had sworn to avoid such bonds, this one had flourished before his memory was clear enough to caution him. Marcus would catalog and remember the kindness and wisdom of the old shaman. He would carry the memory of him like a talisman added to the bag of jewels collected and slung across him over the centuries. The burden of so many fine souls sometimes buoyed him, but more often they weighed him down.

The sacred ceremony began after sunset under an expanse of a million stars. The old shaman burned juniper branches and berries, beseeching the Fire Mother. The ritual was long, and the entire clan attended, bringing gifts and offering sacrifices and gratitude to Tengri and the ancestors.

After many hours of ceremony, song, and meditation, surrounded by pungent aromas and having been deprived of sleep and food, the shaman placed the eagle headdress on Chilger. The beak hung over his forehead and camouflaged his face. From the thick smoke, an image was conjured. The shape of a snake slithered from the red-hot coals, and slowly the smoke rose foot by foot, morphing into the silhouette of a man.

Chilger saw a powerful chief with hair like fire and eyes like emeralds. It was not the first time Chilger had seen him. He had been having dreams and visions of him for years. It was a warning. Instinctively he knew that this man would bring war and bloodshed to the steppe. Chilger had never met the man whose face appeared in the ritual fire, but his wind horse was familiar. His Marcus-memory recognized Helghul's energy. He was not surprised that once again their paths would cross.

He is clearly a khan, but where? What clan? And where is Theron? he wondered, not for the first time. But finally, the answer came.

The face of the little girl from the market immediately appeared in the smoke—Borte.

You said you would never leave me, she had transmitted through Chilger's delirium when he was near death.

Borte is Theron!

He had already met Theron in this lifetime! As a boy, before his Marcus-memory had been reawakened, he had known her, played with her, and watched her be carried away by her stern father. Chilger was overcome with emotion, and the smoky faces of Temujin and Borte dispersed, as sparks rising into the air.

Chilger fell to his knees, feeling physically ill. Borte was his soulmate. He knew it now. For the first time in countless incarnations, they had found each other and were unrelated— male-female contemporaries. He was determined to find her and create the family and life they had dreamed of together in Atitala.

But how? His vision clearly told him his purpose in this life- time was to counter the red-haired menace. He would do what he must, but he felt torn. He was determined to find Borte first. He convinced himself that together he and Theron would be a more powerful force to combat the evil taking power in the Iron Age. It was an Age unknown to him, and he searched for light in the darkness.

Chilger did not know that Borte had already met the figure in the smoke, and to her he was much more than a red-haired stranger.

Chapter 11

Temujin Returns

Temujin had not come for Borte on his twelfth birthday, as had been agreed. Nor had he come in the years following. Borte's father became concerned that his clever daughter would be left to wilt like a field flower, so he had trained her in riding, hunting, and other skills typically reserved for boys. He eventually learned that Temujin's family had been cast out after Yesugei Khan's death, but he had heard no more.

The marriage agreement was still in place even though the suitor was no longer the strategic and valuable alliance he had once seemed; it would be dishonorable to act otherwise. Borte's father could only hope and pray for news that Temujin had been killed. Then he would be free to make a better match for her.

Borte, however, had met no other man who earned her fidelity, and year after year, she grew more independent when no word came. She accepted that she might never marry, and her mother blamed Borte's masculine indifference on her father.

"You taught her to ride and to use the bow. No man will be enough to dominate her," her mother complained.

"She is like no other woman. You see how she rides, how she notices every detail of the weather and stars. She was not born to be dominated," he replied.

"Hmff! You spoiled her, with all the sun you shone onto her. She is self-important and proud."

"She is confident. I regret nothing. Now hush before your grievances turn my mind to worry and steal my serenity," he said.

It was an evening in mid-autumn. Borte was in her seventeenth year and had grown muscular and strong, but she maintained the outward appearance of fragile loveliness. Her soft brown skin was red and toughened where it had been exposed to the elements. She had worked ceaselessly all day, using a thick bone needle to stitch seams through dense skins that would aid in the winter comfort and survival of her family. Her father, the chief, was alerted that a rider approached. As the unexpected stranger grew nearer, his red hair and green eyes were unmistakable. Like a spirit from another time, Temujin returned unannounced to claim his bride.

"It is Temujin, daughter. Make haste to be ready," the chief ordered. Borte was frozen in place, staring, as she realized the significance of the rider. Her heart raced at the vision of Temujin rising like sacred fire, red and blazing across the landscape.

"Hurry, daughter!" the chief snapped, unnerved by the image of Temujin crossing the plain, looking more like a spirit than a man.

"He comes to us like a raven on the wind," Borte's mother remarked from behind them.

"Soon he will arrive, and we will see he is just a man. We will welcome him, hear his tale, and promise nothing," the chief said, returning to the calm, controlled voice to which they were accustomed.

Borte's mother and grandmother had both joined them outside, and the chief steered his daughter toward them. "Take her inside. Prepare for our visitor."

Borte was led inside, her pulse and mind racing. She had waited many years for Temujin to come, and she had not even realized until that moment that she had given up on him. She felt uncertain. He was a stranger, and he was coming to them so suddenly. Borte felt a great charge in the air, and she knew that change was certainly upon them.

Once inside, she collected herself nervously and helped organize an honorable seat for their guest near the corner that housed their ancient ancestors. Borte said a prayer, requesting guidance and blessing in the night ahead. She was attended by the other women, and they all flitted about their home.

"At last he's come. Our prayers have been answered," her mother said respectfully, nodding in almost a full bow toward the fire in the center of the room and to the sacred vessel on the northern side of the shelter.

"It is all so sudden. I can barely breathe. Like the wind, this stranger appears, and I am to marry him? A boy I met when he was half this age? To see him riding solo toward us is to feel invaded . . . under siege. But he is to be my husband, not my conqueror," Borte said aloud, all the while busily placing down carpets and furs, and then rebinding her waist-length black hair with laces of well-softened leather.

"It is one and the same," her mother chimed in, and the older women laughed knowingly.

"It is a relief you will not grow old and sour in your father's care. Soon you will have children of your own," her grandmother said with a wrinkled, gap-toothed smile. Her skin was so aged from the sun, wind, and brutality of life on the plain that she looked well beyond her years.

Will we know love? Borte wondered to herself, but she kept quiet for the remainder of their preparation. Those were musings she would never share with anyone. Silly and impractical, there was no place for such frivolity.

Borte had known since childhood that her duty as a daughter was to become a good wife and the mother of a strong, hearty brood. She would know love through her children, and she would grow to respect her husband if he was gentle and kind. She hoped he would have smiling eyes like her father that twinkled and spoke to her, and a quick wit like her brothers. She hoped he would not be severe like some of the men of her clan.

Borte loved to laugh and tease, but as she peeked slyly through the slim opening where the door flap fell closed, she could not imagine the stern, red-faced Temujin doing either one. She saw no smile, no soft kindness in his face. He looked all business. Her father gesticulated, spreading his arms wide to the Heavens and then to the Earth as they spoke. Borte deduced that their guest was explaining his long absence, and her father was suggesting it must be the will of the Universe that things be as they were.

Temujin and the chief soon entered the ger, and the curious clan members, who had been feigning disinterest, adjourned to their own chores and homes to speculate in private. Borte confidently came forward to greet Temujin. No longer a skinny child, she had become a sturdy, beautiful woman. She offered a restrained smile, and Temujin nodded in return.

Once again, Helghul was accosted by Theron's shine. The thick bands of color and the life force that surrounded and flowed from her confronted him, parrying with his life soul and sending him spinning. He saw her emanations woven intricately through the ger, flowing in and out of her parents and family. They all looked upon her adoringly, deeply affected by her but oblivious to the corporeal radiant force enveloping them.

Temujin remembered her powerful wind horse from their first meeting, and her shine had grown as she had aged. She had overwhelmed and filled him, and she continued to do so. He knew she was special, and over the years, with the help of his ancient ancestors—his Helghul-voice—whispering to him constantly, he had come to understand that she was Theron. After all these Ages, she would be his. The Beast recoiled from the shine, clenching Temujin's guts into a knot. Though the entity fed the desire to possess Theron, he rejected any yearning not born of ego.

"I hope your eyes are bright and clear, and your songs are strong and true." Temujin said respectfully, presenting her with the thick sable fur he had been holding.

Borte was startled, having assumed the gift was for her father, and she took the luxurious prize in her hands. It was the loveliest thing she had ever felt or seen, and she wrapped it around herself, expressing her simple gratitude as she held it out to her family so they could feel its softness. It was an extravagant and valuable token, and she was honored.

"You will have many beautiful things when I am a powerful khan," Temujin said matter-of-factly, happy she was pleased by the offering.

"I am grateful," she said, searching his face and meeting his eyes. "I want only to live a simple life and to be of use to others, if it pleases the gods," she added.

Temujin's chemistry exploded as their eyes met, and his entire body boiled under her gaze. Every hair follicle and cell was electrified and tingling. Borte also stirred; she felt the air of something she did not understand swirling around them.

"I have asked great Tengri and Mother Earth for many years to bring me back here," Temujin explained, as he was ushered in to sit. He took his place of honor on the floor, surrounded by warm furs and carefully woven carpets and blankets.

He reluctantly shared the story of his family's downfall, starting where they had left one another, with the assassination of his father, Yesugei Khan. He left out the most gruesome and murderous details of his family's life when they were abandoned on the plains. Instead, he explained he now led a tribe of his own, comprised of his siblings, their families, and others from the old clan who had joined him. He said he had come to honor his promise to Borte and to the gods, if she would still have him. He intentionally mentioned the spirits with a reverent nod to Heaven and Earth and to the ancestral vessel sitting before him, subtly manipulating her to accept him.

His Helghul-consciousness whirred and ticked calculatingly. He wanted her. She would bear him sons who would become great warriors and generals, and together they would rise as intended. The Beast was pleased that Temujin's weak emotions had retreated, and his stony reason had returned.

Upon listening to his tale, and surrounded by her family, Borte confirmed her intention to honor her accord with Temujin. She was profoundly spiritual and had been brought up to respect commitments. In addition, she felt a familiarity and connection well beyond their affiliation. Still, a nagging, unexplained feeling of angst tugged at her heart, and she secretly hoped their affection for each other would grow.

There was no reason to wait. The lush oranges and golds of autumn would soon be replaced by the frigid whites and greys of winter. Though Temujin was nearly a stranger, Borte prepared to leave her family and join his clan.

Within days, the couple had completed the marriage ritual. They would wait to consummate their union until they returned to Temujin's clan and their future home. Temujin's Helghul-consciousness was feeling intense love for Theron—the same possessive love he had known since he was a child in Atitala, but it still irked the Beast within him. Borte heard the bells, smelled the smoke, and saw the glowing fire that sealed their sacred path onward as one. She took her place as Temujin's wife, and the couple set off to join his tribe. Borte was sad to leave her family and hid her tears as they traveled.

After three days of being jostled on horseback and diverted by tales of his grand plans, they arrived in his camp. Temujin's mother, Hoelun, was the first to greet her, and Borte was quiet and composed, as a daughter-in-law should be. She graciously accepted her gifts and well wishes, and Temujin watched proudly as her glow washed over his people. He was certain they all felt the mysterious attraction and euphoria springing from her, and he was aware that his once notoriously beautiful mother was resentful. The Adversary Solenna had always been jealous of Theron, and Helghul's preference for her. Though Hoelun did not know why she instantly hated Borte, she wholeheartedly embraced her loathing. Helghul knew he would have to watch his mother. If permitted, she would make life unbearable for his new wife.

The settlement was larger than Borte had anticipated. There were ten gers in all and a good assortment of sheep, goats, and yaks, which were corralled for the night to protect them from wolves and other predators. Borte remained quiet and unable to shake the sadness she felt upon leaving her family. Despite her melancholy, her beauty was unparalleled, and curious clan members offered gifts of food and congratulations to please their chief and get a glimpse of her.

Temujin's ger anchored the northern tip of the nomad camp. He had welcomed Borte to her new home, and she settled into the eastern-facing quadrant, making it her own.

Borte took her place among the other village women. Her duties included collecting berries, roots, and fuel; curing and drying skins; and preparing the daily meal. She was not challenged by her chores but thanked the great birch spirits for the branches she burned and sent blessings to the animals that gave their lives to feed and clothe them.

The terra-cotta grasses blew in waves as a warmly bundled Borte helped tend the sheep being led out to graze. They had been gated tightly together in their pen of birch branches to preserve their body heat through the cold night, and they sang a myriad of pleased and annoyed bleats as they enjoyed the water she offered them.

Borte scanned the horizon and took in the beauty of the snow-capped mountains, purple and blue around her. There were stories about the great mountains, legends of a magical, mythical place, and the extraordinary people who resided there.

Temujin spoke clearly of his plans to build their family and extend his clan. She knew that he would come to her as a husband that night, and she was both nervous and curious. She had heard whispers of what it meant, old ladies crudely poking and pinching, but she did not know what to expect. She knew that sometimes her father had joined with her mother, and it seemed to make them both happy and sleep well. She knew it was the way babies were implanted if the gods wished it, and she longed for a child of her own to adore. Her mother had briefly warned her that it might hurt and there might be blood, as there was on her Moon cycle, but she had smiled and soothed her when Borte had become concerned.

On their fourth night of marriage, Temujin sealed the door of their ger for the night. He announced that the first snowfall would soon come, and before then, he would leave on a hunt. It was on that night he first took his husband-place beside Borte. She heard him moving and breathing in the dim light, and he silently lay down next to her. He was not rough—he moved carefully and said nothing as he slowly peeled away the layers of her clothing and exposed her naked body. She lay stone-still, unsure how to respond.

She was soft and round and more enticing than he had imagined. He studied the curves of her breasts in the firelight, and her cold, erect nipples fascinated him. His rough, calloused hands explored her, and she sucked in her breath as he moved his hand from one hip bone to the other. Gooseflesh erupted over her body.

At the sound of her gasp, his arousal heightened, and his breath quickened in response. He ran his hand from her hips to between her thighs, and he felt a warm place there—a soft, woolly patch that guided his way.

Borte realized how rigidly she was holding herself, so she tried to relax under his hand, swallowing the lump forming in her throat. Her thighs opened slightly, and he sought the deeper, warmer place within her. Her eyes remained tightly closed. He was not harsh or rushed, but after a few minutes of discovery and temptation, he shed his lower coverings and moved on top of her. She did not see his naked flesh, but she felt it, hard and urgent, pushing against her. She felt confused and slightly nauseated.

Temujin, now atop her, breathed loudly in her ear, flesh to flesh. She let herself be maneuvered as he opened her legs to him. He entered her, more urgently now, and she let out an involuntary cry of pain. She felt a warm trickle as her hymen was ruptured, and she was uncertain what to do and was afraid to move. The pain did not last long, and Temujin quickly became more rigid between her thighs and then, grunting, he arched and rolled away. He was done, and Borte had a new understanding of the business of men and women.

Borte covered herself and rolled over to sleep, crying silently in the darkness, though she was not sure why. She felt embarrassed by the wet stickiness between her legs and, for the first time in her life, felt disconnected from her own body.

Temujin, having heard her weeping, wondered if Theron had intuitively felt the struggle that had thundered inside him. The Beast was lustful and craved control and conquest. There was nothing tender or loving in his burning, licentious nature, but Helghul had counteracted the Beast's desire as best he could. Where the Beast had wanted him to be rough and cruel, he had been gentle and slow. Theron was too important to him. He wanted her cooperation in everything. Just as Chilger had done, Temujin imagined he and Borte would have the family and life he had so wanted to share with Theron in Atitala. Temujin was unable to sleep, and for the remainder of the night, he restlessly resisted the desire to mount her again. In the morning when she stirred to wake, he finally did.

Armored with a thick leather vest, sword, and bow, Temujin prepared to leave on his hunt, assuring Borte he would soon return.

"Take me with you. I can ride, and I am good with a bow," she said. He looked at his wife, her eyes staring into his rugged face. He felt a twinge of pride that she belonged to him, and his manhood stirred in response. He adjusted himself and mounted his horse.

"Stay here with the other women. Perhaps in the spring we will break the tradition and let you come, unless you are fat with child," he said, amused. Temujin departed, joining the hunters already awaiting him on the plain. Borte watched him go and then returned to the ongon altar at the north side of the ger. She humbly asked the spirits to postpone blessing her with a child. There was plenty of time for that. She wrapped herself against the cold and began her daily chores.

Hoelun watched them from the ger she shared with her daughter, having been displaced by the arrival of her son's new bride. She saw how Temujin looked lustily at Borte, and she recognized the sensual blush of a new wife. She had no generous thoughts and whispered no blessings for her daughter-in-law's fertility.

Temujin had been gone two days, and Borte was busy collecting late blueberries to dry for winter. She had followed the other clanswomen on the long walk from the sheltered mountain location of the camp to an abundant field. The temperature and winds were still fair, Borte was happy to be free of the mountain's shadowy protection, and she was enjoying the warm sun of the open plains. The women whispered all around her, and the young children approached her shyly, giggling and retreating as she playfully smiled and waved to them.

Even though Borte and Hoelun were now family, the envious older woman did not welcome her as she should have, and the others hesitated to act. They were afraid to raise the infamous ire of their matriarch. Borte was patient with them and worked stoically, though she felt sad and alone. She found herself looking forward to Temujin's return.

The blueberry field was worth the walk, and the women filled sack after sack with the sweet fruit. They ate while they happily worked, rushing to get back before twilight descended. The horizon was violet blue, and for every inch the sun lowered in the sky, the temperature dropped significantly. The few remaining summer birds feasted on the bountiful fields as they prepared to migrate, far from the cold and hunger of the punishing northern winter. Borte drank in their song and likened their chirps to the laughter and peals of the berry-smudged children around her. Hunched down in front of an abundant bush, expertly plucking and storing without damaging the tender fruit, Borte did not notice the multiple dots on the landscape as they approached.

The other women began to call out and gather together, herding their children, as a horde of more than twenty unknown riders neared. Borte scanned the fields in alarm.

"Merkits," Hoelun announced fearfully as the men made their final approach. The Mongols and the Merkits were not allies, but they were not at war. Borte fell in line behind Hoelun and the others. Though the visitors were unexpected, the women only watched, more curious than afraid. A dozen riders stopped at the edge of the blueberry patch.

"Which of you is the mate of Temujin?" a rider asked roughly, his leather face scowling as he spoke. He was a stern, weathered man of vaguely familiar dress and colors.

The Mongol mothers drew their children in closer to them, and the youngest cried out to run freely. Borte was distressed and did not answer the armed warrior. The heads of the other women immediately turned toward her suspiciously.

"She is," Hoelun said wickedly, stepping aside and gesturing toward her new daughter-in-law.

Borte was stung by the woman's betrayal and indifference. Her black hair whipped against her face as the winds picked up. She adjusted her fur cap snuggly around her cheeks and waited for an explanation.

The village women decided it was wise to put as much distance between themselves and Borte as possible, and they backed away, abandoning her. There was nothing they could do . . . and besides, she was a newcomer, not one of their own. She would not be missed.

Borte didn't have time to shift before the lead Merkit made his move. The center rider grabbed her by the back of her coat. She shouted, her legs dangling uselessly, as he slung her across his horse. The blueberry sack she had carefully filled flew from her grasp, spilling its contents onto the grass. She struggled angrily to right herself, but he used his elbows in the back of her neck and lower spine to push her snug against his mount, which was already at a full gallop. She felt the bruise of his touch through her heavy clothing, but she continued to resist. She'd heard stories like this—kidnappings, war tactics—but she could not believe she was being used so. Her mind raced. She would be given away, a prize to be won, rewarded, or used up.

Hoelun watched as her son's wife was scooped up and carried away. The Adversary listened to her terrified cries of protest without sympathy. She had been stolen from her Merkit husband by Temujin's father in much the same way. She knew the alarm and confusion the girl must be feeling, but she had no empathy. She hid her glee behind a phony veil of concern that she wore back to camp.

It was two weeks before Temujin returned. Hoelun informed him his new bride had been hauled away by the Merkits, no doubt in retribution for her own kidnapping by Yesugei Khan so many years before.

"When? How long has she been gone?" Temujin asked, enraged.

"Two days after you left," Hoelun replied. The son looked at his bitter mother with anger, easily seeing the glee beneath her phony sorrow. He wished the bandits had freed him by taking *her* instead.

"Why did you not send for me immediately?" Temujin shouted.

Hoelun dropped her head but did not respond. Like the old woman, the Beast within the Adversary rejoiced that the Emissary was gone. Helghul pushed past his mother, sending her stumbling to the ground. With a satisfied smile, Hoelun massaged her hip and bruised knee while Temujin rushed to rally his fellow tribesmen. Despite her son's fury, Hoelun was pleased she had prevented anyone from alerting him sooner. The season had now taken a harsh turn; she would enjoy at least one more winter comfortably free of Borte.

That night, Temujin plotted his wife's rescue and vowed to vanquish the abductors.

Chapter 12

Shambhala Calls

Chilger had become desperate when he realized that Borte, the girl from his childhood, the girl he had been unable to forget, was Theron. As a shaman, Chilger had accepted a profound obligation to ensure the spiritual well-being of his tribe. Despite the guilt he felt for leaving them, he set out to find her, telling himself he would return soon and that the old shaman could handle anything that should be needed. Though this was true, it did not disguise the fact that he was shirking his responsibilities to pursue personal desires.

It had been many years since he and Borte had last crossed paths in the market. He only knew her first name, and it was not a particularly unusual one, but he did remember her father. He rode unaccompanied to distant neighbors, often traveling for days without seeing another human. His companion eagle soared above him, hunting for both of them when its human companion was too preoccupied to care about eating.

The nomadic people could be anywhere, and hundreds of miles separated them from one another. He knew that Borte would be near her nineteenth year by now, and the chance of finding her alive, unmarried, and able to join him was unlikely, but he would not quit. She might send him away, but he would persist.

In the evenings, while huddled next to his sacred fire, Chilger sought direction through medicine-altered states and chanting. The visions came and shook him with powerful images. He saw Borte and the red conqueror, but there was someone else—a surreal, majestic figure appeared like fog on the periphery of the visions floating, legs crossed, yogi-style. The plump, colorfully dressed character wore the robes and crown of a king. He reached out, urging Chilger closer.

"Shambhala calls," the magical father whispered, placing his fat bejeweled fingers on the young shaman's cheeks. His touch was soft yet surprisingly solid, despite his ethereal appearance. "Bring her to Shambhala," the magical father said, and his eyes twinkled and disappeared.

Shambhala was a world within worlds, a dimension layered upon the one in which he was living. This spiritual dimension was in a symbiotic relationship with Outer Earth.

As he traveled, Chilger was inundated by visions of war. He concentrated on finding Borte, and the whispers continued:

"Shambhala," the birds seemed to sing.

"Shambhala," the fire crackled, and in its flames, Chilger saw the fabled lotus-shaped city unfold like a map before him. He and Borte were being called, but why?

Chilger's problem at the moment was not finding the city, but rather, finding the woman. It was late fall, and after several months, there was still no sign of Borte. Chilger had waited as long as he could, but the season had changed, and he knew he must return to his clan, unsuccessful. He would have to wait and search for her again when the harsh winter retreated in late spring.

Each sunrise and sunset without her had cut into him, creating a cross grid of suffering. Shrouded in disappointment, the young shaman went back to his tribe. Upon returning, he built a warming fire in his ger before he sought the counsel of his khan. The energies of the Adversary and Emissary had never mixed well, and neither man sought the company of the other unless absolutely necessary.

A large circle of men sat around a bonfire. The flames were blown violently side to side by shifting gusts, but the hardy men were untroubled by the elements. Most evenings they would talk, laugh, smoke, and sometimes wrestle, but on this night they were more serious. There were many men from their tribe who had been sent out and were yet to return for the night. The others would sit vigil until they did.

"I trust your journey brought you the answers you sought, and you are prepared to serve our people above yourself from this day," the chief said to Chilger in a low mumble. His ruddy cheeks were gently battered by the warm fur hat flapping loosely around his face, and Chilger could see the disdain in his eyes. Chilger's Marcus-consciousness reminded him that he was in the Iron Age, where people, Adversary or not, would descend to their lowest depths, and he needed to be wary. They passed a pipe slowly around the circle, the bowl protected from the harsh wind.

"As yet, I have been unsuccessful."

"I have been patient with your selfish impulses, shaman, but the old one chose you to succeed him, and someday soon he will join the ancestors. You cannot ignore your role. My patience has ended. The woman is not likely to be found," said the chief, inwardly pleased that the young man had failed.

It was just as Chilger had feared. The chief, though happy to have him away, would no longer support his search for Borte. He would have to give it up or, come spring, abandon his clan forever, which was the chief's secret hope. It was only the khan's superstition that prevented him from eliminating Chilger.

"I see great change coming for the people of the plains," Chilger began gravely, changing the subject. "Blood will run like floodwater from the mountains to the steppe and as far as the desert. A red devil seeks to rule the clans under one tribe and will kill all who oppose him," the young shaman prophesied.

"The young think everything is bigger and harder than it truly is," an elder tribe member interrupted, eliciting chuckles of appreciation for the sexual innuendo. His eyes creased and sagged as if being pulled down by hooks. "I have lived many years and have learned that even the harshest winter ends eventually," he added.

"Chilger speaks the truth. I have seen only a sliver of what he knows. We must listen to him. The gods give us the gift of his great insight. Would it be wise to ignore it?" the old shaman asked, irritating the chief.

The men around the fire expressed their concern and support for the young spiritualist with grunts and nods.

Finally, the evening's last riders returned, drawing their attention. The chief made his way to them while Chilger watched. His clansmen dismounted, except for one small man who remained seated with his head down.

The young shaman stood, and a lump gripped his belly, twisting. Even before Borte raised her head, in the firelight, Chilger recognized Theron's shine.

"Temujin will never give up. My husband will come for me," Borte said defiantly, her eyes full of fire. She surprised the men with her fearlessness.

"You are so special?" the chief grunted doubtingly. He looked her over carefully, aware of her beauty even in her angry, disheveled state. His emotions churned, and he looked forward to dominating her and putting her in her place.

"She is," Chilger answered, and as he approached, her shine filled him. His robes blew wildly, and his shaman song filled the air as the metal and glass of his costume chimed. "Is Temujin the Mongol with flaming red hair?" he asked, dreading her answer. He took the head of the mare to which she was bound in his hands, and the tired horse nuzzled him tenderly.

"Yes, that is him, and he and the gods will be displeased," she snapped proudly.

She was so close—her skin, her eyes, her hands. Chilger's body floated beneath him, barely feeling the ground at his feet. He watched the tendrils of air as she breathed, and he longed to take in every particle she exhaled. His Marcus-memory whooped and cheered and scattered his energy as widely as he was able.

"Oh ho, and now she speaks for the spirits! You tell a shaman the will of the gods?" the chief chastised, angered by her insolence. "You are in no position to speak. You have been brought here to right a wrong perpetrated by Yesugei Khan before you were born. Hoelun was stolen from us, and the rape of a Merkit wife cannot go unpunished."

"Hoelun?" Borte gulped, thinking of the cold, distant woman she had only just met. "I am here because of Hoelun?"

"You know of her?" the chief asked.

"She is my husband's mother."

"She lives?"

"She became the wife of the khan. She was near me when I was taken." Borte was stunned. Hoelun, who had betrayed her to the kidnappers, was the cause of this predicament? Borte's distress was plain in her face. "You must return me to Temujin before he seeks revenge. I do not wish anyone to suffer because of me."

"Temujin will not be thwarted, He will wage war no matter what we do; it is his role in the world," Chilger said.

"What war? He has no army. He has not the impressive clan of his father before him," the khan replied dismissively.

"But certainly he has allies?" Chilger said.

"He has been cast out, and we have righted a past wrong. There may be no consequence at all once the months have passed and he has had time to consider our justified retaliation. In any case, there is little chance he will try to rescue the girl as winter sets in . . . we have used the season to our advantage," the chief said.

"Have we started an unprovoked war?" asked one elderly clansman who had been silent. "My totems lead me to be more hesitant of such careless disregard for my life and the lives of my kin."

"I am tired of this cold wind for tonight. My prize intrigues me," the khan proclaimed, turning his bulky frame toward Borte with a lustful glint in his eye. She was now the Adversary's property, stolen or not.

Chilger urgently took his arm and whispered, "This is Borte. This is the girl I left in search of!"

The leader was astonished by the revelation, but rather than moving him to charity, it triggered a base possessiveness.

"Her beauty is undeniable, but I am chief, not you. I will discover for myself if she is worth the bother," he said, taking the head of the mare from Chilger and leading Borte toward his ger. Borte watched the men, seething, aware from the chief's words that the two men had entered a discussion as to who would take possession of her.

"Khan!" Chilger said, anger and urgency reverberating through his voice.

The chief turned his head slowly, glaring at Chilger. "You forget your place," he warned.

Chilger knew he had no claim on Borte, though his Marcus-memory shouted their connection. The shaman stepped back submissively, and the chief took her into his home.

Borte allowed herself to be led, not wanting to alert her captor. She did not resist the commands of the Merkit chief as he sent his sleepy family to separate lodgings for the night, but she secretly surveyed the ger for supplies and weapons she could easily appropriate upon escape. His wives looked at her curiously, but without contempt. It was common for women to be taken in this manner. Women were the property of the man who possessed them. Kidnapped, married, or rescued, she was his, and there was an understanding that he had rights to her. It was wrong, and Borte knew in her soul she belonged to no one, but it was the way of things on the steppe, where survival depended on banding together to survive the harsh elements.

After offering the appropriate blessings and thanks to the fire at the center of the ger, the chief led Borte to the north side of his home. It was the place for honored guests—though soon she would take permanent residence in the east side of the circle with the others.

The chief directed her to undress. She moved slowly, filled with loathing, but knew there was no point in refusing. He was stronger than she, with weapons and men within earshot of any command. Her having the courage to leave by starlight with winter approaching would be wholly unexpected, but she had no hope of escape until he was sleeping. She would feign compliance until then.

The older man shed his thick coat. With his fat belly and missing teeth, he was no equal to the youthful, muscular husband Borte had already known, and she gritted her teeth, boiling with resentment and anger.

"I will change the look on your face soon enough," the chief said, chuckling to himself.

Borte was still removing her thick outer-clothing layers when the chief was beckoned by a call to the entrance flap of the ger.

"Üldeekh—leave!" the chief shouted to chase away the intruder.

"I was wrong to make claims above me. I have come to make amends. Drink this and have the girl do the same. It will guarantee you both pleasure for an extended . . . firm night," Chilger called out. The chief considered the offering and untied the straps securing the entrance. Borte peered through the slip in the door and saw Chilger's face in the moonlight. "Stay *up* all night with this one," Chilger promised again, sounding casual but feeling desperate.

The chief, tempted by the idea of fortifying his stamina and increasing the passion of the resistant woman, pushed his hand through the entrance flap, grabbing the bladder from Chilger. The aphrodisiac contained a mixture of plants and mare's milk.

"It is good you recognize your place, shaman," the chief said, sending him away. Without a second thought, he drank three-quarters of the mixture and passed the rest to Borte, who hesitantly emptied the vessel of its sweet remainder.

With his limbs already tingling from the drink, the khan was certain his timber had been fortified. He urged Borte to continue undressing, but she did not comply. She would not resist, but she would not participate willingly. Instead, she would become stone, sending and receiving as little feeling and warmth as possible. His nose sniffed and rubbed against her neck and cheek as his hands clumsily groped her, removing the under layers of her clothing. Borte held herself rigidly, making it more difficult. Once nude, she moved to lie among the furs and cover herself, but he stopped her, enjoying the look of her as she stood glaring defiantly in the firelight. She was a perfectly proportioned woman: strong arms and legs, wide hips, a flat stomach, and full breasts, and her nipples were firm from the cold. The chief was struggling to pull his pants down over his buttocks with one hand, holding her with the other, when he suddenly slumped away from her. He landed at a haphazard angle with a thump and began snoring.

Unimpressive little thing, she thought as his penis shrank against his thigh. She wondered if all men were the same. Temujin's had certainly *felt* larger, though she had not seen it. Unlike small children, men were modest and covered their bodies in the light, so she had no way of knowing.

Borte, her head fuzzy and her hands tingling, had begun frantically throwing useful supplies and tools into a sheepskin bag hanging nearby. She guessed that the chief was several years older than her father. He had small breasts like a fat little woman, and his belly was thick. His bore-like grunts and snorts were repugnant and made her grateful to have avoided intimate contact with him.

She wondered when it would be wisest to steal a horse and bow and sneak away, but it was only a brief contemplation. Soon, just as intended, the shaman's tonic sedated her as well, and she fell into a deep sleep.

Borte and Chilger were nine frigid hours ride away from the Merkit camp when she woke, confused. They would all be waking soon—the chief and the men designated to stand watch. Chilger had offered the guards a cocktail he had said would ward off lingering evil. It was the same sedative he had given the chief and Borte, and the deception had ensured him a hearty head start. In doing so, the young shaman had made a definitive, life-changing choice. Though he was guilt ridden, thinking of his mentor, parents, and friends, his Marcus-memory had been too powerful to resist and had once again complicated his life. He had chosen his soulmate, Borte. He would never be shaman to his tribe again. They would soon realize what he had done and pursue them.

While asleep, Borte had been fully redressed and was now bent across a horse on her stomach, carefully strapped in place, surrounded by thick blankets, furs, and supplies. Chilger led her and a third horse, also laden with gear. Her head pounded painfully—not from the drink but from the blood, so long rushing to her head.

"Where are you taking me?" she demanded, her words slurring slightly as she licked her dry lips. He felt her alarm, and it stung him like salt to a wound. He longed to hold her and comfort her. She was overcome with doubt and apprehension, but her shine was transmuting colors in a spectacular array, like Northern Lights.

"You will endure no hardship or ill treatment so long as you are with me," he assured her.

"Why should I trust you?" she asked, and her tongue felt fat and slow between her lips.

Chilger stopped and dismounted. In the starlight, his face met hers squarely for the first time. Hope and love were plain in his deep-brown eyes. His face was familiar, and she noticed the tension in his jaw.

"I am your friend," he replied earnestly. "I am Chilger . . . surely you remember me?"

Chapter 13

Forbidden Love

Borte *did* remember Chilger. She had affectionate recollections of her friend from the market. They had played more than once, and he had repeatedly presented her with little gifts and treats. As is often the case with children, his generosity had endeared him to her. She was flooded with warmth at the recognition. Chilger watched her effervescent glow and the brilliance of their entangled shines.

Her gut told her the shaman would not harm her, but she was angry to once again be hauled away, like livestock, without consent.

"You must help me get back to *miini nokhor*, my husband," Borte said.

Chilger did not speak, but he knew he would never help her get back to her husband. Telepathically, he was telling her every-thing she did not remember. He knew she was receiving the infor-mation, if only she were conscious of it.

"It doesn't matter that we were friends long ago. Temujin will find me and right this wrong. He will not spare you," Borte con-tinued, determined to reason with her captor. He was a shaman, not a warrior, and she had watched him kowtow to his own chief, humbled when the leader had led her away to his ger.

"I hope you will come to see that all is right as it is."

"How can it be right when I am kidnapped again, stolen from my abductor and riding upside down on a horse?" Borte replied, her anger and indignation clear.

"I hope you will come to see," Chilger repeated.

"Let me ride!" she demanded, struggling and kicking against her bonds from her place among the supplies. "Unleash me, Chilger. No friend would do less!"

"I tied you for your safety while you slept. Of course I will let you ride, but I will lead your reins until I am certain you will not try to escape," Chilger said, unlacing the ties at her wrist and waist and feeling terrible upon seeing the red welts that had formed despite his best efforts to avoid them.

"You say we are friends, but in truth, I am a prisoner," she accused, jerking her chin at him severely and pressing her fingers into her temples and cheeks to soothe the pain of engorgement.

"No," Chilger countered.

"Then I will take my reins and make my own way," she said, easily swinging upright on her horse and holding out her hand, as if he would turn them over.

"You must not leave. Besides, to do so would be suicide," he said, tightening the straps in his hands.

"My life, my problem. Let me go!" she said.

"No," he said, filling with frustration. Borte watched as his mood swiftly changed. Chilger's face flashed with bitterness at being forgotten, and she could tell that he was resolute. He would not allow her to leave, and she did not wish to once again ride tied to a horse. She had no fear of him, and she could feel that his nature was peaceful, but she did not wish to force a confrontation. He was muscular and strong, and despite her skill with a horse and bow, she could not outrun or outmuscle him if he was determined to subdue her. She would also need to take reasonable supplies with her if she escaped, for she could not survive alone on the steppe without them as winter closed in. She would have to be cunning and create an opportunity to escape, if Temujin or the Merkit chief did not find them first.

Chilger wondered how long he should wait to tell Borte they would seek Shambhala. How would he convince her to willingly come along when her bearing was so cold and resistant? She understood nothing of their connection, nothing of the Emissaries, and Chilger desperately wished Theron had memory, as he did.

He had wished many times that she had memory. The night of the exodus from Atitala, Marcus had lifted the memory serum to his lips, sipped, and then discarded the flask, thinking it empty. For the first time, he wondered: *What if I had taken the vial with me when I went to Theron the night of the Exodus from Atitala? Perhaps there were remnants of the syrupy liquid clinging to the sides? She might be in my arms, helping me search for Shambhala rather than scowling at me defiantly.*

Every lifetime he had endured since the Golden Age in Atitala might have been different but for that one choice. What if he had shared the memory elixir with her? Was it a choice if it had not occurred to him then? Now, thousands of years later, he was tortured by his thoughts. A new regret sprouted roots in the shadowed soil of the Dark Age.

In the distance, a fork of lightning lit the sky followed by a ground-shaking clap of thunder. Borte gasped, and the horses startled.

"We must take cover," she said. All the people of the plains feared thunderstorms. Every year there were countless deaths caused by lightning strikes, flash floods, and wind accidents.

"Do not be afraid. Tengri wakes to help us," Chilger said, hoping the storm would slow the Merkits or any others who might already be pursuing them.

"You do not fear the angry gods?"

"I do not fear the unknown."

"What makes you so daring?" Borte asked, uncertain as to whether he was brave or foolish. The distant clouds flashed and thundered again.

"I can judge by its placement in the sky whether this storm will trouble us. Until it does, we will push forward. I have let fear rule me many times, but I have learned it usually prevents better outcomes, so I confront it when I can."

"You do not talk like other men," Borte said.

"I will share with you a story my mentor told me about a great khan. He ruled his people well and was a merciful master. His people respected him. Many times he was forced to defend his lands against invasion, and always he was successful because he was righteous. He would ask enemy prisoners to choose their fate. Would it be the first cave that led to a quick death by sword, or would they choose a second that led to an unknown end? Most men, more afraid of the unknown than of death, chose certain death by sword," Chilger told her.

Borte wanted to know what was in the other cave, but she stubbornly refused to ask him. She was not prepared to befriend him again.

"Freedom," Chilger said after a moment. "The other cave led to freedom."

"You speak to me of freedom?" Borte asked incredulously, infuriated by the irony of his monologue.

"Consider that you might have more choices than you think. There are greater fears you might face than whether to stay under my protection."

"Your *protection*? Do not congratulate yourself that you stole me from your chief. I can easily survive on my own until I am rejoined with Temujin," Borte said.

"You might choose not to go."

"Why would I do that? You are nothing to me. I have a husband," Borte said.

Chilger winced upon hearing it. The facts were crueler than she knew, and they wounded him deeply. Surely, she must feel their shines intermingling as he did? How could she be so dense and cold in the face of their shared connection? They were soulmates, yet she remained distant and icy.

There was another flash of lightning, followed quickly by thunder.

Seek Shambhala! the thunder boomed. Both Emissaries heard it clearly.

Borte looked at Chilger, but he appeared lost in his thoughts. Though he had heard the call, it had not surprised him as it had her. For Borte, it was the first time, and she doubted her senses, but the thunder pounded again and again:

Shambhala! it said. The Emissaries rode in silence, each of them hearing and contemplating Shambhala in isolation, unbeknownst to the other.

Shambhala had been described as a city of light, hidden between the physical and the nonphysical realms. Borte had grown up hearing the legends of the mystical, supernatural kingdom around communal fires. Ascended souls and ancestors were said to gather there, selectively and carefully assisting those on the physical plane.

Chilger was certain Shambhala was real. He vaguely remembered the Willowy Man—the Tunnel-Keeper from his lifetime as Marcus. He had been from Shambhala, had he not? The memories were jagged and fleeting, but he clung to them. In his dreams and visions, he and Borte were called. In the days to come, like Chilger, Borte heard the powerful call: on the winds, in the crackle and flames of the fire, and in her dreams, but she said nothing. Still, Borte planned to escape. Her only uncertainty was whether she would search first for Temujin or first for Shambhala.

The chief of the Merkits and several of his tribesmen had awakened fuzzy-headed from Chilger's concoction, and their rage woke with them. The deceived khan led a retrieval party to track the pair. His lust for Borte remained strong, and the bite of Chilger's betrayal would sting until the shaman was caught and executed for his treachery. The Merkits would take days to catch up if Borte and Chilger kept moving as long and quickly as possible.

"Following them into the mountains will be suicide," one of the senior Merkit riders said, knowing the season's first snow would soon come.

"Where a woman rides, you fear to go?" the chief snapped, his ego inflamed. He would not rest until Borte was returned. He would have revenge. The Adversary and his men rode hard.

><< ><< ><<

Chilger was quiet and respectful and made no attempt to lay with Borte. She thought it was only a matter of time before he would claim what society decreed was rightfully his. She was pleased to be unmolested and wondered if the shaman was celibate. She considered that he might have no sexual interest in her at all, but she was wrong.

Chilger longed to touch Borte, to hold her in his arms and to physically and spiritually reunite Marcus and Theron, but he had no desire to force her. He knew that no custom or situation changed the fundamental truth that he had no rights to her. He knew she was not his to take, though he fervently hoped she would choose him. He would wait, and hope that their connection would grow naturally.

Chilger's eagle stayed inside the shelter with them, making Borte's escape even less likely. Though the raptor was always blindfolded when on the ground, even without sight, the eagle squawked and alerted Chilger when the prisoner stirred in the night. The bird was fiercely protective of the shaman, and in a moment could relieve Borte of a useful finger or eye. She quickly realized that any plans to flee would have to be complex and perhaps ruthless.

Borte would only resort to violence in self-defense, and Chilger's treatment of her had not warranted it. Could she bind him as he slept? What, then? Leave him to die of thirst and hunger in his shelter alone? She would not do it. She *could* not. Borte's situation was more complicated than she had first thought, and over and over she continued to hear the confusing call to Shambhala.

A light snow had fallen during the night, but the next morning it was bright and clear. The mountains rose majestically before them, and the darkness retreated as the sun spread across the expansive blue sky. Chilger had planned that they would leave the steppe and enter the mountain pass that afternoon.

"It does not matter how deep into the *uuls* you take me. Temujin will follow. He will not relent until he finds me, either dead or alive," Borte said from her horse.

"I am sure you are correct," Chilger replied from ahead, where he was carefully leading them up a narrow path. Their horses were remarkably sure-footed as they navigated the jagged rocks. Their warm breath pushed out in white puffs from their flaring nostrils.

"Why risk our lives? You explain nothing," Borte said, leaning forward in her saddle and gripping tightly with her thighs. There was no response forthcoming. It was a delicate situation, and Chilger would wait until she was ready to hear what he had to tell her.

Borte felt the goodness in Chilger, and though he was a vast improvement upon the fat Merkit chief and was more handsome than Temujin, he was not her mate.

Borte watched in awe when Chilger and his eagle hunted. Chilger released the bird from a high ledge, and it swooped while the man hooted and called. Dipping through the fresh snow, the prey was no match for the predator. The bird wrapped its powerful talons around a fox and twisted until the struggle ended and the kill was secured. The eagle returned, dropping the kill at Chilger's feet.

Chilger and Borte made camp late, and a fox was skinned, cleaned, cooked, and shared. Their bellies full, he reached past her for a thick blanket. Borte misunderstood his intentions and became rigid, bracing herself for the sexual invasion she believed was inevitable.

"I feel your fear like the sting of a thousand hornets," Chilger said. "I will never put myself upon you uninvited."

You will never be invited, Borte thought, but Chilger was an enigma to her. He was different, thoughtful and gentle. The shamans in her tribe had never married; perhaps they were of a different sort. She wondered but did not have enough experience to know.

Chilger lowered himself and the fur onto the ground beside her inside their shelter. As he sat down, their elbows met. It was electric, as if he had touched her with fire, and she flinched, inspecting her arm.

"There is so much you do not understand. So much you do not remember," Chilger said.

"Tell me, then," she said, and so he began.

Chilger started slowly, reminding her of their interactions in the market, the chance meetings, the joy and freedom they had felt running together as children, and the bond they had formed. He brought her to a familiar and comfortable place in their time together, reminiscing about specific, minute details and warm childhood memories. Despite her wish to remain aloof, she was softened by the recollections.

"But there is more, so much more . . . our connection is an ancient one," he said. He let the words hang in the air, his Marcus-memory desperately hoping and wishing, as always, for Theron to know him as he knew her.

"Ancient?" she repeated, but the word was far from simple. The notion sent shivers through her, and she stared at the shaman warily.

"Do you know me?" he asked, willing her to see his shine.

"I always remembered our time in the marketplace, but you feel *too* familiar," she admitted.

"Do you feel a tingle here, in the Tengri-god center of your head?" he asked, touching the center of her forehead.

Borte shook her head no, though it was a lie. She did feel it, and it was twice as strong at his touch.

"I am familiar because this is only one of the many lives we have shared," he said.

Though reincarnation was an accepted tenet of their spiritual beliefs, only a rare few ever professed to have recollection. The idea excited and intimidated Borte, and she longed for more information.

Chilger described their lives as Theron and Marcus, and he told her of their coupling within the Universal Grid, where they had become soulmates.

"We came together as one? I was your body and you were mine?" Borte repeated, trying to understand. He told her of their lifetime as mother and son in Stone-at-Center, and as Plato and Aristotle, though he left out the most harrowing details and said nothing of Helghul. Borte's head was spinning with the ramifications of the stories, and the massive scope of the possibilities made her feel alive.

The warmth in the ger had grown, and Borte gulped as her stomach fluttered and lurched strangely. Temujin suddenly seemed like a distant memory. They'd had so little time together that he was more like a stranger to her than a husband, and Chilger was here, filling her with powerful, confusing feelings. She remembered him from her childhood, but he was more. The energy of her shine was completely immersed with Chilger's, and she could no longer pretend she felt nothing.

"I am called to Shambhala, and I am meant to take you with me," Chilger finally divulged. Borte gasped audibly.

"I, too, have heard the call!" she admitted in amazement.

"You have heard it?" Chilger said with relief and happiness.

"Many times. It is sung on the wind and in my dreams," she said, smiling, though she was overwhelmed by what was unfolding.

He longed to hold her and kiss her. It had been so long since Marcus and Theron's energy had been together. It had been so long since she had known him and loved him with her full awareness. They sat in silence for a long time. Chilger would wait. Marcus was used to waiting.

Chapter 14

The Journey

Only days after Borte's disappearance, knowing he was significantly outnumbered by the Merkits, Temujin appealed to his blood brother and childhood friend, the Khan of Jadoran, for assistance. Temujin had looked up to his friend when they were boys, but as his Helghul-consciousness awakened, he recognized that the khan, Jamuka, was part of his soul group, and his admiration had subsided. The Adversary had been called Abaddon in Atitala and had proved himself loyal and useful many times, but Helghul's expanding ego esteemed no one above himself. Temujin and his clansmen rode hard and long to reach Jamuka as quickly as possible.

"Jamuka, I need your help, my brother. The Merkits have taken my wife—we can use this abduction to our advantage. It is a reason to bring war upon them and take them over. Blood brother, I ask for your assistance in retrieving what is rightly mine. There is great benefit in it for both of us," Temujin reasoned, pacing beside the evening fire, his horse tended and settled for the night.

"Your father started this when he kidnapped Hoelun, but I agree, we can use it to our advantage. It is not only us with an interest here . . . your godfather, Toghrul Khan of Kerait, should be brought in . . . you come with too few warriors. He has a vast army of more than twenty thousand men." Jamuka stroked the thin beard that barely covered the birthmark across his left cheek and ear.

"You are right, brother, I will go to him. We will unite our tribes and crush these Merkits," Temujin said.

Jamuka rose from the log on which he was seated, and the blood brothers embraced and smiled widely at each other. Just as it was when they were boys, their clinch became a competition, and soon the Adversaries were laughing and grunting as they wrestled. Heads down, shoulder to shoulder, they pushed back and forth, side to side, struggling to unfoot the other.

The spectators cheered and hooted as the men grappled in the frigid dust. Then, in one quick motion, Temujin was down, flat on his back, his chest heaving, with his friend's body pressed hard against him. For the first time ever, Jamuka had bested him. After a moment of triumph, the khan, pleased and beaming, stepped off and held out a hand, helping up a surly, sour-faced Temujin. It was not until later that night that Jamuka found himself wondering if Temujin had let him win to curry favor. The suspicion significantly soured his feelings of victory.

The first snowstorm of the season forced Chilger and Borte to make camp early. He had chosen a ledge where he could see the valley behind them, and the biting snow took hold quickly, virtually blinding them while they constructed their shelter. The snowstorm immobilized them, obscuring the transition between day and night, and Chilger hoped those who might pursue them were delayed similarly. While they waited to move on, the shaman continued to entertain Borte with stories and details of his lives before. She was awed and overwhelmed. She did not necessarily accept what he was telling her, nor did she reject it. Chilger felt her opening to him, and he was hopeful.

Shambhala! the wind whistled, sneaking through the flaps and tearing at the seams.

Shambhala—Shambhala—Shambhala, the icy pellets reminded as they drummed against the felt. Borte looked at Chilger, smiling, aware of the magic in the moment they were sharing.

"You hear it?" he said, reading her eyes.

"Yes," she admitted.

When the storm passed, the Merkit chief and riders, still refusing to turn back, had crossed the steppe and had reached the sacred lake where the path entering the mountains forked.

"The summit terrain is difficult. They will have traveled the ridge to stay ahead," the Merkit tracker said.

"The shaman will anticipate your thinking. He will take the summit to escape us," the chief correctly guessed, steering his horse toward the highest peak.

From the advantage of his perch, Chilger saw the smoke of the Merkits' extinguished fire. They were gaining ground, and at this pace they would catch up by the next afternoon.

Borte had not distinguished the smoke from the snow clouds in the morning, but now she could see the men speckled on the distant path below them.

"Riders!" she announced.

"It is my tribe," Chilger replied. He had been watching them since they had cleared the last peak.

"What will we do?" Borte asked anxiously. She thought of the fat Merkit chief and cringed. He would kill Chilger for his betrayal and take her for a wife.

"Can you use a bow?" Chilger asked.

"I cannot kill a man, Chilger. A fox or polecat, but not a man," Borte said. But Chilger knew she was wrong. She *had* killed a man. In her lifetime as Inti, Theron had thrown a rock, accidentally killing the tyrant Katari and ending Helghul's vicious reign over Stone-at-Center.

"If things go as planned, you will not have to," Chilger replied.

The Merkits approached, and Chilger and Borte crouched where snow had gathered on the bluff.

"Now!" Chilger whispered urgently. One after another, the couple rained arrows onto the lip below them. Not one arrow hit the Merkits, but every one of them hit their mark. What began as breathy poufs of powdery snow then separated and slipped, becoming an avalanche. The collapse was larger than Chilger had anticipated, and as he and Borte departed, the cloud of fine snow that had been pushed into the sky above the heavy fall had not yet cleared. He hoped his tribesmen would safely return home, abandoning their pursuit.

As intended, the Merkits were not buried by the avalanche, but their way was now impassable. They would have to retreat before finding another point forward, and it would put them days behind.

"To continue is to put one fool in front of the other," the chief said. "If Chilger and the girl survive the winter, spring will reveal them, and I will have my revenge then."

The Merkits, frustrated and disheartened, turned for home.

The following day, though there was no sign of the Merkit khan or Temujin, Chilger held no delusions that they would be left in peace. The sky was a vibrant lapis blue, and the beauty and difficulty of the landscape rendered them speechless. As they traveled, the air thinned, and it became harder to breathe. Borte ignored her pounding headache and pushed forward, called by Shambhala. Their breathing was shallow and rapid as their bodies struggled to find oxygen. They climbed over the windblown ridge and across a series of high plateaus. The landscape was easier to traverse where it was flat, despite the blowing snow.

That evening, once their shelter was constructed and a small meal was shared, Borte prompted Chilger to tell her more stories. She was enthralled, and he watched her response, gauging how much she would accept. He left out the most brutal and upsetting details, not wanting to cause her any unnecessary pain. He was burdened with knowing *all* the gruesome specifics, but she need not be. Still, he did not mention Helghul.

"What happens between the lives . . . after death?" Borte asked. Her eyes glowed with curiosity, though her upbringing had made her fear everything connected to the spirit world. She had long been told that spirits could be vengeful tricksters and were not to be fooled with.

"It is a place where we have all been many times. There is nothing to fear in it. We will meet again in the Meadow, a vast landscape more like the steppe in summer than any other land I have ever known. Like here, the trees, grasses, flowers, and animals speak to the souls around them, and they flow together in harmony. We are all One, and the connection and joy we feel there is indescribable. Never fear death; beyond it is paradise."

"So why come back?"

"To find you," he replied, and Borte was overwhelmed with feelings of love. She could not see their shines intermingling and embracing one another. For her it was baffling, and she resisted, attempting to rationalize it away.

"Your stories attempt to seduce me."

"The truth is recognized. You are swayed because you are remembering our truth," Chilger corrected gently.

Borte entertained the notion that Chilger's Marcus-memories might be the truth, but her feelings for him remained suppressed, and she silently reminded herself that what had passed did not change the present.

While Borte slept, Chilger lay awake, wondering if he had been deluded, duped by his own selfish wish to awaken Theron. Perhaps he was a victim of the *Muu yoryn sÜns*—or as he knew them in Atitala, the Elementals, tricky spirits who liked to play with humankind and watch them flounder. Borte rolled over, and he studied her face in the firelight. Chilger resisted his physical desire for her, but eventually it became too uncomfortable, and he stepped outside to cool off.

Wandering the perimeter of their camp in the frigid starlit night, Chilger stared up at the many clusters of stars splashed across the sky. His Marcus-consciousness admired the beauty of the Universe, and he lit his pipe and longed for the altered state it offered. He had inhaled only two puffs when he heard a deep, unrecognizable vibration close by. The horses whinnied and stamped, and his heart gained pace, filling his limbs and brain with fight.

With his adrenaline racing, Chilger drew his bow and arrow. The sound did not repeat, but in the silent darkness he felt as though he were being watched. Nothing. Hour after hour he waited. He finally returned to the shelter, cold and exhausted.

The next morning, just before sunrise, Borte served a humble breakfast of warm mare's milk while Chilger bundled up to check on the animals and start dismantling the ger. As he exited the shelter, Chilger stopped short. There were long, wide footprints in the snow all throughout their camp. They were not animal tracks that he recognized, but rather, something humanoid. The prints circled their shelter, and the horses were gone! The tracks were easily visible in the snow and led directly to the sheer mountain face, where they abruptly stopped.

"The *almas!*" Borte exclaimed fearfully from behind him, referring to the mythical, yeti-like wild man rumored to inhabit the mountain passes.

"But where did he go? Surely he cannot scale a vertical cliff . . . and with horses!" Chilger said, confounded.

"We must go, Chilger!" Borte urged.

"We cannot carry our shelter, blankets, and supplies. It is a fool's journey on foot, without horses," Chilger said.

"It was always a fool's journey!" Borte cried out.

"We have no choice. If we stay, we die. If we move on, we might make it," Chilger said.

Chilger and Borte bundled only what they could carry and set out. Borte looked back at their shelter. It went against everything she had ever been taught to leave it behind.

They moved slowly; even the few supplies they had clung to were a great load to bear.

"I feel we are being watched," Borte said a few hours into their journey. Chilger had felt it, too, and continually scanned the glowing white peaks and rocky crevasses around them.

It was then that they saw it. On the path ahead of them stood a creature nearly twice their height, covered in reddish-brown fur. The almas's long, hairy arms were relaxed against his body, and he subtly bowed his head. He did not growl or snarl at the sight of them. The fur around his face hid his eyes, but he seemed to be carefully considering them. Borte was terrified. As a child she had heard stories of the almas, and how they terrified travelers who were foolish enough to attempt the mountain passes in winter. She pulled her bow in front of her, lining up an arrow defensively.

Just then, Chilger's companion eagle, which had been soaring overhead, landed next to the almas and playfully pecked at him as though he were a long-lost friend. Chilger reached across Borte and lowered her weapon. The message was clear: this creature posed no threat to them.

The almas motioned with his long, thick arm, beckoning them.

"We must go to him," Chilger said to Borte, nudging her in the creature's direction. Borte paused, not wanting to move in the almas's direction.

"He bids us closer," Chilger said bravely. Borte followed the shaman, her hand on her bow, and they stopped a few yards away.

"Who are you?" Chilger asked.

"Emissaries, your disguise is not as good as mine. My cloak is effective for warmth, but it can be misleading," the almas replied in a slow, whispery voice. Borte was stunned and tried to make out the details of his face within the fur.

The creature reached up his fur-clad hands and peeled back the hood Borte and Chilger had taken to be his head. There stood

Willowy Man. His fair hair and complexion matched the white of the snow. His smile was radiant, and he appeared as he had when Marcus had known him in Atitala. Thousands of years had deepened few lines and creases, and he was virtually the same: ageless.

"Willowy Man!" Chilger exclaimed with relief. "Borte, he is the answer to our prayers, for he is the Tunnel-Keeper!"

Borte studied Willowy Man's strange pale skin and pink eyes, wondering what a Tunnel-Keeper was.

"What a wonderful reunion," Willowy Man said. "Your shine reached me long ago."

"Will *you* be taking us to Shambhala?" Borte asked.

"Shambhala is not a place of this dimension, like Inner and Outer Earth. Only the King of Shambhala can reveal its entrance, for it is not stone or soil based," Willowy Man replied. "But I will take you to its secret threshold."

The Tunnel-Keeper removed his mittens, and with operatic flare felt the frigid stone wall. He read the notches with just the touch of his fingers. With intricate swiping motions and a low mantra under his breath, the rocks began to morph and soften. Borte stared in amazement as the stone opened into a cave.

"Ah, it's cold," Willowy Man said, putting his mittens back on and ushering them into the large opening. The eagle swooped down from above, joining them, while the Tunnel-Keeper waited. The shaman's apron clanged as he shuffled deeper inside.

Though their legs did not move, they sped through a maze of tunnels with lights, sounds, and colors flashing past them. They rode the telluric current, unharmed as the solid rock seemingly melted away. Chilger remembered traveling as a boy in Atitala. Hidden in the atlantium crates, Marcus, Theron, and Helghul had set off together, determined to save their world. They hadn't succeeded; Atitala had crumbled and fallen into the sea, but they *had* visited Inner Earth. It had been so long since Chilger had thought about that: the Inner Earthlings, the Arya, feeding off the Sun at the Earth's core, their technology and inner peace, and the Guardians! He had not forgotten about the monstrous Lion-Dogs that protected the separation between the worlds. Were there any such creatures guarding Shambhala?

Suddenly they stopped and exited through another portal on the other side of the Altai mountains. Their eyes squinted, adjusting to their sun-drenched surroundings. They stood in a spring-like, grassy field, and before them stood a formidable stupa, twice Chilger's height and twenty paces around. Its silk flags waved greetings to them in the wind, and its stones were piled and balanced precariously all around its ancient base. They ran their hands admiringly along its stone exterior, and then, as their traditions had taught them, they began to pray and walked clockwise around the miraculous temple respectfully.

As they completed their third turn, Borte gasped. There before them stood two extraordinary snow leopards with cobalt eyes. The southern wall of the sacred monument had opened, and standing there next to Willowy Man was a fat robed man resplendently reflecting the sunlight in multicolored prisms, as if he were made of crystal. A glorious crown glowed like a halo on his smooth, dark hair, and his multi-ringed fingers rested on the heads of the snow leopards at his side. Particles of light and silver sparkled all around them like tiny swarming lightning bugs.

Chilger and Borte knelt, touching their heads to the floor.

"Please rise, my friends. I welcome those who are called and trust to seek," the King of Shambhala said. The rainbow emanating from him cast far and wide, and birds and animals gathered in a semicircle around them, peacefully observing, perched on the stupa. Chilger looked at the sky and saw that his companion eagle was within view, soaring on warm updrafts and watching him with interest.

Borte huddled next to Chilger. The vibrations of the holy king made her teeth chatter, so she placed her palms flat against her side to steady her tremors. Willowy Man was standing to the right of the cherubic king, watching the humble Emissaries with pleasure.

"Many are called, but so few are listening. Too few trust themselves to venture out beyond their lives to honor a higher calling. Shambhala has much to share with you. Come!"

"We are honored," Borte and Chilger chimed in, unpracticed but in unison. Chilger was filled with joyful anticipation.

"Before we enter, you do understand that there is a cost to everything? With greater awakening comes greater responsibility. Do you choose to enter?" the king asked.

"Yes!" the Emissaries exclaimed, nodding. They had accepted the terms of Shambhala, and the king stepped aside.

Chapter 15

Shambhala Revealed

As the dark opening of the stupa, which really should have led nowhere, was exposed, Borte and Chilger rose from their knees and climbed the high step into the doorway. As they passed near the king, the silver rain that swirled around him encircled them like a cool mist and smelled of sweet lotus flowers. The king placed his hand on their shoulders, and they were overcome with feelings of pure, loving bliss.

They moved into the darkness, expecting to butt against hard stone at any moment. The king and Willowy Man moved in behind them as the archway disappeared. The king continued glowing, and once the portal was sealed, he held up his hand, illuminating a single bright, vibrant crystal he used like a torch.

The king placed the crystal in a small notch cut into the solid stone wall, and Chilger could see that a beautiful looping flower symbol had been carved inside the indentation. Immediately, his Marcus-memory recognized the Flower of Life—the sacred geometry symbol representing the *Unus Mundus*—Oneness.

As the crystal was placed in the wall, a chain reaction occurred. The light from the first crystal traveled like a laser down into a deep chamber and ricocheted magically time after time and from wall to wall, illuminating a world unlike anything on Earth. There was no stone or soil. Shambhala was a world made entirely of light and energy, manifested as ever-moving tunnels of shifting geometric shapes.

"Is it real?" Borte asked, awestruck.

"More *real* than anything you have known," the king replied, using Borte's limited language to assure her.

"Are you Tengri? Have we died?" she asked, though unafraid.

"You have not died. Your flesh and bones accompany you. We are all great Tengri manifested in infinite experiences. This is merely an alternate plane of existence next to your own."

Borte was light on her feet and felt as though air was blowing up beneath her, barely touching anything. Chilger held her hand, and they both succumbed to tears of happiness and relief, embracing each other before they moved on.

As they followed the king, all around them balconies, alcoves, and precipices magically appeared, creating the impression of walls in the tunnels of light. The people of Shambhala were illuminated, emerging like chameleons changing color. Each one of them was as different and varied as the people of the world can be, but they all raised their right hands to their hearts and bowed, smiling, as the honored guests passed by.

"What a beautiful display for the king," Borte whispered to Chilger. But her supposition was rebutted immediately by way of thought from every direction.

It is for you, good Emissaries of Atitala, the citizens answered without words. Their multitude of voices were like a symphony in the minds of the couple, and Borte and Chilger were staggered. He had told her they were Emissaries, but before that moment, it was just a word, a whimsical idea. To witness this reverence and to be so venerated filled Borte and Chilger with a sense of humility and responsibility.

The beautiful music of the spheres that filled them continued, and as they moved on, they, too, placed their right hands on their hearts and nodded gratefully to the thousands who welcomed them. They were overwhelmed by the outpouring of love.

The sensation of a tunnel ended, opening up into vastness. All around them the people of Shambhala emerged. Their soul-songs echoed like the deliberate beats of a shaman's sacred drum, and rainbows of shine interconnected the many as One.

A platform stood in the center, and on each side of it, there were seven white marble stairs. The King of Shambhala stood on the platform, patiently waiting for his astounded guests to join him. Borte made her way up the left-side stairway, and Chilger was directed to the right side.

"These good Emissaries come from Atitala, and though to them time seems long and arduous, we know that one cycle, ten cycles, a thousand cycles on Earth are only a flash in space and time and are but a tiny part of the Great Cycle. The Emissaries are the world's light in this time of the great darkness, and we have called them here to reward their diligence and aid them in their purpose."

Borte did not understand anything he was saying, but the buzz in the room was electrifying. The king directed Chilger and Borte to hold hands. All around them, white-robed people of every race supported them.

The king rested a tender, plump hand on each of their heads, and his touch buzzed like an electric current that was pleasantly ticklish. Immediately, as his hands connected them, a charge surged through every vein, artery, and cell of their bodies. Brilliant, healing white light radiated from their eyes, ears, mouths, and noses.

"*Aum, Aum, Aum,*" the people chanted, and a ball of light began to form over Chilger and Borte.

The citizens of Shambhala sang as the light ball expanded. Chilger and Borte stood face-to-face, their hands tightly clasped and their eyes locked on each other. They felt a jolt, and their spirits lifted; then their bodies moved as if in slow motion. Chilger and Borte shed their human shells, becoming light. Their bodies slowly drifted to the floor like discarded garments buoyed by the wind, assisted by the people of Shambhala until they rested gently on the platform. Their material shells were left behind, unnecessary in this moment.

The ethereal light beings of Marcus and Theron had emerged. Their spirits were emancipated. They were now pure, bright light, feeling no concern, fear, or any sense of loss. Theron's spirit took on the misty appearance of the lanky girl she had been in Atitala. All around her she saw images that told the stories of who she had been. Her vibrant purple aura rained over her like a waterfall as she became aware of how much more she was than just her material body. She marveled at her Theron-self.

Right in front of her, Theron saw Marcus: golden brown, muscular, with waves of shiny black hair. Her joy was compounded, and in that moment, she *knew* him! Her love, her Marcus . . . and she recalled being kept from him by Helghul on the deck of the ship on the night of the Exodus, though she felt no pain at the remembrance. She stared at him, glowing purple and silver, his shape dark and muscular, glistening in the light of eternal energy around them.

Marcus watched Theron discovering herself. He, too, felt the same euphoric recollection and connection she did, and all the memories blossomed, vibrant and alive.

With a single intention, Marcus and Theron kissed, uniting their energies.

Bliss, intensity . . . *intensity!*

Their souls were recharged, and the filmstrip of their memories became available—everything, all at once, accessed at the speed of thought. Marcus and Theron experienced moments caught in time, layers like sheets of music, reaching them in vibrating tones, one upon the other. She remembered saying goodbye to her dear friend Plato, her Marcus. He had been her mother, her child, her lover, her friend, and so much more. There had been so much love, in so many forms. She remembered that he knew her . . . he *always* knew her.

There, in the multitude of memories. Marcus also saw Plato and Aristotle in their final moments. Plato lay on his deathbed whispering to Aristotle, "Socotra . . . Socotra holds the key to the end of the world."

And then, still at the speed of thought, the scene changed, and Marcus observed Theron's memories. He watched as Aristotle, upon being pressed and plied with clever questions, had innocently told Alexander of Macedonia, "Plato's dying words? Yes, I remember, though I have yet to understand his true meaning," Aristotle said as he and the younger man walked together.

"What did he say?" Alexander asked.

"He was quite senseless at the end," Aristotle began. "He said, 'Socotra holds the key to the end of the world.'"

Marcus and Theron watched the memory as Aristotle and Alexander—Theron and Helghul— spoke about Socotra. Without knowing any better, Theron had helped Black Elder, the King of the Adversaries, gain possession of the Emerald Tablet.

Marcus and Theron watched their memories continue to be played out. Immersed in the bliss of Shambhala, the Emissaries were insulated from the emotions that would eventually attach to what they were seeing, but at that moment, there were no negative vibrations of fear, regret, or anger.

The images collapsed as the King of Shambhala called them back to their bodies. How much time had passed? Perhaps it was seconds, days, or years, for time was relative to the perceiver. Once called, they returned, changed but the same. The spirits of Marcus and Theron entered their material bodies through the crown chakra at the top of their skulls, like a thread through the head of a needle. Their spirits traveled down, occupying each subsequent chakra, animating them and becoming upright. Their eyes opened slowly; they swayed as if they had ingested a powerful drug.

Helghul has the Emerald Tablet. This is the reason we have been called to Shambhala, Chilger thought, now understanding. Chilger's love and gratitude were profound, but he could not escape the realization of his terrible failing—Plato's mistake! Telling Aristotle the whereabouts of the Emerald Tablet had had monumental ramifications. Red Elder had told him to tell no one, and now, because of *his* memory, because he had recognized and trusted Theron, who did not know any better, Helghul had the Emerald Tablet!

Chilger and Borte were led down the left staircase. The people of Shambhala queued up to greet and embrace them. They were Lemurian and human . . . flesh-and-bone beings who had overcome the limitations of the suits of armor they inhabited and reached enlightenment.

"How do you bear it? Always having memory?" Borte asked when the receiving line was finished.

"Because sometimes it brings me to you, and when it does, knowing you is worth all the longing that has come before.

"I saw it all. You took a potion in the cave," Borte said.

"I did not want to forget you," he admitted. "I have regretted my decision a thousand times. But then every time we meet again, I am so grateful to really know you that it makes it all worthwhile," he said.

"Temujin is Helghul," Borte said, but she understood much more. She had watched Marcus's memory of the young ones being sacrificed and Helghul opening his veins to the Beast that emerged from the chasm as it split the Earth. She had watched the sinister entity enter her former friend, her current husband, and she had remembered him holding her back on the deck of the ship, keeping her from Marcus on the night of the Exodus from Atitala before drowning himself days later.

"In this Age of Duality, it is my role to counterbalance Temujin's darkness," Borte said.

"We will do it together, but first we must retrieve the Emerald Tablet," Chilger said.

"This knowledge is why you are called," the King of Shambhala confirmed from beside them. He turned to Willowy Man and said something to him telepathically.

"Theron, please come with me," Willowy Man said. Before Chilger could protest being separated, the king put a loving arm around him.

"There is nothing here to harm her. She will join you again later," the king assured him, and she was gone.

"Good king, Helghul must be stopped! He is a ruthless khan, and I am a shaman with no army and no clan to return to. How will I prevent him from the evil he will unleash?" Chilger asked.

"Rest now, Emissary. Take this opportunity to sleep with both eyes shut," the king said.

Suddenly the place where they stood became a private bedchamber with walls and a floor, and without another word, the king dissolved into the wall and vanished. Marcus pressed the wood of the posted bed with his palms, testing to see if it was real. It was, and he dropped, exhausted, onto the silk and pillows. Borte was in good hands, and he was worn out. Within seconds he enjoyed a deep, dreamless sleep.

⨯⨯ ⨯⨯ ⨯⨯

Chilger woke alone in the simple white chamber. On the right side of the room, there was a small fountain flowing from the outer wall and continually filling a beautiful crystal bowl with clear, jasmine-scented water. There were glass doors that opened to a wild garden, where every plant flourished and burst with fruit and blooms. It was alive with the sounds of a million thriving creatures, and each living thing glowed with a shine of its own. There were no fences, gates, or pathways; the entire garden looked as if it had been planted a century before but had never been pruned.

The smell of paradise was intoxicating. Chilger walked to a nearby tree and plucked a golden yellow pear, taking a bite. He enjoyed its juicy, sweet perfection as juice ran down his chin, and he brushed it away. He had never tasted such delicious fruit.

Chilger returned to his bed, feeling at ease for the first time since childhood. He felt that his purpose was renewed, and though Chilger heard his inner Marcus-voice urging him to continually do righteous acts, it was a difficult task in the dark Ages because survival was challenging, and his soul was rooted deep in his lower chakras.

Chilger was sleeping soundly when Borte arrived. He woke as she slipped into the bed beside him. He opened his arms to hold her, and he felt her warm skin against his torso, arms, and hands.

He was suddenly wide awake. *Skin!* Borte was Theron, and she knew herself. At last, she was as filled with love and hunger for him as he had always been for her; and she kissed his shoulders, neck, ears, and lips. Licking and savoring, the kisses were sent from deep within her belly, centered in her heart. They carried passion and urgency, sending waves of erotic excitement through him. She pressed her naked body against him. Centuries of sexuality and passion swirled between them. There was no shame, guilt, or false humility. Borte fully embodied her feminine power and the material perfection that allowed for physical union and sexual adventure. Chilger's hands caressed the curves of her body, and they explored and enjoyed each other. She removed the silky pants he was wearing, and with deliberate focus and loving intention, they united their bodies, as long ago they had united their souls.

Borte looked down at Chilger, rocking forward and back, rolling her hips with their fingers intertwined against the bed. Their eyes were locked on one another, their bodies clenching and building toward climax. He lifted his hips to meet her over and over until the final peak gripped them. Squeezing, pulsating, they rode the wave of intense physical ecstasy together.

As their orgasm subsided, Borte lowered herself onto him, her breasts against his, their hearts beating together. *Bliss. Connection.* Chilger did not want to cry, but pure happiness never fit well inside a human incarnation. Energy had to move and flow. The light and gratitude of a soul that was realized had to pour out, so joyful tears flowed from both of them.

Finally, they lay in each other's arms, spent, and began to speak.

"Where did Willowy Man take you?" Chilger asked.

"For more lessons," Borte answered.

"What do you mean 'more lessons'?" Chilger asked.

"The Tunnel-Keeper is not magic, he is learned, and he taught me the ways of the tunnels as he did in the White Pyramid at the fall of Atitala."

Marcus remembered that Theron had gone off with her mother, White Elder, but so much had been happening that he had never had a chance to ask what they had done.

"Why is he teaching you to use the fire lines? Surely the Tunnel-Keeper does not wish you to take his place," Chilger said, suddenly dreading that it might be so. He did not want Theron in such high service. For her to be so would be a solitary commission.

"He did not say. Though I told him it would have made more sense to teach *you*. You are the one with memory."

"And what did he say to that?"

"He said it *must* be me. That was all—it must be me. This time he just wanted to see if I still remembered what he had taught me in the past," Borte said.

"You will be powerful beyond all Emissaries!"

"Temujin knows who you are. He knows who I am. Helghul has memory and uses it to his full advantage," Borte said, her mind shifting to more pressing matters.

"I know," Chilger said, stroking her hair.

Borte remembered how Temujin had felt so familiar. She had waited for him and had taken him willingly as a husband. She remembered how inexplicably conflicted and troubled she had felt after their lovemaking. He had not been cruel or unkind to her. Was it possible she had sensed the Beast within him?

"His power will grow more easily as the Great Year descends farther into this Iron Age," Chilger said. "Over and over he has been a force of evil in the world. Temujin will be no different from those he has embodied before. Helghul is a warmonger and murderer, and he must be stopped."

"How will we find the Tablet? If he has memory, we cannot manipulate him as he did me," Borte said, ashamed. "I saw no evidence of the Emerald Tablet among Temujin's possessions," she said.

"It will be hidden. There is no telling where it is now. It may be too far away to find in this lifetime."

"Unless we use the tunnels?" Borte proposed.

"It makes sense, but we do not know where to travel. The Tablet could be anywhere."

"I will have to go back. He will never suspect I have memory," Borte began, but Chilger interrupted her.

"Never!"

"He does not know we have come *here*. If I make him trust me, he will take me back. I can search for the Tablet! It is the only way," Borte said with urgency, certain her plan made perfect sense.

"No! It is not an option. There must be another way," Chilger said with determination. "We will stop him together."

The two lovers held each other, contemplating their dilemma. The shaman was resolute that Borte never return to Temujin. He would do anything to stop that from happening.

Eventually, with no solution reached, Borte fell asleep wrapped in Chilger's arms. Time was slow and dense in the linear Outer World. Months on the Mongolian plains equaled only days in Shambhala. The king had warned them there would be a cost.

Chapter 16

Borte's Sacrifice

It took eight months for Temujin and his allies to prepare the armies and to wait for the ideal season to arrive. Temujin offered a valuable sable fur as a gift to his ally, the same fur he had once given to Borte. Toghrul was a smart khan, and he easily understood the strategic and financial benefit of a Merkit defeat, but he wisely insisted they wait until Tsagaan Sar, the celebration that heralded the coming of spring. Only then would travel and warfare be possible. Toghrul had no reason to rush. Temujin had to wait, but Helghul used the time to plot his rise to power.

The weather cooperated, and days before the celebration of Tsagaan Sar, a bedraggled Merkit patrol returned to the camp and informed their chief that a vast multitude of warriors was amassing two days' ride away. The men of the tribe immediately mobilized. Arrows and bows were bundled and readied, and the clan planned to move to a more strategic location in preparation for war. Though Borte was long gone, the Merkits would pay for her abduction.

"What woman is worthy of this?" the women whispered to one another as Chilger's clan readied for the inevitable attack. The nomads packed up their gers, their families, and their livestock and made for more favorable locations. The warriors set out toward the gathering enemy horde. Families tearfully said their goodbyes.

The Merkits positioned themselves strategically, and though the Merkit khan was an Adversary, they were not united. Temujin's warriors and allies attacked. As Chilger and Borte journeyed the timeless world of Shambhala, his countrymen were under siege. The battlefields were bloody and cruel, and the Merkits were being slaughtered. Temujin's force was too strong—there were too many men—and the battle would be over soon. One small group escaped to higher ground, but they were pursued.

The plains, hills, and marshlands budded with the first scents of spring but reeked with the stench of death. The frigid winds had become cool breezes, and the sun shone high and long in the sky while blood soaked the ground. Some of the dead were retrieved and laid hundred by hundred in ordered rows for cremation, while many others were left to become the food of scavengers.

Temujin, in full war armor, prepared to lead the final assault. He had proved that he had no equal as a military strategist, and Jamuka and Toghrul Khan now listened carefully to his innovative plans. Toghrul had helped conquer the majority of the Merkit territory and had returned to his lands jubilant and enriched, leaving the last stronghold to be conquered by his worthy allies.

"My brother, I find myself grateful we do battle on the same side," Jamuka said, lifting his eyes from the map Temujin had laid out before him. "I have no doubt you will rise as a great khan someday . . . perhaps almost as great as me!" he chortled, clapping his blood brother on the back.

Temujin smiled wryly. He knew full well he would surpass Jamuka's power as khan; the Adversary Abaddon could not compete with Helghul. The Beast liked the idea of having such a close ally, a blood bond for life. The Adversaries were the only people Temujin trusted—his blood brother, Jamuka, and his jealous but devoted mother, Hoelun. Abaddon and Solenna had proved their loyalty long ago.

"We will strike when the sun is high in the sky, and ride at them with the glare on our side. They will not see the arrows fly, blinded by the brightness," Temujin declared, and then his voice changed slightly. "Has there been any word of Borte? Is she with any of the women and children we have taken so far?" he asked.

"No word since she was last seen traveling with the shaman."

"We'll catch up with the last of his clan today. They will not be far off. I will have her back by nightfall," Temujin said confidently. He expected to rescue Borte in the valley of the giant beasts. When he had interrogated the first group of Merkit captives, they had confirmed that Borte was with a shaman who wore the feathers of an eagle.

Temujin prepared for combat. He mounted his strong horse, which was heavily armored. He adjusted his battle helmet and shifted the thick nose shield that was obscuring his vision. Together, he and Jamuka rode out to address their troops. They would lead an attack from the east.

Temujin's Helghul-mind assured him of victory ahead. He imagined Borte in his custody soon, and he was excited by the prospect. Against his will, he had been drawn to her more powerfully than to any other person in any other lifetime.

The sun was rising in the sky, and the plains were in motion like an active comb of honeybees. Thousands of hooves gently swished through the budding grass as row upon row of men on horseback and on foot moved through the fields. Straight-faced and prepared to die, they surged forward at the command of their leaders, looking more beast than human in their war skins and masks. The horde stank of coagulated blood, sweat, and murder. The procession stopped and prepared to be addressed by their khan.

"Your day of triumph is here! You have fought hard and well. Today we will crush our enemy, and tomorrow we will journey home victorious!" Jamuka shouted. He looked to Temujin, who took his cue to speak.

"You have honored your gods, your chief, and your people. At the end of this day, you will share in the celebration *and* the riches we reap!" Temujin promised, and his words were met with a great cheer. Helghul had learned from his past mistakes, in his lifetime as Katari, that his greed alienated his warriors, so he knew that maintaining their prosperity would keep them grateful and loyal. Jamuka looked at him sharply, but he continued undaunted. "Every soldier will return richer. Every man will be rewarded for his loyal service and sacrifice. Now join, and we will crush our enemy! We will share this victory! Share in the glory!" he roared, as the air shook with thunderous shouts, and his warriors elevated their bows and swords high over their heads in jubilation.

In response, Jamuka raised his arm and signaled for the first assault to begin. The soldiers' horses bolted and crossed the half-mile distance to the waiting enemy lines.

"Big promises," Jamuka cautioned, steering his horse past Temujin, and Abaddon's gloomy shine grew darker.

"Mine to honor," Temujin replied, unperturbed.

"That they are," Jamuka snapped, whipping his mount and galloping away. With a slash of his arm, the Mongol horde surged forward.

The skilled warriors fired their arrows into the sun's path, blinding the last of the Merkits while Temujin's warriors stormed through their barricade. With a Mongol saber in each hand, Temujin was slashing left and right, holding his seat with solid, determined thighs. His leg and arm muscles rippled as his blades tore through flesh and bone. The noise and clatter were deafening. Horses whinnied, and warriors attacked—grunting, crying out, and falling to the ground.

Temujin's face was covered in the thick, sticky blood spray, making it difficult to see. Blood soaked his vest and gloves. His arms ached from brandishing the swords and from the weight of the resisting corpses as they crumpled. His throat was raw and burning from his sustained shouting. His eyes gleamed in anticipation of his victory. The Beast within him was fed by the carnage.

The troops pushed forward, scattering their foe, gory and broken, across the landscape. The battle was won, and the males of the Merkit clan were virtually annihilated.

As was the custom, the women, female children, and property were collected as the spoils of war, and the leaders claimed them. Temujin honored his promise, and his filthy, haggard troops celebrated their increased wealth and the generosity of their leader, Temujin. Jamuka watched his blood brother with wary interest but gave up none of his own spoils to compete for popularity. The troops tended their injured and set up camp upwind to the grotesque battlefield, allowing the horses to graze among the dead. They made offerings of thanks to the gods of the Earth and Sky for their victory. Tengri was honored with dance and wine; and the exhausted warriors, husbands, and herders enjoyed the celebration. The gods, as always, had been called upon by both sides.

Borte had not been among the women and children captured. The sun had set behind the mountains, casting deep reds and oranges across the sky. Temujin spent the twilight questioning and torturing the Merkits for information on the whereabouts of Borte. He was told that the shaman had kidnapped her months ago. A Merkit woman who hoped to ingratiate herself with her captors had spotted the shaman's ger in the Forbidden Valley when the horde marched them back over the mountain.

Had the shaman been hiding in the Forbidden Valley all along? Temujin wondered.

Temujin prepared to set off in search of his wife. He tied a thick fur bag to his mount.

"Jamuka, I am riding into the valley to retrieve Borte. The shaman is there. This was his clan, his people, who died on the battlefield, yet this coward hides and keeps what is rightly mine."

"I will ride with you, brother, if you wish. Or better yet, rest till morning. Let us send a search party, and they can bring her back to you here if she is found," Jamuka offered without moving from the comfortable spot where he sat cleaning himself over a carved wooden bowl.

"She is there. I will go," Temujin assured him, and wordlessly signaled to a small group of his clansmen nearby to join him. They obeyed and followed their chief.

Beyond the camp, the mountains rose, and the valley narrowed. It was as Temujin knew it would be. The giant, ancient skulls of monsters, long dead, were posted to ward off enemies—dinosaur remains pitched high to frighten away the superstitious and skittish. Temujin was neither. He knew the animals that had left the bones were long extinct. He had no fear of the Forbidden Valley.

Helghul had thrilled at the brutality and harshness of the battle, and the Beast fed greedily off the violent energy. He was further exhilarated by the search ahead. He shifted the weighty fur bag awkwardly on his saddle and continued to ride. The warriors at his flank dared to pause, unnerved by a menacing Tarbosaurus skull and massive bones arranged on the hillside to scare off intruders. It was even more frightening set against the night sky.

Temujin's clansmen were exhausted after riding all night, following the battle. The morning sun rose, and along their path, a second large Tarbosaurus fossil was propped on a rock the height of two men and shrouded in a patchwork of second-rate animal skins. Temujin's cohorts were visibly troubled; they called under their breath to the great gods and to their personal totems to protect them. Their leader said nothing. He offered them no reassurance or kindness but simply rode on, and they had no choice but to follow.

By midmorning, a single ger and three horses came into view. A large golden eagle circled clockwise above the dwelling, and Temujin felt a jolt of excitement at the realization of his goal. Helghul thrilled with the anticipation of being reunited with Theron.

※◇ ※◇ ※◇

Borte awakened, confused. Though she was safe, comfortable, and warm, she did not know where she was. She woke in a ger somewhere on the vast plains, remembering she had been kidnapped from her husband and then from the Merkit khan by Chilger. They had traveled . . . but how far? Her mind was muddled as she rose to look outside. It seemed like such a short time to her, and it made no sense that winter had turned to spring.

All of it was gone! She had no memory of reaching Shambhala, or searching for it. Shambhala had welcomed them and had now spit them out on the steppe at the very beginning of their journey. They were waking at the location where they had first entered the mountains. Time, layered upon itself, had been altered by their visit to the higher realm.

The brief time in Shambhala had equaled nearly nine months on the plains of Outer Earth. Borte's stomach protruded sharply where it had once been flat and smooth, and she rubbed her hands on her pregnant belly, unperturbed, as though it had been there all along. Almost full term, the fetus kicked and pressed into her ribs.

"Shaman!" she whispered, shaking him. "Wake up!" Chilger opened his eyes dreamily, finding himself inside his ger, and he immediately realized that Shambhala was gone. They were once again in their travel clothes rather than the flimsy, silken garments of the tropical Nirvana. Borte had pulled back the ties on the shelter. They were on the edge of the mountains, and for hundreds of miles there was nothing but grassy steppe. Chilger was overwhelmed with despair, but he knew what they had to do.

"It is gone," he said sadly, looking at Borte. He had not wanted to return—not yet, and truthfully, not ever.

"What is gone?" Borte asked, trying to calm his obvious anguish, assuming he'd had a terrible dream.

"Shambhala—it is gone. We are back."

"Shambhala?" she repeated in confusion. "You must have dreamed, or perhaps the pipe smoke?"

"It was not a hallucination! We reached Shambhala, Borte! The call was answered, and you remembered . . . us!" Chilger said.

"You are scaring me," she said nervously. His erratic, emotional behavior was terrifying. His eyes flashed desperately—angrily—and nothing he said made any sense. He could see the fear in her face, and he grabbed her shoulders, looking at her square-on.

"You have to remember! The Willowy Man? The King of Shambhala?" he said, staring wild-eyed. Borte did not remember. The veil between realities had been restored, and now Chilger was no more or less to her than he had been the day he kidnapped her.

"Maybe it was your shaman pipe? I have heard it can carry a man to another world," Borte said. Chilger shook her, as if he could restore Theron's memory by force. "Chilger, the baby!" she said, and as if his fingers had been scalded, he let go. He stared at her belly. A child! She was pregnant with his child!

"Your pregnancy! How do you explain it?" Chilger asked. Borte was clearly frightened, and she pulled away from his grip.

"I was pregnant yesterday, and I will be so for at least a few more tomorrows. It is not too late. Return me before the baby comes."

"Return you?"

"Temujin may be forgiving. We will tell him you rescued me from your chief with the intention of returning me to him . . . that we were friends from childhood. He cannot fault you for that. He might even reward you!"

It was torture!

She does not remember! It was all for nothing—the journey to Shambhala, the reconnection, the remembering. The Emerald Tablet! Socotra! Chilger remembered with a nauseating lump churning his gut.

Plato told Aristotle, and Aristotle told Alexander. In Shambhala, the loss of the Emerald Tablet had been received as information; in the Outer Earth, on the material plane, the weight of the loss and the task ahead of him hit with Dark Age force. It was an enormous burden, and his guilt was heavy. It was his fault! He had failed Red Elder! He had gone against his instructions to tell no one, and the Tablet had fallen into the hands of the Adversaries. Perhaps Alexander would not have become a great conqueror had he been without it? Had he accessed Indra's Web to his advantage? What would Temujin accomplish with the Tablet in his possession? Chilger slumped to the ground.

I must think! I must convince Borte once again who we truly are!

At that moment, a horse whinnied. Chilger heard movement outside the ger, and he rushed to the door and tossed the flap open. His horses were there. The same horses that had disappeared in the snowy mountains. They were grazing as if Shambhala had truly never happened.

Had it happened?

Chilger exited, and behind him he heard the pounding of hooves as three riders rode full gallop toward them. Temujin's clansmen held their bows and arrows taut. Chilger turned to reenter his ger just as an arrow grazed his cheek, stopping him in his tracks. Temujin's wild crimson hair streamed behind him in its many plaits as his fat pony slowed to a trot, carrying the red menace closer.

Marcus! Temujin's Helghul-memory realized as the Emissary's shine billowed and swirled. He had suspected as much. Temujin was thrilled to see Borte peeking out from behind him. His heart pounded at the sight of her.

"Temujin!" she cried, attempting to push past Chilger and run to him. Chilger held her, preventing her from going any farther.

"Get inside!" Chilger commanded. Borte ignored Chilger, but she could not loosen his grip on her arm.

"Please, husband, do not hurt him. He rescued me," she began, and Chilger cringed at hearing her call Helghul husband. Temujin, however, reveled in her words but was stunned by her pregnancy. How long had she been gone, exactly? Nine months . . . slightly more?

"Oh, Temujin, spare him!" she begged. Her hand was slung low under her bulbous middle, while she bent and twisted, trying to escape Chilger's grasp. "He intended to return me to our clan," Borte lied. Though she no longer remembered her bond to Chilger, she did remember her childhood friend and did not want to see him harmed.

The tightly bound fur sack on Temujin's horse moved slightly as he dismounted. He had drawn his sword and held it loosely in his left hand.

"Let her go, and I will care for *my* wife and child as though they have never been gone. Borte, you must promise never to search for this man. If you agree, I will let the shaman live," Temujin proposed, stone-faced.

"No!" Chilger shouted.

"Let me go! He will spare you!" Borte said, pulling against Chilger's grip, but he did not release her. He pulled her back while Temujin watched their dance gleefully. The clansmen continued to focus their arrows on Chilger.

"You do not understand! He lies!" Chilger shouted.

"Chilger, let me go! He will save you," she demanded, twisting violently in his arms to free herself. Temujin did not intervene, but Chilger was finally forced to release her arms or risk inflicting injury upon her.

Chilger wasted no time and charged past Borte toward Temujin. He had pulled the knife from his waistband, and with the feeble weapon in his hand, he attacked. Borte screamed as an arrow entered Chilger's right shoulder, causing him to drop the knife and fall to the ground.

The Beast within Temujin fed on the despair and rage surrounding the fallen Emissary. Temujin's nostrils flared as he breathed in the scent of it.

"Stop! Do not hurt him!" Borte shouted.

"He will be calmer when you are gone, Borte. I will spare him once you have safely departed," Temujin lied.

On her husband's command, Borte wrapped herself in warm layers, and with the help of the clansmen, she heaved her heavy pregnant body onto her horse.

"Take her to the valley's entrance, and wait for me there," Temujin commanded over Chilger's cries of protest.

"Do not go, Borte!" Chilger shouted, but Borte obeyed her husband.

"He is confused in his mind, Temujin. Promise me you will free him when I am gone?" Borte confirmed.

"I will," Temujin assured her. He could tell that Borte still had no memory. Though she exhibited pity for Chilger, she had not been swayed by the Emissary.

Chilger struggled to stand, reeling from the pain caused by the arrow sticking straight out of his shoulder, having penetrated through the front and piercing his back. He was desperate to stop her, but Borte rode away, blind to the truth, and the morning sun swallowed her up.

"Have you enjoyed *my* wife, Marcus?" Temujin sneered, dismounting.

"We both know she is *my* true wife. Your crippled soul does not belong near her," Chilger said, enraged.

"You will be only one of the many Merkit I will have killed, but you will be the one I most enjoy," Temujin said.

"She will never love you," Chilger snarled, holding his hand against his wound and wincing.

"She chose to leave you, Marcus. Remember that as you die," Temujin said, stalking toward him and brutally tearing the arrow from Chilger's shoulder. The shaman involuntarily screamed in agony as his legs buckled. Clutching the gaping wound, he fell hard onto the ground. Chilger's death would not be quick, or humane.

Temujin tied up the wounded man, who was weak from loss of blood, and sank stakes in the ground nearby. He then tied the struggling but outmatched Chilger to them, one arm and leg at a time until he was fully outstretched, his wounded shoulder searing with pain. Chilger had resisted, but Temujin was bigger, stronger, and more powerful.

Is it a symptom of the Dark Age? Chilger wondered. *Can darkness be defeated in this era?*

Chilger was bleeding heavily, and he was dying. He knew he would soon fade away. Once the Emissary was securely tied, Temujin retrieved the fur sack from his horse. He would show no mercy to Marcus.

"The child will be the image of me as a man. They will be mine . . . body and mind . . . and I will bend them and shape them both to my will," Temujin mocked, his eyes glowing in evil pleasure. He kicked the helpless prisoner in the ribs, and Chilger grunted.

"And you . . . you will be dust . . . nothing! She might remember you for a while, but eventually she will forget. Her tiny slip of time with you will be nothing compared to a lifetime with me," he taunted.

Marcus realized with certainty that he would not see Borte again. He would not find the Emerald Tablet in this lifetime. It was a monumental task that would saddle him in lives to come. As blood continued to leak from his wound, he saw his companion eagle circling counterclockwise, swooping and diving above them.

Temujin opened the fur sack he had safeguarded for weeks and tipped its lumpy, jumbled contents onto Chilger's chest. The prisoner immediately howled in response, his composure shattered by the electric sting of the hideous Mongolian death worm. The worm was a fabled creature rarely seen, but which all the nomads knew existed. It resembled a pile of red, lumpy internal organs and was as long and thick as Chilger's leg. It continued to sting him, regurgitating its ferocious burning acid onto him, liquefying his flesh on contact so it could be easily ingested. The smell of sizzling flesh was unmistakable. The victim writhed in excruciating pain.

Temujin stood nearby, his beastly soul rejoicing in the misery. Chilger's eagle swooped down to attack the worm, but as the bird tried to pluck off the creature, Temujin loaded his bow, and the arrow whistled as it tore into the bird. The eagle dropped near Chilger with a thud, and he looked in to its dead eyes. The murder of his eagle momentarily hurt more than his melting flesh.

The worm continued to torture the nearly unconscious Chilger, moving on to its next sinister phase. Chilger would be eaten.

So this is how I die this time, he thought briefly, through the pain. He welcomed death but found no peace in his final moments.

Borte was waiting anxiously for Temujin at the foot of the Forbidden Valley, frightened by the monster fossils that stared at them from the hillside. Finally, Temujin approached.

"Did you let him go?" she asked.

"He will live on," Temujin grunted roughly.

Borte was relieved and leaned back in her saddle as they returned to camp.

Temujin had many questions, and Borte shared her confusion about the winter-that-never-was, and Chilger's ravings about Shambhala. She still believed she had only been with Chilger a short time, but Temujin assured her it had been many moons.

"Did he say anything else? Do you remember anything else?"

"He asked if I remembered the King of Shambhala and a . . . willow man? But it must have been something in his shaman drink. It makes no sense."

Temujin spent hours, days, and years trying to trigger a recall of where Chilger had taken her and how they had gotten there, but Borte had no answers.

Borte's child, Jochi, was born four days after her return with the help of the clanswomen. Hoelun attended her delivery and glared at her through the entire painful ordeal, enjoying her suffering.

As was the tradition, Borte was sequestered with her son after the birth because, as a recent portal for new souls, she was believed to be slightly dangerous.

Jochi grew and thrived and had the dark hair of his mother, or perhaps of Chilger.

Months passed, and as summer ended, fall was proving to be bitterly cold. Borte worked tirelessly to prepare their ger for winter. The torn felt needed repair in spots, and she mended it using an ingenious bone needle and fine leather strips. She crouched in front of the sacred fire at mealtime while her young baby suckled hungrily at her breast. Temujin had been gone a few days, hunting, and she had not bothered to eat since he had left. She was surprised by how little appetite she had. Since returning to Temujin's tribe, Borte had felt forlorn but did not know why.

Theron's memories had been left behind in Shambhala, and Borte could not recall much of her time away. She was told that she had been gone more than nine new moons, though she could not recall more than a week of it. Had Chilger drugged her like he had done the night he had stolen her from his chief? Had her pregnancy played with her mind and emptied her head? She had definitely been changed by the ordeal, and now she found it difficult to find her happiness. She thought of the shaman often, confused by the feelings of loss that welled up in her.

What if I never eat again? she wondered. *What if I let this dry, dusty seed stuck in my throat grow into a bulb and then take root? What if I welcome this despair and let it envelop me? Finish me from the inside out?*

You are stronger than that, she heard in her head. *Your son needs you. Your people need you.*

She put down her sleeping child and pressed her forehead flat to the ground. Crouched with her knees pulled in underneath her as tightly as her bulky wardrobe allowed, she prayed. She understood that to exist was to be a part of the gods, but she could not find it in her. She had fallen so far into her desolation in the past few months that she worried she could not pull herself out and fulfill the role ahead of her. She must begin to speak out, to heal, to teach, but she was tired, and it seemed so hard.

She took a bite of bread and a sip of thick mare's milk. Perhaps there was a greater purpose. Perhaps she had something to offer the world . . . but not today. On this day, she would immerse herself in her chores and survive as her people had done for centuries. Today she would be nonphilosophical and unthinking. Theron did not realize that the Iron Age was diminishing her light. She would not consider what might have been if she had married her childhood friend Chilger rather than Temujin. She would think of the work yet to be finished—the child to be cared for, the fuel to be collected, the animals to be tended, the furs to be cured, the grains to be packed and dried. She would leave no room for the haunting, nonsensical thoughts about the shaman.

Was he somewhere in the world thinking of her? Someday she would become a great teacher and healer and empress; today she would simply take a bite of food and choke it down.

Chapter 17

The Rise of Genghis Khan

Temujin continued to show great skill and ingenuity and was soon khan to a rapidly expanding tribe. His relationship with his blood brother, Jamuka, became strained since the ego and drive of his fellow Adversary Abaddon did not allow him to submit to Temujin's demands for power. There was only one king. Eventually Temujin went to war with the Adversary and killed his former ally. Temujin assumed Jamuka's leadership and his property, significantly expanding his wealth and power, perfectly satisfied by how the relationship had unfolded.

Despite his absolute assertions that Jochi was his son, doubt and gossip would batter the boy throughout his life.

Before Jochi's second birthday, his first brother was born. Borte was a good wife and a fertile mother, though she continued to wonder about Chilger. She imagined him happily living as a shaman and healer somewhere on the plains. She never forgot him, and she was surprised by how often he came to mind. She attributed her affection to their childhood bond, and to her gratitude to Chilger for risking his life to rescue her from his own tribe. She searched for him in passing caravans, at markets, and in the faces of riders who passed, but she never saw him again. Though she loved all her children, Jochi held a special place in her heart.

Temujin spent the first ten years of their life together, obsessed with the idea of finding Shambhala. Though he searched, he was never able to unlock its secrets. He was never called to enter, and the city remained hidden, somewhere on another level or dimension and out of his grasp.

By Jochi's fifteenth year, there was little in the world that remained out of Temujin's reach. Temujin had become a feared and celebrated leader and was given the honored title of "Genghis." Genghis Khan continued to battle ruthlessly for decades to come, and Helghul and the Beast conquered and decimated a huge territory stretching from China to Persia to Turkey, amassing one of the largest empires ever created.

The Emerald Tablet remained securely hidden underground in a desolate basin along the silk route where Helghul had placed it in his life as Alexander. Genghis had traveled there to reassure himself, but he had left it safely buried in the remote location. He would bide his time until consciousness had descended to a level that it could be used. He would have to better understand its power and prepare the technology to use it.

Borte was honored as the Empress of the Mongolian Empire and was the most respected and valued of Genghis Khan's many wives. Temujin used every means possible to unlock Borte's memories of her time with Chilger, but nothing worked.

Helghul wreaked havoc in the world of man, as was his role, and he basked in his ever-growing power and glory, sowing his seed literally and figuratively across the continent and personally fathering tens of thousands of children.

As Jochi aged, his striking resemblance to Chilger was obvious, and resentment grew. Genghis and his other sons never accepted the boy, though he remained his mother's favorite. His likeness to Chilger offended the khan, though the Adversary knew Marcus's soul was elsewhere.

Jochi was poisoned and died in his forty-first year. According to tradition, he was buried in an unmarked grave on the plains under the stars. Borte never suspected that Temujin had murdered him, just as he had murdered the boy's look-alike father decades earlier.

Chapter 18

Eden's Purpose

Present day, Seattle, Washington

Excruciating! Is it more painful not knowing where, when, or how Theron will appear, or knowing exactly where she is and being unable to see her? Quinn wondered. He contemplated the question as he smoked a joint. He knew he shouldn't. It was an escape, a break from reality, and now that he'd found Eden, he felt guiltier than ever in doing so. He had just showered after arriving home from a disgusting night in jail. He'd learned that Eden was now halfway around the world. Despite his better judgment, he toked and brooded.

Nate had accompanied Eden to Athens. He remained committed to the project and was infatuated with Eden even though he was skeptical about all the New Age spiritual stuff. He had been blown away by her award-winning film about soldiers suffering from PTSD, and he was determined to work with her. When his agent mentioned the opportunity, he had jumped at the chance. Eden had impressed him more in person, and she had been easy to fall in love with. He was thrilled when she was able to convince Oswald Zahn to fund the project. It was a good move for Nate . . . and his career.

"Seducer-Producer" Oswald Zahn was a billionaire inventor-philanthropist who had recently turned movie producer. He had a massive platform and a spotless reputation, and his charity crossed all religious and national boundaries. His nickname had been affectionately bestowed on him when he'd first entered the movie industry, since no actor, producer, or director seemed capable of resisting his charm.

Quinn was stuck indefinitely in Seattle, and Nate was embarking on months of uninterrupted travel with Eden. As they ventured around the globe with her son, interviewing the Crystal Children, Nate would have time to win her over. Quinn and Eden had had little more than one afternoon together, and now she was across the globe. The muscles in Quinn's jaw tensed and contracted as he tried to swallow the resentment welling up in him.

As the first few weeks passed, Quinn worked hard, committed to helping the Crystal Project succeed. He and Eden video-chatted a few times a week. Paris, Lyon, Rome, and Geneva had been successful, and she was excited about their progress. She chattered on Quinn's screen, announcing she had amazing footage she couldn't wait to share with him. They both eagerly looked forward to their blog and video-conferencing time together.

"My court appearance is next week. The guy recovered. My lawyer's sure the charges will be dropped based on the witness accounts. I'm flying out to meet you as soon as I get the all clear."

"That's wonderful! Wait till you get here. Oh my God, these kids are amazing. We've only found one poor little victim so far . . . argh . . . hideous parents! This poor little thing was barely five, and her parents were parading her around like a . . . a circus animal! They were so obviously faking stories and then drilling her for memorized information. She was a sweet kid, but not . . . gifted. In the end, I just told them they wouldn't be getting famous or rich by exploiting her with *our* help."

"You're being careful?"

"Absolutely. Totally running under the radar. No public shoots. Honestly, no one suspects what we're doing. The website looks fantastic, by the way! Thank you."

"The first trailer is seeing a lot of traffic; send another when you have time."

"Are we ever really gonna get this done? I seriously feel like I'm running out of time," she said.

"Patience. It'll happen. If you're working toward it and envisioning where you want to go, you'll get there."

"*We'll* get there," she corrected. "We're a team, aren't we?"

"Teammates. Yeah, I guess we are," Quinn said. They had been so much—so many combinations and complications—and he wanted to be more in her life.

"Where are you headed next?" Quinn asked, aware that she was talking to him from the Sydney airport lounge.

"Christchurch, New Zealand, got added to our schedule unexpectedly. This keeps happening—everyone knows someone else amazing. It's quite a connected little grid. We find five kids when we expect to meet only one."

Quinn smiled at Eden's use of the word *grid*.

"Hey, I gotta go. I have so many notes to finish up, and we fly out in an hour. Elijah's itching to get on here. Let's talk soon," she said.

"Have fun in New Zealand. Be safe," Quinn added as her image blinked, froze, and disappeared from his monitor.

When Quinn woke late the next morning, he jumped in the shower. He was interrupted midsuds by a slow rumble and sway. At first, he was disoriented, but his Marcus-memory quickly recognized the sensation and alerted him.

Earthquake! In Seattle? Shit! he thought as the motion intensified. Bottles and shelves began to crash around him. There was no time to think; adrenaline flowed through his body, and his survival instincts kicked in.

A terrifying roar reverberated through the air, and as the earth violently bucked, it reawakened a host of ancient memories in him. Flashbacks and confusion overtook Quinn as he stumbled out of the shower and steadied himself under the doorway, while the ground continued to shake violently. He felt as though he were a young child, lifted and shaken by strong adult arms.

Naked and cold, Quinn was growing more alarmed; the quaking was extreme and was lasting too long.

The "big one" had been long anticipated for the Pacific Northwest, and now here it was. Quinn's was an old building and low, not a skyscraper. Downtown buildings would be swaying, and the old ones would be crumbling, dropping tons of glass and brick on the sidewalks below.

Finally, the shaking subsided. His cologne lay shattered, stinking, on the floor. Quinn sidestepped the broken glass at his feet, haunted by memories of streets with bombed-out windows and dead bodies. He was sweaty and trembling and took deep breaths, using the skills the Emissaries had learned in Atitala to keep his PTSD in check. He pulled on his jeans, stunned by the destruction in his apartment. The large gilt mirror that had once hung above his bed had been ripped away from its anchors, shattering against his headboard and landing where he had lain sleeping only hours before.

Books were in heaps on the floor, emptied from shelves and tables, joining the many that had been piled there before the quake. The kitchen was a mess. Most of the cupboards had fallen open and had spilled their contents onto the floor.

Quinn flicked the lights. No power. He thought of his battery-powered radio . . . somewhere. As he began to search for it, the ground once again began to shake. He heard an ominous ripping sound as an opening to the outdoors was cleaved into the plaster of the apartment's southern wall. The building was collapsing. Quinn knew he had to get the hell out. There was no time. He found shoes near the door and moved stealthily into the outside corridor, shirtless and stumbling under the power of a second tremor.

The earth continued shaking, more violently than the first time, and Quinn rushed to the aid of his neighbor, who was also trying to escape. The young mother had two crying babies in tow, and they were being thrown mercilessly about as she struggled to keep her footing. Her knees were bloody and scraped, and a third child, about six years old, was fighting to stay in the crumbling apartment, too terrified to leave. He was planted firmly on his bottom, his cheek pressed to the doorjamb, his eyes squeezed shut. The desperate woman's arms were loaded with the two wailing siblings, and the boy was immovable as she begged him to release his hold. Quinn swooped in and picked up the older child, easily loosening his grip.

"I gotcha, buddy, I gotcha. Hang on to me," Quinn said calmly over the screech of fire alarms and wailing babies. The boy attached to him like a monkey to a branch and buried his face in Quinn's neck. "This way, this way!" Quinn commanded, supporting the young mother with his free hand and guiding her to the distant stairwell. He had seen the south side of the building listing and crumbling; he hoped the stairs on the north were still passable.

Once safely clear of the wreckage, Quinn left the traumatized young family lying in the grass a hundred yards from the building, grateful that the May weather was warm and dry. He rushed back to see what further help he could offer.

Neighbors were clamoring about, though many were away at work, which sadly may have proven fatal for them. The second tremor had ended, and the sobs and calls continued as Quinn cautiously reentered the building, making certain there were no unattended victims.

The building was destroyed, completely unsafe, but thankfully there had been no deaths in his small patch. Sirens, smoke, and alarms were ominous in the distance, and no one expected medical attention anytime soon. Keys, coat, laptop, and wallet in hand, Quinn sat in his car and listened to the alarming satellite reports of the damage to the Pacific Northwest.

The entire West Coast, from San Diego to Alaska, had felt the quake. Seattle was in discord, even though the epicenter of the 8.0-magnitude quake had struck hundreds of miles north, hitting Vancouver Island, Canada, directly. The large Canadian island and the smaller surrounding islands had been completely devastated, and tsunami tides threatened inhabitants on both sides of the Pacific Ocean.

Noetic scientists had random-number generators set up in more than seventy cities around the globe, and in this time of tragedy, just as had occurred moments before the events of 9/11, the numbers became subtly structured. Somehow the collective consciousness seemed to register the coming event. The generators synchronized, and the noetic scientists saw it as evidence of a unified field of consciousness. The same unified field had been described by sages in all cultures.

The news stations discounted the random-number generators despite the evidence, reporting that the effect was due to chance.

Eden and Nate didn't eat or sleep as they watched reports coming out of North America with horror. Finally, seven hours after the largest quake, they learned via text that Quinn had survived.

Sadly, tens of thousands had died in Seattle when office buildings, hospitals, shopping malls, the courthouse, and three schools had collapsed. There had been looting in places, especially the big cities, but in many instances, people had acted with surprising generosity.

For some, the tragedy had reawakened them to what was truly important. Suddenly there was more to life . . . and less. Simplicity: an epiphany. A light went on, and people wondered how they could have missed what it was all about. How could they have lived so robotically, in a fog, unconscious? Would they remain conscious, or would they slip back into their old patterns?

Quinn's court date was postponed; therefore, his plan to join Eden and her crew was also postponed. Over the next two months, the aftershocks continued, and cleanup commenced. Quinn couldn't help but think that the Earth was voicing its displeasure. Plato had discussed the idea of *anima mundi*, the world soul. Would things get worse before they finally got better?

Eden's initial instinct had been to return to the Pacific Northwest immediately and assist with the cleanup. Quinn had spent hours debating and counseling her in her helplessness, but as much as he wanted her near, Seattle was a mess.

The Crystal Project documentary would wrap production shortly. The citizens of the world would soon witness the human potential that the children exhibited: the telepathy, the telekinesis, communing with the elementals: harnessing fire, wind, earth, and air. They were able to diagnose and predict ailments and death dates. The documentary would show people there was more to life than fear and survival. Evolutionary change was coming, and there was a brighter future ahead.

The headlines changed, and the "Great American Quake" was quickly old news—everywhere but the West Coast, that is.

The world seemed to be getting worse as the planet flooded, froze, and burned. Governments wobbled and fell. Dictators were democratically voted in and became a permanent stain. Man-made disasters such as wars, riots, and terrorist attacks were the norm; and countries that had been living in Mafia states for a long time were deteriorating. People didn't know whom to trust. Only money and power had a voice. Governments and police were corrupt. Students had to pay under the table for the opportunity to take their exams, and babies in day care only had their diapers changed if their parents paid extra. People were miserable and enslaved, and charity and compassion were uncommon or hidden from view.

Quinn wished the ascent through the Bronze Age could be sped up; sometimes it felt as though the Dark Age had somehow been extended.

⋈⋈ ⋈⋈ ⋈⋈

It was an important time for Eden and Elijah. For the first time, the boy didn't feel isolated and abnormal. Instead, he felt that he'd been chosen to do something important in the world. Eden quelled his natural tendency to grow proud and self-important by reminding him to stay humble and compassionate. It was a struggle.

Nate and Elijah grew to be friends, and Nate continued to flirt with Eden. More than once, across a dinner table, she had considered him romantically. He was kind, funny, and eager to please, but her heart belonged to another.

Eden kept in regular contact with Quinn, who had found a temporary place to live and was spending most days toiling with disaster cleanup. Rebuilding had begun, and as he helped, despite wishing he was across the ocean with Eden, the Emissary spoke in his calm, hopeful way and inspired those around him. His life suddenly seemed to have direction.

Quinn was grateful that Eden was safe. She was in France but was scheduled to proceed to Morocco and then home. He was anxious to see her again, but he knew that Washington State wasn't the best place for them to be. The relief and cleanup had been bungled, reminiscent of the Hurricane Katrina debacle in Louisiana; and many of the citizens of Washington, Oregon, and California were angry about the water and food shortages. Alaska, always hearty and independent, had fared much better, but summer was passing quickly, and there was much left to do.

"I should come meet you in Marrakech, and we can move on . . . maybe we can stay in Spain to do the post-production? Things are still a mess here, and I don't know when they'll be back on track . . . hopefully before winter comes," Quinn said. He wanted to get to Marrakech.

"It's still *that* bad? I haven't wanted to worry you, but it's bad here too. It's pretty chaotic in the streets. I don't even know how you can get here! It's so bloody expensive. I was going to tell you—we've decided to postpone our return to North America another month. I don't know what we'd do without Zahn paying the expenses. It's way beyond what we initially expected, but he's been amazing."

"He has the money. Listen, I'm coming to meet you," Quinn said.

"What about your hearing?"

"It could take years now. I'm coming," he said. He would not be swayed. Theron had been separated from him for too long, and he didn't know what the Universe might throw at them next.

"That sounds great, and I can't wait for you to meet Elijah and the other kids. We met a girl, yesterday, Anjolie. She's fourteen. She's been keeping a journal since she was four! She has fifty-one completed notebooks, about fifty pages each. No one taught her to write, she just writes . . . but that's not the amazing part. She writes in perfect Sanskrit, Russian, English, and other languages I can't even recognize!"

"Fantastic! What does she write about?"

"Sometimes it's terrifying—about floods and ancient ceremonies. She can't even read the stuff in the other languages; she only speaks French. She says her 'inside-brain' writes it all for her and tells her in French what it's about."

"Fascinating. I'd love to meet her," Quinn said honestly, wondering who she was but certain she must be an Emissary. Quinn was thrilled that so many of the Crystal Children seemed to have ancient knowledge. It had to mean the darkest part of the cycle was over. Would Theron soon have memory too?

"Do you ever feel like you're one of them?" Quinn asked hopefully.

"Me? No! Well, not exactly, though I must admit, lately I've been having the strangest feelings of déjà vu. I'm dreaming a lot, and my dreams are so lucid, showing me places I've never been to but that I can recall in fine detail."

"Such as?" Quinn asked.

"I dreamed we had a school, you and I. We didn't look like ourselves, but I knew it was us anyway. I was standing with you on a high set of white steps, and we were surrounded by students. We all had white toga-style clothes on, and I could see every face and eye color and cloud in the sky. You had a craggy old-man face but a gentle smile . . . I woke up deliriously happy from that one. It must be the idea of the school, so weird."

"Maybe the dream is in our past?" Quinn said hoarsely, filled with emotion by her recollection of Ancient Greece.

"I didn't think of that . . . I was thinking about our future."

"Mmm," Quinn murmured, happy that she was thinking about a future with him. "I like hearing your dreams . . . any more?" he asked.

"No, it's silly. Anyway, when are you coming?"

"As soon as possible. I'll let you know as soon as I'm booked," he said.

"Great! Um, Quinn, do you really think we knew each other in a past life?" she asked sheepishly, and he knew she was embarrassed.

"I am certain of it," he said, his voice full of longing for her. He heard a quick intake of breath.

"You'll have to explain that certainty to me one of these days," she said demurely. "We're leaving Lyon tonight for Madrid, and then we proceed to Marrakech in three days. Keep me posted," she added.

"See you soon," Quinn said, and for the first time, he hung up before she did.

The turbulence was terrible, and the man next to Quinn gripped the armrest with his eyes tightly closed. Quinn eyed the barf bag in the seatback in front of him, just in case. He wanted it ready if his seatmate showed any signs of losing his lunch.

The vimanas, the advanced flying machines he had flown in a previous lifetime, had been so smooth, so reliable and fast! He longed for the days when he could fly in a tenth of the time that it took these archaic metal birds. It had only been just over a hundred years since people had rediscovered flight, and in his last lifetime, the one before Quinn, Marcus had become a pilot early. He had been determined to take full advantage of air travel. It made searching for Theron and the Emerald Tablet so much easier.

Looking out the window, Quinn thought of all the training, the endless hours and the navigation systems, he had invented in his last incarnation. He still had all the knowledge and know-how, but his exploration back then had been misguided. To reach his goals, he had become a soldier, and therefore he had gone to war. It was an ugliness others would usually forget when they died, though past-life trauma was real, and sometimes people had residual effects and flashbacks that were difficult to understand and navigate in their new lives. Quinn's awareness and past-life traumas would plague him forever.

He had spent an inordinate amount of time in the frigid poles in that lifetime, contemplating loneliness and separation. He had been reminded that the planet Gaia was alive, and she had protectors of her own.

....

Chapter 19

Consequences of Evil

....

Nuremberg, Germany, 1946

On October 25, 1888, Marcus had incarnated as Richard Byrd. He was now in his late fifties and was an admiral in the navy. He had won the Medal of Honor for valor in his time as an American naval officer, but he didn't care about accolades and awards; the Emissary had bigger things on his mind.

The Iron Age was at its climax. Two World Wars had kept the world chaotic, and the pinnacle of human darkness had been realized with the mass murder of millions in extermination camps and the use of nuclear warfare.

Good side, bad side, it was difficult to tell in the Dark Age when people were so unconscious and densely separatist and nationalistic. If the atomic bomb hadn't been launched by the Americans, it would have been launched by the Germans. There were Emissaries and Adversaries crisscrossing all borders.

It was 1946, more than two thousand years since Theron had unwittingly betrayed Plato's confidence to Alexander, and Marcus still had no idea where the Emerald Tablet was. Byrd had single-mindedly searched, and though he had nothing else to cling to, he was losing hope. He relied on synchronicity to light the way through the darkness.

Synchronicities were signs; they might show up as meaning-ful coincidences, repeating phrases, or numbers. Marcus relied on the subtle energies around him. He knew that when he followed his instincts and not his ego-based emotions or rationalizations, guidance would come.

Marcus was aware that humankind was nearing the end of the Iron Age. As a sailor and explorer, Byrd understood the impor-tance of the stars, but as an Emissary, he knew they were valuable for far more than mapping. Understanding the zodiac and the Great Year Cycle allowed Byrd to have insight into symbolic and cosmic influences affecting the world. Pisces was currently inter-facing with Aquarius, and the Emissary had come to understand that he and Helghul embodied the essence of the Pisces polarity. They were two souls, like fish, swimming in opposite directions yet joined together and unable to break free from one another.

The fragmenting of societies into opposing political parties and religions was also characteristic of the Age of Pisces. The era was dominated by the overwhelming drive for money, power, and control, but Aquarius was dawning; and with it, the expan-sion of love, unity, and brotherhood. When would the collective consciousness shift in a new direction? Byrd longed for the days when the illusion of separation would be over. Not yet. There had been so much war. The bombs in Hiroshima and Nagasaki were so recently dropped that the world still felt hopeless, sick, and dark.

Byrd redoubled his determination to find the Emerald Tab-let. He had managed to retrace the steps of Alexander the Great, and by cross-referencing that lifetime with what was known of

Genghis Khan's movements, he'd come up with a vast and daunting map covering thousands of miles across Asia. He didn't know if the Emerald Tablet was buried in the vast desert, untamed wilderness, or hidden in one of the great cities, but he knew that Genghis Khan's tomb was yet to be found; perhaps it was there.

The Emissary also considered that it might have been moved many times and could be protected by some secret order. Helghul, whoever and wherever he was, might currently have it in his possession. Byrd read little-known texts in many languages and visited obscure libraries and locations, searching. Despite rumors and fables that whispered of the Tablet, he found nothing. He knew that Sir Isaac Newton had written a translation of the Emerald Tablet and had hung it on his wall his entire life, but Byrd could only wonder if Newton had seen the actual Tablet.

In his goal to find the Tablet, Byrd had become an accomplished pilot and explorer. He had been the first to reach both the South and North Poles by air, and he was now tracking escaped Nazis. He knew he would find Helghul and other Adversaries among them.

When the war ended and before, many of the German scientists and engineers had switched sides and had been granted immunity by the Americans. Officially it was so they would not fall into the hands of the Russians, but truly, the United States couldn't wait to press forward with the discoveries the German scientists had been working on.

Byrd had been personally interrogating the relocated scientists for months. He'd interviewed Hermann Göring at Nuremberg while the creator of the Gestapo and former Luftwaffe commander awaited trial for war crimes.

Byrd and Göring had first met in Berlin in the late thirties. Byrd's Marcus-memory had immediately recognized the shine of the Adversary Thaddeus. Because of Byrd's prowess and reputation as an aviator, Göring had invited him to join an expedition to Antarctica. Though Germany and America were still years from declaring war on each other, the Emissary had declined. He remembered Thaddeus's lifetime as Lycon, when he had been instrumental in Socrates's death. He was an Adversary, and Byrd wanted to stay as far away from him as possible. He had, instead, been part of an American expedition shortly after.

Years later, in Nuremberg, deflated and desperate, Göring had been willing to tell Byrd everything he knew if he didn't incriminate himself. The Nazi complied when he was promised morphine, a substance he had become desperately addicted to.

"Oh, those early days! I live on those memories now. Do you remember my beautiful Carin? Did you meet? She was the perfect hostess, and then after she died, my Emmy. Oh, we had nothing but the best caviar, champagne, and fashions," Göring reminisced absentmindedly, rubbing the stiff sleeve of his prison shirt while Byrd briefly indulged him.

"My Emmy's in prison now. It's a travesty. She has suffered enough in this war. Her letters break my heart. They have charged us both unfairly. I was on the outs with the Führer long before the surrender. There were many with more information than me," Göring said.

Byrd listened, unable to muster up any pity for Göring and his actress wife. They were notoriously proud and pretentious; there were no extravagances too grand for the couple, and the admiral knew the Nazi was a villain, far from innocent.

"What have I missed, Hermann? If it was not you next to Hitler at the end, who was it?" Byrd asked, intentionally opening his hand and showing the syrette used to inject morphine. Göring's eyes widened, and he licked his lips.

"Talk to Hans Kammler. He was one of the Führer's closest allies. He did not love the spotlight and opulence like me," Göring said. "I thought he was boring and missing the point of life; he seemed averse to the joys of existence, but now here I sit. Who is missing life now?" he added, feeling sorry for himself.

"Where is Kammler now?" Byrd asked.

"Honestly, Dick? You don't know?" Göring said. His ego liked this. He felt important and valuable, having information the arrogant Americans needed.

"Know what?" the admiral said, flinching at the Nazi's familiar use of his first name.

"So, you Americans don't know everything . . . ," he said, smiling. "He was one of the first to find a safe haven in South America. But, of course, officially he's dead—suicide, they said. No doubt he will continue his work developing the ultimate flying machine. It's his obsession," he said, his eyes gleaming. Byrd wanted more before handing over the syrette.

"Why was Neuschwabenland so important?" Byrd asked. Neuschwabenland was the German name for the Nazi base in Antarctica.

"I never saw the value in it . . . damn brutal conditions, but the goal was world domination, and nothing less. The Führer and Kammler were obsessed with annexing the South Pole, no matter what argument I offered against it," Göring said. "We might have won the war if they hadn't splintered off our resources."

"Antarctica," Byrd repeated, and Göring nodded.

"The development there is extensive," Göring confirmed, licking his lips and staring, mesmerized by the morphine. Byrd's sympathy swelled. Thaddeus had the demon of addiction attached to him in this lifetime. His Marcus-memory remembered Thaddeus's handsome face as it had been in Atitala, and he could imagine it glowing beneath the bloated, soft jowls warbling before him. He wondered why he had chosen to become an Adversary. It was shocking, for he had never observed in him the hateful nature he had seen in Helghul. Had it been there all along? Hidden? Or was there a potential for extreme evil in everyone?

As an agent of darkness, Thaddeus had certainly caused terrible suffering, yet there Göring sat, unaware of his inner self; his extensive history was unknown to him. His allegiance to the Reich was easily betrayed to feed his addiction.

Byrd handed over the syrette and was quickly forgotten. He left Göring to his ecstatic veins.

In previous visits to the South Pole, the Emissary hadn't found what he'd been looking for, but the race for technology and strategic lands had only just begun. Marcus knew what was ultimately possible, and to allow the Adversaries to wield those capabilities would be catastrophic.

Chapter 20

The Beautiful Lie

World War II

France and Britain declared war on Germany in June of 1939 after Hitler invaded Poland, but other than propaganda, preparation, and anxiety, little else had changed until the beginning of 1940. The situation in Paris quickly became more strained. The New Year brought greater hardship, and sirens shrieked, causing panic and mayhem when the bombs fell and when they did not. People were afraid.

Theron had been born a baby boy: Milo Pierre Blanc. Milo's childhood had been marred by the death of his father, who'd been killed fighting for France in the trenches of the Western Front during the First World War. He had grown up in hardship.

Milo had married young, and despite his poor, unfortunate start in life, he was respected and successful. Thanks to his natural brilliance, Milo had become a self-taught engineer and inventor. In his late teens, after visiting the university for weeks and months on end, appealing to the professors with his theories and inventions, he was offered a scholarship. The work he went on to do, advancing theories of flight technology, was beyond anything that currently existed.

Milo, his wife, and his daughter had not been together on June 14, 1940, when German troops and tanks rolled freely through the streets of Paris, crushing the hearts of her people under their hooves and treads. As the Nazis paraded down the Champs-Élysées, Milo rushed home to be with his family. The apartment was north of the Arc de Triomphe, a few blocks up the Avenue de la Grande Armeé, and having heard shouting from their top-floor apartment, the women had rushed down the spiral staircase, five floors to the boulevard. There was not a dry eye among them. Their neighbors had sobbed and proclaimed their despair. All normal activities were abandoned, for Paris, the City of Light, had lost her precious liberty.

By June 22, an armistice had been signed, and the politicians had scurried to Vichy, leaving the undefended heart and soul of France to be greedily consumed by the German invaders. Milo and his fellow citizens were horrified as red-and-black swastikas polluted their walls, gardens, and street corners as constant reminders of the unwanted presence.

Milo was active in his community, and his socially conscious daughter, Sophie, had become a Zazou, one of the French youths gathering at the Pam Café on the Champs-Élysées. Her dramatic hairstyle, garish clothing, and rebellious nature were the least of Milo's concerns. Sophie's overt public disdain for the Nazis and the Vichy government had brought negative attention to her family, but the teen felt invincible. Though Milo had told her to desist and behave more subtly, she had ignored his pleas defiantly, and along with her Zazou friends, she smoked, danced, and sang while fearlessly shouting anti-Nazi slogans from the café balcony.

Sophie, like her father, was an Emissary, and she was unwilling to silence the rebellion within her. In Atitala's Golden Age, Sophie's name had been Yashoda. She had been a schoolmate and friend to Theron, Marcus, and Helghul, and she had helped distract the giant Nephilim with enormous balloons on the day the trio had entered Inner Earth. Sophie was a free spirit, but her Emissary soul was stirred with indignation at the occupation of Paris and the complicity of the Vichy government in the Nazi agenda. She railed against the treatment befalling the Jews, and though she seemed ignorant to the danger, she was not.

"The propagandists are disparaging the Zazous as crude and indecent; they poison your fellow Parisiennes against you, citing your extravagance and disrespect," Milo cautioned.

"If good people remain silent, tyranny will have free reign to take hold!" Sophie argued.

"You are too boisterous and free. We are an occupied city, and you fail to adapt to that reality."

"Would you prefer I was afraid? Hiding and cowering? Plain and grey and in the shadows?" his daughter said.

"Remember the words of Molière, Sophie: 'Man's greatest weakness is his love for life.' When you are too attached to your happiness, it is more easily snatched away."

Without a moment's pause, Sophie replied, "Life asked Death, 'Why do people love me and hate you?' and Death responded, 'Because you are a beautiful lie, and I am a painful truth.' Would you have me embrace the beautiful lie, Papa . . . or should I shroud myself in black and live every day fearing the truth of certain death?"

"Sophie! Enough! How can you resent your papa so? He only worries for your safety!" Madame Blanc said, scolding her daughter.

"He worries for my reputation and his own. I will embrace life! I will sing. I will dance and have sex! I will speak against the wicked Nazis! I will love the beautiful lie," Sophie said, and she strutted away, closing the door loudly as she departed.

"So I must be the painful truth," Milo said to his wife while she consoled him. Milo would ponder those words for many years to come.

⊱⊰ ⊱⊰ ⊱⊰

Before the occupation, life in Paris had been lived in the streets: romantic, cultured, and built around community. Milo Blanc and his family had strolled with their neighbors in the evenings, enjoying open cafés, gardens, art installations, and street performances. But now, the German trespassers overtook daily life. Their boisterousness filled the bars and cafés as they badgered and intimidated the men and harassed the women. They made life difficult for the French at their whim. Shops closed, and families left in mass exodus to other parts of Western Europe. The roads were jammed, damaged by bombs, and motor vehicles and petrol were difficult to acquire. It wasn't until 1943 that the stark cruelty of war deeply affected Milo and his family.

Milo returned to his lab to find it overrun by SS soldiers crating up his papers for removal. One of his associates was seated silently in the corner with his head lowered. There was a large red welt visible on his cheek, and he didn't dare look up.

"Heil Hitler," the German in charge said, clicking his heels. Hans Kammler's underbite pushed out his lower jaw crookedly as his face stretched with a forced, ghoulish smile. His Helghul-consciousness was jubilant. He was giddy to have found Theron.

Milo's arm and neck hair bristled. Theron wasn't capable of recognizing Helghul when confronted by him, but Milo knew he was in the presence of an enemy. Milo hated the Nazi invaders and had done what he could to undermine them. Had his subversion been discovered?

"I am General Doctor Hans Kammler," the general said, smiling with self-importance, showing his uneven peg-like teeth. "You are Milo Blanc?"

"*Oui, je suis. C'est moi,*" Milo said, acknowledging who he was.

"I have exciting news for you, *Herr* Blanc." Kammler grinned.

"The German army requests your service."

"Surely, non, it is a mistake. What use am I?" Milo asked.

"Come, come. Let's not pretend . . . ," Kammler said.

His shine had invaded Theron's, and together their energies struggled against each other in a confused indigo-black eddy. The Iron Age was at its peak, and the Beast was at his strongest. The relationship had corrupted any human qualities remaining in Helghul, ridding his soul of all love. Blanc and Kammler both felt slightly nauseated by the blending of the dark and light, though only Helghul witnessed the spectacle. The oblivious Emissary was at his mercy.

"I have read your theoretical papers. You have made some miraculous breakthroughs that we look forward to developing," Kammler said in perfect French, planting himself casually atop a table, masking the discomfort Theron's energy caused him. The contempt-filled Beast attached to Helghul's soul snarled from deep within Kammler, reminding him of past mistakes.

"I assure you I have nothing to offer," Milo said. He did not want to offend, but he would not help the enemy who had invaded his nation. The unarmed engineer looked bravely into the general's impenetrable grey eyes, and the soldier slackened his phony smile. The viciousness concealed deep within him rose. His eyes flashed, warning of a cruelty Milo could not yet imagine. Ripples of fear shot through the Emissary.

"Careful, *Herr* Blanc," Kammler warned. "I am not an enemy you want to make. We are aware you are one of the gifted. Your work *will* be realized."

Again, Milo began to humbly protest, assuring Kammler that he had no information, no inventions, that the Germans had not already surpassed, but Kammler cut him short.

"A difficult man should be alone in the world to make careless choices . . . but you? How are your wife and pretty daughter?" Kammler asked, standing.

The beak-nosed German began to pace. He was much taller than Milo and loomed over him like a bird of prey. Helghul's dark energy had expanded and fiercely engulfed Milo.

"What have you done?" Blanc asked. All the color had drained from his face.

The Nazis had proven themselves to be ruthless. Milo had spent nearly every penny he had to help shuttle endangered families away from Paris. It had never occurred to him to send away his own wife and daughter—they were not Jews. They were not the condemned race. Most nonpolitical Parisians had gone on with life—sadder, poorer, and desperate for emancipation, but surviving, and Milo had assumed that he and his family would do the same.

"*Herr* Blanc, you will find your women have been . . . relocated," Kammler said, reaching out and seizing Milo's chin with a leather-clad hand. "You can kill them or save them—it makes no difference to me. The choice is yours," the Beast hissed through Kammler's throat, only inches from Milo's ear. The devastated father leaned against his desk for support.

"What have you done to them?" Milo repeated. He felt his panic rising but realized he also felt more courage than was sensible.

"Nothing yet. If you cooperate, they will be *fine*," Kammler said, searching Milo's eyes for a flicker of recognition and any sign of Theron's strength.

General Kammler hadn't met Sophie and Madame Blanc himself. Helghul had no idea that Sophie was Yashoda, an Emissary. However, even if he *had* known, he would have made the identical order he had already issued. Sophie and her mother were currently being transported to the Drancy holding station in northern Paris, where they would await deportation to Kammler's greatest accomplishment to date: Auschwitz-Birkenau in Nazi-occupied Poland. Kammler had been chiefly in charge of creating the vast network of extermination camps as well as the gas chambers and crematoria within, and now he had additional diabolical projects underway.

"We must go. We have a war to win," Kammler snapped briskly. The Beast within him was angry that Theron's shine had unexpectedly unearthed Helghul's weaknesses. The Beast was ruthless and powerful, and his nature had dominated for decades. He regarded his human soul as an affliction. The Beast did not desire one moment more bombarded by the clinging goodness of Milo's shine.

You make mistakes when it comes to this Emissary! the Beast scolded in the man's head. It punished Kammler for his weakness, grating on his nerve endings and sending painful tingles through him as Theron's residual energy separated from them. Kammler grimaced at the searing pain. After nearly thirteen thousand years, the foul partners were at their most wicked and depraved in the darkest depths of the Iron Age.

Milo was distraught as the SS officers roughly escorted him out of the building to a waiting truck. General Doctor Kammler watched from his private car as Blanc was loaded in. The Nazi instructed his driver to depart, and he did not look back. Helghul *never* looked back. His mind was already turned to business even more foul.

Chapter 21

Die Glocke, the Bell

Die Glocke, the Bell

Milo arrived at the gloomy train station of central Prague escorted by two SS officers. Worn out from the excruciatingly long ride and many stops, he was hungry and miserable as he was handed off to another group of Brown Shirts. Their truck navigated the narrow cobblestone streets; its headlights bounced and ricocheted violently off the old buildings. The Germans ignored their prisoner and chattered back and forth. Milo didn't recognize his surroundings. He was lost in so many ways.

It seemed like hours before the truck stopped at a building that could not be described as anything less than a castle. Milo was ushered through a giant, ornately carved set of mahogany doors.

Even in the dark, the manor house was impressive. The grand entrance had a sweeping staircase of the same dark mahogany as the doors, and the floor was intricately designed inlaid marble.

"*Bonjour, Monsieur Blanc,*" a woman said in French with a thick Czech accent.

"What is this place?" he asked rudely without greeting her.

"I am not the enemy, Blanc. We are all scientists here . . . just like you," she said, her sympathetic eyes peering at him over her glasses.

"Ah . . . *oui*, forgive me, Madame," he said apologetically.

"Follow me, please."

She walked quickly for such a small person, and Milo had to hustle to keep up with her choppy penguin-like steps.

"Why don't you leave?" Milo whispered, once he was certain the Brown Shirts could not hear.

"I have three sons," she said, her eyes flashing with emotion. "There is no choice to escape, monsieur; you would not be the first to die trying, trust me. . . . You will be well treated. It is better to focus on your work."

Milo considered her words. He knew that while Kammler held his wife and daughter, he would not risk endangering them. They passed through several beautiful old salons, and the oil lantern in the woman's hand swung like a head on a rope, casting light sporadically. She stopped, and Milo, in his distracted state, bumped into her. He looked at the paneled wall directly ahead of them and assumed she had lost her way in the shadows. The woman stepped aside and waved her hand to move him as well. She lifted a thick wool carpet at their feet and pushing it back, revealed an old and intricately inlaid marble floor. *Push, twist, push.* She proceeded through a sequence of actions, and a trapdoor lifted open. Milo found himself standing over a secret passageway. Two top stairs were now visible. He was dumbfounded.

"Follow me closely. It is steep, and there is no railing," she explained. Milo counted twenty steps, and he followed her as they descended into a well-lit corridor. The woman placed the oil lamp at the base of the stairway since electric lamps were now hung at regular intervals. Their shoes clicked on the stone beneath their feet, and Milo heard a steady buzz and hum reverberating through the passage. They walked for ages before the tunnel ended. Finally, they entered a massive, brightly lit room as large as an airplane hangar carved into the rock. There were at least fifty white coats, presumably scientists. There were more people in civilian dress whom he was sure were engineers, and a scattered unit of heavily armed German soldiers. There were other tunnels leading away from where they'd come.

Milo observed an important-looking man whose attention was being sought on all sides. He learned later that the man was Klaus Habermohl, the creator of the first radial flow engine. It was his other invention, the Haunebu disc aircraft, which was being worked on in this installation. Everyone there was working on flying machines, rockets, or weapons of some sort. Milo had been recruited to assist with *Die Glocke*, the Bell, as well as other inventions beyond the current scope and achievement in fight and flight.

⋈ ⋈ ⋈

Milo had only been working in the underground lab a week when Kammler showed up and handed him a file describing the exact dimensions of a solid tablet and listing the chemical properties and atomic makeup of the Bell's intended power source. It was unlike anything Milo had ever heard of.

"But what *is* it?" Milo said, rereading the document.

"Can you work with it?" Kammler asked.

"No . . . not if I don't know what it is. Nothing remotely like this exists on the *tableau périodique*, the periodic table."

"It exists, I assure you, and it will be available to you when it is absolutely necessary."

"It would be easier to have it here. I do not know how it will respond. I need to test its properties. It might be unstable," Milo said, speaking frankly as he would have done in his former academic environs. It was a mistake, and Kammler backhanded Milo, sending him reeling to the floor and splitting his lip.

"Never question me! Everything you need to know is in that folder. The element will be available when you make progress, understand?"

"But you ask the impossible," Milo said, holding his bleeding lip.

"I am sure, knowing your wife and daughter are waiting, makes it more . . . possible," Kammler said.

"Where have you taken them? Can I see them?"

"They are safely confined. I only wish to ensure your loyalty, *Herr* Blanc. The sooner you complete this work, the sooner Paris will welcome you all back home," Kammler assured him.

Milo contemplated the man. He wanted to believe him, but everything about Kammler contradicted his words. Theron's instincts knew better.

The Bell would be a huge advance in flight, and finally had the potential to be realized under Blanc's guidance. In harnessing the antigravitational properties of atlantium, they would revive the flight technology of a higher, forgotten Age. The Bell wouldn't require any fuel and would be capable of unlimited distances and speeds that defied the human eye. It would be virtually impossible to shoot down. As designed, the Bell could hover, attain perfect vertical climb, not require a landing strip, and could easily be fitted to carry the new atomic bombs under development. One or two of those, released over New York or London, and the Allies would have no choice but to surrender.

Helghul was uneasy having the Emerald Tablet anywhere near Theron. However, as he expected, Milo's creativity and intuition had already proved to be well beyond that of the other scientists. Kammler would have to manipulate the Emissary carefully, but he was confident he could do it. He had done it before, and Aristotle had innocently confided in Alexander.

With no past-life memory, the Emissaries can be easily used, he thought.

Do not underestimate Theron, the Beast telegraphed to him. *Our time is running out!*

⤫⤫ ⤫⤫ ⤫⤫

Drancy was a transit center in the north of Paris where prisoners were interned on their way to the Nazi "work" camps. It was a five-story housing complex that had been transformed into a ridiculously overcrowded temporary prison near the rail line. By 1943, when Madame Blanc and Sophie arrived, Drancy held thousands more than capacity. Living conditions were deplorable, and the guards showed no pity.

Sophie had never spent time in this neighborhood, but she knew that just outside the barbwire gates, there were cobblestone streets lined with blooming flowers; and people going to market, work, or school. Sophie knew, if only they were free to leave, in just minutes they would pass a patisserie, a bistro, and people chatting in the street. They could walk the miles back to familiar roads and faces, and by nightfall their aching feet and legs could deliver them to normal. Oh, how they longed to go home!

On the first day in the holding center, the women witnessed cruelty and suffering beyond anything they had ever fathomed. They watched as two sisters, women in their early twenties, were singled out. They wore the telltale Jewish stars on their arms, and their curls were hidden beneath dark scarves. Despite their attempts to be invisible, their beautiful brown eyes and full lips had caught the attention of a sadistic SS guard nearby. For his comrade's amusement, he circled them, taunting, pinching, prodding, then slapping. The girls didn't resist. They didn't fight back. They stood, unresponsive and slack faced, having often endured random cruelty since the Germans had invaded Paris. They had not expected Drancy to be any different.

The barely postpubescent guard mistakenly perceived their behavior as indifferent, superior, and defiant. Easily embarrassed and infuriated, the young man's fragile ego incited him to brandish his pistol to further demonstrate his dominance.

"You Jews are all the same. Will this wake you?" he shouted, waving the gun. Still, they stood limp, clutching each other by the arm and staring at the ground. They were afraid to move and were sleepwalking through their nightmare, enduring it as best they could. The soldier was blinded with hatred.

These prisoners are an infestation, less than human—animals! he thought. It was what he had been taught. The rhetoric had sunk in, had been accepted, and now the dehumanizing lies made it easy to be pitiless.

The SS guard lifted his gun, and there was a shot—just one—to the forehead. One woman slumped to the ground, and the second screamed and dropped to her sister's side.

"Better," he said, pleased by her reaction. The man laughed at their suffering, looking to the other guards for affirmation.

"Nazi bastard!" the surviving sister screamed. She was restrained, beaten, and bound by the other guards, who had observed and laughed along. Strict instructions were given that she was to remain alive. To kill her would be far too merciful.

The murderer walked away, whistling. He whistled as if he were walking through a meadow of edelweiss, rather than through a pool of blood. Sophie couldn't imagine that things could get much worse.

After a sleepless week, Sophie and her mother were loaded onto a windowless cattle car and transferred to Auschwitz-Birkenau. The railcar was cruelly overloaded, without food or water and with barely enough air supplied by the single barred window. Some cars had a bucket, but not all. There were no toilet facilities, and the passengers were mortified when reduced to urinating and defecating while crushed against their horrified neighbors on the long trip to Poland.

Hour after hour, the train jerked and rocked, and the tortured passengers were carried into the night with their legs aching to sit or lean, but they were packed in too tightly. They stood, without any relief. The journey was too much, and there were cries and moans as people realized that there were dead among them.

"I'm so sorry, Mama!" Sophie whispered, pressed against her mother.

"*Mon dieu*, what for?" Madame Blanc asked.

"It's my fault we're here! It was my outspoken disdain! I wore the fake star. I thought we Zazous would be the difference, but we were fools! Sitting ducks!"

"Oh, *ma chère*, don't blame yourself," Madame Blanc soothed.

"I was such a fool, feeling invincible! I should have worked underground. In secret."

"Your father did," her mother whispered, with her mouth directly beside her daughter's ear. Sophie could feel the wetness of her mother's tears on her cheek. "It is just as likely *he* was discovered, and that is why we are here."

Sophie hadn't known! She was proud of him . . . and oh, she was ashamed of herself! She remembered the terrible things she had said.

"I belittled him. I chastised him for doing nothing. How blind I was!" she cried out miserably.

"Blame *them*, not yourself," a kind older man interjected from beside them. "Everyone has a story or a moment of regret when they should have done more or done less. I should have gone to my brother in London. I could have. How could we know what *they* would do? Whose nightmares could prepare us for *this*?"

At that, Sophie became quiet. The man was correct. The Emissary should not blame herself for the madness around her—none of them should.

The passengers wondered what would happen next, and hoped that the work camp ahead of them would be bearable. They thought of their regrets and what they might have done differently to avoid this predicament. Nothing—for many of them. There had been no escaping, no alternatives. The truth was, none of them deserved what was happening to them.

The prisoners thought of the family members from whom they'd been separated and wondered with aching hearts and limbs if they would ever see them again. As they worried and suffered, the train rattled on.

The dehumanizing, excruciating journey ended a day and a half later in the middle of the night when the heavy doors clanged opened at Auschwitz. Sophie stumbled into the frigid night, squinting into the glare of the harsh spotlights as her stiff legs buckled. The German soldiers barked as loudly as their dogs, and the prisoners jumped and the children cried. Sophie readied herself for the worst she could imagine and was later stunned by how optimistic and naive she had been. She had expected a work camp. She could not have anticipated the depth of the brutality and evil she would witness. The vicious depravity ensued almost immediately.

They were pushed and pulled from the cattle cars by the Kapos, prisoners like them who performed administrative tasks within the camp. The SS officers evaluated the new arrivals like livestock at market, designating whether they would go to work or to slaughter. All humanity was abandoned as they ruthlessly tore children from their parents. Hysterical protests and gunshots followed, shocking and devastating every soul within earshot and sight. Sophie's mother stayed close to her as they marched with their heads down through the mud to a large building that resembled a vast corridor. Along with all the prisoners, male and female, Sophie and her mother were forced to disrobe, and their clothing was carelessly thrown aside, added to a massive pile.

In view of all, Sophie and Madame Blanc were inspected— invaded by callous, rough-handed guards. Following that, their bodies and heads were shaved by male Kapos, and their arms were painfully tattooed. They all wept and gulped in shame, regardless of their gender. The freezing-cold delousing occurred, and the terrified prisoners then dressed in ragged camp-issued garb and were herded across the grounds to the barracks.

We look like animals, Sophie thought. People she had seen only minutes before were unrecognizable. She knew that was the intention.

Sophie could not identify the dreadful aroma of burning flesh and hair that choked them and turned the sky red. She comforted her mother, who was less able to accept what they were experiencing. The older woman did not have the inner beacon of hope and light that the Emissary Yashoda did, and she resisted their circumstances. The smothering density of the Dark Age coupled with her dire predicament had quickly drained her optimism.

The overloaded quarters of Drancy had been bearable compared to this dark hell. Sophie counted sixty-two hard wooden bays, and the women were housed three or four to a roost. The camp was enormous, and she could only imagine how many poor souls languished there.

Were there tens of thousands? More?

July 14, 1939, years earlier, there had been a parade for Bastille Day. The Champs-Élysées had been lined with beautiful, happy Parisians. Sophie had remarked then that it was the most people she had ever seen gathered in one place. She couldn't help thinking that this seemed like a gathering of their shadows.

The sinister darkness of the camp clung to her, coating her skin and lining her inside and out. She called on God for guidance and strength, as her parents had taught her to do, and she sent her energy and love to the people around her, longing to comfort them all. The Emissary had no way of knowing the good her loving energy did, or that her thoughts and intentions flowed through her shine, reaching out and easing the darkness.

Sophie quickly understood the sinister purpose of the camp. The Final Solution was diabolical and senseless, founded on hatred and ignorance and targeting people who had lived normal, simple lives during which they'd harmed no one. The only work here was the work of murder. In the following weeks, she assisted many dying souls into the next world. They had been there longer—worn down, sick, starving, and destroyed. She comforted them with words and hugs, but there was nothing but prayer she could offer to the thousands of others who were never even given barracks assignments. They were killed immediately.

On Kammler's command, Sophie and Madame Blanc were dubbed *preferred status prisoners*, though they were never privy to this knowledge. The daily threat of being killed loomed over them. They were given work details in the Sonderkommando, processing the belongings of the new arrivals. They went through personal effects and separated items, preparing them to be shipped to Germany. Sophie saw other workers pilfering from the piles of belongings, and she realized she could help her fellow prisoners by smuggling out footwear and by trading items for food. She risked her life month after month, secretly distributing shoes and trading small jewelry items to certain Kapos for extra rations of black bread, or cheese that she would give away.

Sophie's empathy and compassion wore on her, but her purpose-driven inner Emissary-Yashoda fueled her drive to help others. She shared everything she had, but there were too many hungry people haunting the filthy place awaiting their fate. There were always terrified new faces, and the awful sound of the trains arriving followed by the screams, crying children, snarling dogs, snapping whips, and the harsh, berating tones of the German soldiers. Everyone knew that more people would end up in the barracks or go directly to the crematoria.

Sophie's eighteenth birthday came and went. Time passed, and only the newcomers cried, filing in and filing out. People were reduced to names on paper and the scratch, scratch, scratch of an emotionless pen until eventually they were reduced even further to the soot of a chimney. Sophie covered her mouth when she was outside being marched to and fro for daily inspections with the other prisoners. She tried to breathe in as little of the airborne dust and smoke as she could. Every time her despair threatened to overtake her, she thought of her mother, and the women she would comfort at night, and she knew they would have no one. She thought of her father, and she felt Theron's energy reaching out to her.

Sophie often heard Milo in her head encouraging her, loving her from afar, and she dreamed of seeing him.

Be strong, he said. *I love you, I'm coming,* he telegraphed over and over, but she never knew if her father was dead or alive. Would he come for them? They had heard nothing about him since they had been dragged out of their apartment and transferred to Drancy.

Milo truly did call to them telepathically. In his mind, he sent them love, encouragement, and peace. Had Theron been aware of herself within Milo, the father would have been comforted to know that Sophie subconsciously received, and felt comforted by, his wishes.

Madame Blanc was silent and wide-eyed. She was a ghost of her former boisterous self. Sophie and her mother wondered when their numbers would be called. Would they die in the hospital or showers from which no one returned; or by gunshot, baton, or dog? They never knew. Day to day, they wondered, shooing away rats and scratching at lice. They had no idea that it was Milo's work for Kammler that had designated them *preferred status* and kept them alive . . . if only barely.

At night when they lay down, exhausted and crammed together in their coffin-beds, Sophie would whisper stories of liberation, hope, and love. The other prisoners flocked to her, buoyed, if ever so slightly, by her loving energy.

"The British broke through the gates and liberated them all with milk, bread, and strawberries—enough for everyone," she might finish. She entertained and distracted the women for hours, sweeping them away to another time and place. The Emissary's smuggled items, her voice, and her affection, made their lives one shred better, and that was something.

As the days, weeks, and months passed, Sophie thought less about her father and more about food, warmth, and survival. The warm boots and clothing in her closet at home, once ignored and taken for granted, haunted her. The ice box, the market! They had always been so easy and convenient. Her body and her thin short hair were alive with parasites, and there was little left to her voluptuous frame but flesh and bone. She and the other prisoners found the strength to survive in the knowledge that they must bear witness. They had to live to tell the world of the unimaginable evil and inhumanity that existed there.

Chapter 22

Contact

Milo hoped, rather than believed, that upon completing the project he would be free of Kammler's lab and be reunited with his family.

The time finally came that Milo needed access to the secret power source. The Bell had been redesigned with Milo's improvements, and construction of the prototype was nearing completion. Kammler was summoned, and was informed that the power source was absolutely required for the final stages.

Milo was excited, but he was also filled with anxiety. There was something about Kammler's presence, beyond the other Nazi soldiers, that vibrated Milo's bones and percolated the blood in his veins. He did not wish to further the proliferation of the Nazi regime by completing the project, but though he searched for a creative solution, he saw no opportunity to alter his present circumstances.

When Kammler arrived at the installation, he emptied the laboratory except for himself and Milo. Not even the SS guards could stay. The atlantium was enough reason for secrecy, but the Emerald Tablet was not merely a piece of exceptional crystal, it was much more.

The general finally laid the Emerald Tablet on a table in front of the full-size Bell prototype. The Tablet was not the rough, unfinished block Milo had expected from its description in the file. It was clearly an antiquity of significant artistic value beyond the qualities and dimensions described. It looked like beryl or possibly green sapphire, but it could not be, for the elemental properties did not match. There were traces of familiar elements in the slab, but its chemical composition was different from anything Milo knew existed.

The edges were finely honed, and Milo felt inexplicably drawn to it, like a powerful magnet. The Emissary was astounded by the immense energy surging through him while in its presence.

"C'est magnifique!" Milo said, reaching out to touch the strange bas-relief lettering on the shining surface.

"Nein!" Kammler snapped, his hand flying to the leather whip attached to his belt. Milo quickly pulled his hand back.

"Surely, *Docteur*, I must touch it? How can I work with it if I cannot touch it?" Milo asked with exasperation.

"I will move it . . . by your direction, but do not waste my time. You said you are close, *ja?*"

"Yes, but there is much yet to do. It will take days!"

"I will assist as needed, but before you contemplate sabotage, remember that I will eliminate your family most painfully, before I eliminate you."

"I will do whatever it is you require," Milo said. *There is no doubt that seeing this treasure is my death sentence,* Milo thought.

To everyone's confusion, Kammler remained holed up in the lab with Milo for days. He acted as an assistant to the Emissary, interrupting work on all the other projects, since no one else was permitted in the lab while the Emerald Tablet was present. The scientists were ushered in and out of the hangar by guards; whenever Kammler needed to present the Emerald Tablet, only Milo was permitted to stay.

The electromagnetic field around the Emerald Tablet was strong, and Milo felt almost euphoric being in its vicinity. The Beast within Kammler detested Theron's shine, and each hour in Milo's presence intensified his rage.

Though the Bell was advancing, the final touches took time. Milo knew that if he'd had the green crystal from the beginning, the advancement would have been significantly more rapid, but clearly Kammler would never have allowed it. Instead, Kammler returned numerous times in the following weeks, traveling between Berlin and Prague. He hid the Emerald Tablet rather than traveling with it, nervous that it could fall into the wrong hands if his car was randomly hit by enemy fire. Helghul did not want to lose track of the Tablet should he meet an untimely death.

Kammler was frustrated that the Bell was not ready for outdoor trials. The indoor tests had been marred by accidents and misfires. The failures created all kinds of problems. Pieces of sheet metal flew across the hangar, damaging other equipment. A mass of iron from an intake fan flew off and chipped the concrete floor before lodging in the wall behind Milo's head. The Iron Age vimana could not handle the power generated by the atlantium and succumbed under the intense pressure, just as the Wright brothers' aircraft would have done in 1903 if someone had suddenly strapped on a jet engine.

The Bell was reinforced and rebuilt. Kammler was chasing victory, and the state of the war was growing more dire. The Adversary was losing patience with Milo, and he scowled and gritted his teeth while they worked side by side.

"I have made the adjustments. Please place it in the inner housing," Milo said to Kammler for what felt like the hundredth time. Milo was desperate to know more about the crystal's origins, but Kammler shared nothing.

"Leave!" Kammler ordered, and just as he had every other time Kammler had attempted to activate the crystal, Milo climbed out of the Bell and stood behind protective glass nearby. This secrecy slowed things down, but Milo had no choice, and he watched from a distance, staring at his gauges and gathering data while Kammler faced failure. The Iron Age consciousness could not command the atlantium easily, as Helghul had once done. He had to rely on Milo's technology to fill in the gaps and harness the atlantium's properties mechanically.

There were small nodes at either end of the casing that held the Tablet inside the Bell. A current ran through a ceramic cylinder to tap the power of the atlantium and channel it into the craft. Kammler focused his thoughts into the Emerald Tablet carefully. Finally, they generated propulsion, but more fine-tuning was needed to achieve lift.

Milo did not realize the turmoil he provoked in Kammler. The general sat beside Milo, steeling his shine against Theron's invasive positive surges. Every question the scientist asked about the crystal inspired Kammler's inner Beast to react violently.

We are nearing the end of the Iron Age. There will not be many more opportunities like this one. We must firmly establish world power before the Great Year begins its ascension, the Beast reminded him.

Kammler bristled at the nagging, like a resentful child. He was all turmoil and urgency within. He did not need obvious prodding by the impatient, emotional Beast.

They were getting close. The plans had advanced, and the engineering and design had been adjusted with the Emerald Tablet in place. The Bell was a towering masterpiece that filled the massive bunker, and it was now nearly operational.

It was during some final adjustments, while working on turbulent flow tests, that Milo reached past the glowing crystal to adjust a node—*contact!*

Milo inadvertently touched the Emerald Tablet, and his synapses fired. At the speed of thought, Theron's DNA was electrified, and Milo received a download of information. The astounding potential of the Emerald Tablet and its momentous secret had lain dormant in Theron's psyche, attached to her consciousness.

Instantly, Milo's Theron-consciousness had been awakened. She remembered the Elders in Atitala gathered around The Emerald Tablet inside the White Pyramid with its golden capstone.

The Emerald Tablet! Atlantium! Helghul! Milo's mind raced as information was downloaded.

The characters on the Tablet became legible, and Milo recalled the ancient language that had been memorized by his soul. The Emissary suddenly knew exactly what it said. The words were contemplative, enigmatic, and explained the secrets of the Universe. But there was more; the information kept coming.

Milo knew himself as Theron, and he suddenly realized that his beloved daughter was Yashoda, his fellow Emissary. Milo saw Helghul as he truly was, with the terrible entity bound to him—intertwined with his soul. The vision was startling, but Milo did not show fear. His scientific thinking allowed him to observe objectively, gathering information and resisting emotion.

By simply touching the Emerald Tablet, a transfer of knowledge had occurred. A window into the Akashic field had been opened, and in a nanosecond, Milo understood the complexity of the Universe. But the opportunity was brief, with Kammler watching beside him.

Milo tried to act normal, unchanged, but his heart was pounding in his chest, and he reminded himself to breathe. Theron's purpose was revealed, and the Emissary wondered if he would have the opportunity to duplicate the experience. Milo went on with his measurements but longed to touch the Tablet again and get more information.

Kammler was watching him with suspicion, as if he suspected the Emissary had somehow tapped in. Had Helghul detected the ripple in Theron's shine? Had he sensed the surge in Milo's sense of purpose and determination? Kammler placed himself between Milo and the Tablet, so the opportunity for further undetected contact was denied.

"Keep your hands clear, Blanc. Do not reach across again. Do I make myself clear?" Kammler ordered. Milo knew the Nazi could easily put a bullet in his head if he disobeyed.

"*Oui*, yes. As you please," Milo said.

That day when Kammler finally departed for Berlin with the Tablet, Milo had time to contemplate what he had experienced. He wrote out the words of the Emerald Tablet in French and read them over many times, committing them deliberately to memory before burning the paper. He contemplated the meaning and was filled with newfound clarity and confidence. That night Milo took a stand.

"Inform *Docteur* Kammler I will not work one more day until I see my wife and daughter and I am assured they are safe," he said to the chief scientist.

"*Ach, mein Gott!* Be reasonable, Milo. Kammler is not to be threatened," the chief warned, genuinely frightened. He had grown fond of Blanc; they all had. The comradery in the lab was without borders. Germans, Slovaks, Dutch, and Poles—they had all been gathered together, and many were prisoners. They had been well treated and afforded good meals, wine, and cigarettes. And the work! My God! What they had been able to accomplish with Blanc's unparalleled creativity had been thrilling. The chief scientist knew Kammler was far more likely to shoot Blanc than meet his demands, and he did not wish to deliver the message, for he, too, might bear the general's infamous wrath.

"My work will cease until I see my family and know they are alive," Milo said, and his supervisor had no option but to relay the message. The ultimatum was not well received.

✄✄ ✄✄ ✄✄

Sophie and Madame Blanc were hauled out of their barracks by an SS guard early the next morning. It was not a good thing to be singled out; those who were, never returned.

"What's happening?" Madame Blanc cried out, clinging to Sophie.

"Move! Hurry up!" the guard barked.

Is this the end? Sophie wondered, her panic rising with every step and command, though outwardly she remained brave, reassuring her mama.

It had been sixteen months since they had been plucked from their home. They had grown used to fear and suffering as a way of life, but their will to survive was strong, and they dreaded what might lie ahead. As they walked, Sophie's mind raced. Her Emissary nature exuded positivity and helped her mother maintain some semblance of hope despite their dire circumstances, but being singled out caused Sophie to expect the worst.

Instead of being marched to *Kommandant* Höss, they were taken in the opposite direction, where they were stripped and scrubbed by a rough, heavy-handed female Kapo. They were then marched naked, without explanation, to a building they knew well. It was their work station, piled high with clothing, shoes, and stacks of empty suitcases.

They were trembling with fear and cold, certain the numbers tattooed on their forearms had finally been called, when they were ordered to dress. They were told to pack a small bag, and suddenly their confusion birthed the tiniest shred of hope. Had Milo come for them?

"Choose anything you like . . . nothing drab . . . something colorful," they were told.

"We are not Jews," Sophie said to the guard, pointing to the yellow Star of David that had been sewn onto every piece of clothing. Of course, she had no bigotry toward the Jewish people. She had worn the Star of David defiantly with her Zazou friends in solidarity with them. She had since learned the dangerous reality of being forced to wear the insignia.

"It's all the same for you now," the guard sneered.

Sophie chose a cherry-red dress with wide white lapels, and she realized her passion for fashion was long gone.

Frivolous, ridiculous, she thought, though she longed for a time when she'd been blind enough to the darkness of the world that such things could matter.

The dress hung on her bony frame, but the long sleeves and skirt disguised her skeletal arms and legs. There was no mirror, but she didn't desire one. Sophie looked at her mother, dressed in a dark-green wool suit with a white ruffled blouse, and she felt tears in her eyes for the first time in months. The pretty clothes could not disguise the trauma that had ravaged them; it was made only more obvious. They chose hats, and were reminded of scarecrows, with tufts of straw hair poking out, standing in the fields, pretending to be something they were not.

As they were marshaled to the exit, Sophie looked across the mud at the barracks where she'd languished for so long. She felt a glimmer of relief that she was leaving, and guilt filled her. How could she hope for herself? How could she leave them behind? Who would barter food for them now?

The women were loaded into a smelly, empty railcar, still wet from being recently hosed out. A small pile of mothy blankets had been thrown in as a last consideration, to assure their "comfort." An armed SS guard traveled the nearly three hundred miles to Bohemia with them. He was clearly annoyed at the detail he'd pulled, and he alternately ignored or glared at them. Inside the car, there was a bucket for toileting and a generous basket for the prisoners containing water, meats, bread, cheese, fruit, and pastries, as if they could be fattened up in one short journey. As if they were human once again.

Chapter 23

The Skin-and-Bones Blanket

Czechoslovakia, 1945

Milo was amazed. He had expected a confrontation with Kammler, but it had not come. Kammler, though enraged, had temporarily returned to Berlin; and once there, he had arranged for Blanc's family to be temporarily transferred to a camp just outside of Prague. Helghul knew he was running out of time. He needed Theron to cooperate, and as much as he resented Milo's demands, it was in his best interest to comply quickly. He would unleash his anger later, once the Bell was operational.

Milo was pleased. He had achieved his goal of being, at least briefly, reunited with his wife and daughter.

I should have insisted sooner! he thought. *I was a fool! I had the leverage all along. I should have realized that.*

The Theresienstadt camp was touted as a center where highly valued political prisoners—Jewish writers, artists, and musicians— had all been gathered. Milo was led to believe that his wife and daughter had always been there, comfortable and close by, waiting to return to Paris. A propaganda film had featured Theresienstadt as proof to the Red Cross that all was as it should be, though in truth, *nothing* was as it should be.

Theresienstadt's *Kommandant* Rahm had spoken personally with Kammler regarding the arrival of the Blanc women and the importance of Milo's visit. Rahm was an expert at creating false impressions of the work camp, but he was nervous. Kammler was powerful and terrifying to even the most hardened Nazis. He must be sure it went well. It was rare to have such a high-ranking official take an interest in individual prisoners; they tended to deal more in the tens of thousands than twos. It made slightly more sense when Rahm discovered that the Blanc women weren't subhuman Jews. They were French—not equal to German, but still superior to Jews, in his warped opinion.

It was a terrible mistake bringing Milo near Theresienstadt. Even from miles away, Theron could feel the sickening energy of the place. It was heavy, desperate, and so full of darkness. The fortress, standing since the 1780s, had been repurposed by the Nazis as a prison ghetto in 1941. If Milo's resolve had been weak, just approaching this place would have fortified it.

To ensure the best impression for Blanc, a wooden table covered with a crisp white linen cloth with pretty flowers embroidered on the edges sat surrounded by three wooden chairs. It had been laid out with a picnic on the banks of the River Ohre, outside the brick walls of the camp. Sophie and Madame Blanc were seated and waiting when Milo's car arrived.

The women stood, and Blanc's first thought was that there had been a mistake. They must have brought the wrong women. *Mais, non!* This was a different version of his Sophie. The effervescent young daughter he had known was gone. Her high pompadour Zazou hair was shorn, and only tufts were visible under her hat. Her rosy cheeks and red lipstick had been replaced by sickly grey skin and fearful eyes. She looked too old to be his little girl, too thin and frail.

"Papa!" she called to him, and they rushed into each other's arms. Madame Blanc joined them and held on tightly. Her husband . . . her daughter . . . and a picnic in the sun—she hadn't dreamed it possible only a week ago.

If the Dark Age had not been so dense, everyone for miles would have witnessed the astounding indigo-and-white shine swirling around Sophie and Milo as the two Emissaries, Theron and Yashoda, connected.

Kisses, tears, and more kisses; they hugged one another until a guard forced them to let go.

"Sit! Sit! This lunch has a time limit," the guard shouted roughly, his Adversary shine cloaking him in layers of grey. Madame Blanc and Sophie sat immediately, like kicked dogs, and Milo was dismayed by the intensity of their fear.

Though the auras of the Emissaries were imperceptible to the soldier, he scowled and rolled his head on his neck as tension pooled there. He was thoroughly irritated by the lightness of Milo and Sophie's combined shines invading him, and he wanted this lunch to be over as soon as possible.

Sophie and her mother had been threatened by *Kommandant* Rahm earlier that morning.

"Make the father happy. No complaints or stories to burden him. You understand?" he had said. *Happy?* It had been so long since happy was an option that Madame Blanc thought it impossible, but she kept her mouth shut.

Rahm was now watching through binoculars from the high walls. The guard had been told to intervene immediately if the women said anything that undermined Milo's cooperation with the Reich.

The women understood that they were pawns, and they did not wish to burden Milo. Nor did they wish to deceive him. Afraid the guards might cut their visit short if they suspected an honest transfer of information, Sophie made her face as light as possible as they talked. Madame Blanc was less able to hide her emotions. She held hands with her husband and sobbed into his shoulder.

"Have they hurt you? What has happened to you?" Milo asked.

"We're fine, Papa," Sophie lied. But she knew she had to get him a message as covertly and quickly as possible. She didn't know how much time they had. It was clear to Sophie that her father was important to the Reich, or they would not be there. *They will not save us,* she wanted him to know. Whether he acted for the Nazis now or not, she did not want him to falsely believe that any of them would be spared beyond their usefulness. She had witnessed the darkness in the enemies' hearts. She had lived in the midst of their unfathomable inhumanity. *Do not imagine you can make a deal with the Devil. Le Diable will win!* Sophie thought, her Catholic upbringing remembered.

"Tell me, how have you been treated?" Milo asked, not wanting to believe his own eyes. He wanted to hear better than he saw.

"You are a beautiful lie, and I am the painful truth," she whispered, still smiling. Her angular jaw creased her skin, with only deep pockets where her cheeks should have been. She was hoping he would recall their conversation, hoping that, all this time later, he would understand her as she quoted Molière back to him. Milo *did* remember. He had thought of their conversation many times.

Death, Molière had said, was the painful truth. She is telling me that my hope for her is misguided. They are as good as dead, Milo realized with horror, comprehending her hidden message. Milo's eyes clouded, his emotions plain. Sophie saw that he understood.

"*Non,* my dear, I am almost finished. We will have our lives back soon," Milo said.

"Man's greatest weakness is his love for life," Sophie replied, and she added, "I no longer have *that* weakness." With the guard watching them suspiciously, confused by their nonsensical French chatter, Milo could only listen without protest.

Sophie no longer loved life. Life was hard, brutal, and ugly. She no longer feared death, and she certainly didn't want Milo to help the Germans save her. There were worse things than death.

He felt tears, but he held them back. He stared at the wasted versions of his wife and child and tried to smile to ease their suffering. The rebellious, life-loving nature of his daughter had been irreparably destroyed. As much as he wanted to, Milo could not sweep the bone piles into his arms and make them healthy again. He could not turn back time.

It was then that his wife seemed to come back to them. She found some piece of her former self and directed him confidently, as she often would have done.

"Be the man you have always been, *mon cher*. Nothing more, nothing less," she said.

"Do not worry, *mes chères*, do not worry," Milo said, hugging them closely.

The lunch ended too soon—it had barely been an hour, and the Nazi soldier was relieved to see them all go.

"Resist, Papa!" Sophie the Emissary whispered, barely audibly, as they hugged for the last time. The guards pried them apart, for not one of the three would willingly let go. The ladies were herded through the gates of Theresienstadt beneath letters reading *"Arbeit Macht Frei"*—work sets you free—more lies, more illusion. The same words were on the gates of Auschwitz-Birkenau.

Milo stumbled to his waiting car. He called back to them, reassuring them they would meet again, though none of them believed that beautiful lie.

Kammler was waiting for Milo when he returned to the lab later that day. Germany was being devastated by the Allies, and the success of Kammler's scientific initiatives would mean the difference between victory and defeat. Helghul was determined to put Theron back to work and ensure triumph. The Emissary had been manipulated before. In her lifetime as Aristotle, she had told Helghul where to find the Emerald Tablet. In her lifetime as Borte, she had been his faithful wife and empress. Helghul had come to think of Theron as a tool to be carefully used; he still believed she had made a mistake choosing Marcus.

"You saw your women?" Kammler said.

"I did."

"They are well?"

"They're alive."

"And they will be, as long as you cooperate. You will finish your work, and your family will return to France. I have no more patience for your delays," Kammler said.

Milo nodded, feigning belief. He was no longer blinded. The Tablet had lifted the illusory veil of maya and had ended Theron's lack of understanding in this lifetime.

"Tomorrow we will be ready for liftoff," Milo said.

The Bell had been ready to go since Milo had demanded to see his family. He had no doubt the machine would work. It was simple science and engineering.

It is the crystal that made it possible, not me, Milo thought humbly.

Kammler was thrilled, but he did not show his pleasure.

Sophie thought about her afternoon with her father. He had looked worried, and his hair was streaked prematurely grey. She had tried to appear brave and strong, but she hadn't been able to ease the shock of her physical transformation.

By the end of the week, they would be transferred back to Auschwitz. The cattle car would be jammed full again, bursting with innocent victims who had already been through so much and who had no idea that a deeper layer of hell awaited them. Sophie didn't think she had the strength to endure the horrifying journey a second time.

She laid down for the night in Theresienstadt, her mother behind her and a newcomer in front. The new girl was only seven and had been separated from her parents. She was terrified, and Sophie hugged her close, comforting her as best she could.

Sophie's hip bones ached as she lay on the cold wooden plank. She whispered and sang to the distraught child in low, melodic tones until her breath became even and calm. Together they fell asleep, the older girl enfolding the younger.

Sophie never woke. She had kept the child warm through the night, but at the end of her life, she was reduced to a skin-and-bones blanket. The Emissary Yashoda's spirit was free. Her consciousness lifted out of her dead body and floated over to her mother. Yashoda stroked Madame Blanc's cheek and kissed her softly on the forehead before passing on to the Meadow. There, the Emissary was reunited with loved ones who had passed before her, and her spirit was welcomed by the many souls she had cared for during the Nazi siege. Sophie was gone, and when her death was discovered in the morning, there was only the sobbing of her desperate mother and a confused child.

A clipboard marked Sophie Blanc absent—scratch, scratch, scratch. Her body was pulled out of Madame Blanc's arms with a slap to the mother's head. A clipboard marked her: deceased. A clipboard noted the place and date, as a gravestone would have done in a humane, sane time. Madame Blanc never returned to Auschwitz. She survived only four days beyond her daughter. She lived three days past the day when the final trial of the Bell Project was to commence.

Chapter 24

The Resistance

After the reunion with his wife and daughter, sleep did not come. Milo's tears closed his throat, and his head ached with grief upon seeing the dying, emaciated pair. Their bones had stretched their skin like tentpoles forcing up gossamer.

Milo looked at his hands. He had never thought about fingers and the fat that plumped them out. He thought of it now. His wife's and daughter's hands had felt fragile and brittle, like dead branches fallen beneath the trees in Luxembourg Gardens. They had picnicked there, with better bread, wine, and cheese than they'd shared that day at Theresienstadt. They hadn't been prisoners then. Sophie's eyes had been excited and hopeful, and

Madame Blanc had been beautiful, elegant, and refined. They had changed inside and out. It seemed like so very long ago.

Milo knew they were dying. He was unable to save them, or save himself, but he was far from useless. Theron's purpose was urgent and unambiguous. The profound download from the Emerald Tablet, and the tragic state of his loved ones, allowed Milo absolute clarity.

The Emissary had an advantage Kammler had not counted on. Theron was self-aware—awakened—and her knowledge of being an Emissary brought with it compassion and unconditional love for the whole. Helghul assumed that self-preservation was too important, and because of it, he underestimated Milo.

⚬⚬⚬ ⚬⚬⚬ ⚬⚬⚬

The Bell was being moved the next morning through tunnels that had been carved into acres of hillside toward the town of Ludwigsdorf near the old Wenceslas mine. There, waiting in anticipation, was a circular launch site of ten standing stones resembling an ancient henge.

The Nazis had used slave labor to extend miles of tunnels, and the extensive passages were able to transport the Bell unnoticed beneath the Earth, avoiding Allied reconnaissance.

Milo had taken stock of all the materials stored within the compound, and his scientific expertise recognized dangers that the Nazis' inexpert minds had overlooked. Ammonium nitrate used by the miners as they expanded the tunnel system was being stored on wooden crates in the deep corridors, the same corridors through which the Bell would pass the next day.

On its own, ammonium nitrate was stable, but with aviation fuel mixed with oil and a spark, he could cause a collapse. A collapse onto the ammonium nitrate, if heavy enough, would create a large shock wave that would explode with the power of twenty thousand pounds of TNT.

>=< >=< >=<

To Milo's relief, all the scientists and engineers were vacating the lab, having been ordered to the launch site to witness the glory of the Reich's greatest invention, along with Kammler.

The Bell rested on an open-bed trailer-truck ready to transport. The loaded truck began its journey through the large tunnel. In some spots, there were only two feet of clearance on either side. The guard driving the vehicle and his passenger were soaked with sweat. They knew their lives depended on the Bell's safe passage. Any slight mistake would more than likely result in their execution.

Suddenly, up ahead, there was smoke filling the tube, blocking their vision and eating the oxygen. The methodical procession stopped, and calm was replaced with urgency.

Before dawn that day, Milo had arrived at the lab and had begun the walk through the tunnel toward the launch site.

"*Herr* professor, you can't go there," the sentry said, and he and his drowsy partner blocked the way.

"I am taking measurements and making final preparations in the tunnel for the passage of the Bell. If I do not complete my work, the demonstration will be delayed. Would you wake *Kommandant Docteur* Kammler at this hour to get permission for me to do my job?" Milo asked.

The soldiers had no scientific understanding to draw upon. Milo might very well have important preparations to complete. The soldiers were swayed. The last thing they wanted to do was annoy Kammler. They let Milo pass.

Milo had stashed a battery with a timer within the wooden ammonium nitrate crates to allow enough time to clear the compound. The battery did its job, creating a spark, and as it did so, the aviation gas-and-oil mixture he had placed beneath, ignited. The flames under the ammonium nitrate heated it, changing its molecular structure and making it highly combustible.

The fire blocked forward progression through the tunnel, toward the launch site.

"Back up! Watch out!" the passenger shouted to the driver, but thick, black smoke had filled the tunnel, and as he shifted the truck into reverse, the trailer turned slightly, just enough, and it was stuck. He could drive forward into the fire, but reversing was impossible.

The guards ran into the smoke but returned, coughing and choking.

Milo hadn't wanted anyone killed by his sabotage. He had timed the fire perfectly, but the soldiers guarding the lab that morning did not flee, as Milo had hoped; they didn't dare. Even as the guards who had been driving the truck came sputtering and panting into the lab, the other guards rallied fire stations and returned to the smoke-filled tunnel with sand and water pails in hand.

"Fire!" Milo heard as the radio message reached Kammler, who was standing near him at the launch site. Kammler's eyes immediately flew to him, and Milo feigned surprise.

"What have you done?" Kammler roared at Milo. Helghul could see Theron's energy swirling, and though Milo shook his head innocently, Helghul knew better.

If the Emissary was successful, the laboratory would be destroyed with not only the Bell but all the other prototypes within. However, the sublime Emerald Tablet would, unfortunately, remain with Kammler. Milo had not been able to configure any plan in which he could take control of it. The most he could hope for was that the explosion would set the Nazis far enough back to give the Allies an opportunity to prevail.

The trapped Bell was only twenty feet from the flames as they expanded, burning deathly hot and entirely filling the area. The fire rapidly heated the small droplets of water trapped within the rock ceiling above it, turning it to steam. As Milo had intended, the steam put immense pressure on the rock, forcing fissures and shards to begin breaking off. A large fragment dropped onto the highly unstable, flaming ammonium nitrate, causing an enormous and devastating shock wave and a massive explosion.

The blast rippled through the entire subterranean complex, reaching its full potential—equal to twenty thousand pounds of TNT; and wiping out every hangar, work station, and prototype, just as Milo had hoped. The rockets and other fuel that had been stored inside added to the chaos, and the ground where Kammler, Milo, and the others were standing, shook. Flames burst from the tunnel exit, and the boom was deafening for those waiting at the launch site.

"I can't hear!" a man near Milo yelled. Scientists and soldiers were shouting and disoriented. The sound of the blast was so loud that their ears hurt, and some lost their balance falling to the ground; their equilibrium was discombobulated. Had they been attacked? Had the Allies discovered the secret complex somehow, knowing that it was launch day?

The lab was destroyed. Milo had maneuvered the scientists and engineers away from the flames, but many Nazi soldiers died inside.

I am death, and life is a beautiful lie, Milo thought sadly.

Kammler radioed for contact, desperate for an update. He wanted the status of the Bell, but there was nothing. There was no one left to answer his calls.

"Collapsed. Nothing left," an SS officer radioed from outside, observing the rubble and massive hole that had once been a fine manor house and the entrance to the hidden caverns.

Blind with rage, the Beast's darkest tendencies overtook Kammler.

He did this! Foolish human, the Beast hissed inside his head. His pistol was already drawn, and he cracked Milo across the face with it.

"Line them up!" Kammler shouted to the SS officer.

It only took a minute. While thick black smoke continued to pour from the tunnel, sixty-seven baffled, terrified scientists and engineers were placed in a long row in front of the standing stones that had been rigged with ropes and pulleys to help launch the

Bell prototype. The men and three women, Milo among them, stared at Kammler. The general began shooting.

"Blame Blanc!" he shouted as he shot, stopping to reload many times. Kammler's outrage at losing the Bell overtook him. As happened more and more often in the Dark Age, the Beast's homicidal instincts reigned over Helghul. Killing the scientists was far from the smartest plan; it was an angry, vengeful act.

One by one, he ruthlessly murdered the innocents who stood crying and shaking. He paused between kills to look at Milo. The terrified people sobbed and begged, clamping their eyes shut and hoping Kammler would stop, praying his cruelty would run out before reaching their spot in line.

The Beast within Kammler fed on the fear exhibited by those in the lineup, and he expected Milo to exhibit his own regret, fear, and sadness, but the Emissary's eyes and surrounding shine reflected compassion, peace, and acceptance. The touch, the download of information from the Emerald Tablet, had been enough to remind Theron of the truth. The treasure still within its golden box now sat in a leather haversack at Kammler's feet.

When the rest were dead, Kammler turned to Milo, who spoke softly.

"Poor Helghul," Milo said, and the Adversary and the Beast realized that Milo had somehow regained his Theron-memory.

"I told you to call me Black Elder!" Kammler said, shooting Milo through the right eye with absolutely no feeling for Theron.

Theron's shine expanded across the grounds, sharing energy with three or four other ethereal souls who, confused by having been so suddenly and violently torn from their bodies, were slow to depart and hovered above their corpses. She helped the few who were unable to accept that their bodies were dead by wrapping their lingering souls in her energy. Theron swept them up with her, taking them back to the Meadow and home into the Light.

The Emissary had done her duty. The Bell had been destroyed. Without the Emerald Tablet–powered secret weapon, the Nazis had been neutralized and had no chance of defeating the Allies' advance, but Helghul was far from beaten.

Kammler's allegiance was to no specific country. His Helghul-memory rendered nationalism, along with racism and sexism, ridiculous, since he knew he could be reborn as anyone, anywhere. His purpose as Black Elder would be fulfilled, uniting the Adversaries and engaging in further chaos and darkness, wherever he was.

When news of surrender and Hitler's suicide reached him, Kammler had already regrouped and launched his Plan B.

Chapter 25

Plan B

Argentina, 1945

The Argentinean hosts stood in formation on the dock, looking out across the calm bay, waiting. The water rippled silver in the sunshine as three U-boats breached the surface. Water washed over their finlike conning towers, and once clear, Kammler climbed the ladder into the upper control room. The electric motors were turned off and set to charge as the noisy diesel engines kicked in.

Permission to land in Argentina had been financially guaranteed, and later that evening, President Perón welcomed Kammler personally, surrounded by his military.

"General, I hope your journey was pleasant."

"I prefer aeronautics over sea travel," Kammler replied stiffly, shaking Perón's hand. "Is everything prepared?"

Kammler did not display the deference to which Perón was accustomed, and the German's presumptuous, demanding manner in the face of his stature and generosity irked the president. Perón hid his displeasure and answered with a polite smile.

"I will provide everything you've asked for: funds, supplies, and access to the best scientists available," Perón promised.

"Germans?"

"Of course. There are many here to choose from."

"*Sehr gut*, great."

"What about the Americans? They have a vested interest in these scientists. What will I tell them?" Perón asked, his eyes glowing with ambition.

"Fuck the Americans," Kammler said, reading his desire. "We have done far more for you than the Americans ever would. I am a man without a country. Argentina will reap the benefits of any gains I make. Who do you think will benefit from an accord with the Americans?"

Perón grinned, amused by their illicit agreement. His initial distaste for Kammler was forgotten.

"Come, let's eat and drink and enjoy the splendor of Buenos Aires. Tomorrow we will talk business," said Perón.

Perón was disappointed by Kammler's unwillingness to join the party. The general sat dully at the opulent club table, separating himself from the singing, dancing, and conversation. He was biding his time until he could excuse himself without insulting his hosts.

"These Germans are wound so tightly, it chokes out all the fun," Perón complained to his young wife, Eva, while they danced. She agreed, and the newlyweds gave their guest no further thought that night.

Kammler had just finished his third scotch and stood to leave when he saw a familiar face approaching him from across the dance floor. He could not believe it. Even with her hair cut short and wearing tinted glasses, he knew her immediately. He had believed the woman dead.

"Is *he* with you?" Kammler asked hopefully.

"*Ja!* Come with me, Hans," the attractive blonde with the little mouth replied in German.

"They said you were dead," he said, following her in anticipation of a momentous reunion.

"I heard the same of you . . . convenient, *ja*?" She smiled.

It was an hour's drive to their secluded bungalow. Once they were alone in her car, the woman explained how she and her husband had escaped from Germany.

"The plan was set long ago, just in case," she finished. "This entire area is German now . . . our new colony," she said lightly, with a smile. Kammler was confounded. Why had he not known of the plan? Why had he been left out of the escape?

The home in the countryside was small but elegant, with a long gravel drive, a large vegetable garden, and flowers planted in beds. As they approached, Kammler saw the guards on the outer portico of the home leaning at ease. The men were dressed in plain clothes, with their rifles slung across their backs. They smoked cigarettes, then merely nodded politely as the woman and Kammler entered.

The home was decorated with antique furnishings, and as Kammler followed, winding his way to the back parlor, his stomach fluttered with excitement.

Adolf Hitler sat there, his starched white linen shirt buttoned to the neck. His appearance and demeanor were as they had been in Berlin. He had made no effort to alter or hide his identity, though he looked more relaxed, and his suntan made his blue eyes glow.

Hitler felt no need to portray himself to Kammler as he did to the outside world: intense and neurotic. Instead, he embodied inner peace and confidence only Helghul knew to be his true nature.

"*Heil* Hitler!" Kammler saluted, and the Beast within him recognized his evil ally and was pleased.

"Welcome, Hans. Thank you, Eva. Leave us to talk business," Hitler said without rising from the tropical print chaise longue. The comrades watched her with admiration as she gracefully exited.

"Grey Elder, sir, it's a relief you're here," Kammler said once she was gone. It would be easier for him to achieve his goal with his mentor by his side.

"Helghul, surely you didn't believe the reports I had committed suicide?" Hitler said.

"*Nein*, but I was concerned of reports of your death, since I did not hear from you," he replied, hinting at his dissatisfaction at having been kept in the dark.

"I was delighted to read reports of your uncertain death and disappearance only ten days after my own. Here, have a drink. It has fresh mint; it is quite refreshing," the Elder said, nodding to the chair in the corner.

"*Danke*," Kammler said. "Eva explained your route, but how did you escape undetected?" Kammler inquired.

"I see your displeasure though you try to mask it. Perhaps feeling abandoned, hey?" Hitler said, pausing. The mentor's face changed, and he looked irritably at Helghul. "The student learns nothing if the teacher solves his problems."

Kammler's jaw unclenched as he considered the Elder's words. Grey Elder had led the Adversaries throughout the Ages; Helghul need not worry. Together, they would rebuild the Reich.

"Now, listen. I have news! The entrance has been found," Hitler said. Kammler knew immediately what he meant.

"Has anyone explored the tunnel?"

"They shuttled supplies in as deep as they could. The last unit never returned. They await your arrival. The discovery is nothing without our knowledge . . . and without the Emerald Tablet."

"When do we leave?"

"Not 'we'—*you*. This is your command," Hitler said.

Late into the night, the men plotted their next scheme.

It was the first lifetime since the fall of Atitala that Grey Elder had taken the spotlight rather than Helghul. Ideally, the Elder preferred to work behind the scenes, letting Helghul rise to power and draw the attention. This time, Grey Elder had shouldered most of the attention while Kammler flew under the radar, expanding the conflict and hatred that was ripe in the world. It had worked—almost—however, discord had grown among the Adversaries; they were not united. Without memory, they were self-interested, nationalistic, and intolerant, thinking themselves superior to others. Separateness and selfishness filled them, and their individual desires for power tore them apart. Grey Elder knew he would have to appeal to their greed and egos to organize them.

Unlike the Adversaries, the Emissaries instinctively acknowledged the artifice of national borders and had no intrinsic thirst for power over others. Across the globe, they were rebuilding hope and chronicling the horrors of the previous decades, determined that through education and compassion, history's errors would not be repeated. They were united, but their unity seemed wholly insufficient to combat the weapons and torture Grey Elder intended to unleash.

Chapter 26

Operation Highjump

Antarctica, 1946

"We know high-ranking Germans are fleeing Europe. We have intel that Kammler is one of them. We lost track of him after he arrived in Argentina, and no one has seen him in months, but I just received news he's headed to Antarctica," Admiral Byrd said to his captain.

It was just as Hermann Göring had predicted when Byrd interviewed him.

"Goddamn Perón, housing all those Nazi bastards! Why Antarctica? Hiding?" the captain speculated from the seat across from Byrd.

"Most likely they have a well-stocked base. Reconnaissance says he has serious brainpower with him. We're heading down. Our mission is to locate those German scientists and destroy their base. We need to take Kammler alive, and if possible, take control of whatever weapons they're developing," Admiral Byrd said.

"No problem. That won't take long."

"They've been annexing the South Pole for decades. There's no telling what we'll find. Assume we're in for a helluva battle."

Byrd turned toward the horizon, and within him, his Marcus-consciousness was tired and desperately frustrated by the political and religious strife that had been tearing humankind apart for centuries. World War II had ended, but he knew the battle to over-power the Adversaries was far from over.

Chapter 27

The Arya

Antarctica, 1946

Dispersed among the myriad of tunnels radiating out from Inner Earth's central sun, the Arya were contemplating "the human problem." The slender creatures hovered without touching the ground and were translucent and humanoid, with no discernible gender. Their skin was transparent, and under the surface, effervescent blue energy flowed through their veins.

It was the Arya who had first discovered the properties and uses for atlantium that they shared with humans of Outer Earth during the Golden Age. However, through the dense Silver, Bronze, and Iron Ages of Outer Earth, humans could not be trusted to wield the power of atlantium; and the Arya had no communication with their unconscious Earth-mates. The humans had recently become a growing threat to the peaceful existence of the Arya and the planet they shared.

It was a conference of the Inner Earthlings' council. They had no king, emperor, or designated leader, nor did the physical distance between them hinder their communication. All the inhabitants were equal, without any need for hierarchy or central government, and they did not communicate in a manner humans would understand or even detect. They were aware that they shared one consciousness. From their locations speckled along miles of coiled caverns, they spoke through mental vibrations and shared understanding. Information was passed among them at the speed of thought, across vast distances, like starlings murmuring. They channeled millions of voices, but ultimately, they were of one mind communicated by the Council of One.

There was no illusion of separation among the Arya, and consensus was assured since all decisions were made in the interest of the greater good. Had they been limited to verbal language, their interactions would have sounded as if every thought, idea, and possibility had been spoken in chorus. The considerations went something like this:

The humans have entered the northern tunnel.
The Guardians will respond.
These humans have information about what lies beneath.
They are no threat to us, in or out. The humans have yet to realize their purpose.
They are in a war-obsessed Age.
We are not their judge.

The Arya were so thoroughly entangled with one another that they were able to process waves of information, simultaneously.

The Elementals warn that the planet might first be destroyed.
Mother Earth must be protected.
The awakening comes.
We all feel compassion for the humans at this time.

The Willowy Man appeared through a portal within the solid rock wall, and he spoke as he emerged from its opening, entering their reality from another dimension.

The humans have the Emerald Tablet with them, the Tunnel-Keeper said.

Shall we intervene?

Intervene?

Intervene? The question echoed among the Arya.

Chapter 28

The Council of One

Outer Earth, South Pole

Only a few hundred miles separated Kammler and Byrd as they crossed the Drake Passage below the tip of South America and entered the Antarctic ice field. Once again, Marcus's and Helghul's destinies would intersect.

Admiral Byrd's official mission was to fortify American claims in Antarctica; however, his actual directive was to retrieve the Nazi high commanders and any scientists they might be harboring, then wipe out any remaining German bases. Byrd's fleet was comprised of thirteen ships, ice breakers, seaplane tenders, one aircraft carrier, dozens of planes, helicopters, and a submarine. The Task Force Commander was Rear Admiral Richard Cruzen, a forty-nine-year-old navy man with the experience and confidence to command the nearly forty-seven-hundred men under him.

Byrd had liked Cruzen immediately. He was collaborative and intelligent, but more than that, he was a fellow Emissary. Bapoo had been a friend to Marcus in Atitala, and Byrd had been thrilled to recognize his shine emanating from Cruzen. Trusting was a difficult thing to do. Recognizing an ally allowed Byrd to lower his guard. It was a relief, when so many of Marcus's years had been spent feeling isolated. Together, the combined energy of the men was intense, and the sailors under their command were rightfully awed.

The swells were massive, and the steel ships were tossed, crossing the strait. Byrd and Cruzen navigated through several hundred miles of ice blocks and icebergs. Beneath the surface, an American submarine was up ahead, periscope up, silent and searching. Breaking through the ice took longer than expected, and more than once the ships were in danger of sinking. The twelve various icebreakers and battleships accompanying them broke from formation and spread across a two-hundred-mile stretch. Like a large fishnet, they combed the waters as they positioned themselves to attack. The icebreakers led the battleships, setting a careful course around the bergs. One wrong move and a ship could be torn open like a tin can.

Upon reaching their intended destination, they found that the location wasn't much more than a superficial claim on the continent. The stars and stripes had been planted, but there was not much else there. The American base, dubbed Little America, was too far away from this location to be helpful.

Bulldozers were unloaded, along with more than fifty dogs and ten sleds. A tent city was erected for the forty-seven-hundred-man force. They began digging a runway while the reconnaissance planes were fixed with skis that would allow them to take off and land.

An extensive temporary base was established, accomplishing the first of Byrd's three tasks for this mission. Now there was only the monumental task of finding and destroying the German head-quarters without killing all the scientists.

The Emissary had his own mission. He suspected the Nazis, under an Adversary agenda, had come to Antarctica in search of the atlantium he and Helghul knew lay miles beneath the conti-nent. Marcus knew he had to prevent Iron Age people from find-ing Inner Earth, especially Helghul.

Most of their reconnaissance was done by aerial photographs, and Cruzen and Byrd were alone in the meeting room adjoining his quarters, studying the images.

"The photographs themselves don't reflect increased activity. We suspect that they are tunneling under the ice. We don't know how many troops they have, or how well provisioned they are, but these shots indicate at least three U-boats in the area. We have to assume they are a considerable presence and may still be develop-ing atomic weapons," Byrd said.

"Is it possible *he's* here?" Cruzen asked, not wanting to sound ridiculous. There was speculation that Hitler hadn't killed himself in his Berlin bunker. It was possible the bodies burned in haste on April 30, 1945, by his closest allies had been nothing more than a dramatic show. The Russians said they discovered his corpse, but no evidence had yet been offered.

"We won't know until we go in. This is their last stronghold, and they'll resist with everything they have," Byrd said, and the men saluted each other respectfully.

The Germans had been developing Neuschwabenland on the Queen Maud peninsula since the late 1930s, and the extent of their development in Antarctica was far beyond anything the Americans could see in surface photos. Neuschwabenland looked like a small settlement; however, as Byrd suspected, they had tun-neled deep underneath the ice and created an extensive base with a large population and stockpiles of weapons and ammunition. The base housed hundreds of soldiers as well as various engineers, climate specialists, and enough supplies to carry them through the next five years. One good thing about working in the ice envi-ronment was that it was a natural refrigerator.

Kammler's Helghul-memory knew the atlantium that allowed for antigravitational flight had been transferred to Inner Earth before the fall of Atitala. As a young boy, Helghul had seen the thousands of advanced flying discs, warehoused and idle, on the outskirts of Inner Earth. For Kammler, the war was far from over, and world domination was still his goal.

Hitler and Kammler had initiated missions searching for the elusive entrance to Inner Earth, hoping to exploit its advanced technology and resources. Finally, the entrance had been discovered. Just one of those flying discs could turn their loss around. Scientists would deconstruct it from top to bottom, allowing for mass production. Their goal of world domination could then be realized.

⨯⨯⨯ ⨯⨯⨯ ⨯⨯⨯

Byrd had returned to his perch with his bitter coffee in hand. He stared out across Ross Bay from the tower island, high at the center of the aircraft-carrier flight deck. A rescue helicopter hovered at starboard. The chopper was the eyes of the fleet, while flight squadrons remained poised to launch at a moment's notice.

"Sir," the sonar officer suddenly said, his ear pressed to his gear, "I have something."

"Is it one of ours?" the Officer of the Deck (OOD) asked.

"No, sir, not this time. We don't have anything in that location."

"Notifying the admiral," the OOD said.

"Aye, notifying the admiral," the radioman replied.

Byrd had just received word of the possible U-boat presence when they were fired upon.

"Torpedo in the water!"

"Torpedo in the water!"

"Man battle stations!" the OOD commanded.

"Aye! Man battle stations!" the helmsman repeated.

Sirens pealed as the American sub sustained a hit, and sailors scrambled to their posts to manage the damage. One compartment was flooding, but crews were quick to respond, and the destruction was manageable. Had the torpedo exploded under the keel, they would have been sunk.

"Under fire!" the radioman transmitted. The OOD was dangling from the rigging above his head to avoid being tossed. The submarine was blasted for a second time, and the direct hit tore open a large hole. The vessel was now breaching at a sharp angle. Loss of vessel and crew was imminent. The rescue skiffs were launched into the icy water to gather the struggling survivors. Eight minutes in the water would mean certain death.

⋈ ⋈ ⋈

The Nazis were relying on their strategic embankment and the element of surprise to overpower the Americans and delay their arrival.

A week earlier, when Kammler had arrived, he had been taken to the newly discovered tunnel. Decades of German searching had only barely missed the mark, but now after years of drilling and tunneling, the entrance to Inner Earth was finally laid bare. They had uncovered miles of ice.

The tunnel was massive; it had originally been created so the Aryan vimana could easily come and go from Inner Earth. The exit had not been used in hundreds of thousands of years.

The floor of the tunnel was rough, but with good trucks, the terrain was maneuverable. Kammler would send in 4x4 all-terrain vehicles to carry his soldiers, but the tunnel was large enough so that Kammler would use the Flettner FL 282 Kolibri helicopter to enter. It was a small, single- or double-seater, with outstanding speed and control—the best in the world. The *kommandant* had arranged for three of the helicopters to be brought to the cave's entrance. He had ordered the trucks and supplies he needed to begin transporting toward Inner Earth, and a platoon had set up camp about a week's distance inside the cave. They saw no sign of their missing comrades.

When Kammler left to finally began his journey toward Inner Earth, he left instructions that the Americans must not be permitted land-side at any cost. Kammler left the following morning. The helicopters entered one after another, and Kammler took the middle launch position. The Adversary estimated that, without any major delays, it would take at least a month for him to reach his goal. The helicopters and troops were heavily armed, but only Helghul knew what awaited them in the caves.

><><><

"Launch fighters!" Byrd ordered, and in turn, two waiting planes were catapulted along the thirty-foot runway of the USS *Philippine Sea*, into the crisp blue sky. Thick plumes of exhaust trailed behind them.

Rescue operations in the frigid waters were complicated by the ongoing battle. Scoping through binoculars, Byrd saw the faces of the men struggling for survival. There were small-vessel rescue operations ongoing while the guns and torpedoes continued to fire. The men worked diligently, pulling their comrades from the icy ocean.

"We're hit. Repeat, we are hit!"

"Confirm, USS *Constitution* is hit."

"Confirm, USS *Constitution* is hit."

"Report damage."

"Aye, report damage." The radio crackled as the degree of damage was ascertained. Radio contact frantically continued among the ships and copters, and there was no break in the sound of artillery fire.

Kammler's remaining U-boats evaded Byrd's fleet submerged in nearby bays, maneuvering around icebergs. Kammler had hundreds of soldiers, camouflaged in white parkas, who were shooting with heavy artillery and antiaircraft guns from blinds dug into the ice shelf and leading to the extensive ice bunkers.

One of the American fighter planes was hit, and flames engulfed the wing.

"Bail out! Bail out!" the pilot yelled to his wingman, but there was no time. The plane crashed into the rock face above the shooters, and the Germans braced as an avalanche buried the soldiers embedded below.

Byrd saw the plane strike. The pilots were fathers, brothers, and sons, and they had made it through two wars only to die on the frozen coastline. Byrd's Marcus-consciousness understood that death was illusory, but grief was not. They would have no heroic death tale. Their top-secret mission meant that their deaths would be logged as accidental. Nazi-hunting in Antarctica? He couldn't tell their families that.

Black smoke billowed into the sky, and missiles filled the air. The entrenched Germans connected once again, and one of Byrd's six helicopters exploded in midair, scattering in flames across the snow and ice. More family members . . . more inadequate explanations. Marcus hated this Age. The waste and sadness of war made no sense to the Emissary.

The American destroyers continued to blast the ice shelf, hitting the troops concealed there with both metal and ice shrapnel. The hidden U-boats launched torpedoes, striking a battleship. Sirens wailed as the Americans rushed to seal the breach, and water flooded in, overtaking them—killing dozens. The men slid through the hatches and sprinted down the tight corridors to seal off the damaged compartments.

⋈ ⋈ ⋈

Beneath miles of ice, the Arya floated in their labyrinth of ancient caves, hovering among the stalactites and stalagmites, contemplating the dense, destructive humans and how to respond.

A human has the Emerald Tablet and has ill intentions.
This human has been here before.

The Guardians?
They are in position.
The humans must be brought to the Council of One.

The Arya telegraphed together.

Kammler ventured deeper into Inner Earth. He piloted his craft and had room for a gunner at the rear. The lead pilot flew solo, and his copter was mounted with a BFL—big fucking light—to illuminate their path. The caverns were so large that they allowed the helicopters to alternate between V-formation and single file. Kammler started to notice an increasing number of smaller off-shoot tunnels appearing, and he was pleased. With everything they had successfully transported already, they had enough supplies staggered along the route for months, if needed.

Stalagmites rose up from the ground, and stalactites lowered from the ceiling. The choppers had to carefully avoid the unpredictable and increasingly dangerous terrain. The pilots reached the base camp after only two days—far faster than the week it had taken the trucks. They landed side by side at the end of the passable road where the tunnel made a sharp ninety-degree turn straight down. There was an enormous vertical hole, with geological striations that made it resemble a cinnamon Danish. They would have to continue without the trucks.

"How far is the descent?" Kammler asked as they angled the BFL in to look, but no one had been able to tell yet. They couldn't see the bottom, even with the light, so he lit a flare and dropped it. Going, going . . . the flare was soaked up by the darkness. They would have to send a scout.

"We will send the lead copter with the light. Once we establish what we're dropping into, I will follow. The rest of you will rappel down and continue on foot." Kammler would never go first. He was not expendable.

"Should we leave the corporal behind to winch us out when we return?"

"No. Everybody in the hole," Kammler replied. He had no intention of climbing out; he was flying out in a vimana. There was no other acceptable outcome.

Once he landed, the pilot radioed: "It's massive. It goes on forever!"

It was quick and relatively easy for the helicopters to lower into the hole, but it was an ordeal for the rappellers. They had knotted together a thousand-foot stretch of rope and secured it to the winch of one of the trucks. They threw all the remaining rope, about forty pounds, to the ground below. Leaning straight back, perpendicular to the wall with their hands under their buttocks, they jumped to the bottom, one by one. They also lowered hundreds of pounds of supplies, including weapons. It was a slow, arduous process, and one heavy crate of ammunition had slipped out of its knots and fallen, nearly killing four men below, if not for the warning shouts.

"We won't be able to carry it all, *Kommandant*," Kammler's next-in-charge said.

"We'll want the biggest guns we have down here, and I haven't seen any sign of food or water. We'll drop and carry everything we can."

The Emerald Tablet, ensconced in its gold box, never left Kammler's side, hidden in his sturdy leather haversack. Just one vimana was all he needed. There had been thousands of them, just sitting idle, and the atlantium! If he could get more, he would have a fleet! He would annihilate the tiny American opposition, and the Reich would rise again from the depths of the South Pole.

As the soldiers continued their drop, the BFL quit. The absolute darkness was speckled with polka-dotted retinal memory of the light they'd lost. Gunfire suddenly filled the air, and the screams of the soldiers waiting to rappel echoed through the cave. Those below were horrified as bodies started falling, thump, thump, splat, in the dark. The soldiers who had flashlights, lit them. Men were jumping to their deaths to escape whatever it was they were dealing with up top.

Ring, ring, ring.

"The Guardians! *Guns ready!*" Kammler ordered. *We must be close!* he thought excitedly. He wasn't afraid, not with the firepower surrounding him. He was confident that their massive guns would be enough to destroy them.

What's a Guardian? the soldiers wondered in confusion as they drew their weapons, still hearing screams and unable to see anything.

"There are creatures in these tunnels beyond your nightmares. Keep your big guns ready!" Kammler warned.

The hardened soldiers braced in position, their guns poised. The flashlights did little to illuminate the massive cave. Ribbons of light crisscrossed and were eaten up by the abyss before them.

Ring, ring. The sound from the bells on thick chokers around the Guardians' necks bounced off the walls, echoing through the caverns.

"There are two sets of bells . . . these ones are close!" the point man warned.

Kammler realized it wasn't only the men at the top of the hole who were in danger. As the chimes overlapped one another, low, resonating growls became audible.

"*Steady!*" Kammler shouted, but no one was feeling steady. The reverberating chimes were ominous, and their commander's dire warning had rattled their nerves, unsettling their courage.

"What the hell are we up against?" one soldier said to another as they slowly crept forward. Kammler stayed at the back of the pack.

"What can it be?" one of the soldiers whispered nervously. The low grumble was growing louder. "Earthquake?" he guessed, but it was a faint hope.

It became clear that what they were hearing was the deep, resonating snarl of a large creature. Should they stay in the largest open cavern or turn off onto one of the smaller branches? They slowly crept deeper into the damp earth.

The creature let out a sinister, ground-shaking roar that reverberated off the walls, igniting their adrenaline.

"*Um Gotteswillen!* For the sake of God!" the men exclaimed as two flares were thrown.

Standing two hundred feet ahead of them was a Guardian, an enormous beast of solid, rippling muscle. The creature aggressively tossed its mane, which was twisted in rows of tight loops and knots. As its giant head swung from side to side, it rattled the studded, armored yoke around its neck and chest. The Guardian's loud, hollow breathing echoed menacingly through the tunnel.

"*Huff* . . . huff . . . huff," the men heard—and felt. The sound, so near, so calm and deliberate, was far more frightening than the howls had been. The beast snarled, baring its lethal fangs, and the fur on its neck bristled and spiked like barbs.

The Guardian looked more horrible than Kammler had imagined, and its glowing eyes flared like hellfire in the dim light. Kammler backed away from his troops, and the creature crept closer. The rancid odor of decay that clung to it choked them. Its shoulders bulged, and its massive head was extended forward on its outstretched neck.

Helghul was reminded of the shishi lions or foo dogs he had seen so many times in his travels through Asia, their giant stone paws resting possessively on the sphere representing the world and the Grid.

As the monster approached, there was a click of extended claws on the stone, each nail as thick as an ivory tusk. They could not flee. The Guardian would surely be on them, ripping out their insides in an instant. And somewhere nearby, another deep roar resonated. Without another thought, Kammler shouted,

"FIre! Fire! Take it down!"

While the shots rang out, Kammler darted to the far left of the cave, and with all the monster's attention focused on the attacking soldiers, he slunk along the dark edge, past the melee and down one of the branching tunnels.

The Guardian leapt, utilizing its antigravity atlantium collar as it pounced. It almost flew, and it landed, crushing some soldiers and scattering the others. A second Guardian hurtled into the cavern and slaughtered the remaining soldiers.

Once Kammler had escaped undetected, he turned his flashlight back on. He was running for his life. He ran until his lungs burned, and his sides ached in sharp knots. Hideous roars echoed in his ears. Turn, turn, branch off, and turn. He knew the soldiers were only a brief distraction.

How many more Guardians will there be? he wondered.

He couldn't run much longer; his thighs and lungs burned as he sprinted. He had the Emerald Tablet. *It must be somehow useful,* he thought. He stopped and removed the lid covering the Tablet, and it glowed faintly from inside his open haversack.

How had Red Elder used the Tablet to subdue Abaddon and the others? He had harnessed sound, Helghul remembered. Kammler set his intention. Holding the Tablet, he waved his hand toward the side of the tunnel beside him, intending to break the rock and weaponize the Tablet. No vibration was conjured. He was unable to shift a pebble. He placed the Tablet on the floor and stood on it, and despite his intentions, he could not make it hover. He had tried many times over the centuries, but still, it lay motionless. His skill was insufficient.

Kammler picked up the Tablet, defeated, and once again began running, using the glow of the Tablet to light his way.

The soldiers had been decimated and were now a considerable ways behind him. Kammler felt no empathy or sadness for them. He was only worried about his own goal. Soon he would retrieve a vimana, and more atlantium, if possible. He would fly past the Guardians and out of the tunnel. He would wipe out Byrd and his troops, reunite with Grey Elder, and rally the scientists and Adversaries disguised throughout South America.

Helghul, Kammler heard an unfamiliar voice in his head, startling him.

Though his legs were still pumping, as if he were running, suddenly he was not. Long, thin hands had encircled his arms on either side and had lifted him off the ground so that his feet met no resistance at all. It was not the antigravity of Inner Earth; he still wasn't close enough for that to be the case.

Kammler was being propelled forward by two Aryan super-soldiers wearing shiny black armor. They held him by both of his arms as he glided inches above the ground. He had forgotten how tall they were, and sandwiched between them, he was tiny by comparison.

"Release me!" Kammler demanded. He had grown accustomed to his venerated stature and resented being manhandled.

You have been summoned to the Council of One, the Aryan escorts informed him telepathically.

This is unexpected! What will this mean to my plans? he wondered frantically, but his struggling brought no release.

The Adversary had no alternative but to be carried deeper into the Earth. He wished the Emerald Tablet was somewhere else as he clutched it tightly to his chest.

The Arya approached a wall of solid rock and stopped abruptly just before hitting it. As they waited, the stone morphed into an opening, and Willowy Man ushered them into the glistening, liquid-like portal.

Though the Tunnel-Keeper recognized Helghul, he did not address him. Pushing his arms straight out in front of him with his palms perpendicular and fingers facing the ceiling, Willowy Man willed the Emerald Tablet to him. The treasure was pulled from Kammler's grasp by an unseen force and landed in Willowy Man's outstretched arms. The Adversary was left holding a torn and empty haversack, and he howled in protest. His rage was nothing compared to that of the Beast escalating within him.

"No!" he bellowed, but his objections were futile. Even with his hands free of the Tablet, Kammler was unable to overpower the super-soldiers restraining him. Kammler's eyes glowed red, and his mind raced, searching for a way to retrieve the treasure.

You were a fool to bring it here! the Beast snarled in Kammler's head.

What alternative did I have? Why didn't Grey Elder anticipate this? Kammler thought. He had planned for the Guardians, but he had underestimated them, and he hadn't considered the Arya at all!

The prisoner was transported deeper into Inner Earth with the help of the Tunnel-Keeper, and flanked by the Aryans.

As a new portal opened, Kammler could see the white glow of crystals imbedded in the walls illuminating the jagged cavern where the Council of One patiently waited. The council floated effortlessly above them and was comprised of twelve Inner Earth-lings who represented all of them. A small division of Aryan super-soldiers filled the tunnels. They were wearing the same black, lightweight, graphene armor of his captors. The council addressed Kammler in unison.

Chapter 29

Return to
Inner Earth

"Give 'em hell, boys!" Byrd said, drowned out by the blasts.

Suddenly a squadron of six disc-shaped vimana emerged out of the icy embankment. Like shooting stars, they arched out of the enormous cracks in the sparkling-green glaciers. They appeared and disappeared as they swooped and circled in formation. They briefly dipped into the frigid ocean before reemerging unaffected. A surge of white water was pushed up by the vimana as they burst through the surface. The waves rolled off the metallic discs as they flew with remarkable speed and agility back into the sky.

"Are they German?"

"Are they American?" the sailors on both sides asked in wonderment, unable to comprehend and not knowing whether to fire. The technology was well beyond anything presently known to them, and the speed of the vimana allowed the aircrafts to disappear and reappear at will. Awestruck and still firing on one another, both camps turned their weapons against the aircraft, guessing they were advanced enemy technology.

"Are you seeing this, Admiral?" Cruzen shouted into his radio.

"Don't shoot! Cease fire," Byrd commanded, recognizing the vimana. His order was immediately echoed across the radio waves, and the confused Americans stopped firing at the Germans and left the vimana in peace.

My God, what we can become, Byrd marveled. *It's the Arya!* he thought. *But why have they revealed themselves?*

"They are not the enemy. Strike the colors!" Byrd ordered.

"What are they? Who are they?" the soldiers wanted to know. The confused shipmen followed Byrd's orders and unfurled their flags in an act of surrender.

Without Kammler to advise them, the Germans had not stopped shooting. The vimanas targeted those who continued to fire upon them. With laser perfection, their advanced weapons incinerated the troops entrenched in the icy embankment. The Nazis were burned and fell, as black ash against the white snow and ice.

The deck-mounted guns of the American aircraft carrier remained silent as the vimanas continued to dart overhead. Byrd's troops awaited his next command, watching unharmed while the remaining Germans continued to futilely attack the vimanas. The Arya were compelled to defend and retaliate, and the outgunned Germans were easily and systematically wiped out.

The Council of Arya spoke to Helghul telepathically, and Kammler could not tell from which being the message had come.

Adversaries and Emissaries are tied to one another in an opposi-tional relationship. We are joined with you in this Age.

Human, you have brought violence to our border, and wrongly believe we are indifferent to your trespasses and your intended misap-propriation of our technology. We are not unaware, nor indifferent; your choice forces us to intercede.

It is not your place to intervene! Outer Earth is beyond your domain! Kammler replied, displaying his arrogance as Black Elder. *Inner Earthlings have declared nonintervention in Outer Earth matters,* Kammler telegraphed to them wordlessly with his thoughts.

This is not Outer Earth. We will not be accomplices to your attempts to prevent the rise of consciousness.

You must not intervene. The consciousness evolves as a whole, not one polarity over the other, Kammler insisted, his face distorting as the Beast within struggled for control. Its dragon-like shadows peaked through Kammler's skin, as though seeping out of the boundaries of his chin and cheeks, morphing his face before it once again sank back, subdued and hidden.

Nothing can prevent change, the Beast hissed.

This is where you are mistaken. You misunderstand the covenants.

The Arya, whom Helghul had once admired so much, were now his enemy and a threat to his plans.

Your people initiated the aggression on your command. We have eliminated the threat, the Arya told him.

The possibility that his troops, and his entire base, had been wiped out was sinking in. Kammler's desperation rose, and his awareness focused intently on the Emerald Tablet suspended in the air and surrounded by the council members who floated around the cavern observing from different angles.

As the glistening, slender vimana lowered, hovering just barely above the deck of the aircraft carrier, Marcus was called:

Emissary!

Byrd was startled. He looked around, but no one else had heard it.

Emissary! You are called before the Council of One, he heard, and he realized he was not hearing through his eardrums but rather through vibrations in his head that were telepathically strumming chords that only Marcus could hear. It had been Ages since he'd used the skill, and the high, pure notes made his head throb.

Come to us, the Arya requested from within the vimana, conveying the echo of millions of united Inner Earthlings.

Byrd made his way toward the deck, and as he did so, he instructed the confused men around him.

"Do nothing! I am going aboard. Send the message throughout the fleet to await my next command," the Emissary said.

"Aye, Admiral, going aboard."

"Sir? Who will ride along?"

"I'm going alone. Collect our dead, and recover what you can. No one is to go ashore," Byrd said.

"Aye, sir."

Byrd descended the stairs onto the flight deck. He heard his captain reporting a play-by-play to Cruzen as he descended to the waiting craft.

"Yes, sir," the captain said. "Admiral Byrd is going aboard the aircraft. No. I don't know . . . he's approaching it now . . . Admiral Byrd is on board. I repeat, Admiral Byrd is on board!" he continued.

The soldiers on the deck watched in awe as the iridescent silver disc lifted, and in a flash zipped away with their highest-ranking officer. It accelerated instantly and was virtually invisible as it flew straight up over the destroyed encampment of Neuschwabenland and disappeared into a crevasse, back to Inner Earth.

Byrd attempted to speak to the pilot both verbally and telepathically, but the Arya did not respond. The admiral looked out of the vimana as it flew expertly through the tunnels, lighting its own way. The darkness was soon behind them, and the warm glow of Inner Earth's central sun warmed them. There was an ocean, vast and clear, and they flew inches above the surface.

Byrd witnessed a splash, but it was not a mammal or fish that he had ever seen. It was something else: a creature unknown to Outer Earth. They once again entered the latticework of tunnels and finally landed. The honeycomb tafone rock sparked Byrd's ancient memory of a time when Marcus and Helghul had been best friends and allies, and the Emissary was briefly nostalgic for a childhood long gone.

Chapter 30

The Burden

Helghul! Willowy Man! My God, the Emerald Tablet! Byrd's Marcus-consciousness recognized it as he was led from the vimana to where the Council of One was convened. The Adversary's shine was filling the space with smoky-grey bands, and though he had seen photos of Kammler, Byrd hadn't known until that moment that he was Helghul.

The Emerald Tablet hovered high at the center of the cavern, and the council members were dispersed at various distances floating nearby. Helghul stood with one towering super-soldier behind him. The others were positioned at the exits. The ground was even in the vast room except for the stalagmites that protruded sporadically. They were the only thing between Kammler and Byrd, who also had one formidable super-soldier behind him.

Byrd respectfully bowed to the Inner Earthlings. As his eyes met Kammler's, he could see that the man was seething. It was then that the Arya began to communicate telepathically.

The end of the Dark Age is a time of personal and collective evolution. As you have come to us connecting Inner with Outer, so, too, must your opposite come to you, in this unification of opposites.

Then silence. They floated, waiting and watching.

Forced together, Marcus and Helghul now stood face-to-face, twenty feet apart, in full recognition of each other.

"I'd hoped you were already dead," Kammler said through gritted teeth.

"A Nazi . . . no surprise there," Byrd scoffed.

"American? Hmph! You hypocrite! Hiroshima? Nagasaki? The innocents screamed while their skin peeled away, and you feign superiority?" Kammler snarled.

"We both know it wasn't Emissaries who dropped those bombs," Byrd countered.

"Ah." Kammler smiled. "Yes, we do cross all borders. Those bombs plunged the world into beautiful new depths of fear and darkness."

"Your time is over, Helghul. It's time for light to return to the world. The Emissary's time has come."

"No. Not yet. Maybe not ever. You've been fed information, but you don't challenge it and question. Faced with the fear and despair of my death camps, even the precious Emissaries lost their hope! Your dear Theron was bent to my will by the mere threat of it."

Theron! Is she alive? Does he know where she is?

Even though Byrd said nothing out loud, Kammler recoiled. The shine emanating from the Emissary had become unbearably saturated with loving energy.

"Your weakness for her will be your undoing!" Kammler said bitterly.

"It's love, not hatred, that requires strength," Byrd replied. "Your selfishness makes you weak."

At that, the Arya interjected, and their attention returned to the hovering council.

The defining purpose of this council is to protect Mother Gaia, they said, referring to the physical well-being of the planet. *There will be no mercy should you ever return uninvited to our world.*

Kammler filled with relief. Was it possible? Would they be sent away with a warning?

The rise of the Great Year has begun. The Iron Age is ending, giving way to the ascending Bronze Age. Light will again appear. We will release this prisoner and the Emerald Tablet into the care of the Emissary, the council continued, stunning them both. Kammler and the Emerald Tablet were to be handed over to Byrd!

"You are biased!" Kammler shouted.

Your choices have created your reality, the Arya replied.

The Emerald Tablet, still hovering at the center of them, floated down toward Byrd and the two super-soldiers guarding him, and Kammler closed in around the Emissary, blocking him protectively.

However, Kammler lunged. It was not at Byrd, nor at the Tablet that Kammler launched himself. Rather, with the Beast in control, he sprinted the short distance toward a jagged stalagmite protruding from the cavern floor. The Beast had no intention of wasting precious time stagnating in prison. This vessel had come to the end of its usefulness. The dark entity bound to Helghul took him over. Helghul was an unwilling passenger as he brutally impaled himself. The earthen sword tore through his stomach and exited out his back, and Kammler screamed in pain, arching and then slumping lifelessly, his head and legs hanging, murdered by the entity within him.

The murky shine surrounding Kammler's body lifted away as his spirit departed, like a ghoulish knight passing through the confines of a suit of armor. Though Byrd couldn't see it, the soul of Helghul looked as he had in Atitala, taller and younger than Kammler, with fair hair, skin, and eyes. He was ethereal and light except for a malevolent shadow that clung to his right side and wrapped like a succubus around his arms, legs, and torso. The Beast hid nine faces against him within its smoky blackness, but the tenth head was on a long dragon neck and was wrapped like a turban around his head. The largest head now rested, dragon-face out, on his brow. For a moment, the sinister hat blinked back at Byrd, smiling with its jagged fangs reaching down either side of Helghul's face and covering his ears as he floated.

The Beast hissed from atop Helghul's head, its fangs snapping angrily in Byrd's direction, and then the energy was pulled. It slipped into another realm—thinner and higher, and dissipated into the ether.

It felt like hours, but only minutes had passed when Byrd was returned to his fleet. He adjusted the Tablet wrapped in his coat as the vimana departed the carrier deck. He had a lot of explaining to do, and none of it could detail what had occurred, nor could he reveal the Emerald Tablet. Byrd's mind raced to conjure up a cohesive tale he could share, though his first thought was to hide the Tablet before too many questions were asked.

Byrd pondered what to do next for a long time. He contemplated every option and possibility, nervous that the Tablet might be discovered, and tormented by the enormity of his responsibility. Finally, he settled on a hiding place for the Tablet. Marcus could avoid his responsibility no longer, but whether the the treasure was in his hands or somewhere well hidden, he was never at ease.

"Leave him be," Eva Braun snapped at the men guarding her door as they frisked her skinny bespectacled guest and ruffled his perfectly pressed suit. The guards offered no apologies for their rigor.

"He's expecting you," she said kindly to the beetle-eyed little German with a large birthmark covering his left cheek and ear.

He, too, had been one of Hitler's key henchmen, and had escaped Germany to Argentina's open arms.

"The outpost has been wiped out. We believe Kammler is dead," the Adversary once known as Abaddon said in a rush as soon as he saw Hitler. Grey Elder was unreadable. His first concern was for the Emerald Tablet. Before he could ask anything further, he heard warning cries from his guards, and Eva screamed. There was the rapid fire of machine guns. Nimbler than he appeared, Grey Elder dropped to the floor as bullets splintered the chair he'd just vacated. His visitor had not been so quick to respond; he lay bleeding beside him.

Hooded assassins dressed in black charged from the entryway and broke through the rear parlor window, fully surrounding Hitler. The Führer was flat on his chest with his gun in hand. He shot and missed his mark, but it didn't matter; he was outnumbered and outgunned. The assassins opened fire, and Hitler's body was torn apart by bullets. Blood poured from the wounds, and his life force lifted out.

Grey Elder's soul surveyed the scene as the murderers checked the bodies to make sure they were indeed dead and wrapped them for transport and disposal. They had been told to render Hitler unrecognizable and to dispose of him where he would never be found. The Andes were vast and difficult, and no one was looking for Hitler there.

Perón had been rightfully distressed when he learned that Hitler was hiding in Argentina. He wanted nothing to do with the Führer. A few scientists were excusable, a reasonable amount of German wealth trickling in was understandable, and everyone was doing it . . . but to harbor Adolf Hitler? That was another thing. Perón had other ideas for the legacy he hoped to leave. He was relieved when the call came that the deed was done.

Grey Elder, like Helghul, had now gone to the in-between, the space from which everything emerged and to which everything returned. One thing was certain: if the Adversaries were going to get the treasure back from Marcus, they wouldn't do it in this lifetime.

Chapter 31

Seducer-Producer

Present day, Seattle, Washington

Though the Seattle airport had been damaged in the quake, a few runways had been repaired, and flights had resumed in and out of Sea-Tac. Quinn had booked a flight to London with a connection to Northern Africa. The earthquake, unstable global politics, shortages, and volatility in the Middle East had sent fuel prices soaring.

Supply and demand? Quinn had scoffed, knowing that the oil companies used any kind of planetary drama to fix prices. Begrudgingly, he had secured himself a hideously overpriced flight to meet up with Eden and Nate in Morocco.

Quinn's plane set down at Heathrow airport. The customs lineup was ridiculously long, four hours at least. Quinn knew he would certainly miss his connection to Marrakech.

"Max Quinn? Max Quinn?" An airport security officer was calling out his name. Quinn raised his hand, not wanting to lose his spot, and he worked his way to the edge of the snaking, endless lineup wondering if his unresolved criminal case had gotten him flagged.

"Passport?" the officer said, and Quinn handed it over, his plane transfer folded inside. "Follow me, sir," the man said, abruptly walking away with Quinn's passport.

"Where? I'm already gonna miss my flight."

"You need to follow me," the officer said. Other bedraggled travelers around him looked on with envy.

"Hey, I have a flight to catch too," a pissed-off Swiss banker called after them.

"Where are we going?" Quinn asked. He soon realized that no explanation was forthcoming, and he followed the tightly stuffed uniform in silence.

Inside a lavish private room nestled in a corner of the Heathrow terminal, Quinn was asked to wait and was left alone, without his passport and boarding pass. He helped himself to a complimentary cup of tea and a slice of pie while he pondered his circumstances. His instincts were prickling and unsettled. Was it the police? Or worse, Helghul? Had Marcus been discovered? He thought of Abaddon and the Adversaries who had jumped him outside Café Zazou. They had known him. He was sure of it.

Quinn tried to keep his mind clear. He waited nervously, as he had in front of the school principal's office as a young boy, and he wished he had possession of his personal documents.

The door finally opened, and Quinn was startled to see a handsome, familiar face. He had seen the features many times staring back at him from magazine covers, newspapers, and television interviews. Seducer-Producer, the tabloids called him. The celebrity strongly resembled a forty-something Paul Newman. His salt-and-pepper hair was cropped short, and his blue eyes glowed in his darkly tanned face. He was dressed impeccably and was a striking physical specimen—muscular, trim, and beyond six feet tall.

Quinn was difficult to impress, but the man before him awed him on two counts. Oswald Zahn was the renowned philanthropist, movie producer, and mogul who had been funding Eden and Nate on the Crystal Project, but more important, he bloomed with the shine of Grey Elder. The Elder had the ability to hide his aura, but this time he wanted Marcus to recognize him. It would make their interaction so much easier. Quinn was jolted by the recognition.

"It is good to see you again, Marcus," Zahn said, smiling. He held Quinn's passport in his hand.

"Grey Elder!" Quinn almost shouted, and the two men merrily embraced. "You're the one funding Theron! I should have guessed!"

Marcus was elated to be in the presence of an ally—someone other than Helghul who had memory.

"In my lives I search for the Emissaries, just as you search for Theron," Grey Elder said, with layers of meaning Quinn could not fathom.

"The world is such a mess. It is such a relief to be reunited with an Elder," Quinn said.

"Let's hope it gets easier from here on out," Grey Elder added.

"It can't get much worse," Quinn replied.

Zahn had Quinn exactly where he wanted him. Marcus still had no idea Grey Elder had been the mentor behind Helghul all along. He had no idea the Elder had been Adolf Hitler. Nor that he had hidden his shine in Ancient Greece when he had incarnated as General Anytus and had been responsible for the death of Socrates, Red Elder, and the massacre at the Mystery School. Quinn had no clue that Red Elder had died killing Anytus in Heliopolis.

Had Anytus lived, Plato's consciousness-expanding knowledge would never have been shared. Red Elder, the Keeper of the Records, had died fulfilling his role.

"You remember when you and I first landed in Stone-at-Center, Marcus?" Zahn asked strategically, steering the conversation.

"Of course," Quinn nodded, urging him on, absentmindedly running his hands through his thick dark hair and holding them there, pressing, as if trying to contain the myriad of thoughts hammering against his skull.

"I talked to you then about the burden of having taken the memory potion," Zahn said. "How have you managed it?"

"It's a curse and a blessing, as I'm sure you know," he said, shaking his head. There have been so many lifetimes since then. Why have we met so rarely?" Quinn asked.

"We've been close many times. I listened to you speak in Ancient Greece, but you were out of my reach," he said. "Another time in Jakarta, I was born to you and died . . . it was your lesson, not mine," the Elder continued sorrowfully, successfully reinforcing Quinn's misguided trust.

"Ohhh," Marcus breathed, immediately remembering that difficult lifetime and, for an instant, filling with the grief he had felt as a mother when her newborn had died. That had been such a hard and short life, during which Marcus had met Siddhartha Gautama, the man who had gone on to be called simply "Buddha." Like Socrates, he had not displayed the karmic colors of an Emissary, but in his lifetime, Siddhartha had had an epiphany and found enlightenment. He discovered that by being mindful, he could tap into the collective consciousness and the Akashic field and receive downloads of information. He devoted his life to sharing what he had learned. Marcus hadn't known then how profoundly important that individual would become.

"I hate to cut this short, but I'm sorry, I gotta go *now*. I think I've already missed my flight," Quinn said.

"Don't worry. I'm taking you from here. My jets are at yours and Eden's disposal."

"You're kidding me?" Quinn said in amazement.

"We can go now; our flight plan is filed, and we're scheduled to depart. Please . . . this way. We have a lot to discuss. We can walk while we talk," Zahn said. Marcus was reassured to have the Elder's support, both financially and strategically.

As the men exited the private room and entered the main concourse, an entourage of bodyguards and assistants closed in around them.

"As you suspected, the Crystal Children are Emissaries," Zahn said in hushed tones. All the while, he smiled and nodded at the passersby who pointed, squealed, and rushed to snap photos. Undoubtedly, the Seducer-Producer would have been completely inundated if not for the large circle of bodyguards.

He continued talking. "They have advanced DNA. They are the next step in the conscious evolution. We need to gather them. They aren't safe where they are, and the Mystery School is ready," Zahn said.

"Ready?" Quinn said in confusion. *This is just what Eden and I had hoped for,* he thought happily.

"You forget, Marcus, I've always known what my role would be. I have been preparing for nearly thirteen thousand years."

"Right. Shit . . . I . . . Where? Is it in Egypt?" Marcus asked, thinking *he* should have been doing more . . . preparing *somehow,* building a school . . . and again he felt inadequate . . . though he didn't know what he would have done differently.

"Close . . . Libya."

"Libya? Is that safe?"

"Safer than where they are now. The children are being targeted by dark forces as we speak, and I have a secured location. They're vulnerable, and I hate to say it, but the Crystal Project has made it worse. My security team has reports that those children are in serious danger. The Adversaries are systematically hunting them down, and we must get them to safety as soon as possible. We'll educate them together and reintegrate them into the world exactly at the right time."

"We have to get to her!" Quinn said, panic rising in him. *I knew it! I should have done something!* he thought.

"We'll be with Eden in under four hours," Zahn said, opening the door.

"How will we convince them all to come to Libya? It's hardly a holiday destination, and they'll have to leave their families, their countries," Quinn said as they walked toward a private hangar.

"I will extend a personal invitation, a free luxury vacation for the entire family, and once we're there, we'll have to tell them the children are being targeted."

"Libya, huh!" Quinn said. He wished it were somewhere else, but he had to trust Grey Elder.

"Everything's under control. Wait till you see the setup there—luxury. It's going to blow your mind. I spared no expense," Zahn said.

'Spared no expense' . . . *that's what John Hammond said in* Jurassic Park *about twenty minutes before the dinosaurs started eating the people,* Quinn thought. But the Emissary ignored his niggling instinct in the shade of the Elder's influence.

Inside the private hangar, Quinn saw no less than six jets with Zahn's company logo emblazoned on the side.

"We'll need the Emerald Tablet, Marcus," Grey Elder said, his blue eyes searching Quinn's.

Red Elder told me it's my responsibility? Trust no one, not even Emissaries . . . *but he said it was because they had no memory* . . . *they could be manipulated. Surely Grey Elder is beyond manipulation,* Quinn thought, convincing himself. *Grey Elder will know better how to tap its power and use Indra's Web to influence events.* Quinn knew he had much left to learn.

"I sank it outside the harbor of Alexandria, past where the lighthouse once stood. It's well hidden. I buried it deep, and the current is strong," Quinn said before divulging the precise coordinates.

"Good work, Emissary," Zahn said, clapping him familiarly on the back.

Four hours! That was all Quinn had to wait until he would see Eden again. He felt fortunate to have Grey Elder helping them.

The Emissary had played right into the Elder's hands.

Chapter 32

The New
Mystery School

"Can I get you anything, sir?" the blonde flight attendant asked
Quinn, her buttons straining against her tight-fitting uniform, her
cleavage spilling out the top. He ordered a martini, shaken not
stirred, and chuckled to himself while he watched her walk the
length of the private jet with a sexy sway.

Quinn's rumpled shirt and scruffy jeans were out of place in
the sleek surroundings, but he didn't care. He was just glad to be
in the air, one step closer to Theron and to bringing the Emissaries
to safety. He had sent only one cryptic email telling her he was

on his way and to stay inside her hotel and off the internet until he arrived.

He turned to Zahn. "Nate, the director of photography, is a buddy of mine. We've run into each other more than once over these centuries, though of course he doesn't have a clue. He's a huge fan of yours," Quinn said.

"An Emissary?" Grey Elder asked hopefully.

"No, just a very good soul."

"That's all right. We need all the help we can get," Grey Elder said seriously.

Quinn was excited that his lengthy journey was finally coming to an end, though flying in a private jet was a vast improvement over coach. "I can't believe you've done all this. It's too good to be true."

Clunk. Quinn regretted saying the words. He didn't want to hear them. Old proverbs were full of true wisdom, and Marcus had learned lifetimes before that when something seemed too good to be true, it always was. Maybe getting all the Crystal Children to safety was an impossible feat.

"I saw you and Socrates together. He was a character," Zahn said, smiling a flawless white grin and distracting Quinn from the paranoia prickling deep in his brain.

"One of my favorites. Why didn't we meet in Greece?" Quinn asked.

"I was traveling through there the day six generals were thrown from the Acropolis. You were in the middle of the clamoring mob, and I was guiding a small group of Emissaries to Heliopolis. It was an ugly day in Athens, and we passed through as quickly as possible."

"It was a terrible scene."

"Mm-hmm," Zahn said.

While they traveled, Zahn explained his plans.

"There are other Emissaries already in the safe zone in Libya, but so far they don't understand their full purpose in this lifetime. They've all been led there under the guise of research and preservation. Only *I* know their true mission."

All Quinn could think about was his approaching reunion with Eden and self-recriminations that accompanied his selfish obsession.

The world is in such a difficult time. The Crystal Children are in danger . . . can I really be thinking about myself at a time like this? he thought.

Marcus wondered again if he was ever meant to be an Emissary at all. If not for Theron insisting, he might have died in Atitala like so many others, and never become an Emissary. It occurred to him that he was no better, no worthier, than the people he was supposed to be leading back into the Light, and he shook his head.

Zahn watched Quinn as he silently squirmed, inwardly berating himself. Quinn's aura was violet and brooding, as he forgot his divinity and dwelled on his shortcomings and perceived failures. Grey Elder had found Quinn in a far worse state than he had expected. He was truly an example of the human condition. Despite his absolute certain knowledge that he was spirit, and was One with the Universe, he doubted himself and felt a sense of guilt and responsibility. Driven by an Emissary's purpose, he felt the need to be perfect and to do . . . more.

⋙⋘ ⋙⋘ ⋙⋘

"You're early," Nate said when Quinn called up to Eden's room from the hotel lobby. It was not the warm welcome Quinn had hoped for.

"Lucky to be here at all," Quinn replied into the phone, hoping for more.

"Room 111," Nate said, clicking off without another word. He wasn't happy that Quinn was joining them. Nate had been frantic when he heard about the earthquake in Seattle, and he hadn't slept until Quinn finally made contact. He loved his buddy, but he just couldn't forgive him for interfering with Eden. When Quinn and Eden had resumed their FaceTime chats, Nate's affection for his friend was once again overshadowed by jealousy.

The cameraman hadn't made the progress with Eden he'd hoped to. At times she'd been receptive, and the intimacy and sharing between them seemed promising, but then she would withdraw. He believed if it weren't for Quinn, she would have been open to a romantic relationship with him. His admiration for her grew as he watched her with the children and the crew. Her empathy was astounding. She intuitively related to people and found common ground with everyone.

The door was cracked open when Quinn and Zahn arrived.

"Hello?" Quinn called, pushing it wider.

"Hey," Nate answered from the faded sofa where he sat typing, his laptop on his knee. Zahn was surprised to see that Nate didn't even raise his head.

Quinn was stung by his buddy's coldness. Nate had only perfunctorily responded to his many emails, but Quinn hadn't expected this.

"Gimme a sec, I'm just finishing up here," Nate said.

"I . . . wanna introduce someone," Quinn said, and Nate finally looked up.

"Holy shit! Seducer-Producer!" Nate jumped up, tossing his computer aside.

"I prefer Zahn, or Ozzie, thanks," Zahn said, shaking Nate's hand. Though Zahn had funded their project and Eden had met with him, Nate had yet to see him face-to-face.

"Holy shit!" Nate repeated, looking at Quinn.

"Yeah, you said that. Close your mouth, man," Quinn said, embracing him and giving him a strong clap on the back, trying to infuse Nate with the camaraderie and closeness he felt for him.

"Where's Eden?" Quinn asked, looking around the room eagerly.

"Market," Nate said smugly, aware that Quinn had, without explanation, instructed her not to leave the hotel. Eden was not good at taking orders, and she had stalked about the small room before marching to the market as she had planned before receiving the puzzling email. Nate was happy she hadn't returned yet.

"It's great to finally meet you," Nate said, reaching to shake Zahn's hand. "Thank you for everything! We owe you so much!"

"Happy to do what I can," Zahn said.

"Did you two come together?"

"We met up at the airport. Quinn and I are old friends," Zahn said. "Listen, I'm going to give you guys some privacy and time to . . . reconnect. We can meet up later for dinner. Nice meeting you, Nate."

When Zahn closed the door behind him, Nate rounded on Quinn, his eyebrows scrunched in confusion.

"I can't believe you never mentioned him. Not even when I told you he was our backer. Anyone else would have mentioned being friends with Oswald Zahn, at least once in all these years!"

"Well, I haven't seen him in a very long time . . . it's a long story." Quinn said simply. *I didn't know until now!* he thought, more accurately.

"You're just full of long stories and excuses, aren't you?" Nate said bitterly. "It never occurred to you that *the* Seducer-Producer would be a good contact for me? For my life? My career?" Quinn reached out to put a hand on Nate's shoulder, but Nate stepped back.

"Sorry, Nate," Quinn said sincerely, his rejected hand dropping to his side.

"Hey, you know what . . . forget it . . . no worries. Eden'll be back soon, so why don't you head to *your* room and clean up, and I'll tell her you're here."

Nate sat down and turned his attention to the screen once again perched on his knee, dismissing Quinn.

"Zahn's rented us two entire floors up the street at the Royal Mansour," Quinn said.

"I prefer the sofa here. I've gotten used to Eden's and Elijah's company."

"They need to come too. It's not just for me. Zahn wants us all there."

"Well, I know you're both used to getting what you want."

"Nate, you're going to have to drop this bitter, competitive thing. We're lucky to have him. He's bigger than friggin' Oprah."

"I know perfectly well how big *Zahn* is, thanks!" Nate snapped.

For the first time in many years, Quinn felt a bubbling anger inside him. He wanted to smack his sarcastic friend on the back of the head. *Smarten up!* Quinn thought irritably. What had happened to his pal Amnut? To easygoing Nate? Quinn wanted to mend the gap between them but was unsure how to pacify his friend without promising to deny his love for Theron. That was something he would never do.

"Can we go find Eden together?" Quinn asked, ignoring Nate's dismissive attitude.

"Naw, no point, we'd never find her in the total chaos of the marketplace. She'd end up back here waiting for us while we wander around like a couple of tourists."

"What do you call a camel in Morocco?" Quinn asked, but Nate didn't bite. "A 4x4!" Quinn answered, making a goofy face, and Nate couldn't resist smiling.

It might be okay, after all, Quinn thought hopefully. Then his cell phone rang.

"Hello?"

I've got bad news. An Emissary in Lyon was killed last night. She was one of the Crystal Children," Zahn said.

"In Lyon? How?" Quinn asked, his stomach clenching.

"Foul play, murder. That's all they're saying. Her name was Anjolie."

"Shit, Eden just interviewed her," Quinn said. The Emissary felt responsible.

"We have to move those kids right away," Zahn said urgently. "I sent an email to all the families we know about. I invited them to an all-expenses-paid safari adventure for helping with the film. We'll explain everything once the children are safe. I haven't divulged the final location, but I used the paparazzi following me as an excuse for that."

"What about the ones who don't accept?"

"If anyone declines, we'll have to tell them their kid is in mortal danger. Their fear will move them. My planes board in two days. We must get Theron and the other Emissaries to safety, but you can't tell anyone where we're going. We don't want to bring the war to us, and if that information gets out, they won't be safe anywhere."

"Got it," Quinn said, and they hung up. Nate was making large motions beside him, desperate to know what had happened in Lyon. What was the problem that had Quinn's face so twisted in concern?

Quinn told Nate about the murder of Anjolie the night before. Nate was horrified. He couldn't believe it. His bad attitude was immediately sidelined, and he and Quinn contemplated how they would get everyone motivated to leave in two short days.

When Eden finally returned to the hotel, she rushed into Quinn's arms. Theron's energy staggered him. He stumbled backward, holding her tightly.

"Thank God you're finally here. We're all together, no more worries!" she exclaimed.

Quinn hated that he would have to worry her again so soon. "I'm so happy to see you," Quinn said, holding her longer than was necessary. His hands were buried in her thick, long hair, and his skin tingled at her touch. Eden was flooded by the energy that flowed from him, and Nate watched irritably.

"There's so much to tell you," Quinn began.

"What's wrong? What is it?" she asked, now only inches from his face and staring directly into his eyes.

"The kids are in danger. It's worse than we thought. There's already been a . . . victim."

"What? Who?" she asked, filling with panic and thoughts of Miguel Rodriguez. Quinn led her to the couch as he answered.

"The girl in Lyon, Anjolie," he began.

"Oh my God! Is she okay?" Eden asked.

Quinn shook his head. "She was . . . killed, last night. Zahn's security confirmed that the Crystal Children are being targeted," he explained.

"Noooo!" Eden howled, bursting into tears. "Oh my God! Ohhhh," she cried, pushing her fingers into her temples and pressing the skin of her forehead together. She couldn't sit. She jumped off the sofa.

"Who would *do* that? Why?" Nate asked. He was stunned.

"The Crystal Children have the potential to change the world, and there are people who don't want it to change."

"Who?" Eden and Nate both asked desperately.

"I'm not sure," Quinn replied.

"We have to protect them!" Eden exclaimed. "I have to get Elijah! He's at the pool. We have to contact the rest of the parents and tell them to keep their kids close and be careful until we figure out what to do!"

"Zahn has it under control. He doesn't want to panic them if he can help it. He's contacted all of them offering them a free African safari. I think they'll find it hard to resist. Wait, I'll come with you," Quinn said, following Eden as she hurried out to find her son.

"We'll all go," Nate said, jumping up. He didn't want them out of his sight.

"This is a nightmare," Eden said, still wiping tears away as they walked. "We can't release this film. Mrs. Rodriguez was right! It's my fault! I exposed them!"

Quinn put his arm around her shoulder, and their energies soothed one another. Eden felt their connection in every blood vessel, like oxygen pumping through her body.

"Poor Anjolie! Her poor parents! We can't endanger anyone else!"

"They're already in danger; they probably always were. Zahn has a secure place prepared where they will be protected. We can set the documentary aside until everyone is safe. Eden, he's already built the new Mystery School," Quinn said cautiously, not wanting to appear happy under the circumstances.

"Are you serious?" she asked as they opened the doors leading to the hotel pool. "It makes sense now! The kids knew! More than one of them asked me if I'd come to take them away. I thought it was such a strange question, but now I understand . . . they *knew* this was coming."

"It's not safe here. You, Elijah, and Nate need to come back to Zahn's hotel with me. He has guards, it'll be safer, and he's rented us a beautiful suite."

"We're still packed; it won't take long. I'm going to need more details, Quinn. This is all so overwhelming. Start again at the beginning, and tell me everything," she said.

Just then, Elijah saw her and gave a shout.

Chapter 33

Helghul Returns

Eden interrupted her conversation with Quinn and embraced her soaking-wet son.

"What's going on, Mom?" Elijah asked in surprise, shrugging his shoulders toward his ears and waiting for her fawning to stop.

Quinn stared at the eleven-year-old boy in horror.

"We're going to a new hotel for a couple of days," Eden said, without explaining.

"Why?" the youngster asked, but Eden didn't want to remain poolside. She wanted to get her son to safety.

"Elijah, this is Quinn. Quinn, this is my Elijah," Eden said, standing behind her boy with her hands on his shoulders.

Quinn feigned a friendly smile, desperately trying to hide his dismay. Nausea rocked him, and his stomach lurched as he reached out and shook the hand of Helghul.

The skinny eleven-year-old contemplated Quinn carefully and cocked his head to one side. "Do you know me?" the boy asked oddly.

Eden gasped, accustomed to Elijah's strange declarations but surprised all the same.

"Do you know *me?*" Quinn countered.

"I've dreamed you . . . or remembered you . . . I recognize your aura . . . your energy makes me . . . no offense . . . I feel like barfing."

"Elijah! Oh, Quinn, he just says whatever. Sometimes he doesn't think how it will make other people feel," Eden apologized.

"What? I'm just being honest," Elijah said.

"It's okay . . . no offense taken. I feel a bit like barfing myself," Quinn answered truthfully, and Elijah smiled and snorted in appreciation.

Together they made their way upstairs. Outwardly Quinn maintained his composure, but privately his mind was in utter chaos. His Marcus-mind was spinning with the predicament. *Helghul is Theron's son! She will be his unyielding protector in this life— the mother bear! And what would they do now? How can I take Helghul to Libya and put him in the center of all the Emissaries in the Mystery School? He has to be eliminated, contained—something!* But Quinn had no idea what to do. *Grey Elder! Grey Elder will know what to do!* Quinn thought.

Zahn sent two cars to move Theron, Nate, Elijah, and Quinn to his hotel, but when they arrived at the palatial resort, he was nowhere to be seen.

Quinn excused himself to call Zahn in private. While he was gone, Nate was amused by Elijah's unfavorable opinion of his mom's "creepy" friend. Maybe Elijah's opinion would help his cause with Eden.

✄✄ ✄✄ ✄✄

"Helghul? Here? Imagine that," Zahn said calmly. He was already aware who Helghul was, though he had avoided meeting him and alerting Helghul to his presence. He would bide his time.

"This is terrible! How can you be so calm?" Quinn asked in astonishment.

"Keep your enemies close, Marcus. He is less of a threat if we know who and where he is. I am thrilled we have him in our power."

"You think we can influence him? Turn him?" Quinn asked doubtfully.

"Yin and yang, Marcus. Good has a drop of evil while darkness has an eye toward the Light. They are one and the same. I am sure I can influence him if I can get close enough. Did he know you?"

"No, not completely, but he knew something. He might remember everything at any moment."

"We are no longer in the darkest of the Ages, Marcus. The Bronze Age has dawned; it will be getting harder for him to remember and easier for the Light. We may have some time. You'll have to deal with his mother."

"Whaddya mean?"

"Theron doesn't know what he's capable of. Even if she did have memory and recognized Helghul, she would never turn on her child. You may need to keep her away from him, neutralize her a bit so that I can do what needs to be done."

"You wouldn't . . . hurt him?" Quinn said, envisioning Elijah's young face.

"He's Helghul . . . Genghis . . . Alexander. He's a boy now, Marcus, but as his memory returns, he will continue on his path. The Beast that's bound to him will make sure of that."

"Unless we can turn him . . . there is always choice," Quinn interjected hopefully.

"Leave him to me. I will do everything I can," Grey Elder promised. Quinn hung up, more distraught than before.

The Emissaries Nate and Elijah settled in to Zahn's opulent digs. Quinn was unable to fully enjoy the feel of Theron with the threat of Helghul so close, and he worried how Grey Elder would handle their problem.

"I can't believe Zahn already built the Mystery School. How did he know?" Theron said.

"He's one of the good guys," Quinn replied distractedly. "Where's Elijah?" he asked, aware that the suite was free of Helghul's prickly vibrations.

"He's gone to the hotel spa with Nate and some of Zahn's bodyguards," she answered.

"I'm going to meditate. Want to join me?" Eden asked, and Quinn nodded. Together, they moved to the floor with a couple of cushions from the sofa. They crossed their legs and put their hands palms up on their knees. Within moments, they had become deathly still, and their heart rates had dropped to less than fifty beats per minute. It was said that prayer is talking to God, and meditation is listening to God. The Emissaries knew it was true, and Marcus's and Theron's shines combined and expanded.

Thirty minutes later, Quinn opened his eyes, rejuvenated and serene. He took a deep, slow breath. The only message he received was that all was as it should be. It gave him confidence that he was on the right path.

Chapter 34

The Deal Breaker

Zahn expressed his regret for not being able to travel with the rest of the group. Elijah was disappointed at having missed the opportunity to meet him, but he was assured he would be waiting at their destination. Grey Elder and Quinn had agreed it was better not to alert Helghul to the Elder's presence, unsure what level of recollection the boy had achieved. Zahn hadn't admitted to recognizing Marcus, but Helghul was shrewd. There was no telling what he did or did not recall.

Eden was stunned by Zahn's influence, affluence, and power as his employees had arranged no less than fifty separate flights to collect groups of Crystal Children and their families. Some of them Eden had only known through her research or via email, but all of them were anxious to be a part of the Seducer-Producer's gathering. Zahn couldn't lure the adult Emissaries with money, so he tricked them by offering them teaching positions with the Crystal Children. They were corralled with promises that they would advance the collective consciousness and help the world awaken.

For the few who wanted more information, Zahn imparted the story of Anjolie. As the Elder predicted, fear had been a powerful tool of persuasion for the more skeptical and resistant parents.

Only three families had refused Zahn's offer, and then . . . warning. They were willing to take their chances. They didn't trust the Hollywood type at the helm, certain there must be a catch, and, of course, there was. Those parents later regretted their choices when, within a week, as had been forewarned, their gifted children disappeared. They were gone from their swimming lessons, driveways, and bedrooms, all without a trace. The police were unable to find any clues whatsoever. The parents tried to contact Eden and Zahn for assistance but were unable to; they were thousands of miles away by then.

The first flights united a huge group of travelers for a night in London. The Crystal Children and their families were thrilled to meet one another, and they interacted excitedly, coping with language differences admirably as they enjoyed extravagant food and beverages provided for by Zahn in the hotel lounge. They felt like little princesses and princes. The collective indigo shine of the Crystal Children rose in billowing plumes around them. As their energy, connection, and numbers increased, geometric forms began to glisten like silver script in the ribbons of their dynamic auras. Quinn had never seen it before, and he marveled at the sparkling shapes as they morphed—appearing, disappearing, and turning in midair. He wondered if Elijah could see it too.

Quinn watched Eden and her son as they hugged and laughed with almost everyone. It was startling how the pair moved together through the crowd in unison, like drapes in a breeze. They felt the energy pushing and pulling them as they went from one table to the next.

"They have an amazing connection," Nate said from beside Quinn. Quinn didn't answer. He didn't trust what he might say. He still struggled to understand Helghul's and Theron's undeniable connection. How could he voice his resentment and animosity for the child? He would be misunderstood. Elijah had likewise begun to avoid him, near but ever separate, like water and oil. It was obvious, as it had been when Eden first introduced them, that their energies repelled one another.

"It's a bit eerie, isn't it? The way they sometimes make identical gestures at the same time," Nate said. His third beer had loosened his tongue. He was thawing, slowly releasing his resentment, and the Emissary was grateful. They might be okay, after all.

"What do you think of him, Nate?"

"He's just a kid. He's an unusual kid, smart as hell, you know . . . but I still don't fully *get* it. I haven't really seen him *do* anything *miraculous*. We filmed some amazing stuff for the documentary, but he sorta pales in comparison to some of those other kids. He kinda just seems normal, you know?"

"There's more to that kid than meets the eye," Quinn warned.

"Whaddya mean?" Nate asked, draining his beer and holding up the bottle as a cute young waitress passed by with a nod.

"I dunno. Just a feeling."

"You sure you're not just jealous?" Nate said, a bitter edge returning to his voice.

"Maybe I am," Quinn said disarmingly.

"I'll admit, he does seem a bit too old for his body," Nate replied.

The waitress delivered another beer to both men. She had been hovering around, giving them more than their share of attention.

"Where y'off to?" she asked, looking at Nate's funky hair and vest with interest. He was exactly the kind of man who would drive her father crazy, and she liked that.

"No idea," Nate replied with a grin. His straight white teeth stood out against his dark-brown skin, and she smiled.

"Maybe I can help you figure it out," she said with a wink.

"Not this time, Car . . . la," he said, reading the name tag pinned to her breast. "This time, we're only here for a pint," Nate said apologetically.

"Maybe next time," she said, but her eyes had lost their smile, and she just looked tired. She wondered why the men she found attractive were never the ones who tried to take her upstairs.

"It's my chair!" Elijah suddenly shouted from the other side of the room, grabbing their attention. Quinn instinctively jumped up.

"Just get another one," said another boy who had been enjoying a friendly conversation around the table.

Elijah had become irrationally angry. "It's mine! My jacket's there! Can't you see it?" he said lifting the back of the chair and dumping the other boy to the ground. Eden intervened, grabbing Elijah by the arm and pulling him away as the other boy's parents helped him up.

"Elijah, stop! I'm so sorry. He's just so anxious about all this change. Breathe . . . take a deep breath," she said sternly, her arms wrapped around the angry, struggling boy.

"My jacket!" Elijah wailed unreasonably.

"I'll get it. Stop! I'll get it," she said, scooping the windbreaker from the back of the seat and apologizing again.

Once Elijah had his jacket, his demeanor changed completely. "I'm sorry, Mom, I didn't mean it," he said, beginning to cry.

"You need to apologize," Eden said.

Nate and Quinn couldn't help. They both knew it was better not to interfere with people's parenting. Quinn had witnessed a surge in Elijah's murky shine during the outburst. Just as he had feared, Helghul was waking up, and the Beast inside him would be too.

"Somebody needs a walloping," the waitress said to them while watching the tantrum. Quinn sighed. This was not good. Elijah was going to be a problem. He had to be.

Once things quieted down and Eden had taken Elijah off to bed, Quinn and Nate focused on the TV and their beers. Headlines scrolled beneath the talking heads who reported the real and fake news. It was all spun by someone. The same few companies controlled everything, and they were motivated by money, not truth. Unfortunately, no one could tell the lies from the truth anymore. No one knew who to believe. People mostly tuned in for someone to agree with them and ignored the facts.

⋙⋘ ⋙⋘ ⋙⋘

The next day at 5:00 a.m., they boarded a new Boeing 747, accompanied by an understated squad of private soldiers. The protectors wore simple tan uniforms, and though they were physically intimidating, they were adept at fading into the background when they wished to do so. Zahn had hired a cheerful team to reassure the passengers and meet their every request.

Elijah was playing nicely with the other children, the coat incident forgotten.

Three similar flights had departed almost simultaneously from other locations. Zahn had arranged for comforting video footage of the luxurious accommodations and grounds to be shown during the flight, along with the happy, reassuring music pumping through their headsets. That, and the open bar, had worked well to put the adults at ease.

The groups arrived in waves at a massive private airstrip on the northern edge of the Libyan desert, on the border of Egypt. Armed escorts continued to guard the passengers, protecting them from an unspecified outside threat. Upon landing, the passengers were loaded onto luxury buses and shuttled to their destination. The planes had landed late at night. It was dark, and there were no cars on the road and no people. Kenya . . . rural Libya—it all looked the same to the passengers. They still had no idea that their flights had taken them nowhere near the promised safari destination. They innocently looked out the bus windows searching for giraffes and lions.

On the final journey to Zahn's compound, the passengers were dozing off. Elijah sat with Eden, and Nate and Quinn sat directly behind them. Quinn stared at the back of the boy's seat, knowing that ahead of him, in that shell, lived Helghul's memories, his intentions, and his cruelty. Inside that child was Helghul *and* the vile *thing* that had become part of him.

"Dude? Don't you have a book?" Elijah said coolly without turning around, as if he could read the Emissary's thoughts.

Eden looked up from cuddling her son and glanced back at Quinn apologetically. She nudged Elijah with her arm and pursed her lips.

Quinn didn't answer, but he was more uncomfortable than ever. Helghul's energy was heavy, and it pressed on him as he speculated how much Elijah remembered.

Out the window there was nothing but desert. They seemed to be moving away from civilization completely. They passed no cities—only one small village—and that had been hours ago. Finally, the bumpy ride came to a halt, with only stars for miles around.

"Look, it's Orion's Belt, isn't it?" Elijah asked. Nate looked out the window, wondering how he could make out any single constellations in the span of stars.

"Did you know it's actually the birthplace of galaxies?" Quinn asked.

"Yeah, yeah, and it's made up of plasma, helium, hydrogen, and dust. Thanks for the lesson, *Quinn Nye the Science Guy,*" Elijah said sarcastically. His mind flashed irritably as the Beast within him rose up.

"Elijah!" Eden exclaimed. The happy lump in her throat was replaced by embarrassment. Quinn wasn't surprised by the boy's outburst; he knew that Helghul would reveal himself eventually.

Elijah didn't know what bothered him about Quinn, but he felt horribly uneasy whenever the man was nearby. The man didn't say much, but Elijah's impression was that he was smug and self-important. He didn't know where the intuition came from. Quinn had avoided him and had barely said two words in front of him, but he just felt it.

An instinct, the boy thought. *Mom always taught me to trust my instincts.*

But Eden hadn't known the instincts she was encouraging were that of an Adversary; and even worse, an Adversary bound to an eternally dark and evil Beast.

Quinn waved off the slight; he understood Helghul's motivations even if the boy did not.

Eden rested her arm on the top of Elijah's seat, still smiling a nonverbal apology at Quinn. Quinn reached out and touched her hand reassuringly, and a thick ball of loving energy gathered in her chest. Quinn was always surprising her. Every time they touched, she was stunned by the powerful impact. Nate saw the brief caress and bristled as he continued to stare out the window.

The multitude of buses stopped in a line, and their doors opened. Sleeping passengers woke, and casual conversations were replaced by confused chatter. The passengers were unloaded at the edge of a desert speckled with a few tan-colored, army-style tents. It was obvious that this was not the luxurious sanctuary they had been expecting, though they were greeted by four musicians playing happy music next to tables filled with fresh fruit, delicious snacks, and jugs of icy fruit punch. The dusty place looked nothing like the pictures they had been shown.

"We must not be there yet. Is this a stop in between?"

"Mama, where are the animals?"

"Where are we supposed to sleep?"

"I thought there was a hotel? Gardens? There's nothing here!"

"Is there even electricity?"

"There aren't even enough tents!"

The multitude of voices clamored over one another while the people helped themselves to the abundant refreshments. The security forces that had accompanied the groups reassuringly ushered people toward one central tent.

"We have an extremely safe place for you, to protect you from the roaming animals," one of the hostesses said with too much enthusiasm. "You all know Batman, right? Well, this is like the Batcave, except way cooler," she continued.

Quinn was uneasy. *What is this? Where is Grey Elder? Surely he will arrive soon and explain everything.*

The wind whipped at them from every side. Eden removed her sweater from around her hips and put it on, buttoning it closed. The other travelers donned their jackets and shawls. There were torches stuck at angles in the sand; their blowing flames flickered across the low dunes.

"This way, line up here," a guard called. The assembly moved toward a plain fifteen-by-fifteen-foot canvas tent. One after another, the confused visitors entered, and the line shrank quickly. Impossible. People continued to cross the threshold of the tent, but no one exited, and miraculously, the small shelter did not grow full and burst at the seams. One hundred, two hundred—they all filed in, amazed by what they found.

Inside the mysterious tent was a large, perfectly square hole in the ground with an open trapdoor of thick steel. Within the hole was a steep metal stairway with fifteen steps. It was well lit, and the walls were painted brightly. It smelled clean and new, and the Emissaries entered, excited by how chic and hip it was.

"It's amazing down there. It's a secure underground facility with everything you could possibly want, and more," they promised. "Zahn spared no expense."

The foursome was in the middle of the pack. Nate descended first, followed by Eden, Elijah, and then Quinn. They were anxious to see what awaited them below. They could hear the buzz of excited voices ahead of them.

Quinn was skeptical. *What did I get us into?* he thought, anxious to speak with Zahn.

At the bottom of the steps, there was a long, smoothly cut tunnel about seven feet high, painted crisp white and lit with fashionable electric fixtures. There was a multilanguage *Welcome* sign ten feet in length, and the younger children were excited by the streamers and balloons along the path. The tunnel was at a decline, taking the travelers deeper into the cool earth.

At the end of the corridor, a massive elevator door shone brilliantly, reflecting the light. The freight elevator took them deeper—how far, they couldn't tell, but as the doors opened, guests were stunned by what they saw.

They entered an enormous room, modern and glowing with pale marble floors and walls and a ceiling of polished copper. There were so many people—not only the Crystal Children but hundreds of other Emissaries milling around. Grey Elder had brought them all to Northern Africa on false pretenses, making full use of his abundant resources. They were contained, thirty feet below the surface.

Quinn's head was reeling, and he continued to watch Elijah suspiciously for any sign of Helghul-memory. The boy stood innocently at Eden's side, wondering aloud with the others. People all around remarked in astonishment and proceeded farther into the expansive structure, pleased with what they found.

"Toys!" the children shrieked, running to the colorful play center with everything they could want, and shelves packed with books. It wasn't what they had expected, but it was modern, luxurious, and comfortable.

One of the guards walked over and tapped Quinn's arm, saying, "Please come with me. Mr. Zahn would like to speak with you."

At last, Quinn thought, relieved. *Now we'll get an explanation.* He walked toward the elevator. "Bring your friends," the man said, nodding toward Eden, Nate, and Elijah. They followed the guard into the elevator, and when the door opened at the top, Zahn was in the long hallway, waiting. Zahn's tan pants and untucked white linen shirt hung casual and loose, and he still wore his Serengeti shades. The Seducer-Producer was flanked by his massive bodyguards.

Quinn tried to move around the security barrier toward Zahn but was prevented from doing so. "I just need to talk to him," he said in surprise, but the sentries remained silent and impregnable. Zahn scrutinized the foursome.

"Ahhh, Quinn!" he purred. With the flick of his perfectly manicured hand, the guards stepped aside, allowing him eye contact but still blocking Quinn from getting any closer.

"What's going on?" Quinn asked. They stood in front of the elevator, surrounded by at least twenty armed and expressionless mercenaries. He wanted a simple, reasonable explanation. He wanted to hear absolutely anything except the horrible truth that he had only just realized.

"Haven't you figured it out yet, Marcus?" Grey Elder sneered, and Quinn's stomach constricted. The intuition he had been struggling to ignore let loose, and he felt a bitter sting as his Marcus-memory fully recognized the familiar feeling of captivity. He felt nauseated and briefly missed the sanctuary of his apartment. His Marcus-consciousness was feeding him information and explanations he was loath to accept: He had been deceived. He had led them all into a trap. He had willingly walked into his own prison.

"Helghul is *my* creature, Marcus. *I* was in the cavern the night you saw him sacrificed to the Darkness. *I* was the hooded mentor," the Elder hissed menacingly, pausing to allow the monumental declaration to set in.

Quinn pounced—fast and fluid, having mastered many forms of fighting. He skillfully got past the closest guards and grabbed Zahn.

"Get the girl!" Zahn croaked as the other guards took hold of Eden, and one pummeled Quinn from behind with the butt of his automatic rifle. Three more grunting guards pulled Quinn off Zahn. The soldiers had been told not to kill the prisoners.

"Don't make me kill her," Zahn hissed angrily, and Quinn finally stopped struggling, his back severely bruised from where he'd been hit, and a goose egg rising on his head.

"The veins at Quinn's collar were bulging as he strained against the thugs, who were restraining him on either side. Blood ran down his neck from the cut on his scalp.

"She was always your weakness, Marcus. You were so blind. So willing to shirk your responsibility."

Zahn removed his lopsided sunglasses and saw that they had been bent in the fracas. He threw them aside. He remained composed, as if nothing had happened, though his hollow blue eyes had lost their phony sparkle, and the shine surrounding him had turned an ominous dark grey as he revealed himself.

"You killed those children? Anjolie?" Quinn accused, referring to the Crystal Child from Lyon who had been murdered.

Eden gasped at the accusation and tried to break free, but the line of mercenaries barred her way. She hadn't understood why Quinn had lunged at Zahn, but the threat to murder her had been clear . . . and this?

"An unfortunate necessity," Zahn said.

"What have you done?" Eden shouted, but Zahn ignored her. It didn't make sense—none of it made sense! Elijah was crying and fighting to free himself next to her, but she could only console him verbally, since the guards held each of them with crushing fingers.

"Let me go . . . or I'll . . . kill you . . . ," Elijah said, struggling to get to his mother.

"It's okay, honey, it's okay. Stop struggling . . . you don't have to hold him so tight! He's just a kid! Stop struggling, Elijah, it's making it worse. You bastards! Honey, calm down . . . relax, and it won't hurt," Eden cried out. She was helpless to protect him, and it was horrifying to watch her child, so afraid and in pain.

Quinn was equally distraught. He had delivered Eden and the Crystal Children to the Adversaries! The weight of his error was crushing him. How could they light the world now? Would the Dark Age continue because of his failure?

Zahn was only inches from the Emissary's face now. "I was Anytus, Marcus," he said in a low voice. "I . . . was Hitler," he said, pausing to let the heinous truth sink in. "I came close to world domination then, but small failures precede great victories. I have carefully planned for this day. I, like you, have lived many lives, and in each I have conspired and manipulated to arrive at this moment. In this life I was born to a useless pair of simple people, but as you can see, I rose to power, as I always have. Memory and money are wonderful tools. I am proof of the greatness *you* could have aspired to if *you* had used the power you were given," Grey Elder said.

Though Quinn had stopped struggling, the guards continued to dig steely fingers into his flesh.

"There's nothing great about you! You create nothing, you only destroy, and you'll be defeated," he said, determined to keep his emotions hidden. He wouldn't give in to any more outbursts. He didn't want to give Grey Elder the satisfaction.

"Life is illusory, my son. Tell me, who do you believe yourself to be? A pot-smoking blogger? When did you get so *weak*? At what point did the Darkness break you down so completely? You were once the great *Plato*, and you have fallen just like Greece herself, from greatness into ruin. You've had the advantage of memory and have done *what* with it? You were so easily manipulated, Marcus. What a disappointment you are," Grey Elder taunted, pacing back and forth in front of him.

Quinn was filled with rage and shame, but he refused to be provoked. The Elder continued: "With yours and Theron's help, I've found almost every Emissary. You'd like to go back, wouldn't you? Run away with your dear soulmate?"

"What do you want from us?" Eden demanded.

She was afraid, not having understood the disturbing conversation. She wondered who Zahn really was. *Who was Theron? Who had always been Quinn's weakness? What lifetimes? Did he say he was Hitler? He said he was Hitler! What the hell is happening?* Eden thought, desperate to comprehend. It made no sense. Oswald Zahn was a good guy, the best, so what was happening?

Nate was equally confused and glared at the guards binding him.

"Zahn, what the fuck's going on?" Nate asked, but Grey Elder ignored their questions, speaking only to Quinn.

"You gave me everything I wanted, and soon I will have the Emerald Tablet. The Emissaries are here and cannot hinder my progress. You'll be contained, and I will have my way in the world."

"The people will surprise you!" Quinn warned. "There are many good, enlightened people. Socrates and Buddha weren't Emissaries! Consciousness is evolving; you can't change that. The world is waking up. The genetic anomalies of the Crystal Children are now more frequent. You can't stop pure consciousness from being born into the collective."

Zahn laughed, and his guards laughed too, though they were ignorant about the meaning of the conversation.

"What? Like Nate there? The good soul you told me about who tossed you aside for the slightest bruise to his ego? For jealousy?"

Nate was surprised to hear his name, and he colored, shame-faced, as the truth was spoken.

"You underestimate people. There *is* unity and compassion," Eden said.

Zahn turned with a sudden jerk, scowling at her. "But the world looks to *me*! *I* am their idol, the great humanitarian, the Seducer-Producer, the great Oswald Zahn. *I* am their god. Celebrity and money is all they value. You say 'God,' and most of the world tunes out. They shut off, repelled by the word and all its connotations, or they divide into their religious trenches and prepare for battle! They think God is some imaginary old being sitting on a throne in the clouds, not something inside *them*! Something they are!"

"You're wrong," Quinn said.

"You think they've come so far? Look at how broken down *you* were, and you're supposed to be one of the *chosen* ones! Do you really think the rest of them have a chance?" He flipped his hand toward Quinn in disgust.

"This *is* a time of awakening. The conscious revolution has begun. You're afraid or you wouldn't have us here," Eden said.

"The hardship's just starting. I'll fan the flames of their innermost fears and fill the world with so many lies they won't know what to believe. They *will* shed their false cloaks of goodness and light and scatter like cockroaches to hide themselves once again in the darkest corners, protecting only themselves and their precious *things*. I will crush every light-sentient being that walks this Earth, and the Darkness will reign forever," Zahn hissed, enunciating every syllable.

Elijah whimpered. "It's okay, sweetie. We're going to be okay," Eden said, catching his eye and trying to soothe him.

"Why are you doing this?" Nate asked simply. Nate, a man without memory or understanding of the higher consciousness, had asked the most important question of all.

"It is my destiny. It is . . . my *role*," Grey Elder answered calmly.

"But why?" Nate asked again.

When it was obvious Grey Elder did not intend to answer, Quinn piped up.

"Because without choice, there is no true goodness. If there is no evil, and no opportunity to choose *between* good and evil, then there is no real good at all. It is the original intention that we all develop and grow consciousness by our choices," Quinn said.

"The darkest times . . . wake the soul," Elijah interjected from where he stood. His childish voice was high, like a lizard's chirp in the night. Zahn looked at him, hoping that Helghul was awake enough to be useful.

"The Emissaries have failed. The Bronze Age will not rise. The Great Darkness will remain," Zahn announced proudly.

"You can't keep us here!" Eden said.

"This fortress is impregnable. I suggest you prepare for a long stay," the Elder replied. "At least you'll finally have your Theron, Marcus. That's all you've ever cared about."

The intimidating guards aimed their weapons, menacingly protecting their commander and chief.

"Bring the boy," Zahn ordered.

Eden and Elijah punched and howled in protest, but the boy was helplessly restrained and carried like a sack over a beefy shoulder.

"Gently now!" Zahn shouted. He did not wish to injure or offend his ally Helghul further.

"No!" Eden screamed, as they held her.

"Mooooommm!" Elijah wailed hysterically. Quinn and Nate were unable to intervene. None of them relented. They continued struggling and shouting. Elijah was carried away, and Zahn and his guards followed, except for the small group detaining Nate, Eden, and Quinn.

Outside, Elijah was maneuvered into Seducer-Producer's Range Rover and sandwiched in by guards on either side. Zahn climbed into the front passenger seat and did not look back at the crying boy as they departed.

Once Elijah was gone, the others were returned to the bunker at gunpoint. There was no accessible control panel inside the bunker.

There was no escape. They were surrounded by solid stone floors and walls, and Quinn was powerless to stop Grey Elder. He went to Eden, who was sobbing in Nate's arms. Quinn and Nate held Eden on either side as she continued to cry for her abducted child.

"I'm sorry I got you into this. I trusted him. I can't believe I trusted him!" Quinn said, hanging his head.

Eden couldn't register his apology. It didn't make sense. There was nothing anyone could say to console her, but she had so many questions.

"He fooled everyone. The whole world thinks he's a saint or guru or something. He's on the board of half the world's biggest charities. How could you have known?" Nate comforted him, his injured ego forgotten.

"I should have known better. I should have seen through him. I believed he was good," Quinn said miserably. He remembered the night in the cave, the many dreams about it. It had been seared into his memory. Grey Elder had been the cloaked grand master to Helghul on the night of the Exodus from Atitala. It had been Grey Elder who had first separated Marcus from Theron, with what Quinn now surmised had been a phony leg injury. How could he have missed it? He had gone back to the memory so many times. Was he meant to have seen it? Had he failed? Could he have figured it out? Could he have paid closer attention and prevented this nightmare? Socrates's words burned through him. "Question everything," his mentor had said, but the Emissary had failed to do so.

"I have no idea what is going on here," Nate said from Eden's other side.

Chapter 35

A Truth Told

Quinn could see the amethyst karmic code surrounding the crowd in the bunker. Their auras joined together and grew thicker and stronger when they were combined, and he saw the silver outlines of the sacred geometric shapes, once again glistening in the air above them. Despite the confusion the prisoners felt, Marcus sensed that their spirits remained optimistic.

They were doomed, and none of them knew the truth about why they were there or understood how they were alike. They saw the polished marble floors, miles of immaculate bright hallways, comfortable stainless-steel dorm beds, well-stocked kitchens, and they remained hopeful. Only Quinn knew that Zahn had collected them like butterflies pinned under glass. They were neutralized and trapped.

There were Emissaries from every continent, of every age and color. Zahn had sent out pleas, calls for help, donations, and volunteers. In response, from around the globe, doctors, teachers, environmentalists, and artists had flocked to him. The Elder had appealed to their sense of duty and service. He was the Seducer-Producer, after all; his persona carried influence, especially among the philanthropic. Marcus recognized his old friends Yashoda, Holt, and Bapoo, but he could not celebrate the reunion, for they, too, were locked away with their influence stifled. They had each been there a few days, or weeks, arriving from different locations, but no one understood what was going on.

Keep your enemies close; better to know where they reside, Marcus thought. In his life as Sartaña, Helghul had imprisoned him for that very reason. Zahn had said the same thing when talking about Elijah, but Quinn knew now that he had been talking about him.

Zahn had identified and collected the Emissaries easily, like shiny rocks on a beach. He may have missed a few, or there were others yet to be reborn, but he was tenacious. He was determined to silence them and to withhold their energy from the world.

All around him, people sat on modular benches and cubes instead of traditional tables and chairs. It reminded Quinn of a modern university campus. It was amazing that a subterranean world like this could exist, but it did. It must have cost a fortune. Despite having Nate and Eden beside him, Quinn felt desperately alone.

"Where has he taken my son?" Eden demanded, rounding on Quinn. The tiny woman shook. Her throat constricted with emotion. Eden's head was pounding. She was terrified for Elijah, and her mind was spinning with pieces of the conversation between Quinn and Zahn: *Marcus? Theron? Hitler? What were they saying?* She felt as though her heart had been carved from her chest. Elijah was gone, and she was responsible for leading the others into danger. *What the hell was happening?*

Quinn hesitated. He didn't know what to say.

"I don't know," Quinn lied. He knew that Grey Elder would be headed to Alexandria, Egypt, to retrieve the Emerald Tablet, if he hadn't done so already.

I gave him the Emerald Tablet! And an Elder will know how to use it! Quinn thought.

He watched helplessly as Eden once again broke down crying in Nate's arms. Quinn ached to console her, but he was not the one she'd reached out for. A few fellow newcomers hovered close by, anxious to hear anything they could, and those who had already been imprisoned there observed the exchange curiously.

After a few minutes, Eden's sobs subsided, and Quinn placed a gentle hand on her back. They each felt the powerful tug, as though the very cores of them were connected.

"What was all that crazy talk? What the hell is going on?" she asked, her misery caught in her throat. She took another deep breath, summoning her inner strength. Her dark hair was wild around her face, and strands were pasted by tears to her cheeks. Her eyes were bloodshot and glowing bright green, and Quinn thought she looked magical.

"I don't know where to begin," Quinn said.

"Start anywhere! Tell us everything you know that we don't, but just give us some answers!" she demanded, a sob catching on a hiccup as she spoke. She was standing on her own now, and Nate stood beside her, anxious for Quinn to explain.

Quinn was tired before even beginning. He spoke in low tones, not wanting those eavesdropping nearby to hear.

"I trusted him. I had no reason to doubt him," Quinn said, but as he spoke, the words felt like a lie. Once again, he flashed to the images of the cloaked figure in Atitala, and he wondered if he had always known it was Grey Elder. Perhaps he had chosen not to see?

"We were all fooled." Eden said with a gulp. She did not blame Quinn for their predicament. He couldn't have known.

"Eden, this is not the first time we've met . . . nor is this the first time I have explained this to you. We come from a place long ago where we were chosen. We are Emissaries . . . many of the others here and all the Crystal Children are Emissaries as well. We are envoys, chosen to bring love and hope to the world, to preserve the knowledge of Oneness and guide the world back into enlightenment. Like you . . . the rest of these people don't know it."

Eden, and especially Nate, stared at him skeptically, but he had anticipated their disbelief and apprehension.

"Emissaries?" Eden said, repeating the word and remembering Quinn's blog name.

"There are a lot of us," Quinn explained.

"This is impossible . . . I mean, it's too unreal . . . I don't *know* the secret of Oneness. How can I share it if I don't even know it?" she asked doubtfully.

"I've wondered that myself, but you always seem to find a way . . . all of you do . . . you just seem to . . . know."

"Who is Theron?" Eden asked.

Quinn gulped. To hear her say the name was overwhelming. "You . . . it's *you*. Your name was Theron," he said, and Eden gasped in surprise.

Nate listened carefully, the hair on his neck standing on end. Quinn could see and feel the karmic energy around Eden billowing and exploring as it joined with the many auras united in the room.

"Me? What do you mean?"

"We are consciousness having a human experience, not humans having a conscious experience."

"Oh, here we go," Nate moaned.

"Shhh! Go on, I need to know what all this means if I'm going to find my son," Eden said, frowning at Nate briefly. The tears in her eyes had been replaced by determination. She was collecting information now, building a plan to rescue Elijah. "I'm no good to Elijah crying on the floor. We have to figure out what's happening and find him."

She needed to understand everything Zahn had said.

"There is an intrinsic essence in each of us that survives our bodies and connects us to one another . . . if you don't believe that, then there is no point telling you anything else," Quinn said, exhausted both from centuries of enduring his predicament and by the hopelessness of their situation.

"You know I believe it," she said.

Nate did not claim to accept the idea of consciousness or a soul, but he listened with new consideration. He wanted to understand.

"Go ahead," Eden urged, gesturing impatiently. Quinn was going far too slowly.

"Our home was called Atitala. There have been many civilizations before ours. They come and go with the cycle of the Great Year. A Golden Age ended about thirteen thousand years ago. We were chosen as Emissaries and given the responsibility of maintaining the Light and leaving clues of the ancient knowledge for those who would seek it. Our world shifted dramatically, and we were scattered like seeds to the wind. We have been reincarnated many times, driven by our purpose. There is much darkness in the world; this is perpetuated by our Adversaries. I thought Zahn was with the Light—he was an Elder, one of our leaders in Atitala—but I was wrong. Now the Great Year is due to begin its ascent and eventually take us into an Age of higher consciousness, but Zahn is trying to prevent that."

Eden contemplated him intently. She had read the theories about the twenty-six-thousand-year cycle and had seen *The Great Year* documentary. She had researched it while preparing for her shoot. It was everywhere: the notion that human history dated back much farther than historians and theologians believed, and civilizations came and went in cycles.

She looked into Quinn's eyes. There was no guile there, no urgency, no pleading or need to convince her. She saw only patience, weariness, honesty, and longing. With her gaze fixed on him so intently, the ache within him grew like grass yearning to be touched by sunlight.

"And who are *we* to each other?" she asked. Quinn's eyes changed and became smoky, and his lids lowered slightly. Nate grew rigid next to her. The talk about the light and the darkness had been confusing, but *this* he understood. The undeniable bond between Quinn and Eden was about to be explained.

"We . . . are *everything*," Quinn murmured, and his shine was deep purple and gold, radiating in beats around him. "You chose me, and I chose you. We are soulmates. Eternally entangled." He dared to sweep the hair from her face, and he placed his hand on her cheek. Would she push him away? Would she reject his touch? He couldn't stop himself. To be so near, so close to her, and yet apart, was unbearable.

Eden raised her hand, but she did not deny his touch. She placed her fingers over his and kissed him. Quinn swept her up into his arms, and they kissed with the passion of centuries of longing. Nate wanted to stop her, but she was Quinn's, and Quinn was hers. It had been obvious since they'd met. Quinn was euphoric; Eden was overwhelmed. The power of their ancient energies binding together filled them both. Hesitantly, Eden pulled away.

"Why is Elijah separated? Why isn't he here with the rest of us?" she asked, with fresh tears slipping down her cheeks.

"Elijah's . . . special," Quinn answered diplomatically, though even in his joy, his jaw clenched at the thought of Helghul.

"Special *how*?" Eden asked. Their forearms were locked together, and they held each other by the elbow.

"He's powerful, more powerful than most," Quinn explained.

"Is he in danger?" the mother asked, desperate for reassurance.

"I don't think so. I think Grey Elder will try to use him again," Quinn answered.

"Again?" Nate and Eden echoed simultaneously.

"There've been many lifetimes in thirteen thousand years," Quinn said.

"After he was born, I had a vivid dream that he was an emperor," she said.

"He was. Some of them weren't dreams, they were memories. Zahn knew your memory could start returning. It's another sign of the Dark Age having ended. You probably know more than you think; you've just classified your memories incorrectly. They were past *realities*."

"I've had a recurring dream about the Mongolian plains ever since I met you," she admitted.

"We were there," Quinn confirmed.

"Egypt?" Nate gasped.

"Yes, Nate. We knew each other there, but the first time I saw you was in a place called Stone-at-Center. It's called Tiahuanaco, Bolivia, now," Quinn said.

"So, I'm an—" Nate said, struggling to say the right word.

"Emissary?" Quinn finished for him. "No. All living beings are reincarnated. Most people will have flashes of memory and recognition, especially as children; they just don't understand them. Most kids are trained not to believe."

Quinn could see Nate's disappointment, so he added, "That doesn't mean you're not important. We are part of the same soul group," Quinn explained, but Nate was obviously unsatisfied. Soul group, shmole group . . . he wanted to be a chosen one!

Eden jumped in. "So we're . . . soulmates, and my son is some sort of . . . leader, but what now? We're prisoners here? What do we do *now*?" she asked.

"We pray, we meditate, and we wait. The answers will come," Quinn replied.

"Oh, for fuck's sake, really? That's all the wisdom we get . . . just sit and wait?" Nate said in frustration.

"With spiritualism comes trust and acceptance, Nate. Anyway, have you got a better idea?" Quinn asked calmly.

"Hard to have a worse one," Nate snorted.

Eden looked at him with compassion and placed her hand on his arm. "He's right, Nate. We just have to wait and ask for guidance. Do you think they know?" she asked, gesturing to the others.

"No."

"Why? Why are *you* the only one who knows?" Nate asked curiously.

"We weren't meant to remember. I took a memory potion and chose a torturous road."

"Why didn't I?" Eden asked.

"You didn't have the opportunity," Quinn said simply. "I've searched for you in every lifetime," he told her, stroking her wrist as he spoke.

"Did you find me?"

"Too often, I did not."

"It must be lonely being the only one to remember," she sympathized.

"Your depression makes sense," Nate said.

"Was it difficult?" Eden asked.

"I traveled my path . . . and I learned there is no shortcut to enlightenment, even for an Emissary. Separation and loneliness are powerful illusions. It's only on this plane that we experience the isolation associated with the false belief that we are independent beings. *That* misapprehension does not exist elsewhere in the Universe. We come into our bodies to feel this, yet we spend our entire lives trying to get back to unity and connection," Marcus said.

"You have to tell them who they are," Eden said, gesturing to the diverse, multicolored crowd.

"They won't believe me," he answered.

"They *need* to know. I think this is the reason why you took the memory potion. This moment, this time right now, is why *you* have memory. It's so you can help us *all* understand."

"Once again, you imagine me nobler than I am. I stumbled my way into becoming an Emissary, and I may have doomed all of us with my blindness," Quinn confessed miserably.

"You have to tell them," Nate said sternly.

Quinn and Eden looked at him in surprise.

"Well, they have a right to know . . . to make up their own minds. At least you owe them that. I'm trying, you know. I wanna believe this Oneness thing. I want to think I've been here before, and I'll be here again, and that life has some meaning. But it's easy to say. I just wish I *knew* it, *really* felt it, like you two seem to. There's so much faith, and I just don't . . . *feel* it."

"You will, eventually," Quinn answered. "It's like building a pyramid—keystones, base, and then one layer at a time until you reach the top. The light is much brighter closer to the top, so it's easier to see it."

"So you're closer to the top than I am?" Nate tried to clarify.

"No. You can't compare people like that . . . I'm an Emissary, and I have memory . . . there just aren't as many mysteries for me. There are truths that I know absolutely."

"Such as?" Nate asked, intrigued and wanting to be convinced.

"It is not my place to convince you . . . you will come to it on your own, when you're ready."

"Maybe you're supposed to teach me . . . so I can get there quicker. Maybe that's why *I'm* in *your* soul gang."

"Soul group," Quinn corrected.

"Whatever," Nate said impatiently. "Tell me something you know. Tell me the mysteries."

"Okay. But you could have found this information anywhere. That's the thing about the mysteries. They're all around us. People just *don't* see or *choose* to see." Quinn paused, and Nate rolled his hands over one another, gesturing impatiently for him to continue. "When we die, our souls recycle back into the Grid . . . think of it like a web of superhighways, but electric current and light, not matter. We are whole and connected, and we know and see totally differently. We see and taste and hear and experience with every part of our spirit, not through five limited senses, and it's . . . Heaven. Perfection. Words are sorely inadequate."

"I knew it!" Eden said. "You must tell *them*."

"What am I going to say? God help me! What should I say?" Quinn said desperately, and instantly an answer came before anyone could say a word. It was a whisper, a silent instinct inside his head. *The truth. Tell them the truth.*

"The truth," Eden whispered.

They stood together, and Quinn called out to the crowd around him.

"People, everyone, I need your attention, please!" he exclaimed, unsure how to proceed. Would they believe him? Would they think he was insane? The crowd came closer and grew quiet, except for the younger children zooming about. As people grew nearer to one another, their karmic energies grew more brilliant.

Quinn stepped up onto a side table to better project his voice and waited for the chatter to subside.

"My name is Quinn," he began, "and I have a message for you and a story to share." He paused. There were others echoing his words in whispers to one another, translating from English and trying to make sure everyone understood.

"It's about time!" a parent of a Crystal Child grumbled.

"I suspect that for many of you, in your lives you have felt a sense of urgency, a purpose, a need to do good and to heal others in the world." The crowd around him looked on in anticipation. "This might sound crazy . . . but I'm here to tell you that you are all chosen people. Most of you are Emissaries reincarnated into this world as teachers, healers, and messengers. I have just learned . . . too late . . . that Zahn is a fallen Elder, a dark soul, and he has gathered us here to control and neutralize us . . . to extinguish our Light and to cast the world into continued darkness."

The crowd listened intently, stirring with skepticism and emotion. The room was electrified, and Quinn felt the hum of the bonding collective energies as they warmed the air. It was reminiscent of the connections Marcus had experienced in Atitala. He knew that Eden had been correct. Having taken the memory potion was allowing him to play this role. Marcus knew if he had it to do over again, he would make the same choice.

"But what can we do? How do we get these kids out of here?" a male voice called out.

"I'm afraid," a female voice said.

"This is crazy!" someone else said.

"How can we make a difference stuck here?" a deep voice intoned.

"Shhh," several Crystal Children said in unison.

Quinn had the answers they sought. "We have to try. One thing I do know is that fear and doubt keep the soul from moving forward and growing and advancing. By being conscious of that, by choosing to face our fears, we can overpower them. We are all consciousness. We never stop being consciousness. If you believe you have a soul, then you must know that your divinity never leaves you. When we join with others like us, others who understand the power of Oneness and connection, then we can illuminate the darkness around us. We can alter the vibration of the collective world consciousness."

"But we're here. We're trapped God-knows-where. How can we illuminate anything from here?" a woman asked.

"God-knows-where . . . you said it yourself. It is not on a human, physical level that we must battle . . . we can't beat Zahn that way. Those soldiers and their guns are real. Ours must be a spiritual resistance. Spirit cannot be contained by walls or chains. It crosses an ocean or a continent without a moment's passing, fast as the speed of thought. If we recognize that we are One and join with the power of one intention, we affect the odds of probability. We may be able to send hope to the world outside these walls, enough positive energy and connection to link with others and make a difference," Quinn answered optimistically.

"The power of prayer," someone added with a smile.

"Yes," Quinn said. "There will be millions of people reaching out spiritually: good people. They, too, will be struggling to abate their fears. As Emissaries, we each chose this mission and purpose. We can merge our positive energies with theirs. We can fight against the great darkness. Our bodies come and go, but we are not only our bodies, we are so much more," he finished, with his adrenaline flowing, feeling a bit like a crazy evangelist. He was reminded of his lifetime as Plato and his connection to spirit as Chilger all at once. All his lifetimes had prepared him for this moment. He looked out at the many faces, and he readied himself for the arguments and doubts that he knew would certainly come.

"I have to get out of here! I have children, a family! You don't understand, they'll be sick with worry!" one Russian woman near the back called out in despair.

Others chimed in their concern and fears, understandable and essentially human.

"Americans did this!" a Punjabi man near the front said in broken English. "You are one of them. Why should we believe you?" he asked suspiciously.

"We cannot be divided. I know it's shocking. I know it's difficult, but we must trust one another," Quinn answered.

"That will never work!" another exasperated voice intoned.

"We are here indefinitely; we should at least try. It's better than retreating into despair," an African woman near the front, with the shine of the Emissary Yashoda, said.

"I prayed for the monks, and they were killed just the same. It's a waste of time," a Tibetan woman said softly.

"Many died, but many more *lived*; their purpose was not suppressed," Quinn answered.

"I don't belong here," an elderly, thickly accented Frenchman spoke up. "I am not one of those . . . those things you talk of. I am a surgeon. I have a practice. I must get back to Paris. I don't even believe in this soul business . . . when we die, we just die," he said, arching a bushy silver eyebrow.

"Why should we believe you? We don't even know you!" an irritated voice called out.

"What could I possibly want from you? I can't make you believe me . . . I can only tell you what I know is true," Quinn answered, more tired than defensive, and buoyed by the tight grip Eden had on his arm.

"So, *Monsieur*, tell us . . . why do *you* know? What makes *you* so special?" the old surgeon queried with less sarcasm than Quinn would have expected.

"I am not special, *you* are. I don't think I am nearly as special as any one of you. All I ask is that you sit *still*. *Listen* to your own thoughts; the answers are within you."

"'And he shall magnify himself in his heart and by peace shall destroy many. He shall stand up against the Prince of Princes, but he shall be broken without hand.' Daniel 8:25! The Bible forewarns of this time in the End of Days when God's people will resist without violence and overcome the Great Darkness!" the Emissary Holt said. He was now a Honduran priest in his thirties.

The crowd was buzzing, mostly with positive energy and hopefulness. There was doubt and fear, but many *believed*. The Crystal

Children joined in circles and began to meditate. The karmic energy was building, and Quinn could see it all around them. People pondered and contemplated and discussed, and despite their personal losses and misgivings, a loving current pulsated through the congregation. It had grown with every word, as Quinn had confirmed for them what many had already known deep inside.

"How do I start?" Eden asked with a fresh strength in her determined jaw. Quinn met her direct gaze and was electrified by her indigo shine, thick and compelling. Before he could answer, a very young child spoke out from near the front, his shine glowing indigo and tipped with golden light. "We need to merge," the boy said, his innocent voice heard clearly across the large gathering, and Quinn could see Bapoo's shine radiating from the child.

"Exactly," replied Quinn, placing a gentle hand on his head.

One by one, some more hesitantly than others, the Emissaries began linking arms.

Chapter 36

The Revelation

Quinn embraced Eden, and Nate placed his hand on her shoulder. They were soon joined by the others, hand to shoulder from the center out in concentric rings, which from above would have resembled a human web. The energy surrounding them grew exponentially as more joined them, one hand to one shoulder at a time.

"I hope it helps," the tear-choked voice of the Tibetan woman said softly.

"It won't hurt," someone near her said kindly, placing a reassuring hand on her shoulder.

Quinn watched as the Emissaries connected and the combined shines became stronger, thicker, creating geometric forms and illuminating the room. He placed his forehead against Eden's and was shocked by what happened next. *Zip!* At that point in time, facilitated by the powerful energy of the fellow Emissaries, Theron was catapulted into her memories. It was like being sucked skyward in the vortex of a tornado. She gasped at the vivid, colorful show. Her lives became known to her, and the couple rested their heads together with a filmstrip of many lifetimes rolling between them. Theron saw her heart's true love, and she spoke his name.

"Marcus," she breathed as they entwined their hands, their foreheads touching, their eyes closed, sharing visions both could see. Everything around them was forgotten as they came together once more.

You remember? Quinn asked telepathically, in mind pictures. It was his very greatest wish.

I do! Ohhh, I remember . . . everything, she answered, without speaking, as the stories unfolded without any sense of time passing. All her memories came alive inside her simultaneously. Many played at once, but each one remained clear, beautiful and distinct from the others, and she knew them intimately.

This outcome was unexpected. *Is it a result of the Emissaries coming together?* Quinn wondered. He knew it was a gift, and he was overcome with gratitude.

In an instant, Eden remembered and felt everything they had ever been. She saw that she'd been transported to Prague by Kammler and had visited her wife and daughter, Sophie-Yashoda, in Theresienstadt. She remembered being Milo Blanc, touching the Emerald Tablet, and regaining her memories then. She had recognized Kammler as Helghul and had blown up the installation.

The vortex spun, and she saw another life—making love in a ger. Then Inti, the son of Sartaña, and Aristotle, and so many more, with and without Marcus. Nate was there too, and Elijah, always prominently popping in and out. She saw her soul group and understood it as she had never been able to before. There were others in her memories, some of them huddled in the group around her now. Lifetime after lifetime, Theron and Marcus were connected. Sadly, they saw their near misses, when they had been close but unaware of each other. There had been hospital beds in the same building but on different floors, and passing on opposite sides of a marketplace on the same day. Their destinies were beautifully bound together, like a tapestry carefully woven with the finest thread, but they had only found each other when it was intended to be.

Eden was filled with love and gratitude. The vortex slowed, and like a column of ash settling to the ground after a volcanic eruption, Quinn and Eden returned to themselves. Neither spoke; they just held one another, connecting with all those around them.

They had joined and were sending the world compassion and healing energy. Everyone present had had the same experience. The gathering of the Emissaries had produced an unexpected result. Zahn had certainly not anticipated this. Together, they had awakened to their souls' past lives. As they had joined hands to shoulders and connected, they were immersed in memory and knowledge. They had awakened a unified power larger than the sum of its parts.

The cynical French surgeon had seen himself as Joan of Arc and was privy to her every memory and thought. The young boy, Bapoo, who had suggested they pray, had seen his lifetime in Atitala and others as Sir Isaac Newton and as Commander Cruzen. The other Emissaries: Mother Teresa, Louis Pasteur, Charles Dickens, Mirabai, Copernicus, Marie Curie, Leonardo da Vinci, Helen Keller, Edgar Cayce, and so many more, famous and not. They were all there, remembering—swirling magically in the energy and communion of the gathering, and joining in the work yet to be done.

The Emissaries could see their auras and recognize one another. Having come together, they understood completely who and what they were. Even the family members of the Crystal Children felt empowered and more than a little overwhelmed.

Grey Elder was unaware of the vibration rising in the prison bunker and was ignorant of their recollections. He had departed with Helghul to the airport, pleased by how easily Marcus and Theron had been manipulated. The most powerful abilities still slept within the Emissaries, and he hoped to keep it that way. Helghul was just beginning to realize himself within Elijah. Soon, like a bear ending its winter hibernation, the Adversary and the Beast within the young boy would wake.

Chapter 37

Black Elder: King of the Adversaries

The private jet had been in the air for two hours. Zahn occupied a roomy leather seat across from Elijah, who had not spoken since leaving Libya.

"You'll have to talk to me eventually. It would be better just to accept that this lifetime is more complicated, so we can move on."

"Where's my mom?" Elijah snapped, puffing out his puny chest. His hands were bound in his lap. Though the boy was angry and afraid, he was drawn to the Seducer-Producer and had remembered glimpses of past lives with him.

"She's safely contained so we can do what needs to be done," Zahn replied, popping an olive into his mouth from the decadent platter in front of them. "Help yourself. They're Niçoise," he added, chewing while he spoke.

Elijah glared at him and looked out the window. "I'll kill you if you hurt her," he said, and he meant it. Helghul had begun to remember in flashes, but the boy remained powerless and intimidated by his captor.

"I don't suggest you try. I have no intention of hurting her. You and I have so much yet to accomplish."

"What am I doing here? Why me?" Elijah asked.

"I think you have some idea, but it doesn't matter. You'll remember soon enough."

"Remember what?"

"That you are special, Helghul. You are the yin to the yang; you are Black Elder, the King of the Adversaries. With my assistance, you will rise and claim this time for the great darkness. Your many lives have led you to this end."

"I am not what you say," Elijah countered, but Zahn smiled and munched a thick slice of bread with brie and red-pepper jelly.

"Have you ever seen yourself . . . as someone else? Do you have memories you couldn't have lived . . . know things you couldn't know?"

"You know I'm a Crystal Child. My skills are no secret," Elijah answered.

"You are far more, Helghul," Zahn assured him, and Elijah couldn't help but feel a twinge of self-importance at the comment.

"Why do you call me 'Helghul'?" he asked.

"It was your name, a very long time ago, in Atitala."

"So who are *you*?"

Zahn moved from where he was sitting and took the seat next to Elijah. The boy shifted away, but inwardly he was conflicted. His instincts drew him to the man next to him despite his having been the reason he had been separated from his mother.

"I was called Grey Elder. You and I have always been allies. When you search your memories, you will know the truth of our connection. You have had many lifetimes. You can access them if you try, if you haven't already. It will come easier as you get older, but there's no time to waste anymore. You may remember that your mother is Theron—she's safe. I don't want to pit you against your mother; her destiny is her own. You're meant to lead again, as you have always done. There is more going on inside you than you know."

Elijah intuitively knew that it was all true. He was looking through the eyes of a child but thinking with the mind of a man. His daydreams and his random, strange memories had new meaning for him. "I was happy where I was," he retorted, renouncing the emergent thoughts.

"But there is a far greater destiny awaiting you. As the Great Year turns, the Bronze Age will ascend. You are the Black Elder now, but as the Light reemerges, you will lose your strength and power. We must not let that happen. We can expand the entropy in the world system. You can reign forever."

"How?" Elijah asked curiously. His body, the Beast within him, was gradually waking from his slumber.

"Consciousness evolves as a whole, and if we keep the people in survival mode, the Light will be unable to spread. Watch tomorrow's headlines and you'll see just what *we* are capable of."

Elijah said nothing but nodded. He had been having so many strange dreams over the past few months. They were full of shameful thoughts that he'd been unwilling to share with anyone. Zahn seemed to understand. Were they allies, after all? The memories bubbled up, and the dreams and daydreams began to make sense.

"Untie me?"

"Of course," Zahn said, knowing it was safe.

Once free, Elijah reached out to the platter, satisfying his empty belly with a large slice of bread and cheese.

The youngster's mind was a pendulum—one moment he was Elijah, and the next he was Helghul, filled with a thirst for power, and aware of centuries of foggy memories and ambitions. The boy's transition back to Helghul . . . had begun.

Chapter 38

The Nobu Virus

The project did not officially exist. No information about Nobu could be found in any official document, and, until now, no president had ever needed briefing on the program. Only a small handful of high-ranking uniforms, suits, and lab coats had heard of the Nobu virus, but when they watched it decimate an entire continent, they recognized it immediately.

The airborne contagion had been accidentally discovered by Russian scientists in the late twentieth century under the frozen wasteland of Antarctica. It had lain dormant, isolated beneath the ice, where it should have remained, ever harmless. Video footage had captured the scientists' jubilation at having found live bacteria under such conditions, and later had recorded their horrific fate.

Vastly underestimated, the microorganism's ferocity had not been fully appreciated until two full teams had died. Upon contact, the airborne virus tore through the body like fire on brittle branches. Despite their masks, gloves, and suits, precautions had not been adequate, and the scientists had become infected. The symptoms had begun with excruciating internal pain and ended with vomiting blood. Like acid, the virus attacked the linings of the stomach, throat, and nose, as well as the fingernail beds and all soft tissue, rapidly eating its way out of its host.

The loss of the first team was officially blamed on a gas leak, and the second team's loved ones were told that their plane had crashed into the ocean. No one could know about Nobu; it was too valuable. Scientists had learned from the losses, and with extreme caution they were able to contain the deadly virus and move it to a top-secret location for further study.

Suddenly, the virus surfaced in Australia. The world observed in horror as the gruesome images were scattered across the internet and television. Within a few short hours of exposure, a victim's tissue and skin boiled and blistered, liquefied from within by the pitiless germ. As the devastation unfolded, the internet was flooded with footage as terrified Aussies captured images of the shocking scenes, transmitting to the world and begging for help. The virus spread, and the reports slowed. There was no one left to tell the tale. More than one amateur correspondent left his or her video rolling as they were devoured and became bloody, unrecognizable corpses. The audience watched as the victims rotted in eerie silence.

A Sydney traffic camera captured the image of a toddler in only a diaper, faltering blindly through the streets, trails of blood from his eyes where tears would have been. No parent nearby, the child stumbled into traffic while cars honked and swerved, their panic-stricken drivers also suffering and afraid. The boy was crushed under a tire as the helpless audience looked on.

The infected prayed for death, and it came quickly. The virus progressed at an unprecedented rate; a large adult was dead in less than six hours from start to finish. The suffering was not prolonged. The disease was fatal. No human or animal had yet survived exposure.

"That cannot happen here! My God, that poor child! What is it? I'd kill myself before I'd die like that!" people across the globe exclaimed from their offices, living rooms, and shacks.

In their isolation beneath the soil of Libya, the Emissaries were unaware of what was happening outside.

With Elijah by his side, Zahn watched triumphantly from his opulent Egyptian apartment as millions were wiped out in a single day.

"Oh, this footage! We couldn't have hoped for anything better. I love technology. It makes it all so much easier! Fear and panic will smother them. They'll come eagerly now, seeking protection and promises," Zahn gloated.

"You did this?" Elijah asked, both shocked and impressed. Grey Elder blinked a slight nod.

"Won't it make them all sympathetic and mournful? Pull together, send aid, and all that?" the boy asked. He looked back at the television as though he were watching a movie rather than gruesome reality. Helghul had now filled Elijah so completely that he had little time to feel eleven, little time to *feel* at all. He rarely thought about his mother, Eden, the way he once had. However, his mind often wandered to memories of Theron.

"We will easily sweep away the shattered bits of charity left behind. People are compassionate only until they are threatened. When *their* lives, *their* families, and *their* bodies are set to be burned, their sympathy and selflessness disappear."

Zahn had chosen Australia because it had allowed for containment. He had considered other locations—Hawaii, Hong Kong, New Zealand, Malaysia—but they were all too risky or too small. He wanted to make a big impact, but it was imperative that he maintain control of the volatile bug. He didn't want the pandemic to wipe out the entire planet . . . yet.

Some flights had departed from Australia before the threat was known, the people on them unaware of what was happening until they arrived at their destinations, where they were aggressively quarantined for days. Others, who had taken off only shortly after them but had been infected, had crashed midocean when their crews swiftly succumbed to the illness.

Leaders around the globe scrambled to reassure their citizens, with only empty guarantees to offer. None of them knew what had happened or why, but the Americans and British had quickly commanded a quarantine and containment of the infected continent. After that, no planes had left Australian airspace, and no boats had left her harbors, though many, large and small, had tried. They had been turned around or blown apart. Either way, the result had been certain death.

The president of the United States had watched in real time, like everyone else. He had been moved to a well-guarded, undisclosed location and was preparing to address the American people. Just before he was due to go on the air, he received a call from the chairman of the Joint Chiefs of Staff.

"I hope you have something to tell me I can use," the president said, while his hair-and-makeup people fussed over him. They removed the protective paper guarding his collar from thick face powder as he carefully checked his profile. It was more important than ever that he look calm and reassured; the dark circles under his eyes must be well camouflaged for the taping.

"I have information, Mr. President, but I'm not sure how much you can use on the air," the general replied.

The president was intrigued, and he irritably waved away the people buzzing around him. "Go," he commanded, and the room immediately emptied. When the door finally closed, he urged the general to continue.

"The situation in Australia was caused by an ancient virus called Nobu, unknown to the modern world. I don't know how it was released." The general paused, giving the leader a moment to comprehend what he was hearing.

"How do you know this? Why haven't I heard of this 'Noo-boo' virus?"

"It was accidentally discovered by Russia over a decade ago during a mission to Lake Vostok, Antarctica. It's untraceable. I'm sure I don't have to explain."

"Russia? Then how the hell did it get into the hands of people who would do *this*?"

"No one has taken responsibility for it yet," the general replied.

"Don't give me useless answers I already have!" the president barked.

"There's been a pharmaceutical company working with the virus—top secret—that's all we know."

"Which one? Goddamn it!" the president shouted. "Find out who fucked up. Whose plan was it to annihilate half the globe, and why? And don't call me again until you know!"

"We know which one. It's owned by a corporation linked to a friend of yours—Oswald Zahn."

"Ozzie? Now we're getting somewhere!" the president said, hanging up the secure line and shouting to his assistant, Shirley. "Get Zahn on the other line right away!" Shirley heard him through the door. She knew better than to ever venture beyond shouting distance. There were no secrets from her.

The president half filled a tumbler with scotch and tossed back the burning amber liquid in one gulp. Zahn had been an influential donor in his first-term election campaign, and his support was vital for the next one.

This phone call will have to be handled with diplomacy, especially if it really was Zahn's company that fucked up, the president thought.

Moments later, the president made a reassuring address to the American public and the waiting world, imparting no new information. He apologized to the grieving families of the US soldiers who had been stationed, and died, in Australia. He assured public safety. He promised to share information as he received it. He promised to do everything he could for those tourists and others still alive, trapped, in the small scattered towns of the Outback. In other words, he lied. The president had no intention of telling anyone what the virus might be until he had a plan to combat it, and he sure as hell wasn't sending any more Americans to Austra-lia without an antidote.

When the lights and the cameras switched off, Shirley was waiting in the wings. She rushed to her boss, a phone outstretched. "Zahn," was all she said.

"Ozzie," the president said solemnly, with a politically per-fect look of despair pasted to his face, despite the caller's inability to see him.

"Mr. President," Zahn said. Elijah listened from beside him, impressed.

"I'm calling about one of your companies . . . they've done some work with a particularly vicious strain of virus."

"I keep my distance from the day-to-day of my investments. Not my area of expertise. I prefer the starlets and casting couches," he said, chuckling.

"We both know there isn't anything you don't know about your business, Ozzie. I don't care who dropped the ball, which families or influences are behind this. I just need you to look into it and help *my* people out."

"From what I understand, Mr. President, *your* people have already taken over the files . . . the labs and everything else. I got a call an hour ago. I told them to cooperate in every way. I'm just as bewildered and concerned about this as you are."

"We don't want to be next. No doubt the perpetrators are poised to release the virus again. We don't want people out there panicking. It brings out the worst."

"I'll do everything I can," Zahn declared before he hung up.

"Are you going to help him?" Elijah asked.

"Better," Grey Elder responded, and he began eagerly dialing his phone, setting the next stage of his plan in motion.

Two days later, Zahn's call to the president's private line was immediately answered.

"We have a vaccine. We can prevent what happened in Australia from happening again," Zahn declared.

"Thank God! How soon? How many people? What kind of timeline are we looking at?" the president asked, releasing a breath that felt like it had been held in for a week. The deep creases in his forehead eased slightly.

"We can start immediately and keep up production of the vaccine while we expand to less populated areas. I've put all my resources into getting this done as soon as possible."

"How much? What's this going to cost us, Ozzie?"

"Nothing. I'm willing to provide the serum at no expense," Zahn replied.

"To whom? You can't mean to all of America, that would cost . . . millions," the president exclaimed.

"No, sir," Zahn said. "To the *entire* world, and it'll cost billions."

Chapter 39

Hail the Savior

The media, and the internet, focused on every possible aspect of the chaos surrounding the events in Australia. The pandemic hijacked regular broadcasts, cycling the devastating home-shot images over and over. People were riveted to the gruesome show, and Grey Elder was elated by the swell of entropy in the system. Disorder and chaos were building around the globe. The world had tuned in, blogged, and tweeted, theorizing about the vile pictures coming from Down Under. Confusion and terror monopolized all modes of communication, and still no one had heard of the Nobu virus or its vaccine.

There were little pockets of Australia's Outback that had managed to avoid infection, but Nobu would eventually find them unless they stayed far from the infected zones. There was no hope of rescue; the leaders of the World Health Organization declared a global emergency but would not risk contamination to visit the continent. There were no attempts to enter the region, which was completely cordoned off—the airspace and seaports were guarded by allied air and naval forces. Experts on biological warfare gathered at the Central Intelligence Agency headquarters in Fairfax, Virginia, to confer with the US surgeon general and the head of the WHO in a top-secret meeting.

"We have to identify other at-risk populations and define the control opportunity. Then we can review the existing plans and build from there," the head of the WHO said.

"There's nothing like this in your books," the director of the CIA replied.

"It's our job to make a formal plan, so we'll *make* a plan! Create a national task force, alert our international partners," the surgeon general said. She was a politician; she hadn't practiced medicine for decades. Now, two years before her retirement, she was being faced with a world catastrophe.

"Your plans are useless. Nobu is too aggressive. It doesn't allow for social mobilization and local interventions," the CIA director said.

"We'll do it anyway. We'll focus on media management and psychosocial support. When news of Nobu gets out, people are going to panic. Draft a list of protocols and procedures even if they'll be useless. People need some hope!" the surgeon general said. *I should have retired last year,* she thought. *Then Nobu would be someone else's nightmare.*

All around the world, fear bubbled and swelled, and Grey Elder let the pot stew.

The term *Nobu* started to emerge, first on the internet and then eventually in the media, intentionally leaked by Zahn. Still, little was known about what Nobu was or how the outbreak had occurred. Random false explanations meant to incite fear were seeded intentionally through populations by Zahn's social media bots. People speculated on the cause of Nobu and cried out for an explanation. Zahn understood that the unknown caused more chaos and fear than even the nastiest reality, so he offered no more information. He delayed the announcement and the onset of the vaccinations intentionally, reveling in the panic gripping the world. Everywhere there were rushes to hoard water, supplies, and any variety of flu drug available.

Riots had broken out in many places. At a big-box store in Kentucky, a pharmacist had refused to sell unprescribed malaria antibiotics to frantic customers, and three people had died, including a nineteen-year-old stock boy who was crushed by a toppled display shelf.

Theories about terrorism abounded but became confused when people wondered why the Aussies had been attacked, rather than a more likely target.

"They are all disposable. I have faith in the selfish, fear-driven nature of humankind. They will come like rodents to a feast," Zahn explained to Elijah from their secured compound on the outskirts of Giza. It was dangerous in the ancient city now; violence and unrest had become the norm.

The American president once again appeared on television, this time to confirm the rumors about the Nobu virus and to announce the offer of humanitarian aid by Oswald Zahn.

"You have to tell the world it was terrorism, and we don't know the perpetrator, Mr. President. They must know how grave it truly is—no sugarcoating it. People need to fear that it could happen anywhere or they won't agree to be vaccinated. All the countries, even our enemies, have to be on board. There must be urgency and full proliferation. We don't want that virus taking hold and mutating on us," Zahn coached over the telephone.

"I can handle it," the president assured him. He hung up and cleared his throat, preparing his most convincing Winston Churchill voice.

The countdown began. "Three, two . . ."

"My fellow Americans and our friends around the world, this is indeed a dark time in history and for humankind. I am here to tell you that what occurred in Australia was not an accident. It was biological warfare. The innocent people of that unfortunate land were deliberately infected without provocation, without warning, by the intentional release of the Nobu virus. The United States and our allies are outraged by this horrific and blatant disregard for life," he said predictably, failing to mention Russia's link to the bacteria.

"We still don't know who's responsible for this heinous crime, but we will find them and hold them accountable. I guarantee it. It is imperative that we pull together now. Do not panic. The World Health Organization is on top of things, and an antidote to this virus has been produced. American humanitarian Oswald Zahn has rallied his considerable resources in the interest of helping the world and humankind. In conjunction with his charities, the World Health Organization, and the government of the United States, the vaccine will be made available to everyone, free of charge. No one who chooses to be vaccinated will be denied. This man," he said, as the broadcast switched to a split screen and Zahn looked seriously into the camera, "this savior, Oswald Zahn, has come to the aid of his country and the world, and offers the only known protection from this vicious scourge."

The feed flickered, and suddenly a composed Zahn took over the world screens. His chiseled, handsome face and voice were blasted in every language across the globe simultaneously. The world watched skeptically, desperate for answers and reassurance.

"I am not a savior," Zahn began pragmatically. "I come in this uncertain time to lead the way *out* of confusion and fear. I am a citizen of the *world*, not of one country. White, black, brown, yellow—it doesn't matter to me. We are all the same underneath our skin and in our hearts. We are all in this together.

"I have made arrangements to make the antidote available in most major cities immediately. We will expand out from there, as we are able. It is my hope that each one of you will be vaccinated in the coming months," he said emphatically. "You must think of yourselves and your families now and do what *you* need to do to survive.

"We don't know who is responsible for this act against humanity, but we can protect ourselves, though it must be done quickly— we have no idea when and where the terrorists could strike again. We are in more danger than ever, now that they know a vaccine is coming. Of course, vaccination will be your choice. The vaccine has no side effects and will leave a small crescent-shaped scar on your inner wrist. Protected, we can all move forward, unified in this terrifying time."

⋈⋈⋈ ⋈⋈⋈ ⋈⋈⋈

The captive Emissaries were in awe of their collective energy and increased paranormal abilities. They continued the energy healing and prayer they were sending to the world daily. They remained deeply affected as they interacted with one another, now as old friends.

The soldiers didn't go down into the bunker often. But occasionally supplies would come and garbage would go. Muhammed had been helping guard the bunker since the prisoners had first begun arriving. He wondered about the mixed group and had many questions, but since none of the guards knew any more than he did, there were no answers forthcoming.

While Muhammed lifted a few heavy boxes of canned food from his dolly onto the kitchen counter, he suddenly cried out in pain. The muscles in his back had seized, an old and excruciating injury, and he knew that just walking to the elevator would be a slow hell. A few prisoners approached Muhammed with concern, and his security team raised their weapons. "Leave them," Muhammed pleaded as a Crystal Child, barely five years old, who shone with the Emissary Bapoo's aura, placed his tiny hands on Muhammed's lower back.

"You think too much with your body . . . your thoughts are energy, and they get trapped here and here," he said. As he touched the man, the pain and tension disappeared, and the man swung around, more agile and loose than he had been in years.

"How did you do that? It's a miracle!"

"Yes," Bapoo said. "Most of us can do it. We can look at people and see where they are sick. There are shadows. I can teach you."

That was the beginning. Muhammed had been unable to stay silent about what had happened, and word spread quickly among the guards.

"This is good," Quinn said. "If those guards can see what these kids can do, they might just help us."

Over the following days, one by one, the guards made their way down through the elevator soliciting diagnoses and healing, both direct and remote, since just about everyone needed a miracle.

Quinn and Eden had hardly left each other's sides once her memory had been restored. Marcus and Theron were reunited, and her love for him was no longer restrained. She couldn't take her eyes off him. How had she not seen it before?

Eden spent a great amount of time running her hands along the smooth walls and floors of the bunker. She was searching, determined to escape and find Elijah.

"I remember the verse the Willowy Man taught me. If I can find the nodes and read the walls like he showed me in Shambhala, then I can access the fire lines and get us out of here," Eden told Quinn and Nate quietly so that only they could hear.

"What are fire lines? Where do they lead?" Nate asked.

"Did you ever read *A Journey to the Center of the Earth*?" she asked, and Nate shook his head no. "They're portals that link tunnels along the ley lines of the planet. They're ancient, like Atlantis kind of ancient," Eden said.

"It makes absolutely no sense. None of this does. But how can I help?" Nate asked.

The American president was harshly criticized for supporting Zahn and for not unequivocally proving who was responsible for the Nobu outbreak.

"You can't give him so much power and influence! We're American, dammit, the world expects us to lead!" bellowed the senator in frustration. Her red hair flopped up and down on her forehead as she spoke, and her hazel eyes flashed with disdain. She hated this man. The president was a moron, and he had only beat her for the nomination because their party was terrified of having a lesbian in office.

"He has the antidote! I have no doubt that without him, we'll be the next continent of corpses!" the president countered.

"Did you ever think that maybe *he* was responsible for the outbreak?" the senator boomed.

"Why? To what end? He isn't even charging for the vaccine! What's his motive?" the president argued.

"They're touting him as a savior! Did you read the *Washington Post* and the *New York Times* today? Fox News, CNN, even Breitbart! They agree for the first time ever! 'A saint,' they all said. They'd crown him king of the world if they could!"

"We need him," the president argued.

"We have access to the best scientists and doctors in the world. We can find our own antidote," the senator continued to rage.

"How long will that take? How much money will it cost? Are you willing to risk the lives of people you love? I'm not. My ego can stand down and let him pay the bill. If you haven't noticed, our economy is already on the brink of collapse. Popsicle sticks hold the fucker together. We couldn't afford to vaccinate Oregon, let alone the entire planet!"

"How can *he*?"

"That's *his* problem," the president retorted.

"So if he didn't unleash this virus, who did, and why?" the senator asked for the thousandth time.

"I've thought of nothing else since it happened. I've been hoping for a note, a sign, someone taking responsibility. Nothing! Did you ever wonder . . . maybe the fanatics are right? Is it fucking

Revelations? I go to church. I've read the Bible. My wife read me a quote last night from the Book of Zechariah. It says something about 'flesh consuming away while we stand on our feet, eyes and tongues consumed in their holes.'"

"Armageddon? Are you serious? You think it's the end of the world?" the woman asked, stunned.

"All I know is that our people are running scared, and they *need* a savior right now. Zahn fits the bill! The economy is in total collapse, and we were already so divided that we are on the verge of civil war. We cannot fight a war against an invisible enemy! He's offered his help, and I'm happy to take it!" the president shouted, grateful for the outlet of emotion.

"At what cost?" his cohort asked simply.

"I don't know," the president breathed, resigned to their helplessness.

"If it *is* Revelations, we're in bed with the devil," the senator countered.

"If I had a nickel for every time *I've* been called the Antichrist, I could afford to vaccinate the goddamn planet myself," the president said. "And remember this: if Zahn *is* responsible for the pandemic in Australia, then he *has* the virus, and he's prepared to *use* it. *That* is not an enemy I want to make."

Across the Atlantic, half a day away, the British prime minister was involved in a strikingly similar conference call with the leaders of Germany, France, and Belgium. They had agreed to the vaccinations but felt less than grateful.

"It's goddamn Revelations, for Christ's sake! What are we supposed to do?" the British leader moaned, exhausted.

"If you truly believe that, I suggest you rethink your expletives," the leader of Belgium advised wryly over the speakerphone.

"Bloody hell!" the Brit said, downing the sherry in her glass.

"Zat's better," the German chancellor interjected. "Now vut are vee going to do about zis mess?"

Chapter 40

Creating Chaos

After Zahn's broadcast, people around the world responded with desperation and panic. They had naively hoped that Australia was an anomaly, something isolated in their environment. They had hoped they were safe in their distant lands. Many were anxious to get vaccinated as soon as possible, but others were unconvinced.

Grey Elder's campaign for mass vaccination had been prepared well in advance, and he was busy putting the plan into motion. He was interfacing with both the cooperative and uncooperative leaders of the world, but he was in no real rush.

The Chinese head of state had refused Zahn's offer of "protection," but before his refusal became public, he died of what was officially recorded as a heart attack. In truth, he had been poisoned by his second in command, who then assumed leadership and willingly agreed to allow the vaccinations to begin. His life was spared, and his bank account was buoyed. More than a billion Chinese would be given the option of survival through inoculation. Like people across the entire planet, individuals would have to choose for themselves.

There were other leaders who resisted, and Zahn surreptitiously bought his way into many unwilling countries: North Korea, Iran, Pakistan, and more. His wealth and power seemed endless, and the leaders were bribed and threatened as necessary. No one wanted their country to be the next Nobu graveyard.

Clinics were set up in hospitals, schools, churches, synagogues, mosques, temples, and town halls. Immunizations were quick and virtually painless. The individual's identity was recorded, the left hand was placed face up, there was a quick pinch-click to the inner wrist, the serum was injected, and the vaccination was complete. Only a crescent-shaped mark remained. The individual was now immune from contracting the virus.

Millions lined up to be marked, some tentative and some relieved. By car, train, donkey, camel, and foot, people came and waited, sometimes for days or weeks. They had come willingly to receive the vaccination. They had made their choice. Some felt no difference, but others wandered away staring at the scar on their skin, feeling that something profound had occurred. In some cases, a heaviness descended over those who had complied. Could there have been something more to the vaccine, an undeclared side effect? Sometimes they regretted their decision, but it was not a choice that could be undone.

It didn't make any sense, yet some people refused. En masse, publicly and privately, millions of individuals and groups made solemn oaths denouncing the inoculation and refusing to be marked, preparing to live or die with the consequences.

Over the next few weeks, Zahn's immunization initiative monopolized the world news. Families were torn apart by the dilemma of whether to proceed with the vaccinations. The whole world was dividing into friend-and-family groups.

"How do we know they're not going to poison us with the injections?" people wondered fearfully. "Maybe it's a plot, population control . . ."

"He's American. The Americans are behind it all; we can't trust him. They're trying to control the world," a million voices cried, in dozens of languages.

"He's a saint."

"It will turn us into zombies or robots!"

"It's just like in the Bible! The mark of the beast!" others cried, terrified.

"I'd rather die!" some exclaimed bravely.

"I must be first in line!" others vowed.

The Pope, who had gone into hiding, broadcast via the internet from a secret location. He called upon people of all races and religions to unite. "We are all One. Christian, Muslim, Buddhist, Jew. There is no separation. In this time of darkness, renounce the false prophet, and do not be marked! It has been foretold that a beast will come with falseness, cloaked in charm and guile. Do not be fooled! God will protect and reward the brave. Heaven awaits," he promised.

Holy leaders from around the world continued to argue both for and against inoculation. The Pope was called both a saint and the Antichrist by different sides; and the debate raged on social media, in the streets, in bars, and in private homes.

Whatever the response, there was panic and discord that fed the dark souls of the world, strengthening their energy and pleasing Grey Elder. Crime was at an all-time high, especially violent crime. There was a noticeable undercurrent everywhere, like the energy of a packed house on fight night after the main event. The crowds were keyed up, their adrenaline and testosterone pumping. Gangs roamed neighborhoods looking for trouble.

The weak and innocent were afraid to leave their homes except to work, and most avoided the streets, especially after nightfall. Neighbors didn't nod and smile at strangers, afraid of who might take exception. Riots and uprisings around the globe continued to escalate as the markets crashed and banks collapsed.

Merchants preyed on the fears of the people, selling weapons and pepper spray by the boatload, and 3-D printers generated unlicensed guns at breakneck speed. Advertisements for alarms, armaments, and self-defense products screamed from TV and radio with dire warnings and prophecies. Fear-mongering drug companies infiltrated the collective psyche of the population with rumors, comprehensive advertising campaigns, and internet blitzes. They recommended bogus antidotes and prescriptions and warned of inevitable shortages. They claimed that children would be the first victims; and terrified, vulnerable parents hoarded supplies, turning their homes into bunkers.

Headlines and rumors warned the population to comply and be vaccinated.

"The Unvaccinated May Be Carriers!"
"Noncompliance Leads Virus to Mutate!"
"Absolute Compliance Is the Only Protection!"
"Refugees Pose Nobu Risk!"
"Failure to Vaccinate Endangers All!"
"Extraterrestrials Caused Nobu Outbreak!"

No one was safe, but despite the fearmongering and regardless of the threat, many continued to refuse the injection. They congregated anywhere, despite the risk of repercussions. Where they gathered, there was hope and resistance. It ballooned around them, and the positive energy was delivered to the chakras of the world like a salve. The resistance was peaceful, but it helped. People joined hands and prayed, wished for, or imagined better days, and positive energy mushroomed.

"Join hands and send forth your love and hope to the world, and in doing so, we can rise up," an evangelist called to his congregation.

The internet was like a vein of power and defiance. It offered the isolated and afraid an outlet and a community. Knowledge was shared, and the conspiracy theorists gained influence, identifying

Zahn as a corrupt megalomaniac and naming his conspirators and cronies.

People dared to hope. They couldn't have known how much it was helping, how their optimism and hopefulness cut through the inky darkness.

It had been six weeks since the destruction of Australia, and the vaccinations had been extensive. Zahn and Elijah remained in Egypt near the Great Pyramid, observing the chaos that had enveloped the world and constantly fueling it.

"Will we get vaccinated?" Elijah asked.

"There's no need. There *is* no vaccine. It's a placebo. If the virus is uncontained, we're all dead," Zahn replied.

"I don't understand. Why bother with it all? You've spent so much money!"

"I have no shortage of money. The vaccine has fueled people's fears and divided them. If they had been given an absolute death sentence, people would have found camaraderie. When there is no hope, there is peace and resignation. We gave them something to cling to and the uncertainty of what may come. In doing so, we have caused absolute chaos. We have torn apart families, communities, and countries and filled them all with fear and doubt."

"*And*, they call you a savior," Elijah added shrewdly.

Populations in the sacred sites of the world swelled as people left their homes and jobs on pilgrimages. Rome, Mecca, and Jerusalem had all become dangerously unstable, yet people continued to gather. There was a movement of humans throughout the globe as they joined, hopeful and determined. They made their way to Mount Sinai, Giza, Chichen Itza, Stonehenge, Delos, Croagh Patrick, Emei Shan, Song Shan, Tikal, Borobudur, the Temple Mount, Teotihuacan, Angkor Wat, and on and on. In America they congregated on the mountains, in the forests, in deserts, in the cornfields, near streams, or anywhere spirit was felt.

The energy of the Earth—what Plato had referred to as *anima mundi*—vibrated, and the collective consciousness heard and responded. From Inner Earth, the Arya sympathized with the humans projecting loving energy; a powerful burst of divine light expanded up. In contrast, the Elementals that made up all matter refused to intervene and remained neutral. They were still angry at the humans for releasing the Beast from its chasm into their world.

Zahn watched the pilgrims with disdain. If he had his way, they would suffer extended torment beyond the brief agony Nobu would have brought them. Grey Elder's hateful thoughts were interrupted.

"Where is Eden now?" Elijah asked. In the presence of Grey Elder, and with the constant urgings of the Beast, Helghul's memory had grown clearer by the day. It had been weeks since the boy had mentioned his mother at all.

"She remains in Libya, contained," he said.

"Unharmed?" Elijah asked.

"Is it possible you still care for Theron above others, even when she has consistently chosen Marcus over you?" Grey Elder goaded.

"She has been both a thorn and an aid to me. I have used her like a useful tool," Elijah said, wanting it to be true, but he felt his attachment to her deep inside him. Without his Helghul-memories and the Beast in his head for the past decade, Theron's influence had once again increased.

"It would be better not to think of her at all. Instead, remember that you are Helghul. Think of Marcus once again supplanting *you* as the love of her life, and let that anger stir and fortify you. *He* is her soulmate, the masculine to her feminine. You are the dark to his light. It is as it should be."

"And you. What am I to you? I have done nothing since you brought me here but eat like a dog at your table. What's the point of listening to your sermons day and night if you don't let me *do* anything?"

"It will soon be clear. You are a powerful ally, and when the time is right, it is *you* who will stand on the slab and pronounce our victory," Zahn promised, appealing to the boy's ego.

Elijah was placated . . . for now. He longed to join the noise and bedlam of the Egyptian streets. He wished to be amid the violence and feel the hot wind of the garbage fires on his face. He craved excitement and was tired of living in his memories. His Helghul-voice was becoming more vocal, anxious to realize his purpose and role in this lifetime.

"Tomorrow we will reclaim your treasure," Grey Elder said cryptically.

"Treasure?"

"We will retrieve the Emerald Tablet," the mentor replied.

"The Emissary told you where it is?" Elijah said.

"Quinn believed I was his ally. When he recognized me, it weakened him. Not wanting the responsibility on himself, he told me where he hid the Tablet. I hope you can learn from his weakness. Forget Theron," Grey Elder said. Elijah clenched his jaw at the challenge. "We will retrieve it tomorrow," Zahn said, and he left the room for the night.

Elijah was alone, and he thought about the Emerald Tablet. The Beast was alert, waiting for Helghul's ruthlessness to rise.

Rise, boy, and be a man! the Beast growled in his head. Elijah could hear it, and it frightened him. He turned on all the lights and pushed the voice out of his thoughts. He was once again engrossed in the hazy slideshow of his past lives.

>◇< >◇< >◇<

In the bunker in Libya, the guards continued to access the healing powers of the Emissaries. It was through them that the prisoners learned about the Nobu virus. The Crystal Children from Brisbane and Sydney who had been inadvertently saved by Zahn were especially devastated by the horrible news.

The Emissaries remained securely detained. Quinn spent time with Bapoo, Kushim, and Holt, reconnecting and reminding them of everything they had once known. Eden spent her waking hours running her hands along the walls, listening with her intuition through her fingertips. She was determined to find the trigger point that would release them.

Chapter 41

The Return of the Emerald Tablet

Zahn's plane touched down in Alexandria one hour before sunset. Elijah was thrilled to return to the city he had built, which had been named for him so many centuries before when he was Alexander of Macedonia. Helghul felt the power of his life as Alexander the Great surging through him. He filled with recollections, though the city little resembled the perfect specimen he had once designed.

"The site of the destroyed library? Is that where it's hidden?" Elijah guessed.

Zahn smiled mysteriously but chose not to answer. The men were dressed in the robes of the local lower class to avoid attention. They did not want to stand out. Zahn easily managed the black sports bag he had been toting since their flight as they hailed a public taxi to the harbor. The sky was fading into evening when they found the fishing boat tied to the pier, waiting for them. It was nothing special, a filthy little skiff. As Zahn dismissed the driver, Elijah was concerned.

"Why this one? It looks like it's about to sink," Elijah said, scanning the docks. His nose wrinkled, disgusted by the smell of wooden slats stained with the entrails of gutted fish. He saw no less than ten better-looking options in the immediate vicinity.

"We want to blend in," Grey Elder responded, dropping his baggage aboard.

The boat was adequate for their needs, and Grey Elder untied and cast off. Elijah steadied himself on a bare wooden seat, avoiding a dive tank and a tangle of worn nets at his feet. He prepared for a long, bumpy ride. He was startled when the choppy engine cut out when they were barely out of the harbor.

"I don't understand? It's *here*?" Elijah said incredulously as Zahn dropped the anchor. He knew that during his life as Alexander, the place where they now floated hadn't been covered by the sea. Zahn removed his robe and shoes and revealed a thin wetsuit underneath. He pulled a mask, flippers, mouthpiece, and headlamp from his bag.

"Why here, with so many boats around?" Elijah asked as Zahn quickly attached his mouthpiece to the regulator and adjusted the tank at Elijah's feet.

"It's murky, and there's a strong current. The Tablet was well buried."

Zahn tied a rope around his forearm, and a long coil sat in the boat at Elijah's feet.

"It'll be heavy for you. When you see me tug three times like this," he said, jerking the line, "start to pull it up. I'll help. And here," he said, handing the boy a nine-millimeter handgun.

"It's loaded. If anyone comes near, shoot. No hesitation, no questions. Dead."

"Dead," Elijah repeated, turning over the heavy pistol in his hands. He'd only seen guns in movies and on the news. Now, he suddenly felt like a real soldier, like Kammler, and he felt a rush of dark power run through him as his Helghul-consciousness expanded, like mold in the damp.

Zahn raised the red diver down flag to keep other boats at a distance. He dropped backward into the cloudy water, and his light disappeared below the chop. Elijah had plenty of time for contemplation. Five minutes passed . . . ten, fifteen—the sun set, red and orange fire on the horizon, and darkness descended. Elijah began to panic, relying on his Helghul-memory to remain calm. Boaters passed by closely, too self-absorbed and rushed to bother with the straggling skiff. Helghul cradled the gun in his hand and felt power welling up inside of him as the coil of rope disappeared deeper and deeper until there was almost nothing left.

If Zahn drowned, Elijah didn't know what he would do, where he would go, or how. Would he dive, searching for the Tablet? He was on his own in a foreign city, and though he was Helghul, entwined with a formidable Beast on the inside, he was a skinny, penniless American boy on the outside. *At least I have a gun,* he thought. Then he began to wonder if he could get back to Libya somehow and find Theron. Could he trust her now? Could she be manipulated to help him rise to power once again?

After twenty minutes, the boy wondered if the harsh current had taken Grey Elder. The rope had nearly exhausted its length, and he held the end, waiting for the signal. He searched for bubbles on the dark surface but saw none. Elijah's alarm had peaked just as the rope jerked . . . one, two, three. He began to pull, the gun now set aside, and he was soaked by the time Zahn surfaced. Elijah helped the Elder load the heavy sack that Admiral Byrd had fashioned out of thick fishing net. Inside was a second layer of cloth, and then, the Emerald tablet within a gold box.

Elijah rested the edge of the Tablet on the hull to manage the weight, tipping the boat slightly. The boy held on to it tightly.

Once the Tablet was safely on board, Zahn handed up his dive tank and climbed out of the water.

The Elder took out a large diving knife and cut away the netting, alive with seaweed and shells. He opened the box, exposing the Tablet to the air for the first time in decades. Elijah was in awe as it glowed, like a beacon in the darkness. The boy reached out and touched it, and his bones trembled at the contact. The charge of the stone surged through him with a million vibrations, and his identity as Helghul became fully realized. Suddenly the fog was lifted, and Helghul saw himself clearly in Atitala, then as Katari, Genghis, Alexander, and so many other brick-and-mortar lives.

The Emerald Tablet glowed a brilliant luminescent green. Elijah's heart was thumping, and he felt the energy emanating from the atlantium crystal. It had been so long, but the magic of the object had not waned.

"Welcome back, Helghul," the Elder said with a wink. Zahn was pleased that the boy had finally come to his senses, and he placed the precious Tablet in its thin solid-gold box inside his bag.

Ninety minutes later, Zahn reclined comfortably with Elijah on his jet, heading back to Giza, enjoying snacks and sodas. The gold box was on the floor at their feet, concealed in the sports bag, and electrifying the air around them.

"What now?" Elijah asked when the flight attendant had been sent away.

"We use the Emerald Tablet to ensure the extension of the Dark Age."

"Use it? How?"

"The Great Pyramid serves many purposes. It is much more than people currently believe. Remember how they powered Atitala?"

"Yes."

"At the end of the last Golden Age, the Emerald Tablet was removed from its place in the White Pyramid of Atitala. The Great Pyramid of Giza is a resonator, a geomechanical power plant. When the Tablet is placed in the powered-up Great Pyramid, consciousness can be manipulated. The despair and panic we have so carefully orchestrated will be amplified and sent into the Universe. We will blanket the Earth in this energy grid, and we will stop the ascension to a higher Age. Consciousness will be cast back into the Iron Age by the state of the people's will," Grey Elder explained.

"So we'll create a . . . a *dis*–Unity Grid?"

"Exactly," Zahn replied.

"But what about the Emissaries?" Elijah asked.

Zahn searched the boy's face watchfully. "Are you Black Elder, concerned about your enemies; or a boy, asking about his *mommy?*" Zahn sniped. He didn't wait for an answer. He raised his cell phone and began making a call. Elijah had been dismissed.

For a moment, Helghul's thirst for power wavered. He felt a desire to see his mother and protect her. He remembered a simple day in his life as Elijah, by her side, interviewing Crystal Children and being one of them, feeling love and connection. He thought of his hand safely in hers as they laughed at Nate singing from the vehicle's driver seat . . . but that was before . . . before he knew what he really was. It was before the Beast had stirred and strengthened within him like a volcano bound to eventually erupt, and before he touched the Emerald Tablet and knew without any doubt exactly what he'd become. The innocent, childish part of him had been overcome, and the darkness that warped his soul flooded him once more and overwhelmed the child he might have been.

Chapter 42

The Emissaries Unite

"Sir, it's the prisoners," the guard said in Arabic.

"What is it?" the stout man asked irritably, looking up from his meal. The creamy sauce from his dinner had gotten stuck in his black mustache, and at any other time, his cohort would have laughed.

"The prisoners haven't been eating or drinking and—"

"A protest?"

"No, sir, there's more. We wouldn't have noticed, but when Abdul put his lute down next to the fire . . . well, it kept playing. The ground was vibrating so much that the strings . . . sang," he said, searching for words.

Overly full from his meal, the stocky boss heaved himself out of his comfortable chair. "I don't feel anything. It's not vibrating now," the man reassured the guard. He was not the superstitious type. Ghost stories would not get the best of *him*.

"But it is. Listen," the nervous guard said, and sure enough, the twang of the open notes could be heard. The lute lay on the ground, abandoned, and five armed men stared at it with fear in their eyes.

"Maybe an earthquake?" one of them suggested.

"Prepare to go below!" the leader ordered.

Most of the guards had witnessed for themselves the unusual powers of the Crystal Children. From a head cold to a cancerous tumor, the children had healed them and their extended families through direct touch and remote healing. From finding a lost wedding ring to locating a runaway daughter, the Crystal Children's predictions had come true with astounding accuracy. The guards were rightfully nervous as they descended into the shelter.

Seven hours earlier, Eden and Quinn had slipped the bonds of captivity unnoticed. Eden had finally found the location of the gateway. Though the ground and walls on the southern corner of the holding area had shown no sign of ingress, she *felt* that it was there. To anyone else, the foundation was solid. There was no hollow reverberation, no loose stones, no hint of a possible exit, but she found what she'd been searching for.

With Quinn and Nate by her side, Eden had whispered the rhyme she'd learned from Willowy Man while her fingers rolled and slid along the wall. The smooth, polished barrier had divided and shifted, shimmying like a bird rustling its feathers and opening to take flight. The partition had become malleable and liquid-looking as they watched, and then an archway and tunnel had become visible.

"I knew it!" she had hooted happily.

"I can't believe what I'm seeing," Nate had marveled.

Meanwhile, life in the large room had continued unchanged. The Emissaries and the other captives had remained completely calm, grouped in various stages of meditation, precognitive practice, conversation, and games. Their bond was continuing to strengthen and evolve.

Nate had been shocked when the opening appeared in a solid wall. "We should gather all the Emissaries and escape," Nate had said, staring at the archway.

"No! They are safer staying behind. Their purpose remains here. This portal has been opened only for us," Eden said.

"We can't just leave them behind. We can't just disappear! What if Elijah is brought here?" Nate had asked, horrified at the prospect of abandoning the Crystal Children he had innocently helped Zahn find.

"Elijah won't be coming here, *that* I can guarantee. Helghul is far too important to Grey Eld—"

"Don't call him that! I know what you think, I know who he's been . . . but he's my son! He's my *baby*, and I won't give up on him if I have breath left in *this* body! Not as long as *I am his mother!*"

"Of course you won't, and I won't either," Quinn had promised, taking the trembling woman into his arms. "I *do* understand the love of a mother for her child. As you've told me many times, there is always choice . . . we can hope . . . we can help Elijah choose the Light," Quinn soothed. "Listen, Willowy Man taught you this for a reason, and Helg . . . your son is as good a reason as any."

"I'm not going," Nate announced. "Someone has to stay with these people. More than half of them are here because of us, and if Elijah is brought back, then I'll be here for him."

"Thank you, Nate. You're a good soul," Eden said, throwing her arms around him. "We'll get help once we finish what has to be done."

Quinn hugged him next.

"I love you, man," he said.

"You too," Nate replied, tearing up. "Get going. Stop that maniac from doing whatever he has planned."

"We need to go quickly," Eden said, anxious to find Elijah.

"Not yet. Come help me," Quinn said. For weeks he had been practicing the Merging with the captives. When the portal had opened, he had immediately recognized that the time for the joining had come.

Holt, Kushim, and Bapoo helped Quinn gather everyone together. Once collected, the group had built their human web, conjuring the kaleidoscope of colors and energy in the air above them, just below the copper ceiling. It hadn't taken long. The Emissaries' powers had grown intense since coming together. Individually, they were powerful; together, they were a much more significant force. By the time Eden and Quinn passed through the portal, the Merging had created a Unity Grid in youthful bloom in the air above the peaceful Emissaries, but Nate couldn't see it. The small boy with the Emissary Bapoo's shine took Nate's hand and invited him to kneel.

"Do you want to see?" Bapoo asked.

"See? What can't I see?" Nate said, and the child touched Nate on his third eye, between his eyebrows, and suddenly Nate *could* see. A Unity Grid grew and was expanding into geometric forms, from a tetrahedron to a dodecahedron. It was magical, and Nate was stunned as the Grid continued to expand and grow.

"Those are called Platonic Solids; they are a bridge to the higher dimensions. Don't worry, Nate. We are eternal," the boy said. "They will carry you."

"Whaddaya mean, 'carry me'?" Nate asked, concerned.

"Your *consciousness*, silly!" the child said happily, skipping away to join the other Crystal Children.

I'm staying right here. I'm not going to any higher frickin' dimensions! Nate thought.

Chapter 43

The Halls of Amenti

Once Quinn and Eden had passed through the portal, the stone wall had sealed itself behind them.

"Willowy Man said we have to send out our intention of where we want to go. The lines travel in different directions at different times. It's like a crazy superhighway, and I won't be able to control it like he does," Eden said, feeling simultaneously panicked and exhilarated as they entered the portal and it closed behind them.

"Egypt . . . take us to Egypt. I know how crazy that sounds," Quinn replied.

"I need to find Elijah before we do anything else," Eden said.

"Elijah will be with Zahn . . . I made a terrible mistake. I told Grey Elder that the Emerald Tablet was hidden in Alexandria. We have to get there and move it, if it isn't already too late."

"Okay, let's send out our intention to find the Emerald Tablet. If Zahn doesn't have it, we'll end up in Alexandria and use it to help us. If he does have it, the command will take us to him and Elijah anyway."

"Perfect," Quinn agreed, and touching foreheads, they both asked to be taken to the Emerald Tablet.

They zipped forward at incredible speed. The particles around them fragmented, and they were propelled, then slowed. Theirs was a jerky, uneasy journey—nothing like the ease of traveling in the care of the expert Willowy Man. Eden had remembered the Tunnel-Keeper's training perfectly, but she lacked his finesse and expertise.

"This is insane!" Quinn said, happy to be free of the Libyan prison but nauseated by the movement.

"I'm sorry it's so jerky. I'm trying. It's been about eight hundred years!" Eden said. She was nauseated too, and hoped they would arrive before she vomited.

Suddenly ahead of him they saw a swirling mass of rock, looking gelatinous as it shifted and opened. It wasn't a civilized exit. The Emissaries were spit out, tossed through the portal from the telluric energy. Theron landed lightly, sliding like a feather on the shiny floor, but Marcus landed at an awkward angle with a thump, hitting his head. He rubbed the goose egg that popped up on his skull. It was definitely not like traveling with the Tunnel-Keeper.

"Are you okay?" Eden asked.

"Where are we? Do you recognize this place?" Quinn asked her, getting off the floor.

There were scrolls and books and tablets and shelves that seemed to go on for miles. The stone walls were steep and uneven, but there was no sign of the Emerald Tablet. The room had corridors jutting off in many directions, and Quinn couldn't guess which pointed north or south. There was no wind, no cool, no heat—just stillness and the sound of breathing.

"You are two of three from the West who will enter today. Your fates are woven together like the strands of a whip," a voice announced, repeating the familiar phrase Plato had first been told by the Oracle of Amun in Siwa, but they saw no one. "You have entered Amenti, the sacred Hall of Records," a male voice continued.

"The Hall of Records? It's real?" Eden said in amazement. The Hall of Records was legendary and was said to contain a complete collection of knowledge from every Age and to hold all the secrets of the Universe.

"Information is the only thing that *is* real," the voice said, and then a man stepped out from behind a nearby shelf. He was stocky and wore white robes. He had a trimmed red beard, a round nose, and smiling cobalt eyes. Red Elder, the Keeper of Records, received the effervescent karmic colors of Theron and Marcus.

"Red Elder!" Quinn and Eden exclaimed happily. Quinn reached out to touch Red Elder's shoulder, and he was solid, though semitransparent. "How are you here? Are you real?" he asked.

"I am as real as I have ever been. This place is not wholly of your dimension. I remain energy and light and flow within the Grid. I am of a parallel Universe to yours."

Quinn passed his hand through the shelf beside him. The books, scrolls, and tablets that all appeared so real and solid were immaterial, but miraculously, he saw the words in his mind as his hand passed through the writings.

"Dear Emissaries, you have known me many times, even in this lifetime before I passed," he said, nodding to Eden.

"Oh my God! Jamie!" Eden gasped. "Red Elder! I can't believe it! You were Jamie? My husband?" she said, holding back tears.

"What?" Quinn said in confusion. Jealousy rose in him. The Emissary's joy at being reunited with the Elder soured significantly.

"Our son . . . Elijah . . . we're searching for him," Eden said.

"In due time. Your path to the child will be clear."

"Did you know? When we were together . . . did you know about . . . all this? Who we were?"

"Who we are," he corrected gently. "I knew."

"What do you mean you knew? Of course you knew. But what the fuck, Red Elder, this is messed up!" Quinn said.

"In what way, Marcus? We have all shared the flesh with others many times. Your soulmate is not your physical property; she is your spiritual partner. No relationship, sexual or otherwise, can change that," Red Elder said, but it didn't help; Quinn was not placated.

"Why didn't you tell me?" Eden wanted to know.

"Your inability to remember was a merciful gift. It was not my place to take it from you."

"But I remember now," she said.

"That, too, is a gift."

"We asked to be taken to the Emerald Tablet. Why are we here?" Quinn said.

"You are approaching your goal, but the prophecy had to be fulfilled. Three of you will pass through these halls and register your wisdom before the events of this day unfold. Now, it is time to deposit your knowledge; the darkness does not rest."

"I don't understand," Eden said.

"You must each impart into the Akashic records what it is you have learned," Red Elder explained.

"How do I decide? There are too many lessons. How do I choose what to say and not?"

"What do you feel most deeply?" he asked.

Theron thought for a few minutes. "Gratitude," she finally said. "I am grateful that I have experienced the miracle of creation. The birth of a child, motherhood, has let me know the love of the Creator."

"It is a tiny glimmer of the great love our Creator feels for us," Red Elder said. "It is recorded. Proceed quickly and with blessings," he said, and a corridor lit up, showing Eden the way.

"Can't you come? Help us find Elijah; he's your son too," Eden said, pausing.

"I have played my role in your current life. My place is here, but take this," the Elder said. He held out a long silver dagger. The handle was ornately carved with the image of a ten-headed Hydra.

Eden didn't recognize it, but Quinn's Marcus-memory did. It was the same dagger Helghul had used to open his veins and summon the Beast from the chasm.

"Don't touch it!" Quinn said, pulling her hand back. "There is evil attached to that blade."

"There is no negativity in the object itself, I assure you. It is all in how it is used," Red Elder said. He handed it to Eden, but he looked at Quinn while he spoke. Eden took the knife from him and was surprised by how heavy it was.

"Now follow your path. Elijah is in danger—you must hurry!"

Eden began running down the long corridor glowing with crystal lights. Her son was in danger!

"Eden, wait!" Quinn shouted, but she kept sprinting, desperate to save her boy. Quinn didn't want to split up, but as he protested and tried to chase her, he felt his feet firmly stuck to the floor.

"What is this?" Marcus said.

"No one passes through the Hall of Records without imparting knowledge. Marcus, what have you learned?" Red Elder asked.

"I've learned that you can't trust Elders!" Quinn snapped, and he meant it. His feet instantly came unstuck, and he rushed after Eden, calling out for her to wait.

"I see little has changed for you, Marcus. Your deposit has been recorded," Red Elder said, but Quinn was too far gone to hear him.

Chapter 44

The Most Ancient
of Ancients

Quinn ran after Eden, calling her name. He had lost sight of her, and the crystals in the walls began to fade. Quinn was sprinting, but as he turned the second corner, he came to an abrupt stop.

He found himself in a familiar place. It was the cenote of Atitala, the beautiful freshwater pool where Marcus and Theron had spent so many joyous hours, and where Helghul had pulled a silver dagger and tried to stab him. It was unchanged—the enticing blue water and the hanging roots and vines stippling the sunlight that peeked through the skylight above.

But where was Eden?

Tunnels shot off in different directions, and as Quinn wondered which he should take, he saw someone emerging directly opposite him. His heart leapt, but it was not Eden who emerged through the archway. It was Helghul! Helghul as he had been in Atitala—a man in his early twenties, blond and smug, his usual sneer directed at Quinn. Quinn realized that he, too, was changed. His body was young and muscular; the skin of his arms was a deep caramel brown. He was as he had been as well.

"Marcus!" Helghul snarled. "It's time to do what I should have done in the beginning." The two men sprinted toward each other, determined to battle and unleash centuries of hatred and frustration. But rather than colliding, something extraordinary happened. Instead of meeting flesh to flesh, they each hit an invisible barrier that stopped them with a jolt. In perfect symmetry, they sat, mirror images of the other. In exactly the opposite position, they swung and kicked at each other, each blow met with a counterreaction.—each force met with equal, opposing force. Exhausted, they fell back on the stone floor. Marcus stood up, and still in perfect reflection, Helghul did the same. The light and the dark, they stared at each other. Marcus reached out to touch the force field between them. As he did so, Helghul's corresponding arm was pressed back in equal extension. But there was no tangible separation; he felt no screen or barrier, yet the two men were unable to touch.

"What is this between us? Why do you back away so strangely?" Marcus asked angrily. He had no time for these games. He had to find Theron, and he had to do so before Helghul intervened.

Helghul punched toward Marcus, who retreated and countered in the exact same way. The men looked at each other in confusion. Helghul head-faked three times, and Marcus's head simultaneously bobbed backward three times.

"Stop that!" Marcus shouted, once again lunging toward Helghul. Helghul's body responded in exact reversal and therefore could not be touched. For every movement, there was an equal and opposite countermovement. For every intention, an equal and opposite intention. Marcus turned to leave; he would find Theron and be done with this nonsense, but as he did so, Helghul also turned to depart. Their backs faded away from each other.

Marcus marched out of the cave, and twenty yards ahead, he saw an archway. He entered, and to his bewilderment, he was back in the same cenote, and Helghul was entering from the opposite side. Step by step, they were in perfect, but opposite, sync.

"What is this? What have you done?" Marcus shouted.

"It is *you* who has done it!" Helghul snapped angrily.

"Is there something you're not telling me?"

"We are in our primary human bodies. Time is irrelevant in this place. Until we understand it, we are stuck here, together," Helghul said irritably.

"What are we to understand? Tell me so we can be done with it."

"I wish nothing more than to be done with *it*, but the solution to this riddle eludes me, just as it does you. Do not tire me with your demands anymore. It is bad enough that I endure your face, your memory, and your betrayal. Let me think."

Marcus made some more movements, complex and strange, and in every instance, Helghul did the equal and opposite in perfect sync, without effort, each time growing more annoyed. Marcus sat down to think, and as expected, Helghul did the same. They could not leave the cenote, and they could not touch each other, though everything one of them did undeniably affected the other. Each man thought and struggled.

"What are we missing? What are *we* missing?" Marcus asked, wracking his brain.

Suddenly Marcus grew very still. He slowed his breathing, closed his eyes, and instead of trying to think, he tried *not* to think. He emptied his mind and breathed.

Marcus meditated for almost eight minutes, while Helghul sat nearby in the same pose facing the glistening blue cenote and wondering, *Why the cenote? Was it because of Theron? Atitala? The fight so long ago?*

Marcus jumped to his feet, and Helghul stood beside him.

"It's the water! Water is the most ancient of ancients! Everybody who's come before us is alive in the water. Every birth sac and withered corpse returns to the water cycle like a puddle drying in the sun. The water has held all life!" Marcus said.

"So what? What does it mean?" Helghul asked.

Marcus ran forward to jump in the water, but as he did so, Helghul stepped away too. As if a rope held them core-to-core in a tug-of-war, Marcus could not enter. He had been so sure! What could he be missing?

Marcus bent down and picked up a small pebble. He threw it into the pool, and beside him, Helghul mirrored the equal and opposite motion, though he tossed no stone. The single stone dropped in with a plop. In response, a ring rippled out, and then a second. From that zero point were born two rings, and they split one from the other, which is not the way of water. Instead of living within one another, the rings split into the vesica pisces, like the splitting of a cell in the creation of life. The rings rippled side by side, and between them, where they touched, was their point of origin, like an eye. Together they were duality—the yin and the yang, balance—and they created the eternal figure eight, which began to spin. Larger and more quickly, a great whirlpool was created in the center of the cenote, and the sound of rushing water filled the space.

"We jump together, side by side," Marcus said to Helghul over the rushing water.

"It appears it can be no other way," Helghul agreed. They both stepped simultaneously toward the edge. "You are still no friend to me, Marcus."

"Nor am I your enemy," Marcus said benevolently, and together, in agreement, they jumped into the magical eddy and were gone.

Elijah woke with a start. He expected to be soaked, wet from head to toe, after leaping into the cenote vortex with Marcus, but his sheets were dry and luxurious. Had he been dreaming?

Helghul knew better. There were certain dreams that were more than what they appeared to be.

"It's time to go," Grey Elder said, prodding the boy gently.

It was 10:00 p.m. A strong wind had blown the clouds and smog away, and the night skies over Giza were clear and bright. Grey Elder carried the black sports bag over one shoulder. His forearm rippled with the muscles he had maintained diligently, knowing that his duties might someday challenge his aging body. He was dressed in Western clothing and had made sure that Elijah wore similar garb. They got in a waiting taxi, and Elijah was grateful for the occasional gust of air through its open windows. The night remained warm, and traffic was noisy and slow.

"I hate baseball," Elijah complained when Grey Elder tossed him a hat.

"We need to look like tourists. That's how we're getting into the pyramid."

"Can't you just pay our way in?" the boy asked, turning over the Yankee cap in his hand.

"Of course, I've done that too. Egyptian politicians are easily bribed. However, they don't have the same control of their military as they like to pretend. I have papers allowing us access to the pyramids and surroundings, but we must be prepared to deal with potential problems. We cannot be perceived as any kind of threat. As much as the soldiers are happy to take bribes, they're truly protective of the Great Pyramid, and they don't want any trouble. They understand how dangerous times have become."

"Isn't it risky to advertise we're Americans?" Elijah asked, waving the cap in the air.

"It's necessary. When I get close, the guards will know me anyway. This is the body I have to work with. I mustn't look like I'm trying to hide or they'll be more suspicious."

"What if they don't let us in?"

"*You* will get in. Everybody has a price . . . anyway, if I have any difficulty, I have my ways," Grey Elder answered darkly.

They exited the cab and walked toward the Great Pyramid, leaving the streets of chaotic traffic and honking behind.

"Move quickly and don't speak to anyone. The crowds are large and prone to violence," Grey Elder said as they approached the largest pyramid. It was lit around its perimeter, but the evening light shows that had once entertained tourists had ceased months before when Giza had become too dangerous.

The Egyptian army had been staunch, not allowing anyone to enter, but as time passed. the higher-ups had made exceptions to reap the financial benefits. Pilgrims and tourists were willing and able to pay for access to the site, and life in Egypt was a struggle for its people, both military and civilian, so they took what they could on the side.

To Grey Elder's displeasure, despite the warnings of danger and the legitimate threat of harm, the area outside the metal barricade fences was surrounded by pilgrims. There were thousands of people from all over the world who had been arriving for months. There had been a great deal of animosity and violence directed at the peaceful pilgrims—much of it directly engineered by Zahn himself. Despite the danger, they continued to come. From outside the army barriers, they paced, prayed, sang, and just stared at the monuments as though waiting for something miraculous to happen. They had been drawn by the energy vortices, which were the very reason the Emissaries had built the pyramid in the first place.

"Papers? Open the bag," the soldier at the barricade commanded, but Zahn was prepared.

"It's nothing, just snacks and water," he said loudly for others to hear. As he opened the pack toward the man, he held a huge wad of money in his hand. The gold-encased Emerald Tablet wrapped in a black cashmere sweater went unnoticed. The soldier pocketed the bribe quickly and waved them through. He didn't want to be seen taking the money; he might get in trouble, or worse, have to share it. He had earned more in that moment than he would make in five years.

Grey Elder and Helghul had passed through the first barrier easily. Now they only needed to make their way to the pyramid's tourist entrance and into the King's Chamber.

Quinn's arms were outstretched, and he looked around in confusion. He wasn't wet. Had the cenote been a mirage or some sort of daydream?

Where's Eden? Am I too late? he wondered.

He stood in a long, narrow corridor he easily recognized. He was in the subterranean chamber of the Great Pyramid. In many lives, Marcus had explored the hallways and chambers beneath the pyramid. It was one of the only monuments that reminded him of Atitala. He wasn't surprised that this is where his search for the Emerald Tablet would lead. Grey Elder and Helghul needed the pyramid to access the full power of the Tablet.

The pyramids were misunderstood in the present day. They had never been built as tombs. The White Pyramid in Atitala had supported the positive Unity Grid, connecting with other pyramids around the planet and linking every person across the globe under its collective field. Pyramids were power plants. Once the Emerald Tablet was placed within the pyramid, Quinn knew that the energy it was capable of projecting was immense. But he wondered if the marvel could ever become operational again.

The long-misunderstood Giza pyramid hadn't functioned in millennia. It had been stripped of its outer coating and gold capstone, and the Nile had meandered away from the Great Pyramid. The river had dropped so significantly that it no longer flowed near the base of the structure. The pyramid was an instrument that required certain conditions to function. Grounding waters had to flow through the carefully constructed tunnels beneath it and then combine with sulfuric acid to act as the giant battery's electrolyte, converting the vibration of the Earth into harnessable energy.

Grey Elder was aware of the challenges facing him in his bid to resurrect the pyramid. However, many were in league with the darkness, and he had timed things well. That night, explosives placed just south of Aswan had succeeded in collapsing the nearly two-and-a-half-mile-long dam, which had been holding back the Nile in the Nasser reservoir since 1964. Insurgents, terrorists— it didn't matter who would be blamed—the political discord in the country and in those surrounding it made it easy for Zahn to have his way.

Quinn started running. He had to find Eden, and he had to get to Elijah and Grey Elder before it was too late.

>◌< >◌< >◌<

"Where are we heading? I thought you said we were going to enter through the tourist entrance," Elijah said as Zahn turned toward the Sphinx. Even though it was nearing midnight, there were many people milling about the area, pointing at the stars and remarking at their brightness.

"I've arranged passage for myself through the tourist entrance. If that is hindered, I will enter with cash or by force. You must enter through the Hall of Records. Your passage is through the Sphinx. We will reunite in the King's Chamber."

"Why?"

"There is a question that can only be answered in the Halls of Amenti. You must ask what phrase has to be spoken to initiate the process when we place the Emerald Tablet in the King's Chamber."

"You don't know?" Elijah said in surprise.

"I am not privy to this information, but all knowledge is available in the Hall of Records, and all questions can be answered. You must ask for the words to initiate the process."

"Why me?"

"You are one of three who have been prophesied to come from the West and enter the Hall of Records, but I have prevented Marcus and Theron from fulfilling their destinies. They remain confined."

Helghul thought of his dream of Marcus in the cenote. *Was Marcus still captive?* He didn't think so.

"The pyramid will be activated long before the Golden Age, and the Darkness will be perpetuated. We will, as you said, create a dis–Unity Grid," Grey Elder said.

"Why don't you come with me?" the boy asked, nervous about going alone.

"I cannot pass. Only *you* will be granted entry."

"How will I enter? I vaguely remember in my life as pharaoh, there were legends of the Hall of Records and the concourses between the Sphinx and the pyramids. I searched endlessly, but they don't exist," Elijah said as they stepped down into the trench surrounding the giant stone lion with its human head. A pair of soldiers passed close by, watching Zahn and Elijah curiously.

"The tunnels *do* exist. It is all in the timing. Pass the right front paw three times, just as you would have done at a stupa when you were Genghis Khan. The entrance will open for you," Grey Elder instructed.

As Temujin would have done, Helghul thought to himself as he began to pace.

Zahn stepped about ten feet away, avoiding the lights at the base of the monolith and blending into the shadows. The Emerald Tablet was tucked away in the bag under his arm. As instructed, Elijah walked clockwise three times around the Sphinx, beginning at the right front paw. Zahn waited, listening to those passing by, watching for approaching soldiers, prepared to intervene if anyone came near.

Once, twice, three times, he walked clockwise, the nearly 160 yards around the Sphinx. On the third and final turn, the boy was confident . . . but no entrance opened. Nothing happened, and he looked to Zahn for an explanation but saw with alarm that his mentor was in an animated conversation with two soldiers who were looking at him with suspicion.

Helghul was perplexed. *Is Grey Elder mistaken? What will I do if the door doesn't appear? Think!* he railed at himself. *Why isn't it working?*

How would Temujin get in? he thought, but he had tried that, and nothing new came to mind. He circled, making three full turns for a second time, but when he returned to the right paw, nothing! *Was the entrance elsewhere? Did it exist at all? Was there a secret word or deed . . . or a chant?* Pace, pace, pace; he walked back and forth. Grey Elder was distracting the guards, but for how long?

Think, think, think . . . no—feel! I must use my intuition, he thought. *How would Marcus get in?* Just then, the bothersome guards split off from Grey Elder, moving simultaneously in the *opposite* direction of one another. *That's it!* he realized. Helghul's recent dream of Marcus had been a clue! The face of his counterpart flashed through his mind, and he thought of them jumping, strangely united, into the cenote. Marcus would walk around the Sphinx clockwise, just as he had already done. But *he* was not Marcus! Helghul knew he must walk the reverse path of Marcus.

"I have it!" the boy hissed jubilantly to the Elder, who was scanning the sky and looking at his watch with concern. He was confused as to why the boy was unable to open the gate to Amenti.

Elijah proceeded *counter*clockwise three rounds.

"Boy! Boy! What are you doing there?" a nearing soldier called out from the opposite side of the Sphinx.

Elijah began running, and just before the outsider reached him, he made his third and final turn. The Sphinx opened, as if it had lifted its paw, and he ducked quickly inside the narrow rabbit hole that appeared. He slid in, knocking his hat off in his haste.

Elijah didn't hear the astonished exclamations of the soldier, who had been only steps behind and now held Elijah's fallen ball cap. The boy had simply disappeared. He was a world away. Relieved, Zahn made his way toward the main entrance of the Great Pyramid with the Emerald Tablet in tow.

The small Adversary stood inside the narrow tunnel stretching out ahead of him. He dusted off the scraped, bloody flesh of his right elbow, flinching. His light jacket had torn through. He celebrated inwardly at having mastered the portal he had sought so fervently in the past.

The corridor was lit, but Elijah could not understand by what source. There were no torches, no bulbs or crystals. There was no window or crack to the outside world, yet the passageway glowed dimly as he advanced.

Elijah came to a spiral staircase and proceeded downward. At the bottom he found another and another, until he had descended nine steep staircases in all. He worried he was taking too long. He needed to reach the King's Chamber quickly. Grey Elder would be waiting.

The base of the ninth staircase rested in the center of a large stone room that was filled with shelves and tables bursting with scrolls, books, maps—every manner of preserving knowledge. Jutting out from the room, there were nine long passageways.

As he paused, Elijah noticed that his injured elbow was still bleeding. He thought of the cartoon bandages his mother always carried in her purse, even once he had grown too old for them. The insignificant recollection instantly took him back to a time, less than a year earlier, when his ancient memory had been foggy and dull. A time when he was more Elijah and less Helghul. He'd had a home, a bedroom with posters, and a quilt with a ratty corner that he'd often chewed. Back then he had simply been a son to a loving mother. Mom . . . Eden . . . *where was she now?* he wondered.

Movement to his left pulled him out of his reverie. Near the base of the staircase, waiting to greet Elijah, stood Red Elder. His long robe glowed and swished against the tile at his feet. His eyes were bright white and blue and bulged slightly. Helghul recognized the Elder instantly . . . but there was more.

"Welcome, I am the Keeper of Records, known by many names."

"Red Elder, Hermes Trismegistus, I know you . . . ," the boy began, but his words caught in his throat as Elijah recognized his father Jamie's spirit. "You left us," Elijah whispered. The boy's grief bubbled up and overflowed. "You could have stayed with us," he said sorrowfully, as a son to his father. For an instant he was simply an eleven-year-old boy grieving the loss of his dad. Elijah remembered their last trip together, snorkeling and surfing in the waves off the coast of Hawaii. Jamie had promised that his trip to Syria would be brief, no big deal, and they would meet up again in Egypt. This time they would travel as a family for good.

"It was not my choice to leave when I did; occurrences happen outside our personal choices, though I do not question it. You understand that life situations prepare us for what we have come to learn? It is the information that remains," Red Elder soothed.

Elijah stared at the record keeper. "You *knew* this would happen! You said we would meet in Egypt! You're *nothing* to me now," he snarled bitterly. The Beast within him successfully buried the sentimental boyhood pain that had spontaneously emerged. "Tell me the phrase that will link the Emerald Tablet with the activated pyramid!" Elijah demanded.

"As it is below, so it shall be above," Red Elder answered automatically, unable to do otherwise. All questions were answered in Amenti, for information itself was neither good nor bad. It was the motives of people that caused the suffering.

Elijah smirked at the simplicity of it and turned to leave. The mysterious light that had led him through the tunnels up until now was no longer visible. The nine hallways leading from the Hall of Records were dark. He didn't know where to go.

"There are many passages one can take," Red Elder said.

"I must get to the King's Chamber," the boy replied.

"You *choose* your destiny."

"I have already chosen, just as *you* have," Elijah said coolly, rejecting Red Elder's familiar shine.

"Your destiny is uncertain. Find the space in your heart where love resides. There is always choice," Red Elder counseled.

"I wish to go to the King's Chamber of the Great Pyramid," Elijah declared, certain his choice was decided.

"Like everyone who passes through these halls, you must first make a deposit before leaving. What knowledge have *you* to leave for the Keeper of Records?" Red Elder asked.

"There *is* no new knowledge. Since the First Tribe, it has all been done before. The cycle repeats—a balance of all things light and dark, male and female. How am *I* to add anything new? Are these shelves not bursting with that same message—patterns and symbols written in a million ways and languages?" Elijah asked, exasperated. He had to hurry.

"Your deposit has been recorded. Follow the path that lights unto you. Follow the Light."

"I don't answer to *you*; I answer to a higher power," Elijah replied. His vulnerable emotions had been smothered and denied. One of the corridors to his right began to glow.

Chapter 45

The King's Chamber

After the first twenty yards, the tunnel leading from the Hall of Records merged with the ascending passageway of the Great Pyramid, and Elijah met Grey Elder, who had come in through the main tourist entrance. Together, they made their way through the Grand Gallery and into the King's Chamber.

Eden's journey was quite a different experience. She had to climb and step carefully to make her way. Piles of rock and debris littered the corridor. It was taking so long: up, down, over, and under. The way was not easy, but she remained determined. Still leading her, the strange light glowed ahead and dimmed behind her as she proceeded, jogging up the subtle incline. Eden imagined she felt Elijah somewhere close by, and it spurred her forward. She hoped that Quinn would catch up soon.

Quinn had stopped running; his chest was heaving from exertion. He slowed to a jog and then a walk. Where was Eden? Why had she gone on ahead without him? He heard a strange rumble behind him, and it was growing.

As Elijah had entered the Hall of Records via the Sphynx's paw, a torrent from the exploded dam was flooding the Nile basin and overtaking precious ruins, boats, and villages. Thousands of unsuspecting people drowned in their beds. The swell swept up everything in its path as it headed toward Giza. It was naturally drawn to Port Said, where it would dump into the Mediterranean Sea—but not before flooding the site of the Great Pyramid.

The Adversaries had ensured that the dam was built decades before, with a financial agreement struck in 1958. The Adversary, Nikita Khrushchev, had been among them, and the influential leader had stayed in the wings, pulling strings and fulfilling long-term plans and promises meticulously laid out by Grey Elder and his thousands of minions.

Though the Aswan Dam was a significant collaboration, Khrushchev was better remembered for his infamous role in the Cold War, bringing the world to the brink of nuclear war during the Cuban Missile Crisis in 1962. Later that same year, Grey Elder was reborn as Oswald Zachariah Zahn in a tiny town in southern Texas.

Quinn heard rushing wind just as something wet and cold scurried across his foot. He jumped in alarm, but it was water—not a rat or cobra, as he had first suspected. Quinn was pushed violently as the water rushed into the pyramid base, rising quickly and threatening to drown him with its ferocity. Quinn finally reached the Subterranean Chamber of the Pyramid, and it, too, was filling with water. He didn't know how it had come to be, but he knew that Grey Elder must be responsible, and he had to get to higher ground as quickly as possible.

Outside the Pyramid, the Nile had risen suddenly, and palm trees and wreckage were moving across the Giza compound with tsunami force.

To survive the surging river, guards and tourists were clambering up the two-and-a-half-ton limestone blocks. There was room for everyone who was nearby and had the opportunity and ability to climb. Side by side, helping one another, people scrambled up . . . up . . . up. Everyone at his or her own pace. Everyone facing different obstacles and inconsistent stone heights.

When will I be high enough? Will there be room at the top? people thought as they scurried to the pyramid's peak.

Eden was oblivious to the overflowing water rushing into the lower levels of the pyramid. Relieved to be out of the cramped Ascending Passage, she had reached the Grand Gallery—a steep, narrow hallway that led to the King's Chamber. There was no sign of Elijah. The Queen's Chamber had been empty when she passed it, but a strange hum had since filled the air. Up ahead she saw a bright glow near the King's Chamber, and as she climbed, the hum grew louder. Her only concern was getting Elijah to safety. Would she find her child? Surely Red Elder had been correct, and he was here somewhere.

As Eden neared the luminous room, she was anxious about how the confrontation might go. Grey Elder had proven himself to be ruthless, and Eden wished that Quinn was with her as she squeezed the handle of the silver dagger in her hand. She was grateful to Red Elder for thinking of it. She had been rushing to find her child but had been ill prepared. At least now she felt some security as she steeled herself to face the unknown. She briefly contemplated waiting for Quinn to catch up, but she couldn't. She had to know that Elijah was safe.

It never occurred to Eden that her son might refuse her help or be a danger to her.

><< ><< ><<

A massive granite coffer stood in the King's Chamber directly between two vents on either wall. Grey Elder had used the anti-gravitational powers of the atlantium Emerald Tablet to easily move it back to its rightful location after thousands of years of having been displaced and misunderstood. It was a large rectangular granite box that had often been mistaken for a casket.

The so-called tomb had been the subject of extensive lore and conjecture and was even compared to the Ark of the Covenant. Eden had once read to Elijah that it had been intended as a coffin for the pharaoh, Khufu. Incorrect. She had also read that the students of the Mystery School had reached enlightenment by lying for a night within the six-and-a-half-foot-long, three-foot-wide structure. Correct. But never had any scholar accurately discerned the purpose of the box.

Both Elijah and Eden now knew the truth; their memories were full and clear. Eden had lain in the casket herself in her lifetime as Pythagoras but had forgotten. The power of the energy had been inspirational, and Pythagoras had gone on to do great work. Imagine what he might have done if Theron had possessed memory.

Zahn placed the trembling Emerald Tablet on Elijah's chest inside the coffer, and the resonating *A* note grew louder. The note was haunting, and every hair on the boy's body raised with an electric charge. Elijah couldn't see much of the room. He could see the flat rose-granite ceiling and the upper walls from where he lay on his back. It was longer and wider than his slight young frame, and he fit easily inside, hidden from view. The room had grown bright with starlight, drawn in through celestial vents to where Elijah and the Emerald Tablet lay.

When he had first arrived in the King's Chamber, Grey Elder had asked him the secret phrase from the Halls of Amenti.

"As it is below, so it shall be above," the boy had answered. It was a line written on the Tablet, and Zahn had remarked at the simplicity of it.

Though it was carved out of atlantium, the Emerald Tablet was far more than a simple shard. It allowed consciousness to be accessed, and when coupled with the fully powered pyramid, it became a great resonator. The Elder knew that as the Emerald Tablet's energy passed through Helghul and the Beast, it would become a conduit of evil. Influenced by their powerful negative energy and coupled with the current chaotic state of the world, starting the resonator now would reverse the Great Year Cycle and stall conscious evolution.

If everything went according to Zahn's plan, there would be no ascending Bronze Age. The negative energy and divisiveness that had been so masterfully engineered around the globe would eclipse everything.

While Zahn was waiting for the dam waters to reach their necessary height in the lower tunnels of the pyramid, Elijah lay in the coffer, his heart pounding in anticipation of the Tablet. He was remembering thirteen thousand years earlier when he had opened his veins and the evil entity had attached to his soul. He had been intoxicated and thrilled by the idea of power and glory. In many lifetimes since then, the Beast had fortified him against his enemies and had been a powerful ally, heightening his ruthlessness and brutality, but Helghul would never admit it. The two beings resented each other, and the entity had become more uncontrollable in the last century, sometimes overtaking Helghul completely. This did not sit well with the Adversary. Neither he nor the Beast had submissive natures.

Steady, boy! the Beast snarled.

I am Black Elder—not you! I am the King of the Adversaries. It is you *who must submit to me!* Helghul thought to the Beast that was taunting him inside his head.

You hold me back from my greatness. It is time that true, unbridled darkness reigned on the Earth, the Beast growled.

Hold you back? Me? It is I who have lived and conquered in every life. You jibber-jabber in my head, annoying and distracting me. You cannot exist here without me!

Stupid boy, you would still be crying for your mother if I had not overcome you. Your rage. Your calculating ruthlessness . . . that is all me! the Beast said.

"I want you out of my head telling me what to do! I don't need you anymore," Elijah said angrily, this time shouting and surprising Grey Elder. Elijah's outburst concerned him.

Maybe he has not yet regained his full memory, he thought, and he knew precautions had to be taken to ensure the boy didn't react badly or try to flee.

"This is unnecessary! Why are you doing this!" Elijah asked angrily as Grey Elder finished binding his hands and ankles. The boy had resisted by uncooperatively stiffening his body. Helghul boiled inside of him, full of rage.

"When you resist your partnership, especially at this moment, it is cause for concern. You have lived and died many times, Helghul. Surely you realize the dark entity is bound to your *soul*. It does not leave you even when you die. It feeds on you as you feed on it. The Beast requires your human soul to exist in this world and makes you the powerful being you have become. Your bond is eternal," Zahn said.

"Liar!" Eden yelled, bursting into the chamber and running to the Serapeum where her son lay. "The *Source* is eternal; our choices are not! Forgiveness and repentance are *real!*" she shouted as Elijah sat up to greet her.

"Fairy tales," Grey Elder snarled. The last thing he wanted was an Emissary near the Emerald Tablet when he activated the Great Pyramid.

Grey Elder took a step toward Eden, and she raised the dagger in her hand protectively.

"He has choice! It's a grid, and *all* roads lead back to the Light," Eden said, wrapping her free arm around Elijah's shoulders and hugging him. Using the blade, she began cutting the ropes binding his wrists and ankles. She sporadically swiped at Grey Elder, preventing him from coming too close.

"And all roads lead *away* from the Light," Grey Elder said, irritated. He continued speaking, this time to Elijah. "Your soul is unified with the Beast and always will be. You would not have had the lives you've had, if not for the darkness! Your cycle would have been *nothing*. There would be no memory of Alexander! Temujin would have never become the great Khan!"

"You belittle me, Grey Elder. I never needed you or the Beast to achieve what I have. It was I who killed Black Elder and took his place—not you!" Elijah said bitterly.

"Get out of the box," Eden said to Elijah, still holding the knife toward the Elder. "Where there is evil, there is goodness; inside *him* there is goodness," Eden said. Elijah remained in the coffer, conflicted.

Grey Elder watched, calculating his next move. Eden was too late; everything had gone as planned. The vibration shook their bones, and the ominous *A* note grew louder as the Great Pyramid once again tuned to the frequency of the Earth and powered up. The rumble of the geomechanical power plant further wakened Helghul's thirst for continued power as it roared back to life.

She's wrong. She doesn't know the things I've done, Elijah thought. Theron had always underestimated the depths of his wickedness.

"Any goodness that was ever in me is long gone," Elijah said to Eden. "You were a fool to come."

"That's a lie! You *are* good. You *do* feel love!" she said, hugging him with her free arm, but this time he pushed her away roughly. He felt her loving energy, and as her shine radiated through him, the Beast burned angrily inside. It could feel the softening Theron elicited in Helghul, though the Adversary desperately tried to hide it. Elijah struggled against his inner demon. He did not want to admit he still needed the Beast to steel him from his human frailty.

I feel the weakness she elicits in you. Together we are powerful! Remember what we have accomplished! the Beast said in Elijah's head.

Zahn stepped toward Eden and Elijah, his handsome face calm and serene as if he were taking an afternoon stroll. He was confident that Helghul's true nature would usurp the boy's youthful innocence. The dagger carved with the ten-headed dragon shifted nervously in Eden's hand as she felt her son moving against her.

Where the hell is Quinn? she thought.

Chapter 46

The Emissaries' Last Stand

The commander felt the change before he saw it, and the Adversary cringed. Facing the elevator from five yards away, the soldiers could now feel the strong tremor shaking the ground and air around them. The other guards stood back, waiting for their orders before proceeding. Some of the mercenaries felt fear, and some, influenced by the waves of energy caused by the Merging, were questioning their ethics and choices.

The energy was intense, and the commander was enraged when he ordered the elevator door opened. As the doors parted, light burst from the room, and the soldiers were thrown back, blinded, as the energy of pure loving consciousness poured over them.

The Emissaries were sitting arm in arm, chanting deep intonations of *Aum*. Their combined shine had swelled and grown dramatically, so each one was like a thousand more, and they were no longer distinct from one another. Their ethereal spirits levitated well above their motionless, barely breathing bodies. The geometric shapes of the Unity Grid flowered in the air above the Merging group, changing like cymatic sand patterns on a drum as the frequency heightened.

A brilliant celestial bloom filled the room and made a dome around the prisoners. Only the Adversary could not see it. The guards clearly saw, and being at ground zero of the Grid's creation, they were astounded by the energy it produced. The Emissary Bapoo and one other small child walked to the edge of the spectral-hued transparent dome and, facing out, placed their tiny hands palms flat on the invisible, glowing wall and looked at the guards.

"They're angels," the guard Muhammed said.

"Open fire!" the Adversary bunker commander shouted, but the guards did not follow the order. They lowered their guns—they couldn't do it. Many of them had come to know the remarkable children who had healed them and their loved ones, and they were further awed by the miraculous orbs of light drifting around the room. Many of the mercenaries were, at their heart, religious men, and they felt they were witnessing a miracle. They felt the waves of connection emanating from the quickly expanding Unity Grid, and unconditional love flowed through them.

"Shoot, shoot!" the commander yelled again before pulling out his own pistol. Nate had been watching from outside the circle, and as he saw the gun being lifted, he picked up the square ottoman beside him and ran at the shooter, bulldozing the bunker commander. The commander managed to let off one shot before he was slammed back against the wall, at which point his subordinates turned their guns on him.

The single bullet had passed easily through the ottoman. The mutiny was short but lethal. As the guards took away their commander's weapons and restrained him, Nate dropped the footstool and stared at his belly. Blood poured from the wound. The bullet was lodged in his liver, and he fell to his knees. The woman with Yashoda's shine came to Nate's side, and he lay with his head in her lap.

"Thank you," she whispered.

The old French surgeon and several other doctors and nurses rushed to Nate's aid, but his wound was beyond their healing. Just as Yashoda had done in Auschwitz, in her lifetime as Sophie Blanc, she offered comfort and eased Nate's suffering with her kindness.

"You have to get the children out of here," Nate said desperately. He had been anxious for Quinn and Eden to return, visually checking the spot on the wall a thousand times, but they hadn't come. He worried that Zahn had outdone them and that he had more sinister plans for the prisoners.

"Don't worry, they're coming," she said, repeating young Bapoo's proclamation. "We have called the other Emissaries; they are close. Do not worry about us. Muhammed and the other guards are with us now."

Nate was relieved. He had not saved them all, but he had certainly saved one or two by rushing in front of the commander's pistol.

"Go home, Nate. They are all waiting for you," Yashoda said, placing her ebony hand on his cheek.

Nate's spirit lifted out of his body. He was surprised that he was still aware. He was still . . . himself. He saw Yashoda's shine, and then as he looked down at the room, he saw all the Emissaries' shines and the growing Unity Grid, which easily passed through the material walls and ceiling expanding skyward. Nate's soul no longer belonged in the bunker, and a warm glow called him, compelling him to pass on into the Meadow. It was his childhood dog, Gizmo—playful and jumping. The familiar energy welcomed him. Nate was surrounded by the Light, and the loving energy of all the people he had loved and lost. They were happy, and they welcomed him with joy in their hearts. There, the skeptic became a believer, as all his questions were answered.

Chapter 47

Indra's Web

"Stay away from my son!" Eden shouted as Zahn took another step closer.

"Where are you going to go?" Grey Elder sneered.

Eden stood protectively between where Elijah stood inside the coffer, looking down on them. Despite his desire to defend his mother, he was helpless.

Eden was preparing for Zahn to lunge, and she planted her feet squarely. As she held the blade in the air, he kicked the dagger out of her hand. It flew and hit the wall, landing with a clatter. As Eden lunged to retrieve it, he backhanded her across the left cheek. She stumbled and braced herself.

Get the knife and kill her! the Beast demanded inside Elijah's head.

The boy jumped out of the coffer, leaving the Emerald Tablet inside, but instead of retrieving the weapon, he rushed to his mother's side.

The Beast within him, incensed by the boy's pity, sent fiery impulses shooting through his nerves, causing Elijah extreme pain. The Adversary screamed, and Eden turned to him, trying to understand what was hurting him. Zahn retrieved the weapon.

Eden reached into the coffer and grabbed the Emerald Tablet, swinging it at the Elder, attempting to knock the knife away as he approached. Zahn countered, roughly pushing her backward. She stumbled against the coffer and held the Tablet like a shield in front of her and Elijah.

Elijah was torn! He was the Beast, he was Helghul, and he wanted the darkness to reign, but he was also a child who loved his mother and wanted to protect her. It was primal, as his love for Theron had always been.

The Elder charged toward them, the knife raised over his head. As Eden and Elijah cowered behind the Tablet, the Elder faked left, and Eden instinctively shifted. Having drawn her out of position, he switched directions and slashed at her from the right side.

Quinn burst into the tiny room just as Zahn's blade met Eden's flesh, brutally cutting into her forearm and slicing Elijah's shoulder at the same time. She twisted to fight the Elder off, and Elijah screamed in pain and outrage.

"Hear me now, darkness of the night, chained in the fetters of fire by light!" Quinn shouted, as he charged in. He was reciting the chant indelibly burned into his brain from the night so long ago in Atitala, when the Beast had been called up from the chasm and had taken possession of Helghul. He had hated the memory, but now it was serving an invaluable purpose.

"Reach now forth this sacred land, misbegotten Beast; take now this offered hand. See me now, oh wicked eye. Seek this place from whence we die. Offer this, your sacred feast. Rise up now, all-powerful Beast!"

Quinn continued chanting as he harshly body-checked the Elder away from Eden.

Zahn was lifted off his feet and hit the floor, and the blade flew out of his hand. Though Zahn scrambled to his feet, Quinn's words had been faster.

A fierce howl was now coming from Elijah. Eden's hands were covered in blood as she desperately wrapped her fingers around her child's gaping injury, applying pressure. The gash drained onto the stone floor. A dark soup, something more than blood and less than human, stirred within his wound.

Quinn watched triumphantly as a ghostly black serpent with ten heads and the body of a dragon rose like toxic black smoke from the boy's torn flesh. Eden was terrified as the entity slipped through her hands, expanding and becoming material and solid in the emerald glow. It represented a departure from humanity—the evil that lay within all human beings if they opened themselves to it. It was a horrible reminder of what the soul could become.

The horrific Beast filled the air above them, just as Quinn had intended.

"Fool! There is no escape for any of you now. What did you think, that the Beast would just disappear?" Zahn said, laughing, but he was hiding his inner panic. As "real" as it was, the Beast required a human host to exist in the material realm. Its form was temporary. It didn't have much time before it would be once more exiled to the chasm.

My hunger for human flesh burns! the Beast roared.

Elijah immobilized by fear, watched as the creature screeched from ten fanged mouths, swooping and hovering, its barbed tail and vicious talons whipping the air barely above their heads, stretching, free of its confines. Eden kept her hands pressed against her son's shoulder as blood soaked her shirt from where her arm had been cut.

"Helghul, with the Beast, you will reign all-powerful! You are Black Elder, the King of the Adversaries. Together, we will manipulate the great resonator and extend the Dark Age. You must take the Beast back in!" Grey Elder said.

"No!" Quinn and Eden shouted together. The Beast thrust multiple heads with gnashing teeth at the trio. Quinn lifted up the Tablet protectively over the top of Eden and Elijah, shielding them from the attack.

"Careful! Do not harm the Tablet!" Grey Elder shouted to the Beast, though the roar of the pyramid was growing louder and made it difficult to hear. The Emerald Tablet continued to tremble violently in his hands.

"Take hold of the Tablet!" Quinn shouted to mother and child, and they did. He knew it was their only hope of escape.

Eden shifted one of her bloody hands from the wound of her son and placed it on the Tablet.

"Indra-reveal-your-secrets!" Quinn said in a rush, calling upon the knowledge he had stored for more than two thousand years, since his life as Plato. Red Elder had said that Marcus might need this knowledge one day; had he known then? Had he seen it in Indra's Web?

Immediately in front of them, the jewels of Indra's Web appeared and expanded all around. Lifetime after lifetime unraveled in a glistening fractal-matrix extending in every direction. The time-pocket-jewels were visible at each intersecting line of the magical quilt, and every jewel held inside of it an entire Universe. Each existed independently of the other within the multiverse. Quinn could see people going about their normal activities, each living and existing in their own reality.

So many experiences, so many lives, he thought in awe, still holding off the Beast protectively.

"Stop them!" Grey Elder shouted to the Beast, bounding toward the coffer and carefully maneuvering past the multidimensional portals so as not to accidentally send himself into another time. The walls, floors, and ceiling of the King's Chamber seemed to disappear as Indra's Web expanded infinitely in every direction. Scenes of lifetimes were projected onto the Elder's face and body as he rushed to stop the Emissaries from escaping.

"Helghul! You have already committed to the Beast; it cannot be undone!" said Grey Elder.

"No!" Quinn and Eden shouted.

The images of the Beast entering Helghul in the cavern were burned in Theron's memory from her time in Shambhala. Eden would never allow the entity to repossess her son.

"I have a plan! Trust me!" Quinn shouted to Eden. The Beast, its heads swinging violently, was dappled in the glow of the holographic life scenes. It hurled itself at the puny humans who were huddling behind the small block of atlantium as they moved toward one of the portals. Its ten vicious heads had distracted the Emissaries from the razor-sharp, serrated tail, until using it like a spear, the Beast struck them from behind.

Its tail hit Quinn first as he pushed the others toward the jewel gateway. It sliced through the Emissary's side easily, plunging through Eden's narrow waist, exiting through her stomach and impaling Elijah. The tail finished by colliding with the Emerald Tablet.

Eden was injured and dying, but she could see the Beast dematerializing, returning to its ether state and hovering next to her child's body. She heard the severely injured boy whimper, and she believed the entity was preparing to reenter him through his wound.

"I offer up *my* body!" Eden said weakly, sacrificing herself in Elijah's place. This mother's love knew no limitations. She willingly surrendered herself for her son.

"No!" Quinn groaned, for it was at that moment that their intertwined bodies passed through the nearest gateway. Just as they entered the open portal, half-dead, the Beast slipped through the cut in Eden's forearm and took possession of its new host, binding to Theron's soul.

They had made a quantum leap and were being propelled into another lifetime. They were catapulted at the speed of thought, through the Universe to another time and place within Indra's vast tapestry, to a moment that had been randomly chosen.

Grey Elder howled with outrage as the three who were joined together like the strands of a whip vanished along with the Beast. Indra's expansive web collapsed in on itself, sucked at lightspeed into one tiny point and disappearing. Zahn ran to where they had been. There was nothing but dark pools of blood filling the tight spaces between the stones. The Emerald Tablet was gone!

The Emissary had succeeded in freeing Elijah of the Beast only to have it backfire when Eden protectively called the Beast into her, incorrectly believing she was saving her son. By opening Indra's Web, Marcus had succeeded in transporting them, and the treasure, somewhere else in the fabric of time, but at what cost?

Zahn was filled with fury, but he had no time to waste. He had to focus on this reality before all he had worked for fell apart. Grey Elder exited the pyramid and saw the devastating aftereffects of the flooding. Wreckage littered the desert, but he felt no pity or remorse.

Marcus had complicated things, but Grey Elder had now learned the command to control Indra's Web. "Indra-reveal-your-secrets," he had heard. If he were to regain possession of the Emerald Tablet now, and he certainly intended to, he would be unstoppable.

History would tell him where they had gone. It was only a matter of time.

Chapter 48

No Time

Present day, Malibu, California

Shanti radiated a pure soul that made her truly beautiful. She no longer wore the dreadlocks she had been sporting years earlier when Quinn had met her briefly outside a coffee shop in New York, but she had added a silver nose ring. She had been promoting her band back then, but now she was a massive success, having earned her second platinum album.

The band took up their instruments onstage in the golden hour, just prior to sunset, and the light behind them was magical. Shanti took a deep breath before making her way through the party patrons. With smooth, sexy charm, she glided through the crowded Malibu garden to the stage at the edge of the ocean. She was greeted by warm smiles, cheers, and welcoming touches as she passed.

The crowd was full of famous faces. Hollywood's multicultural, sexually diverse who's-who sashayed their way down the steps, drinks in hand, onto the sand for the show. Chilli G, the multi-Grammy-award–winning rapper and producer, sat elbow to elbow with politicians, movie stars, and models.

"And now, I present Seattle Underground," the model-emcee said, towering over Shanti as they hugged. Shanti gave her friend a grateful squeeze before she left the stage. As she stepped up to the mic, a few members of the audience shouted their appreciation.

"We love you, Shanti!" she heard, and she blew them handfuls of kisses.

"I love you all! What a beautiful evening. What a perfectly wonderful group of people you are! I wouldn't want to be anywhere else but here right now, with you," she said as the band played softly behind her. "Can you feel that?" she cooed, and the crowd roared in approval, "That's some good energy, that is. I know the festivities are just beginning . . . but I feel like there is still . . . not enough time." The audience got the reference and knew that a special song was coming. They continued to cheer. "There is just, just . . . no time," Shanti continued, and the band played a beautiful, haunting melody. The crowd listened attentively as Shanti sang in pure tones about the anguish of soulmates saying goodbye to one another.

Shanti had written her first hit single for her parents, when her mother was terminally ill and had only a few weeks to live. Her mom and dad had been lovers since high school, and though Shanti had been filled with her own fear and grief, sadness for her brokenhearted father had overwhelmed her.

How do you say goodbye to the love of your life? she had wondered. How would her parents bear to part? Within thirty minutes, her Grammy Award–winning song, "No Time," had been written.

Shanti looked to the sky while the pianist played his solo, waiting for the drummer to count her back in.

At that moment, she saw pulses of light flash across the sky, revealing intricate, interconnecting lattice patterns displaying the Flower of Life. It was the Unity Grid. The Emissaries had expanded the Grid, and it had grown well beyond the bunker where it had begun. The sky was filled with brilliance and beauty. The colorful lights were brilliant and did not fade in and out; they took clear, laser-sharp form and reached from one side of the sky to the other.

Shanti stopped singing.

"Look! Do y'all see that?" she exclaimed.

With the help of the Emissaries gathered in their secret North African prison, the rest of the world was shifting, but the event occurring across the planet was experienced in many ways. Conscious evolution was an individual human journey, and the experience of all human beings depended on what they were open to perceiving.

To those who saw the Grid, it was awe inspiring. They didn't know what it was, but they felt that they were part of it. The power of the Grid vibrated through Shanti, and her heart felt connected and full. She dropped to her knees and wept with joy, still staring at the amazing scene.

"Thank you! Thank you," she whispered.

Many people *did* see the Grid, but others saw nothing, and laughed, assuming that Shanti was high or having a breakdown. The audience, like the rest of the world's people, were divided, but both experiences were right and true to the perceiver. Their differences confused and scared them, and people struggled with how to cope with the knowledge.

"It's bigger than anything on the planet . . . it's bigger *than* the planet!" Shanti's drummer said, staring.

"Oh my God, it's so beautiful! It's us . . . and we're it!" the governor of California cried out.

It was not only the Cali skies that were lit up. Around the globe, regardless of day or night, people could see the magical energy dancing overhead. The bright lights forced people from their beds, and night workers stopped what they were doing, gazing in awe. Traffic halted as all eyes looked to the skies. The wave of energy was more than seen, it was *felt*. A surge of unconditional love washed over all who witnessed it.

Those who did see tried to explain it to those who did not.

"It's right there! Like a kaleidoscope . . . a laser light show. Look. Can't you see?" they asked, but many were simply blind to it because their consciousness had not yet evolved to a level to see it.

The party became divided. Some people were witnessing a miracle, and others thought their friends were going crazy.

"Where's the cameras at? We gettin' punked here? My wife might see this shit," Rude Boi, a member of Chilli G's entourage joked, nudging aside the pretty scantily clad lady sitting on his lap. The men of the entourage looked around in amusement. The Malibu beach party was now filled with hugging, crying people. They had never seen a party change so fast, and they weren't sure what all the fuss was about. People were staring at the sky and pointing, but Rude Boi saw nothing but the usual twilight.

"What's wrong with all these crazy-ass people? D'you see somethin'?"

"Nah, nothin'. There's nothin' there!" Rude Boi turned to talk to Chilli G, but unlike his friends, the rapper and the women around him *did* see the Unity Grid.

Chilli G's tough façade had softened, and he and the women were crying, overwhelmed with emotion. Chilli tore off the layers of gold chains around his neck that suddenly seemed to weigh him down, letting them fall to the sand.

"What's goin' on with you?" Rude Boi asked.

"It's like when I did ayahuasca! It's just like it," Chilli G replied without looking at his friend.

"It's beautiful!" the woman at his side exclaimed, raising her hands in the air, her hips swaying, and she began to sing.

"Amazing Grace, how sweet the sound . . ."

The other women near her joined in, and when Shanti heard them, she sang along.

"That saved a wretch like meeee . . . I once was lost, but now I'm found, was blind but now I seeeee," they sang, and the band picked up the melody and played along.

"Take me to church!" Chilli G said happily as they continued.

People joined hands, swaying, dancing, singing, and Chilli G added a rhyme.

The division among the partygoers quickly grew more tense. The people who could not see the Unity Grid became increasingly confused, irritated and angry, pushing over drinks and shaking or pulling at their mesmerized friends to snap them out of their reveries.

"There is nothing in the sky, for fuck's sake!" an angry Hollywood A-lister shouted, throwing his chair and walking up the side path to leave, followed by many others. More than one of the guests were so incapacitated by the fight-or-flight response that they froze, and some even fell asleep in their chairs.

"Look, babe, there! The whole sky's lit up. Can't you see it?" a woman was saying, but her blond muscle-bound actor boyfriend saw nothing, and he pushed over a table in frustration.

"Knock it off! It's not funny! You're scaring me!" another woman said, pulling her girlfriend by the arm while she pointed to the sky, trying to explain the miracle she was experiencing.

Those who could not see the Grid assumed it was drugs, a group hallucination, or some massive practical joke.

⋊●⋉ ⋊●⋉ ⋊●⋉

The Emissary Yashoda put a pillow under Nate's head, placed his arms across his chest, and gently closed his eyes before rejoining her fellow Emissaries. The Unity Grid had broken the confines of the bunker in Libya, and the rescuers had arrived to liberate Zahn's prisoners. Emissaries who had not been lured or kidnapped by Grey Elder had heard the telepathic call of the Crystal Children, and they had come or sent help. With the assistance of some powerful political influencers, the Libyan military had been called upon to secure the area and overpower the mercenaries, but it wasn't necessary. The mercenaries had already turned on their

Adversary commander, won over by the Crystal Children, and they willingly opened the doors to the prison.

The captives were ushered outside, and they rejoiced in their freedom, soaking in the fresh air while hugging one another and dancing. The stunning Unity Grid rippled across the sky, set against the vast rolling desert and wrapping its energetic limbs around the planet until it met itself on the other side of the world . . . and then began to retreat.

As it was in Malibu, many people saw and felt the wave of the shift, but many did not. Many wondered what was happening—how could they have missed it? In grocery stores, on highways—anywhere that humans inhabited—there was recognition or confusion. While the Light grew brighter, spreading love, the darkness grew more violent and resistant. Divisions deepened, but awareness climbed, as many people became aware of the metaphysical Universe around them.

The planet was alive, and the beings living upon her soil were reminded that they were more than they had remembered. Inside each person there was the spark of millions of lives. Consciousness would continue to awaken. The Great Year had shifted upward into the Bronze Age, but the remaining darkness in the world, with the help of Grey Elder and the Adversaries, would become even darker. Now the world had been clearly divided, and he would use this division to his advantage.

Epilogue

The Tarim Valley, Asia, 1047 BCE

Expelling the Beast from Elijah had been a terrible mistake. Quinn had never expected Eden to take the entity in as they leapt through Indra's gateway.

The membrane between worlds was thin, and the Emissary took a deep breath as his senses adjusted to his new environment and his consciousness woke to another lifetime. He was disoriented, and he searched for something familiar, some sort of reference point. It was if Quinn were waking from a dream. He was dizzy as he looked down at his short legs standing in the burning desert sand. He didn't recognize himself. He surveyed his youthful hands and feet and guessed he was no more than age fifteen or sixteen. He was no longer Quinn, though he felt and thought just like he had before transporting through Indra's portal.

Where am I? When am I? Where are Theron and Helghul? Marcus wondered, but he was alone.

He searched the ground frantically for the Emerald Tablet. On his left, there was a rolling mountain range that had been worn down by erosion, with layers of boulders, rubble, and blown sand at their base. On the right there was an open, arid desert that looked across a massive, dry lake bed. The Emissary kicked through the sand desperately, but there was no sign of the tablet.

Just then, he heard someone running up behind him. A robust boy, about the same age, smiled as he approached in the dust. He had sun-kissed cheeks, with almond eyes framed by black hair, beneath a tall leather cap that pointed at the top. His legs were double-wrapped in tartan cloth, and he had a large, brown braided scarf around his neck. Marcus recognized him immediately. It was Nate—but no longer Nate. His shine was the same, but he was a Chinese child dressed in Celtic layers.

"Mu! Where have you been?" the boy asked. "The burial procession is about to begin, and the chief is looking for you. Come . . . hurry!" the boy said. It was clear that they would both be in trouble if Mu did not rush.

Marcus's mind raced to understand where and who he was. He did not recognize anything. The Beast had entered Eden, that he knew for sure. He had watched as she had called upon the entity to save her son. She had sacrificed herself for Helghul, not knowing that they were almost free of it.

"Mu? Are you even listening to me?" the boy said, nudging Marcus. "Your ba is waiting!"

"Yes, yes," Mu replied in a language he did not remember learning.

A small village had been built into the craggy rock knoll on the side of the mountain, giving the best protection from the elements. Marcus followed the boy to the waiting queue of men and women squinting against the wind spraying him with desert sand. As he approached, Marcus's eyes searched among the people, sheep, and goats for anything or anyone familiar.

"Pick up your offering, and take your place," the clan chief said sternly to Mu. His father was tall, at least six feet, and had long stringy-red hair. His face was handsome, and he wore the same plaid colors Mu had wrapped around his neck and legs.

"Yes, Ba," Mu said, instinctively knowing their connection though he didn't recognize the man's karmic code. Through Indra's Web, Marcus's consciousness had been transferred into Mu's body. This was not a past life he remembered. He took his place beside the chief.

Mu scanned the villagers, searching for Theron and Helghul. They must be there somewhere, but their shines could not be found. He saw that the people were Caucasian. Their faces had been chapped and weathered by the wind and sand in this difficult environment. They all had red or blonde hair, except for one Chinese woman standing beside Nate.

That must be his mother, Mu thought.

The chief began to sing an ancient Celtic tune, and one by one, people in the circle fell into step behind the clan chief as he followed a horse-drawn cart. The rest of the clanspeople followed behind the funeral procession, some carrying bronze shovels, while one older woman carried a pot of paint and a small brush. Mu's Marcus-mind was revving. It was then that he glanced into the cart behind them.

Mu stared, stunned by what he saw. It was Eden, lying inside the cart. Her arms were crossed, and the Flower of Life tattoos on her forearms were visible, but she no longer had the shine of Theron. Eden was dead, and beside her lay the corpses of Elijah and Quinn. The Emissary's own face stared back at him—Quinn's face, but that body was no longer connected to him. In this lifetime, he was Mu.

Bibliography

Auschwitz-Birkenau Memorial and Museum Wesite http://auschwitz.org/en/.

Auschwitz Memorial @Auschwitz Museum https://twitter.com/ AuschwitzMuseum.

Bauval, Robert and Adrian Gilbert. *The Orion Mystery* (New York: Three Rivers Press, 1994).

Campbell, Thomas. *My Big Toe: Awakening, Discovery, Inner Workings: A Trilogy Unifying Philosophy, Physics, and Metaphysics* (Lightning Strike Books, 2003).

Capra, Fritjof. *The Tao of Physics: An Exploration of the Parallels Between Modern Physics and Eastern Mysticism* (Boston, Shambhala Publications Inc. 1999).

Carlson, Randall. *Randall Carlson Presents: The Great Year.* http://www.youtube. com.

Cruttenden, Walter. *Cosmic Influence.* Podcast http://www.binaryinstitute.org.

Cruttenden, Walter. *The Great Year*, narrated by James Earl Jones. http://youtube. com.

Dalai Lama XIV, His Holiness the, *How to Practice: The Way to a Meaningful Life* (Simon & Schuster, 2003).

De Santillana, Giorgio and Hertha Von Dechend. *Hamlet's Mill* (David R. Godine, Publisher, 1977).

Dunn, Christopher. *The Giza Power Plant* (Inner Traditions/Bear, 1998).

Emoto, Masaru. *The Hidden Messages in Water* (Beyond Words, 2004).

The Grimerica Show. Podcast http://www.grimerica.ca.

Hancock, Graham. *Fingerprints of the Gods* (New York: Three Rivers Press, 1995).

Hauk, Dennis William. *The Emerald Tablet: Alchemy of Personal Transformation* (New York: Penguin, 1999).

Jung, Carl Gustav and Roderick Main. *Jung on Synchronicity and the Paranormal* (London: Routledge, 1997).

Khan, Paul and Francis Woodman Cleaves. *The Secret History of the Mongols*: trans. (Cheng & Tsui, 2001).

Klocek, Dennis. *The Seer's Handbook* (Steiner Books, 2005).

Lanza, Robert, MD, with Bob Berman. *Biocentrism: How Life and Consciousness Are the Keys to Understanding the True Nature of the Universe* (Dallas: BenBella Press, 2009).

Laszlo, Ervin. *Science and the Akashic Field: An Integrated Theory of Everything* (Vermont: Inner Traditions, 1997).

Mandelbrot, Benoit. *The Fractal Geometry of Nature*, 1st Edition (Times Books, 1982).

Marrs, Jim. *The Rise of the Fourth Reich, Project Camelot.* http://www.youtube.com.

Melchizedek, Drunvalo. *The Ancient Secrets of the Flower of Life,* Vol I, II (Light Technology Publishing, 2000),

Newton, Michael, *Journey of Souls: World Case Studies of Life between Lives* (Llewellyn Publications, 1994).

Roerich, Nicholas. *Shambhala*, reprint (India: Vendam Books, 2003).

Schoch, Robert M. PhD, and Robert Aquinas McNally. *Pyramid Quest: Secrets of the Great Pyramid and the Dawn of Civilization* (New York: Penguin, 2005).

Sheldrake, Rupert. *Morphic Resonance: The Nature of Formative Causation, 4th Edition* (Park Street Press, 2009).

The Shoah Foundation Website, https://sfi.usc.edu/.

Stevenson, Ian, MD. *Children Who Remember Previous Lives: A Question of Reincarnation* (McFarland Revised Edition, 2000).

Tarnas, Richard. *Cosmos and Psyche: Intimations of a New World View* (New York: Viking Penguin, 2007).

Tolle, Eckhart. *The Power of Now* (Vancouver: Namaste Publishing, 1999).